April's Secret Storm Seasons of Love and War, Book 5

By

Brenda Ashworth Barry

Published by
Melange Books, LLC
White Bear Lake, MN 55110
www.melange-books.com

April's Secret Storm ~ Copyright © 2015 by Brenda Ashworth Barry

ISBN: 978-1-68046-222-7 Print

Cover Art by Caroline Andrus

Dedications

First, I'd like to thank my husband who always supports me.

Cindy Watson: thank you for being my reading partner, family and one of my best friends.

To my parents who are always there with love and support.

To Mona, my childhood best friend and lifelong best friend.

To all my children: A mother couldn't be any prouder and grateful for all your love and support. Frank, thank you for all you do.

To my dear friends: You know who you are. Thank you for sharing, supporting and being my biggest fans.

My chatter box group: Thank you so much for the encouragement and support that you give me every day. Lisa you rock and have helped me in so many ways.

To my fans and cousins. You are the best and your support means the world to me.

My editor Barb, thank you so much and thank you to the proof readers.

Caroline: thank you for all these lovely covers.

Melange-Nancy: Thank you for making me and my saga a part of the Melange family and for enjoying my stories.

Chapter One

Coming to Dublin had been an enormous mistake. Hadn't Beth Ann said, if she were right about Kaylob and his parents, this was a potential earthquake of an eight-point magnitude, on the scale of emotions? At age twenty-four, after everything she'd lived through, she thought nothing could blow her mind. Yet, here she was, being blown away. Her head was spinning, in the humongous library filled with floor-to-ceiling books, watching Kaylob hug the woman who was supposed to be his long-lost aunt, who just happened to have identical blue eyes and the exact same cleft in her chin.

She knew another storm was brewing.

"I've waited so long for this day," Lillian said lightly and wrapped her arms around Kaylob, while he stood there stiffly.

They had expected Ireland to be gorgeous, that was a given, but neither one of them had been prepared for this kind of lifestyle. It was an enormous surprise when, only a half hour earlier, they had pulled up to the fairytale castle with the ocean drop all around. It took their breath away.

Lillian was miles above the word elegant. Beth Ann couldn't help but stare at her dreamy chiffon dress with all the flowing layers and its embroidered sleeves and collar. Even when she glided into the room, one could tell she had class and charm.

"I'm so glad you're here." Lillian's voice broke. "I've heard so many wonderful things about you, Kaylob, and I can't believe this day has finally come."

Beth Ann examined his face. Uh oh, he was not happy, that much she knew by the irritation etched in his eyes.

In her wildest imagination, she couldn't have thought this up. Not like this. Sure, she had suspected Kaylob's parents may have adopted him, but when she found out Lillian was his aunt, there was no reason to believe anything else.

Kaylob stepped out of Lillian's embrace. Beth Ann could almost feel the frost in his voice when he spoke. "So tell me, *Aunt Lillian*, why is it that we are just meeting?" He leveled a look at her, which held her attention.

Holy thunder. And Beth Ann had thought her childhood was full of twists and turns. This by far was exceeding anything she had gone through. Beth Ann had become the woman she was today because of her bumpy upbringing. She had always measured time by the sound of wheels going down the freeway and watching the landscape go by. There was no question in her mind, living on the road with her family, and spending so much time in the car as they traveled from one state to another, had given her a gateway to her imagination. Even the rain droplets on the window of the old, rundown station wagon had brought her hours of entertainment, she had turned the streaming droplets into race contests.

Beth Ann recognized when things weren't right with people. Now, Lillian's face showed nervousness. And the resemblance between the two of them was uncanny. Jesus, even her hair color was almost the same as Kaylob's.

All these years she wondered why Kaylob had not looked anything like Harold and Jackie, his parents. When they were kids, she had speculated about this difference. He was tall and handsome, with a wide smile and fun spirit. His parents had dark hair, were much shorter, and were rarely happy.

Beth Ann had to close her mouth because it was still hanging open. Just as she did, Lillian pulled a handkerchief from her pocket and wiped her eyes.

"I know we should have met sooner, but at least we are meeting now." Lillian fidgeted with her collar.

"Yes, I would agree, waiting until 1975 is a little long." Kaylob's eyes narrowed. "We should have met sooner, much sooner."

They had waited to take this trip and it was supposed to be relaxing, not uncovering some family secret.

Not after what they'd been through. Beth Ann had been kidnapped, which had been horrifying. The year before she had been attacked by some creepy robbers, right after Kaylob was found alive in a POW camp. Didn't they deserve a break and some peace in their lives? All of it was enough drama to last them a lifetime, or at least sell their story to Hollywood. However, there was no way she'd star in it, even though she'd won a Tony and was an actress and singer.

Lillian cupped his face. "Let's just focus on the here and now." Her lips trembled. "All that matters is that we're together." She glanced over at Beth Ann, then crossed the room toward her.

"It's so nice to meet you. I've heard all about you from Jackie." She pulled her into a warm hug and Beth Ann felt her trembling.

Beth Ann didn't know why, but she couldn't hold back the tears. Maybe because she felt an instant connection.

"Aunt Lillian?" Kaylob's voice sounded stern.

Lillian turned and faced him. "Yes?"

"Just who are you really?" He gave her a pointed look and her smile vanished.

For a minute Beth Ann was expecting her to say, "I'm your aunt of course."

But instead a look of resigned sadness flowed across her face. She waved towards the couch. "Can we sit down? I wasn't expecting to have this conversation so quickly." She busied herself, refilling their cups of tea from the service tray that was sitting on the coffee table, all the while avoiding their eyes. Her hands shook a bit as she poured.

Beth Ann moved closer to Kaylob and took his hand. Right away, she noticed his sweaty palms. Oh God, he didn't need this. Why had she agreed to this trip?

She had mixed emotions about this reunion, and yet, if Lillian was his birth mother and he knew Jackie and Harold had adopted him, wouldn't it be a good thing? On the other hand, maybe his life would feel like a big fat lie. Thinking about everything, made her nauseous and her stomach flipped upside down.

Oh no, she was going to throw up.

"I'm sorry. I need to use the powder room, I know where it is, the butler showed us." She must be turning green because Kaylob shot her a

3

worried look. "I'll be right back." She dashed off to the bathroom, hoping nothing else would happen while she was puking her guts up.

* * * *

Kaylob told himself to pull it together and not sit there in silence, staring into his cup of tea. And why exactly did his wife look so sick? Right now she needed his attention, but before he could get up Lillian drew him back.

"Kaylob," Lillian said softly. "I am going to try to explain everything." She gave him an uneasy glance.

His eyes moved up and connected with hers. A memory hit him like a pound of clay.

"*Come on son,*" *a man said.* "*You can do it. Swim to daddy.*" Who was the man?

He remembered Lillian's eyes; he wondered where the lady had gone. Then he forgot to wonder anymore. Some time later, he forgot her eyes and the man who had called him son.

But sitting here now, he remembered.

"*Don't push him, honey,*" *Lillian had said, with love in her voice.* "*He might be afraid.*" *She swam over and held the little boy he once was.* "*I love you little man.*" *He was embraced and warmed by her voice and touch. He never wanted it to end and wanted to stay with them forever.*

When they had dropped him off that day, he had screamed and cried. "*Mommy, daddy, no go, please, no go. Take me with you*"

"*Go to your room,*" *the other man yelled.* "*And do not come out.*"

Shit, that was Harold the father that never acted like he cared. His hands trembled when he picked up his tea and he felt like he was going to heave.

That was the last time he'd ever seen Lillian, and that was the day his dad, Harold, told him he'd never see them again. He had also smacked his behind for being what he called, *a sissy pants*.

Kaylob stood and drew in a deep breath. "I remember you." he said. "Your voice, your eyes, we were swimming. There was a man that kept calling me son."

Lillian said nothing for a moment, looking as though she was

4

searching for the right words, but he saved her the trouble. "I need to go check on Beth Ann." He left the room with pain in his heart and whispered one word. "Why?" And why didn't he remember until now? Did he bury the memory?

He walked down the long hallway to the bathroom. The door was shut and he could hear Beth Ann throwing up. "Beth Ann, are you alright?" The toilet flushing was all he heard next. He knocked. "Beth Ann?"

No answer. He knocked harder.

The water came on. "I'm okay. I'll be right there."

"Let me in, please," Kaylob said.

The doorknob turned and she opened it slightly.

Dear God, her face was pale as paper. "Oh, baby, you don't look well." He reached in his pocket and pulled out a cinnamon breath mint. "Here, this might help."

She held up her finger, asking him to wait a moment. Then she turned and bent down over the sink, cupping her hand and putting water into her mouth, then rinsing. He'd never seen her throw up over stress before, but he had heard she'd done that when he had been declared dead. And this was another major bombshell.

She dried off her mouth and stood straight. "I'm sorry, that just came out of nowhere."

"It's okay, I just want you to be alright." He handed her the mint and tucked a strand of her curly red hair behind her ear. There was no missing the mass of worry gathering in her brown eyes. "Maybe we should get out of here."

"No, please. I don't think I could handle that right now." Her eyes pleaded.

"Okay, not right now then, but at least try that mint."

"Thank you, honey." She popped it in her mouth and took his hand. "I'm better." She gave a weak smile. "I guess it must be a combination of stress and jet lag."

"Are you sure you don't want to leave here and get a hotel? This might be too much for you to deal with." He wrapped his arms around her.

"No, please, let's stay. Unless, it's too hard on you."

"I don't know yet." He met her gaze. "Let's go talk to Lillian." He released her.

Lillian gave them an expectant look when they returned, but simply regarded them without prying. Once they were seated again, Beth Ann spoke up.

"I love this room," she said and waved her arm around. "So many books. I also love the way these couches face each other in front of this amazing stone fireplace."

"Yes, I don't think I'll ever read all of them." Lillian glanced around. "But, I'm an avid reader, so I've read a lot. I enjoy reading in front of the fireplace."

"Can we talk about the truth?" Kaylob interrupted. "The books are nice and all, but we're talking about my life here."

Lillian gave him a guarded look. "Well, of course, dear."

"I've been lied to by everyone." He stood and started pacing the room. "I really just want to leave." He glanced at Beth Ann.

"No. Please hear me out," Lillian said, with a shaky voice.

"Hear you out? Do you know how old I am? Isn't this happening a little late?" His eyes narrowed.

Beth Ann stood up, but swayed and almost went down to the floor. Kaylob jumped over and caught her. "Beth Ann, are you alright?"

For whatever reason, Beth Ann was taking this really hard. Maybe, with everything else she'd been through, this was too much, along with the long trip. He just needed to get a grip and talk normal.

"Come on, baby. Just sit down. I'm acting like an idiot." He shot a look at Lillian to let her know he was faking it, for Beth Ann.

They all sat back down and he watched Beth Ann slump. She was not feeling well and he could see it. He took her hand and gave it a gentle squeeze.

"Well, Lillian, why don't you just explain who you are. Why is it that I'm just finding out about you? I mean, I didn't even know you existed until recently."

"I need a minute to think about this." She let out a deep breath. "Like I said, I wasn't expecting to talk about this so soon."

"Oh of course, twenty-seven years isn't enough time for you to know what to say," he snapped.

"Please, Kaylob," said Beth Ann. "Let's stay calm." She placed her hands across her stomach.

Kaylob calmed his voice and noticed Lillian appeared pale, but otherwise composed.

"Okay, I'm not trying to upset you, Kaylob, but here goes. I was eighteen when I got pregnant by my fiancé. We were both in college in the states. His family was from here and very powerful and wealthy. My family was from here too, but I spent a lot of time in California and that is where I met Jackie, your mom."

"Don't you mean the lady who pretended to be my mom?" he grumbled.

Beth Ann took his hand in hers, and for a moment he felt a little more relaxed.

Lillian frowned. "Nevertheless, we became inseparable. She was married and I was engaged, so we did holidays and weekends together." She wiped a tear from her eye. "When we found out I was pregnant, we couldn't let Patrick's family know. They would have wanted to put our baby up for adoption." Her eyes showed pain. "They were controlling and had so much power."

"I can assume that baby was me?" he questioned.

"Yes," she glanced between him and Beth Ann. "We are talking about you."

"So you didn't want them to put me up for adoption, but that's what you did. You gave me away. How is that different?"

"Jackie was my best friend and she couldn't have children."

"Well, now, that's just so much better. You dumped me off to a family who couldn't have children, and a dad that was never around. Hell, he never acted like he gave a shit about me." Kaylob wanted to get up and hit something, but had to remain calm for Beth Ann's sake, or at least try.

"No!" Lillian winced, but shook her head. "We saw you twice a month. We were supposed to be able to see you, and we had all planned to tell you when you were old enough." She ran her hand down her dress to smooth it out. "But Harold changed his mind and wouldn't let us come around. We begged and pleaded with him, but we had already signed the papers and terminated our parental rights. Believe me, we spoke to several attorneys and it was too late." There was no missing her hands trembling when she stood and moved over to make a cup of tea. "We never put anything about visitation in writing because we trusted them. They were so in love with you." Her voice dipped. "We thought you'd have all of us to love you."

What was he supposed to feel about that? His parents adored him ... like hell. His mom did, but never his *father*.

He glanced over at Beth Ann, who was turning green again. "I think we need to put this conversation on hold. My wife is not looking so well." He stood and held out his hand to her, even though all he wanted to do was yell and scream at Lillian. This all seemed like a bunch of bullshit excuses.

"Thank you, honey." Beth Ann took hold and let him pull her up. "I'm so sorry. I don't know why I'm feeling this way." She held her stomach. "But my guess is what I said earlier, jet lag and stress."

"You do look a bit fatigued." Lillian studied her. "Jet lag can be really harsh."

"Maybe if I take a nap, I'll feel better. I might not have eaten enough," Beth Ann admitted.

"I'll send up some lunch to your room. That might help you to feel better. Our cook makes the best chicken soup around."

"Thank you, Lillian." Beth Ann smiled and Kaylob took her hand. He would stay until she could travel, then he was going to insist on leaving this place and never coming back. There would be more questions, but right now he needed to let his wife get some rest. After all, she was his number one priority. Everything else could just wait.

* * * *

Beth Ann was relieved that they were going to put off the rest of the conversation. Her stomach churned in all different directions, but was headed downhill. What the heck was going on? Maybe she had caught the flu, or maybe it *was* just all the stress.

They excused themselves and once they stepped out into the hall, Lillian instructed one of the housekeepers to take them up to their room. They followed the girl through the house and up the giant staircase. It was truly gorgeous with its rich wood banister.

She turned and grinned at them. "By de way, my name is Cara. Ha-war-ya?" She had a tiny accent, but not like the cab driver who had driven them here, his was so strong it was hard to understand.

"Good, thank you," Beth Ann said, then nudged Kaylob.

Kaylob gave a fake grin and nodded.

By the time they reached the double doors, Beth Ann was feeling less queasy. Cara opened them up and waved for them to enter.

"If yer be needing anythin', please be lettin' us know. Dare is a phone in yer livin' room dat rings down ter Nathan, de main butler. Naw matter waaat yer might be needin', turn down yer bed, a midnight snack, we'll be 'ere for yer." She smiled and added. "Cheers."

After she closed the door, Kaylob wrapped his arms around Beth Ann and gave her a worried look. "Let's get you changed into something comfortable. I want you to rest until lunch arrives." He nodded towards the bed. "That looks really comfy."

Beth Ann glanced around. "Can you believe this? This room is *three* times the size of our townhouse." She walked over to the amazing rock fireplace that took up an entire wall. "Look, another set of double doors." She opened them and stepped out onto a very large terrace. "Oh my gosh, Kaylob, the views are breathtaking." Beth Ann paused. "Kaylob, come and look." She wondered why he was so quiet. "Kaylob?"

She went back inside and found him sitting in a chair, gazing at the floor mournfully. "Kaylob, honey." She moved near him and squatted down. "Are you okay?"

For a minute she didn't think he was going to speak, but after a long pause, he cleared his throat. "I'm not sure I can be excited about any of this." He glanced around the room. "These people dumped me off and they were my parents. Look how they lived and look at my life. I was always looked at as the kid from the wrong side of the tracks." He inhaled and met her gaze. "Beth Ann, I had to take care of a mother who was depressed, because my dad was never home. I hardly had a childhood."

"You're right, it was unfair and wrong and I understand you're hurt and angry." She pulled him up. "And, it was awful for them to wait so long to tell you. But, aren't you forgetting something?"

"No. Oh, yeah. I'm forgetting how I had to work and save my own money. Sometimes going without things I wanted. Often, I had to hand over my whole pay check to my dad. Why, because he was always behind on something."

"Are you saying you would have rather grown up here instead of Novato?" she asked quietly.

"Hell yeah, look at this place. I would have also grown up with a dad that maybe loved me. Why wouldn't I have wanted to grow up here?"

Beth Ann felt a jab in her heart, then tears sprang out of her eyes.

"Kaylob," she said and ran to the bed crying. It hurt for him to say that to her. If he had grown up here, they would have never met. Why was she so emotional about it though? Maybe it was the disappointment with everything. However, she needed to stop crying like a baby. Taking a deep breath, she tried like heck to reel in her emotions. After a few minutes she exhaled and dried off her tears. This was not about her. It was about Kaylob.

She felt the bed jiggle when he sat down. "What did I say? I thought you'd understand." Confusion moved across his face.

"We would have never met," she said, just above a whisper.

"You're right." His eyes clung to hers. "My life would have been empty without you."

She nodded. "Mine too. When I think about the fact that you might have grown up here, my heart hurts." She placed her hand across her chest. "I'm glad you grew up in Novato. I'm sorry you went through all you did, but still, maybe it was fate."

Kaylob continued to gaze at her, but didn't say another word. With a whispering touch, he ran his fingers down her cheek to her neck. "I love you with all my heart." His eyes were etched with pain.

After a couple of minutes, he rose and stepped out onto the terrace. Maybe he needed time alone and to think about what had happened. It had to be a lot to take in. She laid her head on the pillow and didn't remember closing her eyes.

* * * *

The sound of laughter woke Beth Ann. She glanced around, and for a moment, she felt disoriented, not sure where it was coming from. She rolled off the bed and noticed the clock. Wow! She'd been asleep for over two hours, her stomach growled right on cue. One thing was for sure, she was feeling much better. Pure exhaustion must have caused her nausea, dizziness, and emotional syndrome, which had to be a real syndrome, she was sure of it.

"Kaylob," she called out, but there was no response.

Another round of laughter came from outside. She noticed sandwiches and soup on a nearby tray and grabbed a half of what appeared to be turkey and cheese, then stepped out onto the terrace and let the sunshine warm her face. Down below in the garden, she spied two girls walking along the path, giggling and chattering away. Who were they?

One had beautiful long blonde hair and appeared to be maybe nineteen or twenty. She wore blue shorts with a matching top. Could any girl be more perfect with her tiny waist and long legs? The other one, who had short dark hair, looked really young, maybe fourteen.

Beth Ann took large bites of her sandwich and stared. Then she saw Kaylob jogging towards the two. It appeared he'd already met them, because when he stopped the little blonde stuck her arm through his, then leaned in and kissed his cheek. The food almost got stuck in her throat, but she managed to swallow. Maybe it was time to blast some pillows down on their heads. That would get their attention.

When Kaylob's arm went around the young woman and he kissed the top of her head, Beth Ann saw red.

Chapter Two

"Okay, take a breath." She must have spoken too loudly, because the blonde girl turned and caught her staring.

She moved away from Kaylob and ran closer to the terrace.

"Beth Ann." The girl tilted her head upward, shading her eyes. "Please come down and join us."

Holy double vision! Beth Ann couldn't believe it. This girl was the female version of Kaylob, even down to the dimple in her chin. Only she was tiny, with the same dazzling smile.

"My name is Shawna and I always wanted a sister," she squealed. Kaylob was looking up at Beth Ann with clear amusement as he blew her a kiss.

Beth Ann waved back, feeling slightly embarrassed that she'd jumped to conclusions. It hadn't occurred to her that Kaylob might have a sister. "Wow! Okay, I'll be right there," she called down and returned to the room.

She'd hurry as fast as she could, but needed to eat something first. She sat at the table, finished her sandwich and ate almost an entire bowl of soup. Afterwards, she brushed her teeth and headed downstairs, hoping to find her way out of the large maze, filled with corridors and rooms.

The main butler glanced at her with curiosity as she came down the elaborate staircase.

"Your name is Nathan, right?" Beth Ann asked.

"Yes, ma'am." He nodded.

"How do I get out to the garden behind …"

The butler sniffed and started to speak, but before he could get a word out, she heard her name.

"Beth Ann."

She turned and saw Kaylob walking towards her.

"Never mind," she said to Nathan and took Kaylob's outstretched hand.

"Come with me. I want you to meet my baby sister. She's wonderful." The smile on his face was enthralling. "How are you feeling?"

"All better now," Beth Ann said. There was something about the way he said baby sister that made her feel joyful.

They stepped outside and the first thing Beth Ann noticed was the beautiful gardens and the ocean view that surrounded them. Everything was so perfect and reminded her of what heaven might look like. The green was the deepest green she'd ever seen and the blue skies seemed more colorful than those back home. Kaylob squeezed her hand as they walked down the cobblestone path.

A scream made her jump.

"Beth Ann!" Kaylob's newfound sister ran up and threw her arms around her neck. "I'm so glad to meet you." Her voice trembled. "I've waited all my life to meet Kaylob and now I get a sister, too."

Beth Ann couldn't have been happier. Shawna appeared charming and authentic. Just like her mother and brother, you could feel the kind spirit and Beth Ann hoped this revelation would make up for the earlier shock of finding out his long-lost aunt was really his mother.

The girl's royal blue eyes glistened as she backed up. "Sorry, if I startled you," she said in a quiet voice.

"No," Beth Ann said, then stepped closer to embrace her. "I always wanted a sister and it's so nice to meet you."

The girl with the dark hair stood off in the distance, letting them have their reunion.

"Paula, come here," Shawna called her over. "This is our cousin, Paula, and we are both so excited we finally get to meet the two of you."

Paula walked shyly their way. "I'm your cousin by marriage." Her smile revealed a mouth full of braces.

"Yes," Beth Ann nodded. "That would make us family." She hugged the young lady and noticed the broad smile on Kaylob's face.

"I hope it's not rude of me, but I have to go inside and call Brian,"

13

Paula said. Shawna gave her a teasing look and Paula blushed. "He *is* my beau now."

Beth Ann watched the crimson light up her face.

"I'll be back in a bit." Paula smiled at everyone and went on her way back through the garden. They all chuckled and watched her hurry off.

Shawna was holding Kaylob's hand and there was no doubt by the proud way he was looking at her, that her husband was already taken with his baby sister. It was one of the best days of Beth Ann's life. In the past it had always saddened her because Kaylob didn't have much family.

"Shawna," Beth Ann asked. "Did you know all along about Kaylob?"

Shawna nodded fiercely. "Yes, I was told he'd come home to meet me someday. When I was little, every year on his birthday, I would stand out front and wait." Her lip trembled. "We always made him a cake and would sing happy birthday. I made him something every year and I finally get to give it to him. I hated that he wasn't with us and there were times I threw tantrums. I didn't understand when I was little, why I couldn't see my brother. At least now, I can get to know him and give him all the things I made for him."

"I'm looking forward to it," Kaylob said.

With an expression of endearment, she looked up at her big brother and swallowed. "I wanted to meet my brother so bad. Two years ago when I turned eighteen, mom finally showed me your picture. I have it on my bedroom table." She pointed towards the house. "I always had faith that we'd meet someday." She paused to take a breath. "I know you're mad at Mom, Kaylob. I understand, I spent time being angry with her, too. Remember though, she was only eighteen when she had you. She would call and ask Jackie every year if they could please tell you or at least see you."

"Let's not talk about your mom," Kaylob snapped. "Let's focus on us."

"Okay." Shawna's eyes fell and she looked down at the ground.

"Sorry." He reached out and touched his sister's face. "I just think it might be best if we leave her out of our conversations, for a while anyway."

The wheels were turning, and Beth Ann remembered what she'd overheard between Jackie and Lillian. It was all making perfect sense.

"Now, I understand that phone call when Kaylob was in the hospital," she said softly. "I was suspicious when I first heard it." Beth Ann glanced between Shawna and Kaylob. "I heard Jackie say, *I know it's not fair, it's never been fair. You have the right to see him.* I get it now, and if the truth be told, I thought Jackie might be talking to his birth mother." She sighed. "However, I threw that thought away when Kaylob told me he had an aunt named Lillian. I just figured she and Harold had had some kind of falling out."

"It's okay, baby." Kaylob reached for her hand. "You had no way of knowing the story."

"I do know it was Harold," Beth Ann said. "He didn't want Lillian around and Jackie felt she had no choice. I understood that much."

Shawna nodded. "We all knew it was Harold. I just didn't know if I should say anything." She looked down.

"Let's drop it, okay?" His smile was tender. "It wasn't your job or Beth Ann's to tell me anything." He looked out at the ocean. "It's just a lot to take in right now. I can't seem to wrap my mind around it. I need to go lay down and get my head clear."

Beth Ann nodded. "Do you need me to come with you?"

"No. I need to be alone for a bit. Is that okay? How are you feeling and did you eat something?"

"I feel much better now and yes I ate." Beth Ann met his gaze. "And I understand that you need time alone."

"Beth Ann and I can spend some sister time together," Shawna said.

He gave Beth Ann a quick kiss and took off.

They both stood staring at Kaylob as he walked away.

"This is all just a shock for him, but one thing is for sure, he's happy that you're his sister."

They continued strolling through the gardens, which seemed endless. The trails that twisted and turned gave way to more flowers and amazing trees in a variety of colors. Shawna would pause and point to all the different flowers. Beth Ann was impressed with how she seemed to know all the names. She waved towards the Shell Flowers, Easter Lilies, Amaryllis, along with the gorgeous Lilies, Roses, and Chrysanthemums.

Some Beth Ann knew, but right now there were just too many for her to remember all of them.

Shawna grinned and stopped. "These are my very favorite, Gerberas, Daffodils and Daisies. When I get married, I want to use these in my wedding." She inhaled. "Someday, I hope to meet the right man who will become my husband."

A few minutes later, Paula came running around the corner looking excited.

"There you are," Shawna said. "We are heading inside, you want to join us."

"I have a date with Brian, he's taking me to the movies, so Mom is picking me up. It was nice to meet you, Beth Ann." She was beaming. "We will be leaving next week, to go back to the States. I want to spend all the time I can with him."

Shawna touched Paula's arm. "Have fun."

"I will." Paula nodded.

"Nice meeting you, Paula, and I hope I see you again," said Beth Ann.

"Me too." She turned and practically ran down the path, but just before she got to the corner she called out, "Tell Kaylob goodbye and I'll see him soon."

"I will," Beth Ann chuckled. "Wow, she lives in the States?"

"Yes, they just vacation here off and on. They'll be back for the summer."

Beth Ann got lost in her thoughts. It was funny how much Paula acted like she used to when she first started dating Kaylob. Heck, sometimes she still acted that way.

"Beth Ann," Shawna called her name and waved her hand in front of her eyes. "Did I lose you?"

"Oh, my gosh, you sound just like your brother. He asks me that all the time." She laughed.

Shawna grabbed her hand. "Let's go into the parlor and have tea."

"Okay, but let me sneak upstairs and get my wedding album. I want to show you our pictures that I brought to share with everyone."

Shawna went upstairs with her, but waited in the hall. Beth Ann grabbed her wedding album, and because it was in the outer room, she didn't have to enter the bedroom. She quietly left and they headed down to the parlor.

The first thing Beth Ann noticed when they entered, was how large it was. The room had flower prints everywhere, wallpaper, pictures and even the lamp shades. Holy midnight, the room was busy. Shawna pointed to a red velvet couch near the window, which matched the red carpet. They both sat down side by side.

"I brought these pictures of our wedding to show Lillian. But I had no idea that I'd be sharing them with Kaylob's sister and mother," Beth Ann said.

Nathan walked in with the tea and sat it down on something that looked like a coffee table, then poured them each a cup.

They both thanked him before he left.

"How did he know we were in here?" Beth Ann took a sip of the warm mint tea.

"I think he has radar." A soft laugh escaped Shawna.

Beth Ann chuckled and opened the album to the first page. The memories filled her with total delight, especially since she'd spent such a long time thinking he was lost to her.

The first page showed Beth Ann climbing out of bed with messy hair. They both cracked up. Then there was one of her wrapped in a towel, looking shell shocked. Beth Ann explained as she flipped through the pages.

"Here I am getting my hair done and being rushed around everywhere."

Then when she came to the one where she stood in front of a mirror looking at her wedding dress, the memory caused tears to fill her eyes. "My dress," Beth Ann whispered.

"Oh, my goodness, Beth Ann, it's so beautiful and so are you." They paused for a minute just taking in her gown.

When they got to the next page, it showed Kaylob being woke up and ushered out of bed. Frankie's smile was wide and he appeared to be waving away the camera person, since he and Kaylob's only attire were boxers.

Beth Ann started to turn the page, but Shawna held her hand. "How old is he?" She raised an eyebrow and didn't take her eyes off the picture.

"Frankie's my age. Twenty-five." Beth Ann grinned.

"Oh, he's very handsome." She arched a brow. "Wow! And hot."

"Yes, he is, he's been mine and Kaylob's best friend since childhood." Beth Ann felt amused by Shawna's open admiration of Frankie. He got that response a lot from women.

After a few minutes she let Beth Ann turn the page. Each snapshot made them laugh until they got to the ones of the ceremony. Both got very quiet, then Beth Ann pulled out the papers and let Shawna read their vows. Beth Ann watched as the tears gathered in Shawna's eyes, and she seemed lost in the words.

"You and Kaylob are so in love." She held the vows to her heart. "Someday, I want that too. I'm saving myself for my husband and I know it's old fashioned. I've been teased a lot about it. But I want to wait until my wedding night."

"It's your body and you have the right to make that choice." Beth Ann took her hand. "Nobody should make fun of you."

Shawna nodded and rested her head on Beth Ann's shoulder. "Did you guys wait?"

Beth Ann felt heat rise to her face. "No, but when he got back from the POW camp, we waited until we were married to make love. We got teased a little, too."

"Sometimes you have to go with your heart," Shawna said with a sigh.

Once Beth Ann flipped to the professional photos of everyone in the wedding party, she stopped at the big one of Frankie and Kaylob. In the first picture they appeared serious and were looking right into the camera. The second one showed Kaylob being extremely happy and Frankie had a sly grin across his face. She knew that look well.

Beth Ann heard Shawna suck in her breath. "Oh my," she said. "Frankie is the most handsome man I've ever seen." She seemed taken with him. "I want to meet him."

Beth Ann closed the book. "Yes, he's all that and then some. But ..." She met Shawna's gaze. "He's a major playboy and he has lots of girlfriends."

"Oh, so he's never going to settle down?" Shawna asked, wearing the same impish grin she'd seen on Kaylob's face a million times.

"He said when he's thirty-something he wants to fall in love like me and Kaylob. But, I don't know. He had a live-in girlfriend and that didn't work out. He wasn't in love with her and they parted friends. I just can't see him ever settling down. I wish I could."

Shawna stared off into space. "Maybe he's just not met the right one yet. Want to walk down to the beach?"

"Sure." Beth Ann nodded and took a sip of her almost-cool tea.

Once they arrived, Beth Ann appreciated the slight breeze which brought some relief to the fairly warm day. They watched the sea gulls dip and dive into the green emerald water. One boy was playing fetch with his dog on the sand. Beth Ann loved the salty smell in the air and all the beauty around her.

As they walked, Beth Ann told Shawna more about how she and Kaylob had met. She'd even shared how he'd made her blush so badly the first time she'd ever seen him, that her mom thought she had a fever. They both had a great time sharing stories and laughing. By the time they got back Kaylob was looking for them.

"Where have my two favorite ladies been?" he asked.

"On the beach walking in the sand and we had a whale of a time," Shawna said, then giggled. "I was trying to find out more about your best friend, Frankie." She nudged Beth Ann. "He's a hunk and I want to meet him."

"No, you don't. He's trouble, but we love him anyway." He met his sister's gaze and seemed serious.

"Yes, I really do." Shawna seemed more determined.

Uh oh, Beth Ann smelled trouble, so she changed the subject. "We could all go take a walk in the garden, it looks amazing out there." She glanced at Kaylob then over to Shawna.

"Not me." Shawna explained. "I have some things I need to do before dinner. Don't forget to be in the garden room around six." She kissed them both and ran off.

Before they went for another walk, they made a quick trip up to their room to grab a sweater. A late afternoon in Ireland this time of year was a little cooler than California.

"Okay, I'm ready," Beth Ann said.

Kaylob was pulling on his windbreaker and took her hand. "Let's go."

Beth Ann was glad he appeared to have momentarily forgotten his anger with Lillian. It seemed like the unexpected gift of learning he had a sister had changed his mood. There was at least hope.

Dusk had set in by the time they got back downstairs. The gardens were even more magnificent than they had been before. It was gorgeous how the sun filtered through with its warm embrace and made the flowers glow with radiance. Nothing had ever been so lush.

As they continued to stroll, watching the little lights flicker on, Beth Ann found herself inspired and making up words to a song. "Dusk slides into dawn and lifts you up to find a new day, a new life, and a new beginning," she sang hitting all the right notes, then added. "Dawn is my friend, who waits every day for me, always there to light the way for me. Reach out and touch my face with your light embrace, and never shall I feel alone again." She continued until she was done with the final words. "Never will I be lost in despair again with the love of my life by my side again. The light from the sun will warm my heart and always bring you home, and I'll never … be alone again."

"Beth Ann, I've never heard that song before. It's very touching. Did you learn that on tour?"

"No, I just made it up," she said.

"You just made that up?" He stopped walking and his eyes widened.

"Yes," she nodded.

"Just this very minute?" he asked again.

"I was inspired by all the beauty and grandeur."

"Baby, you should write down those words, and keep that melody. That is a gift."

"I have a whole binder of songs." Beth Ann shrugged. "No big deal, I never do anything but write them down and put them away."

"It's a big deal and you should show them to someone." He pulled her close and nibbled on her neck. "I love it and I love you."

"I love you too, honey." Beth Ann glanced down at her watch, feeling a little embarrassed because he was making such a big deal about a made up song. "I'm starving," she said, changing the subject.

Kaylob chuckled. "You're really starting to sound like me." He rubbed his belly.

They made a hasty retreat upstairs again where they got cleaned up and changed for dinner. Just before they left, Kaylob pulled her into his arms. "Are you feeling okay? Do you think it might be getting close to that time of month?"

"Honestly, I never know anymore since I was kidnapped, things changed. Maybe it was the stress. But I'm not regular anymore. I'm fine though, just very hungry." She paused. "Kaylob ... I know you were upset with your mo ... Lillian, and I'm sure mad at Jackie too. Maybe all of them. Are you okay with doing this?"

"Hell no, but I'm starving and this is not a good time to talk about it." He stared at her. "I'm not happy with any of them. For one, look at how much time I've missed with my sister. Why in the hell didn't they at least help out my parents? The bottom line is, they could have told me sooner. I mean, to wait until I'm twenty-seven, almost twenty-eight," he said. "That's bullshit. Nevertheless, I'm very happy that I grew up in Novato." He leaned in for a kiss. "It was a great place."

She kissed him back. "I thought so, too." She moved over to the mirror and brushed her hair. "Let's go. I'm famished."

"You're scaring me, Beth Ann. Did I give you the hunger disease?" He took her hand and pulled her out the door.

Beth Ann had learned a long time ago not to mess around much when Kaylob gets hungry. Now they just had to find the garden room.

They walked past a multitude of quarters, each different from the other. One had a baby grand piano with tons of seating and marble floors, thankfully none were red and there was no flower wallpaper.

It seemed like it took forever, before they spotted Nathan standing at a set of double doors, as though he were waiting for them.

"Hello Mr. and Mrs. O'Brien." He pushed the doors open. "It's this way." He waved them through to a dining area so massive that it felt as though they were outdoors. It was incredible, with a giant waterfall that was not too loud, but just enough to be relaxing. The aroma from the food was divine.

"Oh my gosh." Beth Ann had to blink a few times.

"How special." Kaylob stopped, glanced around and didn't look happy.

The table itself was practically the size of a football field. Shawna was already waving at them from one side of the table. Lillian sat with her back to them, but turned when Shawna said something and gave them a radiant smile, but the smile faded when she saw Kaylob's face.

Ah ha, at least Beth Ann knew now where Kaylob got that charming smile. She was truly stunning. And, there were no words to describe Shawna, who made Beth Ann feel like a plain Jane.

As they walked a mile towards the table, she could feel Kaylob tense up.

"Are you okay?" She leaned close and asked.

"Yes, I'm fine," he said tersely.

They arrived at the table and Kaylob pulled out the chair directly across from Lillian and Shawna.

Lillian regarded them steadily. "You both look debonair tonight. Beth Ann, you look like you're feeling better. All the color is back in your beautiful cheeks."

"I am feeling so much better. Thank you."

"Kaylob. I'm happy you joined us tonight. I've been looking forward to this all day." She picked up her napkin and laid it on her lap.

Kaylob nodded, but Beth Ann saw the irritation flash in his eyes. He was not happy at all.

Shawna took a sip of her ice tea. "Beth Ann, your singing is beautiful, no wonder you won a tony. I was on my way out to ask Kaylob something, and stopped and listened to that beautiful song."

"See." Kaylob touched her shoulder. "I told you it was good." He glanced around the table. "Beth Ann created that song. She's so talented."

Beth Ann felt heat crawling up her neck. "Kaylob. It was just a silly song. But I do have a question for you, Lillian, if you don't mind." Once again she changed the subject.

"Not at all." She wiped her mouth and looked at her expectantly.

"Why is it that you and Shawna don't have an Irish accent? And many of the keepers don't either. I understand why Paula doesn't, because she lives in the States, but I was wondering about the others."

"I have it," Lillian explained. "But, I've worked hard to not use it. So, because of that, Shawna doesn't have much of one either.

Remember, we spent a lot of time in the States and while in college, I had a speech teacher. I didn't want to stand out or be different."

Kaylob took a drink of water. "So what about your staff?" he asked.

"Oh many of them have thick accents. But Nathan isn't from here. I met him in New York."

"Ah," Beth Ann nodded.

Shawna giggled. "Beth Ann, I'm still laughing me leg off." Her accent was thick, but fun.

"Wow. You did that well," Beth Ann said.

"How about we be eating." Shawna picked up the covers to the platters revealing the food. "Yum. That's a universal word."

The food was plentiful with corn beef and cabbage and some type of potatoes that were rich and creamy. Never had she tasted potatoes that melted in her mouth. It was out of this world and she was sure her taste buds had arrived in heaven. The shepherd's pie was even more delicious, she savored the smooth texture, which had a buttery taste.

Kaylob hadn't said a word, but he was going back for seconds of the shepherd's pie. After a few bites, he finally took a breath. "This is marvelous, the best I've ever tasted." He wiped his mouth and glanced around the table. Beth Ann hoped his mood had settled, but she could still feel tension rolling off him.

"Glad you liked it," Lillian said then took a sip of her tea. "Bethany is one of the best cooks I've ever had."

Kaylob nodded and Shawna agreed.

"She makes a great pie." Shawna took one more bite and pushed her plate away. "I can't eat anything else."

Beth Ann couldn't remember a time when she ate so much. Not even at Gram's. "I hope my clothes fit when I leave here." She took her final bite. "Dinner was delicious."

Kaylob had nodded through dinner at the conversation and was polite, but way too quiet and the tension was clear. Once dinner was over, Lillian and Shawna rose from the table. It seemed pretty clear that escaping was what they both wanted.

"I enjoyed dinner with you both, but I'm afraid I'm exhausted." Lillian placed her napkin on her plate. "I do hope you'll both be here for breakfast. We usually eat around 9:00 a.m. because Shawna is a night owl, and stays on the phone with her friends all night."

Kaylob glanced up at her. "We'll see."

"Alright," she said with sad eyes.

Shawna raised her eyebrow, as Lillian left, but didn't say anything. She merely said goodnight and kissed them both on the cheek before she excused herself to go to her room.

After Shawna left, Beth Ann turned to Kaylob. "Want to take a walk again? I need to shift this food around."

"Sure," he stood and held out his hand, but before they could step away, Nathan walked in. "Would either of you like dessert?"

"No, thank you," they both said in unison.

"I hope I can walk after eating all that food." Kaylob laughed as though he was telling a joke, but she could tell his heart wasn't in it.

As they walked through the garden once again holding hands, Beth Ann could feel the breeze tickling her skin. The moon shed a flickering light across the scenery, giving it a magical radiance. The night was bewitching and the sounds of the waves and other night-time creatures gave her goosebumps. Somewhere, off in the distance, someone was playing a bagpipe. They both paused to listen.

Kaylob took her hand and placed it across his heart. "Beth Ann. I feel so connected here." He gazed into her eyes. "I feel this longing and a need to be in Ireland. But I'm upset at the same time."

She glided her arms around his waist and looked up into his eyes. "It's perfect, from what we've seen so far. I was wondering ..." She took a deep breath. "Do you think you might be able to try talking to Lillian? Maybe you'll start to understand more of what she was going through?"

"No, not right now, I don't even know if we're staying!" He moved away from her. "I don't need to hear anymore. The way I feel right now is not good. I feel full of anger at all of them. I hate feeling this pissed off. I'm grateful for the money I have now, but I would bet there is no Uncle Tony. Remember what the taxi driver said. He didn't recall her having any siblings. Which means, where'd that money come from?"

"Oh, that's right. I don't know, honey, it makes no sense right now. Can we give it a few more days and see if you can get the answers you need?" she asked, gently.

What she wanted was for him to understand, she totally supported him, but really wanted him to give his mom a second chance. How did she do that without hurting him?

Kaylob looked up at the stars, ignoring the question. "Look." He stepped closer and wrapped his arms around her from behind. "Our star followed us all the way here." He kissed the top of her head. "Have I mentioned that you are the love of my life?"

"Hmm." She turned and faced him. "I'm not sure if I've heard that line before? Maybe you better take me upstairs and show me." She stood on her tip toes and kissed his chin, then gave it a nibble.

"Mrs. O'Brien, yer tryin' ter seduce me." He ran his tongue over her lips.

"Very well done." Beth Ann laughed at the accent.

Kaylob knew just how to charm her, from her head down to her toes, which sent shivers to other unspoken regions. Her body was ready before they even got started.

When they got in the room they brushed their teeth and Beth Ann ran her bath water. The tub was giant sized and had jets with different speeds. She was looking forward to relaxing after all the walking.

Her gown had just hit the floor, when she heard footsteps behind her.

"Baby, I need you now." His eyes were filled with desire.

"Now?" She glanced at her tub that was filled with bubbles, then she reached down and turned it off.

"Yes, right now." He pulled her closer and there was no doubt he meant right now.

"Okay," she murmured, as he led her across the room and laid her on the bed. The next thing he did was peel off his clothes and holy smokes, her heart was racing and her eyes were glued to how much he desired her.

"I'm all yours. Do what you will," she invited.

"Just wait until you see what I'm going to do and how good you're going to feel." He started with his lips, slightly grazing her calf, and working his way up. She liked this bath much more than the other one she had planned.

25

Chapter Three

Kaylob had always kept his word and boy did he show her. Two hours later he was passed out on the bed. Beth Ann started to quietly roll out, when she felt his hand touch her.

"Where do you think you're going, young lady?"

"To soak in the tub that I almost got to climb into," she teasingly added. "But someone needed to get ..." She paused. "A little something."

"What were you going to say, Elizabeth Ann Rose?" He pulled her closer.

"Nothing," she said then laughed.

"Like hell. You were going to say I needed to get laid." He arched a brow.

"Kaylob Shawn O'Brien." She scolded, then hit his head with a pillow.

"Oh no you don't. Say it." He climbed on top of her. "My husband needed to get laid."

"No!" She looked away. "I won't say that."

"Okay." He tickled her knees, in the spot he'd known about since she was eleven. "Say, my husband needed to get laid and I loved getting laid, too."

She screamed in laughter as he tickled her some more. She was used to him making her say he was the boss or he was the most handsome, but not this.

He tickled her again. "Elizabeth Ann Rose, admit what you were going to say or ..."

"Okay, okay, my husband needed to get laid and I loved doing it." She felt her face heat.

"There we go. See, we are adding things to our game." He growled and pulled her closer. "Let me show you how hungry I am." He started kissing and nibbling on her belly, working his way down. Then he showed her how many times he could make her call out his name.

After another hour of making love, she lay in his arms, listening to his heart beat.

"Beth Ann, I have something to tell you."

She looked up into his eyes and saw how serious he was. "What?"

"I'm trying to figure out how to say this." He put his hand across his forehead, like he was in deep thought.

"Kaylob, just tell me, please."

"Okay." He paused. "I sure as hell hope these rooms are soundproof." He chuckled. "I wouldn't want anyone to hear you." He teased. *"Oh more, Kaylob. Please now. Ah, oh, yes now. I want all of you honey, please, all of you. Oh, yes, here it comes, it's here."* He mimicked her mischievously.

"You brat!" She took a pillow and walloped him. He grabbed it away and carried her into the extremely cool bathtub. They had to drain it and start over again. It was well after 2:00 a.m. when they finally fell asleep.

* * * *

The next morning Beth Ann stood on the terrace and noticed the aroma was a bit salty, but with a sweetness that clung in the air, like cotton sheets hanging on a clothes line. It was nice. She watched as the birds sailed in the breeze, gliding across the sky. It was as if a slice of paradise was bestowed upon the countryside and she was there to witness it. Although, she was saddened for Kaylob. She would be lying if she said she wished he had lived here, because she didn't. The fact remained that it was wrong of them to hide it from him for so long. Why hadn't they told him sooner? That was just crazy and she couldn't think of any good answer. The best thing she could do is try and help him take his mind off it. That wouldn't be easy, but she could try.

"Kaylob," she shot over her shoulder. "I'm in love with this place, it's so breathtaking."

Then she saw Lillian walking in the garden with a pure white cat on a leash. Now, that's something Beth Ann had never seen before.

Kaylob stepped outside on the terrace and said, "that's different."

Beth Ann was glad to see him looking at the kitty with interest. Maybe he'd start to calm down and not be so angry.

"Good morning up there." Lillian called out. "Would you two like to come to breakfast a little early?"

Beth Ann nodded. "Sure, I'm starving and I'd bet Kaylob is too." She glanced at him and saw his jaw tighten.

"What's the cat's name?" She was trying to ease the tension.

"This is Lazy Boy," she called out. "He's so lazy that I had to teach him to walk on a leash, just to get him to move around."

"We'll be down soon. I want to meet this Lazy Boy," Beth Ann said.

They both finished getting dressed and ready for the day, then made it downstairs. Entering the garden room made her stomach jump for joy. The scent was out of this world and smelled like baked bread, or something delicious.

Kaylob stuck his nose in the air. "I'm so hungry if I don't eat, I think I'll die soon." He sounded pathetic.

When it came to food, Kaylob never let anything stop him from eating. It secretly amused her.

"What?" he asked, as though he could hear her thoughts while they headed towards the long table, which was already set for breakfast. Nobody was there yet, she heard Kaylob let out a deep breath.

"I was just thinking how you never let anything get in the way of hunger." Beth Ann chuckled.

"You're right," he agreed and gave her a sly smile. "Although this situation has come very close to making me lose my appetite."

"Kaylob, I'm so sorry."

"Let's change the subject." He glanced around.

They had just sat down when the servers came rushing in as if they were waiting in the wings for a cue. The platters of food started arriving and the aroma got even better.

Nathan came and stood by the table. "Good morning, Mr. and Mrs. O'Brien. Today we have the traditional Irish breakfast, consisting of fried eggs, beans, black and white pudding." He lifted more covers and continued. "Here we have tomatoes, mushrooms, soda bread and wheat bread, orange juice, plus bacon, and we have some turkey sausage, because we were told that Mrs. O'Brien won't eat pork." He nodded.

"You have a fry-up here and real Irish coffee, but if there is anything else you need, just let us know."

Beth Ann grinned."This looks perfect, don't you think Kaylob."

"Yes, perfect. Thank you," Kaylob acknowledged.

Nathan gave them a nod, then Lillian and Shawna came strolling in. "Good morning. Nathan, this looks fabulous." Lillian turned and smiled at Beth Ann and Kaylob. "And you both look wonderful this morning."

Shawna wasn't so formal, she moved over and hugged them both. "It's so nice to walk in and see my brother sitting at the table with my beautiful sister-in-law."

Kaylob stood and pulled out chairs for them, but before Lillian sat down she cupped his face. "I'm so glad you're here, Kaylob." Her lip quivered.

He tried to smile, but Beth Ann recognized it was fake. He was still upset. That much she knew, but at least he was trying to cover it up and was not as visibly angry as yesterday.

Beth Ann prayed that he would start to enjoy his new family. She could see he was already attached to his sister. Looking at the three of them together made it clear where Kaylob got his good looks. Of course Jackie and Harold were cute in their own way, but these three had it all.

While they dug in, Beth Ann was determined not to eat as much, or so she told herself. Maybe she should get on a scale soon, she touched her belly.

"Beth Ann," Lillian said. "You're glowing this morning. Did you have a good sleep?"

"Yes, I slept soundly."

Shawna caught Beth Ann's gaze. "I did too, and I got to bed before 3:00 a.m. I came up to your room around midnight because I saw the lights on from outside, but ..." She blushed. "I think you were busy."

Beth Ann felt her face heat. Holy cow, from this point forward, she would stuff a sock in her mouth.

"Shawna Cynthia Rafferty. Stop that. You're embarrassing them." Lillian gave her daughter a cross look.

Kaylob laughed. "I'm not embarrassed." He glanced over at Beth Ann. "But my wife appears to be. Look at her rosy cheeks."

Just as he opened his mouth to take a bite, Beth Ann kicked him under the table.

"Ouch. Why'd you do that?" He gave her an impish grin.

She was going to kill him later.

They all seemed to finish at the same time, but of course Kaylob went back for some last-minute bites.

"I have to work today," Shawna said. "I tried to get a few more days off, but they're short-handed."

"Where do you work?" Kaylob asked.

"I'm a cook at Emerald Bayside," she said. "I love cooking and someday plan on being a chef. I guess we have that in common."

"Yes, we sure do," Kaylob agreed.

Lillian took a sip of her coffee and sighed. "She's been hanging around in the kitchen learning how to cook since she was six-years-old."

"Kaylob got his degree after waiting forever." Beth Ann leaned her head on his shoulder. "He's amazing."

"Thank you, baby. I try."

"I've heard only good things about your cooking, Kaylob. I hope to sample some of your food someday," Lillian said.

Kaylob nodded, but didn't smile.

Lillian placed her napkin on her plate. "I was wondering how you'd feel about meeting your grandmother?"

Kaylob sat there looking down for at least a minute. "I have a grandmother?" He swallowed.

"Yes and she's been dying to meet you." Lillian's eyes got glassy.

"She's the best Kaylob, you'll love her." Shawna's grin spread across her face.

Beth Ann watched Kaylob's expression and wasn't sure what he was thinking, until she saw curiosity fill his eyes.

"I would," he said. "What's her name?"

"Edna Finley and she's a lovely lady. Patrick, your birth father, loved her like his own mother."

Beth Ann saw the burning questions flicker in his eyes.

"My birth father," Kaylob's voice dipped. "I want to know about him."

Shawna stood. "I'm sorry, but I have to go." She turned and rushed out of the room.

Kaylob started to go after her, but Lillian waved him down. "She can't talk about her father." Lillian glanced down at her coffee. "She took his death very hard."

Beth Ann's heart broke for all of them, but there was no missing the depth of pain in Shawna's eyes when she ran out of the room.

"Let's go to the Seaside Parlor." Lillian stood. "I have something for you from your father."

They got up and followed her through the formal dining room and went towards the west, down the enormous hallway. Finally, they came to what was called the Seaside Parlor. The minute they stepped inside, Beth Ann knew this was her second favorite room so far. It had one wall lined with books and the far wall had a small white stone fireplace. The room was adorned with seashells and a flower border. Everything was a frosty blue with light pink. The couch was white with throw pillows and looked comfortable.

Lillian made her way to the bookshelf and pulled out a beautiful ceramic box, which she set on the table and opened it up. She took a deep breath and seemed to gain her strength as she pulled out a folded paper.

"This is for you, Kaylob. Your father wrote this before he died." She got a far-off look in her eyes. "He always said, in case anything ever happened to him, he wanted to say these things to you." She handed it over.

Kaylob took it in his hand and stared. Beth Ann noticed his fingers trembling.

He slowly opened it up and started to read.

My dear son, Kaylob Shawn Rafferty,

As you can see, your adopted parents let us name you and kept your first and middle name on our behalf. The nice thing is your adopted dad is Irish, so you got the great name of O'Brien.

If you're reading this, then I am no longer walking this great, green earth. I want you to know something. I loved you from the day you were born and I will love you always. The day you came into the world became one of the best moments of my life. It was bittersweet though. Giving you to Jackie and Harold was something that has haunted me every day of my life. So many times I wanted to steal you back. But, your mother and I knew that would be wrong. We did, however, look into fighting for visitation and because it was never put in the adoption papers, there was nothing we could do. We were young and stupid. We should have made sure it was in there before we terminated our parental rights.

We looked forward to every visit with you, and seeing your smiling face became the momentous part of our existence.

Kaylob, I wish I would have been more courageous and stood up to my family. I wish I wouldn't have let my fear of their power and what they might do drive me down the road to losing the most precious thing a man could have, his son.

Those last two nights we had with you were beautiful. We had no way of knowing it would be the very last time we held you or kissed you, but those moments will stay in my heart forever. I know you won't remember me or what we did, so I want to tell you about it.

That morning we went out to breakfast and watched you eat pancakes with smiley faces. You told us at age three they had vanilla inside. Only you said, "it tastes like banella, Daddy" and you gave me a bite and your mommy, too. You insisted we take a bite of those vanilla pancakes. And son, I knew you were smart right then, because you nailed it. They were vanilla pancakes.

Later we played in the hotel swimming pool where you would hang on to my neck. Together we would laugh while we playfully splashed your mommy. You would swim back and forth between us, as if you were basking in our love. I do believe you knew how much we loved you. And, you seemed to sense when we were sad and we were. It was the day we had to take you back. You would give us kisses and hugs and say, smile mommy, smile daddy, I wuv you. We did our best to be happy, but the final day was always so hard.

We dropped you off and that first night alone without you was spent in tears. We would hold each other in a pain I can't describe. It's like the biggest part of our hearts were missing. Jackie told us when we picked you up that weekend, that she wanted you to come and spend a summer with us. It was supposed to happen that following June 2nd until Sept 2nd. We had already rented a vacation home on the outside of town, where my family wouldn't see us, but it never happened.

Our hearts were tortured. Our souls were empty.

Years later we had your sister, Shawna Cynthia Rafferty and we fell in love with her just as we did you. She never took your place and she never could fill up the space we left for you. But she won her place deep inside our hearts.

You have a wonderful sister and every year we celebrate your birthday and your grandma comes to visit and joins in. My parents passed away and we never made peace with each other. They did, however, leave me everything they owned.

If I'm gone, which will be the case if you're reading this, then know I'm in the wind that blows against your face. Every falling star is me sending love down to you, and every rainbow is the many colors of happiness that I wish for your life.

If you listen closely to the Irish wind you can hear my voice and it will be saying how very proud I am of you, son.

I've seen your picture and heard what a wonderful young man you are. There are other things I've seen too, but I won't put it in this letter. I'll leave that to your birth mom.

I love you and will be watching you from the stars.

Your dad.

Kaylob was silent. When Lillian handed him a picture, he simply took it. "This was taken on our last day together," she said.

Beth Ann swallowed her tears, when she glanced at the photo that showed a happy little boy with two beautiful parents. Not to mention, his dad's physique was identical to Kaylob.

"How did he die?" Kaylob asked.

"It was the worst storm we'd ever had, and your dad wanted to come home early to make sure Shawna and I were safe. The road out here was not paved then." She took a deep breath and wiped off some tears. "It was a mudslide. It took us two days to get to him." Her voice broke.

Kaylob sat there holding the letter and picture in silence. After a long while he stood and left the room without looking back.

"Should I go after him?" Lillian cried.

"I'm going to go up. But I'm not going to talk unless he wants me to," Beth Ann explained and touched Lillian's hand. "Give him some time. He'll come around. This is all a shock for him." She stood and left the parlor.

Everything was quiet when she entered the bedroom, so she walked through the doors and found Kaylob sitting on the bed. Her heart almost broke when she saw his head in his hands and the picture and letter next to him.

She sat beside him, not saying a word.

After about twenty minutes he glanced over at her. "Hi baby. I'm sorry for being so quiet ... Can I ask you a question?"

"Sure, honey."

"Did you ever suspect that I was adopted when we were kids?"

Beth Ann thought about if she should mention the truth to him; it had crossed her mind many times. She had to be honest.

"Yes, I often wondered about it through the years. From the first moment I met your parents, I wondered. But as I mentioned, when I overheard the conversation between Jackie and Lillian, I had a deep feeling that something like that might be going on."

She was waiting for him to get angry at her for not saying anything and maybe she should have. But the truth was, she didn't know anything for sure, and she had no clue how to broach the subject.

"I did too," he admitted. "When I was little, I remember dreaming about Lillian and Patrick for years. I honestly thought of them and remembered their voices. Eventually, the dreams and memories faded." He looked down. "I asked my mom about them when I was about five and she just smiled and said sometimes angels come to us in our dreams. She told me maybe they were my special angels." He took in a long steady breath. "But my mom had tears in her eyes and I wondered why."

Beth Ann kneeled in front of him. "Oh, honey." She wrapped her arms around him. "Your dad is your guardian angel," she soothed.

Beth Ann didn't know what to do for him. He was hurting badly and she needed to support him in any way she could. She couldn't imagine what he was feeling. That was a big question, why did they wait so long? That wasn't fair to Kaylob or to Shawna. So much missed time.

As though Kaylob was reading her mind again, he asked, "Why did they keep the truth from me? Does that make any sense to you?"

Beth Ann had to be honest once again, but she also wanted him to give Lillian a chance too. "Kaylob, you need to sit down and have a long conversation with all of them."

"You're right." He nodded. "I deserve to know why."

Beth Ann hugged him. "You know ..." Just then someone knocked on the door. "Wonder who that is."

There was no way she was going to let anyone in the room right now. He needed some space and she was prepared to tell whoever it was to come back later.

She opened the door to find a lady about Gram's age. Her blue eyes glistened with inquisitiveness. She was tall, with salt-and-pepper hair and a stunning smile.

"Hi," Beth Ann said, staring at the lady.

"Top of the morning to yer. I know this probably won't be a good time for yer, but I really want to be seein' me grandson. My name is Edna, an I've been waitin far too long to be meetin him."

Edna had an accent, unlike Lillian and Shawna. Before she could speak, Beth Ann felt Kaylob behind her. When she turned, she saw his beautiful blue eyes soften with pent-up emotions, so she stepped aside.

Edna moved closer, her eyes pooling with tears. She then placed her hands on his face. "Ah, you're a bonny sight. You would be havin' no idea how long I've waited to touch me one an' only grandson."

She wrapped her arms around him and Kaylob hugged her right back. There was no distance, no anger, and all Beth Ann could feel was the instant connection between the generations. It was truly beautiful.

The hug went on for an incredibly long time, as though they were trying to make up for all the lost years.

Beth Ann placed her hand across her heart and thought of her own Gram. God had blessed her life, and she took that very moment to thank Him. Not just for her own Gram, but for Kaylob's chance at knowing his.

As she stood watching the two, she saw Edna unclasp a chain that held a heart locket around her neck.

"I've been havin' this since the day yer were born, an I've never taken it off," she said, handing it to Kaylob.

He held it in his hand and ran his fingers over it. "That's very special."

"Open it," she requested.

He did so, revealing two pictures, one that was clearly of him as a baby. The other photo was that of a little girl, who had to be Shawna. They could have almost been twins.

Kaylob handed her back the locket, then took Edna's elbow and led her into the sitting room, where they both sat down. He glanced at Beth Ann, who trailed behind, and patted the seat next to him.

"Aye, you'll be joinin us," Edna agreed. "I want to be hearin' all about the both of yer. How yer met and fell in love." She smiled. "I've been hearin some of it from me dottir, but I want to be hearin it from yer."

Beth Ann headed to the couch, but with no warning, the room started to spin. *Oh no! Not now, please, what's going on?* She felt herself going down, unable to stop as the room went black.

* * * *

When she opened her eyes, she was on the bed and the first person she saw was Edna. "Hi dear, I be feelin' glad yer back with us. We be calling the family doctor and he's on his way."

Kaylob was there by her side. "Beth Ann, you scared me to death." He tucked a strand of hair behind her ear. "Beth Ann has passed out from stress before."

"I have?" She couldn't think of a time.

"Yes, remember the time at the ocean when I just got back." He touched her cheek.

"Oh, right," she said and nodded. "I do remember now. That was a while ago, but I was under a lot of stress."

Beth Ann turned her head and noticed Lillian was there too, sitting beside her on the bed.

"Well, you've been through a lot, from my understanding, and *this* may have been too much." Lillian regarded Beth Ann with warm and caring eyes.

"We're gonna be givin' yer sum privacy, and we'll be sendin the doctor up, when he gets here." Edna stood and gave a soft smile.

Beth Ann watched as Kaylob rose and walked his grandmother to the door.

"We can talk about all this later." He gave them a nod.

Beth Ann was feeling better so she sat up and watched Kaylob studying her. "I guess I'm just reacting to stress these days and scaring everyone." She shook her head. "I really don't need to see a doctor. Like you said, this has happened before and I fainted when they said you were missing too. So I don't need to see anyone."

"Oh yes, you do," he scolded and sat down next to her. "And you are not going to talk your way out of this."

"Okay," she agreed.

"Jesus, that doctor better hurry." He got up and paced.

"Kaylob, settle down. I'm feeling fine." Beth Ann wondered why he was so stressed.

"No, you can't be. You just agreed with me way too fast." He turned and grinned.

"Oh, you." She took a pillow and threw it at him, but he dodged it.

"Ha, you missed." They both laughed, but she could see that he was worried about her.

Doctor Mallery, an older man with thinning hair and glasses perched on the end of his nose finally arrived. He concluded that she'd had an anxiety attack. He had a thick accent, which made Beth Ann listen closely.

"I shud really be runnin' a blud test," he said.

"No, that's not necessary, but thank you. If it happens again, I'll get some tests. However, I will follow your instructions and do some deep breathing." Beth Ann smiled, hoping that being cheery and cooperative would send him away.

"Okay, I can't be forcin' yer, but if it does 'appen again, I hope yer'll folly through." He took her hand. "Why don't yer an yir husband be takin a few days an enjoy de sea an be takin sum long walks, an go sight seein'?" He started wrapping his stethoscope up and putting it away.

"We will," Kaylob answered. "That I can promise."

"Well, she looks like de picture of health, so I'm not worried, and since the fainting has happened in the past, I won't be trying to force yer. Just try ter keep de stress away." He addressed that last bit to Kaylob, as though she wasn't there.

"I will, sir." Kaylob nodded and shook his hand. "Thank you for coming."

"No problem."

He walked the doctor to the door.

When Beth Ann felt better, she persuaded Kaylob to take her down to the beach. They spent the rest of the day on the shoreline looking out at the ominous sea. The emerald water stretched out as far as the eye could see. The seagulls were floating high above and casting shadows over the waves as they skillfully dove down, pulling up a fish and flying away. It was entertaining to watch. Although, in the back of her mind, she was wondering about the fainting. The strange thing about it was, in the past she knew when she was stressed, but this time she didn't feel all that stressed, maybe upset for Kaylob, but not the kind of stress she'd had before. Wait, she remembered that time when she was a kid and passed out, freaking her whole family out. That was from lack of food and sun. Oh well, if it happened again, she'd get that blood test.

She caught Kaylob staring at her. "What, honey?" She smiled.

"I was just thinking, what a lucky man I am to have you as my wife." His eyes went soft.

"I'm the lucky one." She moved closer and kissed the side of his mouth. "Yum."

He took his shirt and threw it over his lap. "Beth Ann, be careful." He glanced down.

Beth Ann had to laugh. "I just kissed the side of your mouth, like this." She slowly placed her lips to the side of his, then glided her tongue inside. With her hands on his face, she turned his head towards her to get better access.

"Beth Ann," he mumbled again. "Do you have any idea what you're doing to me?"

"I might," she whispered and continued kissing him.

It didn't take long for them to go discreetly up to their room, where they made love into the late afternoon. They had become the great explorers of each other's body and did things that would scare the birds away. It was magnificent the way they had their little secrets and always spent time showing off for each other. By the time they made love, it was explosive.

* * * *

Later that day, they decided to take a stroll into the town of Dingle and snuck off without telling anybody. It was a little village with shops and food places everywhere.

The store fronts were painted in multi colors of blue, green, and bright yellows, with flowers perched out front, that gave everything an old world feel.

They had been shopping for about an hour when they came across a pub that was fire engine red, with swinging doors. They could hear the echoes of laughter and old Irish music filling the air.

"Want to go inside?" Kaylob asked.

"Yes, sounds like a fun place," she said.

They entered and right away Beth Ann noticed the décor. The bar had frosted and stained glass, with 1930s vintage style mirrors. The mahogany bar lined across the entire west side of the pub.

"Wow." Beth Ann waved around. "This place is really impressive."

Kaylob nodded, then took her hand, and led her to a small round mahogany table.

She glanced around at everything. The furniture complemented the original ornate ceiling with its spherical lamp shades. The hardwood floors matched the mahogany bar. The entire place made her feel as though she had stepped back in time.

The pub seemed popular and from what she could tell it appeared that the people were regulars.

She was just about to say something, when a short guy with white hair approached their table. His cheeks were strawberry red, along with the tip of his nose.

"Wud yer two be likin' somethin' ter draink or ayte?" His smile was warm.

Kaylob looked up at the menu on the wall. "I'd like to order a coffee with cream and sugar, along with two of those biscuits."

The guy looked at Beth Ann.

"I'd like to have the same, please."

"Yer won't be sorry," he said as he walked away.

She noticed that Kaylob's attention had turned to the two guys up at the bar. Their accents were the thickest yet.

"That lad has nutin ova him. Yer wait and see."

The other guy responded. "Lissen ere, tat lad as much ter learn, he's but a wee youngun. I'd bet me earnings on tat other lad."

Kaylob leaned over and whispered, "We are most definitely in Ireland." He wiggled his eyebrows at her. "How are you feeling by the way?"

"I'm better, but I'm worried about the outcome of all this, and wondering if you'll ever be able to forgive your parents, both sets."

"I don't know. It's not going to be easy, but I've decided that I'm going to sit down with Lillian and have a nice long chat and see where it goes."

Beth Ann noticed his jaw tighten, not just once but twice.

"I'm sorry for asking, let's just enjoy the afternoon and try not to think about it."

"I can't stop thinking about it. I'm so pissed at all of them. Like I mentioned, it's not so much that they gave me up, but they waited so long to tell me. They were young and sounds like they trusted my so called dad and shouldn't have, but to wait so damn long. I find that hard to fathom."

Beth Ann saw the server bringing their coffee and biscuits. He set their orders down on the table. "Wud yer be needin anything else?"

"No, thank you," Kaylob said. Beth Ann placed her hands on top of his, holding his strong, warm fingers tightly.

"I wish there was something I could do to help." Beth Ann's voice lowered.

Kaylob gently squeezed her fingers. "Just being my wife and being here has helped, baby." He reached out and touched her cheek.

"I love being your wife." She held his gaze and could feel his love.

Once the coffee cooled for a minute, she took her first sip of the warm rich drink. Holy midnight, it was the most flavorsome coffee Beth Ann had ever tasted in her life, and the cookies were scrumptious too.

The sounds of the Celtic music was soothing, along with the varied accents. It gave the place a fabulous atmosphere. The smile on Kaylob's face warmed Beth Ann's heart. At least for now he seemed to be relaxing and enjoying himself and she was feeling the same.

They watched people coming and going and almost everyone smiled and greeted them. Beth Ann figured they must fit right in with her red hair and Kaylob being a blond.

She leaned closer and said, "I've never seen so many redheads."

"I can't say I have either." He arched a brow and grinned. She playfully stepped on his toe.

"Ouch, I was just agreeing with you." He took her hand and kissed her palm. "Nobody can hold a candle to my redhead."

"You are such a charmer, Kaylob Shawn O'Brien."

They stayed for at least an hour before they left the pub. Once outside, they headed downtown to go through more shops. It was fun buying trinkets and souvenirs for family and friends. It was one of the best days they'd had in a long time. Just the two of them, exploring a new place, while they watched children running and laughing through the streets. The pace was much slower, more so than any place in the States. People were not in a hurry to get to wherever they were going. No horns honking, unless if it was to wave at someone. It was a breath of fresh air, which they both needed.

They turned the corner and Beth Ann saw a little girl sitting alone in a stroller, as a lady, probably her mom, was running around picking up food that was on the ground. The items must have fallen out of a bag that she was carrying.

Kaylob ran over to some runaway apples. "Here, let me help." He bent down to retrieve a few rolling down the sidewalk.

Beth Ann noticed a beautiful little blonde girl watching the lady as Kaylob rushed around helping. The child giggled a few times when the apples seem to be running away. Beth Ann guessed that maybe she was two. When she glanced down again at the little one, her smile warmed Beth Ann's heart. She seemed so trusting.

"Hi," the little one said, in a dainty voice.

"Hello there." Beth Ann grinned and waved her fingers.

"Thank you so much," the lady said to Kaylob as they both grabbed the last few apples and she placed the bag back under the stroller. She wiped her forehead tiredly. "Whew, they just fell out, and everything started going in different directions."

Beth Ann noticed she had no accent and asked, "Do you live here or are you visiting?"

"We are on vacation," she explained. "My husband is in that store." She pointed across the street. "We are taking turns because of all the fragile glass in the shop. She's a bit of a grabber." She nodded towards the baby.

"Ah," Beth Ann said, nodding. Then leaned down to the child. "You're a pretty little girl."

Kaylob joined her and agreed. "She's adorable."

"Thank you, both. Here comes my husband now and thank you again for helping with my runaway groceries." She grinned and waved goodbye, then crossed the street, pushing the stroller.

After spending more time walking through the town, stopping at a chocolate store and tasting so many sweets, they found a bakery where the aroma smelled divine. Of course they had to order another delicacy, which was a pear and almond tart.

Kaylob picked up his fork. "This is a short crust base spread with jam that's filled with almond Madeira."

He took a large bite and his eyes closed. "Oh, yes," he said and licked his lips. "You have to taste this."

Beth Ann picked up her fork, gathered a large bite and slid it into her mouth. The creamy almond flavor melted across her tongue, and all she could do was mumble, "Delicious."

It was so mouthwatering that Beth Ann ate the entire thing. Kaylob, of course, had to name off every ingredient. They had been trying out sweets all day, but had not eaten any real food since morning, so they'd need to do that soon.

After spending time enjoying each other and their surroundings, she noticed it was getting dim.

Kaylob nodded towards the outside. "We better be heading back. Do you want to flag a taxi or walk?"

"I want to walk, for more than one reason." She touched her stomach. "I need to work off all these calories."

"You and your calorie worry. I don't think you need to concern yourself about that. We're on vacation, and calories don't count." He cracked up.

"Oh, is that so." She held his gaze and smiled at her funny husband.

It was time to head back so she let his comment slide. They left the bakery and watched little multicolored lights starting to flicker on around the town. It was truly lovely.

The walk back was amazing with beautiful old style lamp posts lighting the way. They followed a limestone path and she was glad they weren't in any hurry, because the area was something that she wanted to remember.

Every chance they had, they would stop and take in the setting. Beth Ann couldn't help but wonder if they were delaying strictly because of the beauty, or the dread of facing Lillian. Although, in her wildest dreams, she could have never imagined this kind of exquisiteness. The land was lush and green with open pastures all around. The temperature was a tad cool, with a slight breeze that made her shiver. Kaylob must have noticed because he took off his jacket and had her slip it on.

"Is that better?" he asked.

"Yes, but what about you?"

"I'm fine. I'm wearing long sleeves." He lifted his arms.

A little while later Kaylob stopped and the two of them gazed for a while at a beautiful tree that was yellow with luminescent leaves. Never had Beth Ann seen anything so spectacular glistening under the moon.

"Sweetheart, besides you, nothing has ever seduced me more than this place. It's visually intoxicating, with all this awesome scenery." He gestured around. "Even the weather and air make me feel like I've come home. I can almost hear my dad." Kaylob's voice was deep and husky, filled with emotion. "I wonder if he would have waited so long to tell me?"

"Maybe not. It's like he is here with us," she pointed to the sky. "Look, it's turning a brilliant orange with yellow and blue streaks. Your dad is sending us the colors of the rainbow."

"I can feel him around me, but the most important part of all this, is knowing my father loved me."

Beth Ann placed her head on his arm. "I love you too, Mr. O'Brien."

"I love you so much, Beth Ann." He stopped and pulled her into his arms, holding on tight like he never wanted to let go.

"Kaylob."

"Yes."

"How do you feel about Shawna? Do you have any resentment towards her? If you do, I haven't felt it."

"Because I don't. How could I? None of this was her fault and she's suffered too."

"I'm so glad, because it's clear how long she's waited and how much she loves you."

* * * *

The next day arrived and Kaylob was ready to have that talk with Lillian. There were so many questions. Why wait so long? Why didn't they at least help out his family? Jesus, they suffered and couldn't pay the bills most of the time, while his birth parents lived here in luxury. Where was Lillian when he got home from the POW camp? Didn't they ever check up on him or want to know how he was? Sure, Beth Ann had overheard Jackie and Lillian talking, but it didn't sound like she tried very hard. What kind of person leaves a child with someone and never looks back? How could he forgive that?

He noticed Beth Ann staring as he finished getting dressed. "I want to go down and find Lillian. I feel I need to do this alone, but if you want to join me you can."

"No," she replied and shook her head.

He couldn't help but notice how sexy she looked in bed, with her messy hair and sleepy eyes.

"Only if you want me there," said Beth Ann. "I really want to eat breakfast up here. I'd actually enjoy reading and taking in the views from the terrace this morning. I think it would be relaxing and I feel the need for that today."

"Now, that sounds like a great idea. I don't want you under any more stress. Regardless, if Lillian and I work this out, or not, I won't have my wife suffer because of it."

"Kaylob?" Beth Ann's gaze clung to his. "Please try not to let yourself get too stressed either."

"I won't, baby." He leaned down and kissed her delicious lips and a little moan came from her throat. He had to get out of there now or he'd end up back in bed.

Once Kaylob went downstairs, he ran right into the head butler. "Hi

Nathan, I'm hoping to meet up with Lillian this morning and I'm wondering if you can let her know?"

"Yes, I'll tell her right away." Nathan nodded.

"Thank you. I'll be in the Seaside Parlor." Kaylob pointed.

"Could I get someone to bring you some apple muffins and coffee or anything else to eat?"

"Coffee and apple muffins would be great. Also, Beth Ann is staying in our room. Could you be sure someone gets breakfast for her. She's taking it easy today."

"Most certainly, and I hope she is feeling better." His eyes softened.

"She is. Thank you, Nathan."

Kaylob headed to the parlor and felt his stomach growl. He wasn't sure if it was from hunger or nerves. He was also going to talk to his parents when he got home. Doing it over the phone from Ireland wasn't a good idea. They needed to answer to a lot of things as well.

He had called Frankie, who was staying at their place. His townhouse was being redone, something to do with wiring or electrical issues. Also, some painting and new carpets were being put in. He'd given Frankie the scoop about his family, or at least what he could with all the static over the phone. But, he'd get a chance to tell him everything when he got home.

Once he stepped inside the room, he sat on the white overstuffed couch and picked up a magazine, but he was unable to read one word. All he could do was think about what he was going to say. He didn't want to be bitter or angry, that wasn't good for anyone. On the other hand, how the hell could he get past all the lies and how long it took any of them to come forward? Actually, they didn't, he'd had to come out and ask who are you really? That made him furious, just thinking about it. He got up and paced the room. Maybe this was a mistake, maybe he should just leave and never look back. But he couldn't do that with Shawna, he loved her already and the bond they had was strong.

The thought of never seeing her again made his heart sink. That just couldn't happen. Now he could relate even more with Cole and how protective he was of Beth Ann. Of course Cole had taken things a little too far. Even today he had never told Beth Ann that Cole had threatened to send her away. Someday, maybe he'd say something, but what was the point now. He should have told Beth Ann when she turned eighteen, but he was too caught up in self-pity. Why? Because he was poor and got picked on for living on the wrong side of the tracks. Thinking about it made him even more pissed off. Not because he cared about money, he didn't. But hell, he was a kid, worked hard and took care of a mother who suffered from what they now know is clinical depression. At least the medication helped, but back then, nobody knew.

"Good morning, Kaylob," Lillian said as she carried in a big tray of food, which he went and took out of her hands.

"Should I set this down here?" He moved towards the little dining table that looked like it could accommodate two, maybe three.

"Yes, that would be great." She turned, crossed over to the doors and closed them. "I think we need privacy."

Chapter Four

"Do you want to sit here?" She moved back over to the breakfast table.

"Sounds good." Kaylob sat down.

Lillian nodded and seated herself across from him.

They both picked up the muffins, placed them on a small plate and poured a cup of coffee. She picked up the cup, took a sip, then met his gaze.

"Kaylob, I don't know how to make this better. I know it was wrong for us to wait so long and I don't blame you for being angry. But please know," she reached across the table and held his hand. "I loved you then, and I do now."

He moved his hand away. That statement alone made him boil. How could she sit there and say that?

"Like shit." He gave her a hard long look. "Don't hand me this load of crap. Is that how you show love? Giving me away and never looking back, and not telling me I had a sister?"

He took a bite of his muffin and almost couldn't swallow, his mouth was dry and he was shaking inside.

"Kaylob, I can't prove to you that I love you, but, I can promise from this day forward, I will tell you anything you want to know."

"I'm supposed to care about that? A tad late, Mother." His voice was full of sarcasm.

"I know it's late and I don't blame you for hating me." She stared into his eyes.

"Okay, explain to me why you didn't contact me and tell me? I'm an adult. Harold didn't run the show anymore."

Lillian took in a deep breath. "Because I didn't want to make things harder on Jackie. Every time I brought it up, she cried. As I mentioned before, we did see attorneys when you were younger, but we had signed away our parental rights. We had no legal way to do anything. We would have been breaking the law to try and see you." She inhaled deeply, then continued. "Harold told us he'd get a restraining order if we tried. We also tried to support them, give them money to help out. Harold threw it back in our faces—said we were trying to buy you." She blew on her coffee and took a small sip.

"I know this is hard to understand, but when your dad, my husband, died, I couldn't function. Losing him took my breath away and I had to learn to live again. You were eighteen when it happened. I was lost, I didn't think I would survive. By the time I got back on my feet you were drafted into the army, then you were supposedly dead. I can't tell you what that did to me.

"It wasn't until I got the call from Jackie saying you were alive, that I started to breath normally again. I was waiting for the right time. It seemed it was one thing after another." She took another sip of her coffee.

"What took so long after I got home?" Kaylob's heart crushed as he thought about her going through something similar to what Beth Ann had experienced.

"It always seemed the timing was off. I checked up on you as often as possible. Then I heard about what you were going through afterwards. Some type of Vietnam Syndrome. Jackie said it was bad and it wouldn't be wise to let you know right then."

Kaylob had to agree with that. He'd started drinking and was pissed off at Beth Ann, hell, he was angry at the whole world. Sometimes he still had issues with loud noises and fireworks. He stayed away from those things. He met her gaze and she continued.

"I did take several trips out to see you and tell you. But it always seemed the timing wasn't right. That is why I wanted you out here, I was going to tell you. We knew it was way past the time."

He noticed she was blinking hard. Great. If she started crying that would make him a damn ass. Sure, he knew he was being harsh, but how do you forgive something like this? He'd been lied to all his life. Okay, so they'd tried, but was it enough? Did they try as hard as they could?

"Kaylob?" She swallowed. "What can I say or do to make you feel better?"

"Why did my dad let his parents control him?" he asked.

She seemed to be gathering her thoughts. "Your dad was afraid of his father for many years. The truth was, his dad was controlling and seemed to take it out on Patrick's mom when something went wrong. He wasn't a very nice man and Patrick wanted to keep your grandmother safe."

"He hurt her?" Kaylob asked, not sure if he wanted the truth.

"Yes." She nodded. "Your father tried to get her to move away from the abuse and hide from his father."

"What happened?"

Lillian's face was etched with pain. "She packed and was ready to go, but she backed out." Tears pooled her eyes. "After Patrick died, she cut her wrist and bled to death. Nobody found her until the next day."

Kaylob felt sick as he watched Lillian fight back tears. A grandmother he'd never known took her own life. Maybe that was the reason Lillian was so nervous about Jackie and her depression. But still, he needed time to think about all this information.

"Lillian," he cleared his throat. "For the sake of my wife and Shawna, I'll try to move past this. I can't promise you anything, because honestly, I'm not sure if any of these things are a good excuse to have waited as long as you did. But I will try to get along with you, for the sake of everyone and my grandmother."

"Thank you." Her voice dipped and she swiped away her tears. "I am thankful for that much."

Kaylob nodded and ate the rest of his muffin in silence. After he was done, he asked the burning questions.

"I want to know the truth. Who is my uncle Tony and did he really leave me all that money?" He gave her a pointed look. "Was he my father's brother or something?"

"No, that is your inheritance, part of it was what we tried to give your parents when you were younger. Both you and Shawna got almost the same amount. Except you got more, because we added money for the years we didn't get to support you. The million dollars is from your father and your grandmother and the ongoing deposits will be from the trust we set up for you. Please, don't give it back. Your father wanted you to have that money and your grandmother always wanted to give it to you."

Kaylob didn't know what to feel or say; his dad had died. How could he be mad at someone who wasn't even around anymore? That part made his heart sink. If only he could have met his father and known him while he was growing up. However, all the wishing in the world wouldn't make it come true.

"I am grateful for the money. It has changed our lives and I will be sure to thank Edna too."

"Kaylob, no matter what you think of me, I am proud of the man you are. You are so much like your father." Her eyes fell. "He treated me much like you treat Beth Ann. He was the best husband in the world." She set her napkin down.

Kaylob felt his throat tighten, for whatever reason that got to him. He needed to get the hell away from her before he said something he'd regret, like I forgive you, or it's okay, you did what you thought was best, and you had no choice. All his life he had wanted to do the right thing. Jesus, he'd gone back to war because it was the right thing to do, to hell with his fiancée, Beth Ann, who had cried, begged and pleaded for him not to go. What did that get him? Nothing but a vacation in a POW camp for over two years, and he'd almost lost the love of his life.

Kaylob stood and stared at her. "This conversation is over for now, I need to get out of here." He headed towards the door and knew he had a lot to sort out.

"Kaylob, before you leave. I thought you'd like to know where your father and grandmother are buried. In case you want to visit them?"

"I would." He turned to see a tear slide down her cheek. "I could show you or I could give you a map. It's within walking distance."

"I'll take the map."

Lillian went to the shelf. "Here you go." She handed it to him.

Kaylob did feel badly for a grandmother he'd never met. He couldn't help but think of his birth dad as he headed upstairs. It must have been hard for him, to watch his father physically hurt his mother. Kaylob thought of his parents in Novato, the only parents he had ever known and how much Harold had hurt Jackie by being gone. At least he'd never raised a hand and was gentle with her when he was home.

Kaylob arrived back to the room and walked outside to the terrace.

Beth Ann didn't seem to hear or see him, as she watched something off in the distance. The breeze was soft and blew curls around her face. God, he felt like he was home whenever he saw her, especially like this.

He cleared his throat and the minute she heard him, she glanced up, shading her eyes from the morning sun.

"Hey there." She gave him a tender smile. "How did it go?"

"Do you feel up to coming with me to my dad's resting place and I'll tell you on the way? I did get a lot of answers and some I wasn't expecting."

"Of course, I want to go." She stood and held his hand. "I've eaten and I'm ready. Do we need a ride?"

"No, we can walk, if you feel up to it."

"I feel great." She gave him a tiny smile.

Once they arrived at the family cemetery, they entered through a large black iron gate. Right away there was a melancholy theme of death and sadness hovering all around. The place looked like something you'd have seen in *Gone with the Wind* or one of the old classic movies. They headed down the gracefully curving pathways with trees that shaded some of the well-kept lawns. Headstones filled the area as birds chirped and squirrels dashed up trees.

"Wow," Beth Ann said lightly. "I was imagining a small place. Do all these headstones belong to your family?"

Kaylob glanced around then back down to the map. The breeze rustled through the branches, almost blowing the map out of his hand.

"I think so." He clutched the map tighter. "Lillian said my grandmother was buried here too, and I'm guessing these names are from family. A lot of Raffertys," he said, pointing to the different names on the illustration. "I guess my grandmother is buried next to her son and this looks like Edna's husband. Which would be my grandfather of course, his name is Dermot Finely. We need to find the tall angel holding a sheep." He glanced around.

"There." Beth Ann pointed to a place off to the right side, near what appeared to be a running creek.

They strolled over until they arrived in front of his father's headstone. Kaylob leaned down and ran his fingers across the concrete, then onto the lettering. Patrick K. Rafferty, a loving husband and father.

He moved his hand away and his stomach clenched. Maybe he was going to throw up too. His eyes burned until the tears trailed down his cheeks.

"Beth Ann." He sucked in his breath. "I'll never get the chance to know him."

"I'm so sorry honey." She wrapped her arms around him.

It hurt so bad Kaylob felt like his heart was going to explode, he tried to roll back his emotions, but couldn't. All he could think about is that he'd lost a father who he'd never hug, share a cup of coffee with or have a long talk about life. He'd never have a chance to cook for him, or tell him about his wife or share any detail about his feelings. Maybe what hurt so bad was because somewhere in the depths of his soul, he knew that his birth parents had made an awful choice they had regretted. They were only eighteen and his dad's father was obviously a bad man. He plopped on the ground and ran his hands across the cool stone, he could feel Beth Ann watching him, but he couldn't push back the pain.

"Dad," he whispered. "If only."

He heard Beth Ann suck in her breath. So he reached out his hand to her and she came down next to him. Together, wrapped in each other's arms, they let the tears flow.

"Kaylob, I'm so sorry." She reached up and touched his cheeks. "I wish I could take away the pain."

"Thank you for understanding and being here with me." He wiped away the tears.

After letting his feelings calm, a movement behind him caught his attention.

"Hi Kaylob, Hi Beth Ann. I'm so sorry to intrude." Lillian's lip trembled as she stood holding a box in her hands. "I wanted you to have this." She was clearly uncomfortable. "I don't know if this is the right time. I've messed up so bad. I just wanted to do the right thing." She moved around and set it on the ground. "If you have any questions, please ask."

She turned to leave.

Kaylob could see Beth Ann didn't know what to say. So he asked. "What is it?"

"Something I thought you should know. When you said we didn't look back or never cared about you, I should have shown you right then. We were always there, Kaylob. At your first surfing competition, your graduation from jr. high and high school. We attended everything we could, but stayed off in the distance. After your father passed away, I continued, once I pulled myself up again. Jackie knew, but Harold never did." She paused. "The pictures and albums are all there. It was our collection.

"We always loved you, we just didn't want Harold to put a restraining order against us and make it where we never saw you. Plus we didn't want to hurt Jackie either, not after what happened to Patrick's mom. I was at your wedding, I sat way in the back, off to the side. It wasn't easy to hide, but Jackie sent me an invitation and I wore a wig." She wiped away a tear. "It was amazing and one of the most beautiful weddings I've ever seen."

Kaylob saw Beth Ann trying not to cry. After a few minutes, Lillian turned and walked away.

"Oh Kaylob," Beth Ann whispered. "Are you going to look at these?"

With trepidation, he opened the box. Sure enough, there were lots of albums with pictures of many events. Including one of him walking down the street in Novato. Why hadn't he ever noticed? He wracked his brain trying to remember them being there, but didn't. If only he would have known. If only he could have remembered them, like he had when he was little.

Jesus, they had been threatened with never seeing him again. The memory of Cole making that same threat about Beth Ann, hit him hard. He knew the fear of losing any chance of being close to someone you loved. Cole had made that clear as hell, if he dared to get too serious with Beth Ann, she'd be gone.

For the next few hours, Kaylob and Beth Ann spent time going through photo albums and walking through the family grave site. He had more family than he could have ever imagined. They found his great-great-great grandfather, who lived to be eighty-three and that was old back in those days. There was a baby, Nolan Reid Finely, who had passed away at three years old. How awful for the family. He touched the stone and saw Beth Ann's eyes grow glassy.

"I wonder what he passed away from?" She ran her fingers across his stone too.

"So many diseases back in those days. Could have been from anything. I would sure like to know more about all these family members."

"Maybe there are some journals or logs in the library at Lillian's house. I bet there are records," Beth Ann said.

"Good idea," Kaylob agreed. "I want to know more about who they were, and learn as much as I can about my family tree."

* * * *

Almost a week later, Beth Ann and Kaylob had found many records of his family on both sides. It seemed to give him a sense of belonging, although he still didn't want to be around Lillian too much. Seemed Kaylob was deep in thought and didn't want to talk about it. They hadn't spent much time with anyone lately. Shawna had been working late into the evenings and sometimes she'd stop by, spending a minute or two. Beth Ann was happy to announce each time someone asked, that she had not been sick or light headed again. The funny thing was, she didn't feel sick at all. Her appetite was the best it had ever been.

As they sat watching a program a few nights later, there was a knock on the door. Kaylob stood and went to answer it.

"Hi, sis." He grinned and gave her a big hug.

Shawna's smile was weak, but she came into the room carrying chocolate cake, at least enough for six or more.

"I baked this from scratch and heard that it's Beth Ann's favorite." She set it down on the little table.

"Thank you." Beth Ann started to stand, but Shawna waved her back down.

"I have to open tomorrow." She frowned and sighed. "They are shorthanded again. You know, I would quit that job if I didn't love cooking for people so much."

She leaned down and hugged Beth Ann then embraced Kaylob again.

Kaylob shook his head. "You've been working almost double shifts. I hope they're paying you well."

Shawna laughed. "I don't do it for the money. Like you, I have enough to last me the rest of my life and then some. I just love to cook and create." She glanced at Beth Ann. "And taste this." She picked up the fork and gave her a bite.

Beth Ann couldn't believe how it melted in her mouth. "Oh, my gosh." She let it melt across her tongue, and thought she might dissolve right then. "This is the best cake I've ever tasted."

"Thank you. Here, now you, Kaylob."

Kaylob put a piece in his mouth and Beth Ann watched his eyes close in pleasure. "Man, oh man, Shawna, it's truly incredible. The flavor explodes in your mouth."

"Thank you." She put the cake back down. "I'm off to bed, but you enjoy. I brought enough for six, and I've had my fill." She touched her stomach.

Kaylob walked her back to the door.

"Wait," called Beth Ann. "Can you give me five minutes? I need to talk to you."

"Sure." Shawna came back in and sat in the chair. "What's up?" She had a quizzical look on her face.

Beth Ann glanced between the two of them. "Would you ever consider leaving here and working at our restaurant with Kaylob?"

"Leave here?" Shawna repeated. "Work at your restaurant?"

He met his sister's gaze and nodded. "Come on, think about it. If you don't like it, you can always come back home, but test us out."

She rubbed her hand through her hair just the same way Kaylob did. Beth Ann had to smile, because that meant she was contemplating the offer.

After a few seconds she stood. "Where would I live? I'd need to find a place."

"With us," Beth Ann said. "We have two spare rooms and our place is big enough, plus we are buying a new house that will be even bigger. Live with us, Shawna, at least for a while." Beth Ann swallowed. "Please say yes. It would be so nice to have someone with me, you know after everything I've been through. That's one of the reasons we're moving. Too many bad memories."

"Are you sure?" She studied them both. "You two are almost

newlyweds."

A slow grin spread across Kaylob's face. "We'll be fine, believe me nothing will stand in the way of our newlywed moments. Our room is very private and sound proof."

Beth Ann gave Kaylob an annoyed poke and Shawna laughed.

"We will be able to make up some of the time we missed with each other." He paused. "Come on, Shawna, say yes." He gave his sister a hopeful look.

"I'd love to!" She threw her arms around him and squealed. "I want to come and live with my big brother and sister." She moved over to Beth Ann and hugged her.

Together they stood in a circle and Beth Ann believed this would be a new chapter in each of their lives. Now, the three of them needed to figure out how to tell Lillian and Edna. Beth Ann could only pray that they would support this decision.

* * * *

The next morning at breakfast, all three shared the news with Lillian. Beth Ann could not read the expression on her or Edna's face, but at least they hadn't pitched a fit or anything.

Lillian sat there, looking a little sad and lost. Finally, she spoke. "Will I be allowed to come and visit her?"

Kaylob nodded. "Yes, of course, you need to come and see your daughter," he said, then added, "We should have a new house soon and plenty of room."

"I hope dat invite is for me too," Edna asked. "I don't get into de states as often as Shawna and Lillian, but I will be having my passport."

"Great, and of course we want you there," Kaylob said, this time he at least had a smile.

They both nodded and tears filled two sets of eyes.

Beth Ann had to go out on a limb and hoped her husband wouldn't kill her. "Maybe you could spend the holidays with us this year," she said, then glanced at Kaylob.

"That would be nice." Kaylob said, but didn't meet Lillian's eyes. As a matter of fact, Beth Ann noticed how he hardly even glanced her way.

Lillian and Edna looked at each other. "We'll be there," Lillian said, then added, "I'm looking forward to it."

With that decided, they all continued eating and talking about the restaurant.

The next day, Shawna quit her job and sadly for them there was no time to give notice. They were leaving first thing Friday morning and Kaylob seemed glad. Beth Ann could only hope that he would work on the relationship with Lillian. At least Kaylob didn't seem angry anymore, just really quiet when Lillian was around. Maybe in time, now that he'd found out the entire truth, he'd be able to forgive at least Lillian and Jackie. Harold was another story and it might never be worked out.

* * * *

A few days later, Frankie glanced around Beth Ann and Kaylob's townhouse. Everything looked nice. They would be home soon and he was happy about that. Their truck was parked at the airport so they'd be driving themselves home. He sure as hell had missed them. He'd heard about Beth Ann passing out and having some health issues. He was worried about her, even though they kept saying from what he could hear, everything was fine.

He sat on the couch and propped his feet on the coffee table, pizza was on the way. That was the one treat Frankie would let himself have. Eating junk wasn't in his portfolio, and it was way too unhealthy. He leaned his head back and closed his eyes.

Before he could relax, there was a knock. Hell, that was fast.

He went to the door and swung it open. Beth Ann smiled.

"Hi stranger." She giggled and looked cute with her hair pulled back in a ponytail, dressed all in pink.

Frankie embraced her and saw Kaylob walking towards them with suitcases, there was a little blonde bombshell following him. As he let go of Beth Ann he asked and nodded towards Kaylob. "Who's the chick?"

Beth Ann arched a brow. "That *chick* is his little sister."

"His little sister?" It was his turn to raise an eyebrow. "He told me about finding his family and something about it being a secret. At least, from what I could hear. With all the static and bad connection, I must have missed the little sister part."

Before they could finish chatting Kaylob walked up and set down the suitcases. "Frankie, I'd like to introduce you to Shawna, my sister."

Frankie's breath caught in his throat. All of a sudden the air was stuck in his windpipe or he just swallowed his tongue. She was a knockout, he thought, as he scanned her from top to bottom.

Kaylob hit his back, perhaps a little too hard. "You okay buddy?" He narrowed his eyes.

All he could do was nod and stick his hand out to greet her. "Hi, Shawna. It's nice to meet you."

The minute she smiled, he felt his legs turn into rubber bands. Was he going to fall? He held on to the door frame with his other hand.

"Hi Frankie." She placed her hand in his, and the moment she touched him the sky opened up and sent a bolt of lightning through him. "It's nice to finally meet the man in all those photos." She continued to hold his hand.

He was so electrified that his mouth would not work. Kaylob stared at him, cocking his head to one side. "Frankie, you okay?"

Finally, he collected himself and pulled away. "Yes, sir, I'm fine." He turned and walked back inside.

Beth Ann laughed. "Frankie." She pointed. "Aren't you going to help Shawna with those heavy suitcases?" She shook her head. "They wouldn't let me carry anything."

"Oh wait, yes, I mean. I can do that." He was acting like an idiot.

"Are you okay?" Beth Ann asked.

"Yes."

"Did you just wake up or something?" she persisted, frowning.

"No, no, I was just surprised." He lied. God, he couldn't even look at Shawna. He bent down and picked up someone's suitcase. Then when he stood, he glanced up into Shawna's eyes and felt the chemistry all the way into his soul.

Jesus, he was blushing or having a hot flash. No way. He'd never blushed a day in his life. What the hell was going on?

"Frankie." Her voice was like chocolate velvet. "Do you need my help?"

"No." He tried to step back, but went smack dab into the door frame. Then tripped over the door jamb and almost fell.

He set down the suitcases in the living room. "I have to go home. Where are my damn keys?" He almost shouted while he searched for his car keys.

"Why?" Kaylob asked. "I thought you'd been staying here and wanted to wait until they were done painting your place and putting in the new carpet?"

"Yes, but they're almost done and I can stay in my bedroom." He swooped up his keys and clung on tight. "I have a lot of studying to do." He moved closer to the door.

Shawna met his gaze. "That's too bad, I was looking forward to getting to know you better," she said, and he was pretty damn sure she had a mischievous grin spreading across her face.

Just then there was a loud knock on the door.

"Oh, that's dinner. You're having the pizza person for dinner."

Kaylob looked confused. "We're having a pizza person for dinner?"

"I mean, I reserved it for you, ordered it," he finally said, wiping his brow with his hand. "I need to go."

He swung the door open then almost tripped over the door jamb again. The pizza guy looked at him like he was nuts. After he steadied himself, he was gone in a flash and realized he hadn't even grabbed his things.

Screw it, he'd buy new stuff.

All he knew was he needed to get as far away from Kaylob's little sister as he could.

* * * *

Beth Ann stood, staring at the door in shock. What was the matter with Frankie? Maybe he was spending too much time studying. He had almost been rude to Shawna.

Beth Ann caught Shawna's eye. "I'm sorry about that. He doesn't usually act that way and once you get to know him, he's really a fun guy."

Kaylob finished paying for the pizza and shook his head. "A wild hair must have crawled up his backside. I'll call him later."

Beth Ann recognized Shawna's sly grin. "I think Frankie Russo is afraid of me." She chuckled. "He wasn't rude. I just made him nervous."

"I don't know. I've never seen him nervous since we were kids." Beth Ann thought for a minute. "Especially when he gets around women. There was that one model girl. She was older and he was nervous in the beginning."

"Well, you just saw it happen again," she said, and seemed very sure of what just took place. "Yes, that Frankie Russo is a funny guy." Shawna giggled.

Kaylob furrowed his brows and glanced between the two of them. "Let's eat, I'm starving."

Beth Ann nodded. "Me too."

Kaylob pulled out some plates and went back to the dining table and threw the pizza box open. "Wow." He inhaled as he leaned over. "This smells great."

Beth Ann walked over to grab a piece when the smell assaulted her, her head started spinning and she turned and made a mad dash to the bathroom.

After throwing up for what felt like a good five minutes, she heard Kaylob knock on the door again and at the moment she wished he'd go away.

"Baby, are you okay? If you don't open this, I'm breaking it down."

"Hold on." She brushed her teeth, then opened the door. "I better go get those tests tomorrow." She said weakly, fearing that there was something really wrong.

He nodded and embraced her. "From now on please open the door when I knock. You scared me."

* * * *

The next morning, she called and got an appointment with the doctor right away. Kaylob begged to go, but she never liked anyone going to the doctor with her. Usually, he was good and had always respected that. But he had been extremely difficult about it this time. She'd finally talked him into taking Shawna to the restaurant by telling him that being back home had simply made her stress levels go up. Then she told him, "I'm going grocery shopping afterwards." She knew he hated that. Beth Ann saw the moment his face looked resigned, then watched as he got on the phone and spoke with Rene, their Realtor.

Maybe this time they'd find the perfect house. The ones they looked at before they left for Ireland just weren't right, wrong size, not enough land, but the biggest issue was they had a dream area that they were hoping for.

A few hours later, Beth Ann sat in the waiting room thumbing through a magazine, thinking about everything she had been through. Maybe, that's all that was going on. After all, so much had happened and she was still dealing with the memories of first being attacked by two guys, then being kidnapped by Peter.

"Beth Ann O'Brien," A nurse called out. Beth Ann stood. "My name is Nina and I'll be taking your vitals before the doctor sees you." The lady held a chart and led her to the scale.

Wow! Beth Ann had put on five pounds. "Good job," the nurse said. "Seems like you've struggled with keeping weight on for a very long time. You saw a different doctor last time you were here after the incident. But today, you'll be seeing Dr. Pollack. He's very good."

Afterwards, Nina put her in the room and told her to slip on a gown. Beth Ann hated this part, but did what she was told and tried to relax on the table. A few minutes later the nurse came back in and got her temp and blood pressure.

While Beth Ann explained everything that had been happening, the nurse wrote it down and stopped a few times and studied her.

"Is there a certain time of the day the nausea comes more than others?" Nina inquired.

"Not really. I didn't even know I was going to throw up yesterday. It happened early in the evening when I smelled the pizza."

"I see." She stood and patted Beth Ann's arm. "The doctor will be right in."

After what seemed like a century, the doctor walked in.

"Hi there, I'm Doctor Pollack," he said as he stood over her.

He seemed like a nice man who checked her over, listened to her heart, and looked in her ears. He was tall with salt and pepper hair and had kind brown eyes.

When he pushed on her abdomen, it made her wince. "So, you've been getting a little sick and dizzy. And you're a little tender there." He touched her again.

"Yes." She nodded.

He pulled the gown back down and met her gaze.

"I need to run some blood tests today and are you okay with getting a pelvic?" He touched her leg.

"Yes, that's fine." She agreed even though she hated having one.

Once he got the nurse back in the room and put her feet up in those god awful stirrups, she heard him saying things under his breath.

"Uh huh? Yes, sir." He moved his hand away and patted her foot. "Just as I thought." He pulled off his gloves and had the nurse help Beth Ann up.

He washed his hands and picked up her chart. "Nina, can you call over at the lab and see if they can get her in today?"

The nurse gave her a knowing look and said she would.

Now Beth Ann was feeling anxious, so she spoke up. "What do you think is wrong with me, doctor?" She swallowed, waiting for some bad news. But he was smiling. Would he smile if it was bad news?

He pulled up the little round chair and sat by her. "Well, Mrs. O'Brien. Congratulations! You're pregnant. I can't tell how far along, but by the looks of everything, I'd venture to say about two months." He looked at her chart. "When was your last period?"

Beth Ann thought about it and knew she didn't pay much attention, because these days it just wasn't regular.

She counted on her fingers. "I'm at least six weeks late, or more, but that's normal since the kidnapping. My husband and I always use protection. I don't know how this could have happened."

"Well, there are all kinds of ways. Maybe you forgot, or something went wrong. "

"Oh, my gosh, the produce room," she said, then blushed. "I forgot about that."

"Excuse me?" The doctor tilted his head.

Beth Ann touched her stomach and changed the subject. "A baby?" She felt her lip quiver. What the heck was she going to do? She had no idea how to take care of a child. Her head was spinning, but she sucked it up and tried to act normal.

He nodded. "I'll let you get dressed and we'll send you over for those labs. You'll need to find an OBGYN or I can give you a few referrals and you'll also need to set that up right away."

"Okay." She nodded and let out a deep breath. "Pregnant?"

Beth Ann spent the rest of the day in shock and go mode. She went and did what she needed to do, but felt like a zombie walking around in a trance. When she walked through the door the phone was ringing and she froze with groceries, then set them down and ran to the phone.

"Hello."

"Is Beth Ann O'Brien there? This is Nina from the doctor's office."

"This is she."

"Congratulations. You're going to have a baby." She sounded very happy. "I wish you and your husband the best of luck and please let us know when the baby is born."

Beth Ann said all the right words. "Thank you and I will." But she had no idea how to feel? *A baby, their baby.*

She had to call her husband, so she dialed the number at the restaurant and asked him to please come home right away. She could hear the worry in his voice.

Beth Ann sat on the couch to wait for him. She had a hard time even saying the word *pregnant.* She'd never wanted a baby. She reached down and felt her stomach and tears fell from her eyes. How could she be a mother?

When he came in by himself, she glanced around. "Where's Shawna?"

"She thought we might need to do this alone." His face was etched with worry. "What is it, Beth Ann?" He rushed over to her, squatting down.

Seeing his soft blue eyes and the worry lines on his forehead, she knew what she had to say.

"Kaylob, we really have to get a bigger house." Her lip trembled.

"What?" His eyes studied her from top to bottom. "We are going to look at six houses over the next few days. Can we talk about your health and worry about the houses later?"

"No, my health issue is the reason we need a bigger house." she choked out. "We're pregnant."

"We are?" he swallowed hard. "And, we get to keep it?"

Chapter Five

"Of course we are going to keep her." She touched her stomach. "Our baby is growing inside of me, and we made her from love."

"My baby is having a baby." Kaylob reached down and placed his hand on her stomach and tears rolled down his cheeks. "I can't believe it."

"The produce room." She grinned. "Three times."

"I love that produce room." His voice broke.

* * * *

One week later, as she sat at the breakfast table having coffee, she thought about the reactions from everyone when she and Kaylob had called to give them the news. It was a joyful occasion and they were meeting some of them that Friday night for a celebration dinner at the restaurant. There were tears and joy over the phone with each person they called. It was a tie between who had cried the hardest, her mom or Gram. Jackie had cried too, but Harold was quiet, as usual. The happiness from Lillian and Edna had been over the top, even though Kaylob had refused to talk to Lillian. Beth Ann got a little upset over that, but she had to remember he was still going through a lot. After all, his entire world had been tilted upside down. Maybe the baby would help to bring everyone back together. Forgiveness was important, although she realized this was something Kaylob had to do. She would not push it.

He had yet to have that long talk with his adopted parents. Jackie had sobbed when Kaylob called her about the baby. He'd also told her how upset he was about all the secrets. However, from the tone of her voice, he had said he was afraid that it might lead her back into depression, so he dropped that part of the conversation. His dad had said nothing at all. He was cold and didn't seem to care. Maybe it was all just a ruse and he didn't want to show his true feelings. Beth Ann had no way of knowing.

The development that made Beth Ann very happy was Blake seemed pleased and surprised at the announcement and was coming to celebrate with them. He was happier these days and Beth Ann was pretty sure he was dating Melissa, or so she hoped anyway.

When she had been in the grocery store a few days ago, she had glanced at a magazine and noticed the tabloids had hinted that Blake might have a special someone, because he had not been seen out with his usual array of ladies. Of course, these stories weren't right and sometimes they just lied.

When Frankie had returned their call, he had tried his best to back out, but Kaylob had given him the one, two, threes, of why he had to be there. He would be the Godfather and Shawna would be the Godmother. There was no way they'd let him miss it.

What was wrong with him? He'd never done that before.

Beth Ann was sad that her family and childhood friends couldn't be there, but she and Kaylob were going to try to go down to Novato as soon as they could.

Plus, she had promised Lisa that she could hold the baby shower. She had told Lisa about how Frankie had almost fallen, trying to escape. Shawna had insisted it was from being nervous around her, and it did look pretty funny because of the way he was acting. Either way, Lisa and Beth Ann had both cracked up, thinking about Frankie being so afraid.

Tonight she was going to watch and see if Shawna was right, was Frankie nervous around her? By any chance, if he was, this was something Beth Ann did not want to miss. Imagine, Frankie Dean Russo, nervous around a woman. She felt highly amused.

* * * *

Frankie stood in the doorway of the restaurant, afraid to enter, but he didn't have a choice. He had some good news of his own he wished he could share, but not tonight.

Besides, why should he feel nervous? She was just a pint size blonde that happened to be his best friend's sister. There was no way he'd act like an idiot this time. As a matter of fact, there were usually a lot of good looking women roaming around the bar. He'd focus on one of them. He was good at that and Kaylob had always sent the ones that were trying to hit on him, Frankie's way.

In the meantime, he needed to figure out why he had reacted to Shawna the way he did. Tonight he would be cool, calm, and together. Maybe it had been the stress from all his studies. He needed a distraction or something. He strutted in the door, observing the area. The first person he saw was Carol, one of his favorite people. She had always been so beautiful with her mocha skin and cute little Afro. The woman had the best legs in the U.S. of A., and boy had he tried with her more than once. It didn't take her long to tell him he wasn't her type, so they became great pals.

She waved and came running over. "Can you believe it?" She hugged him. "Our redhead is having a baby and she's absolutely glowing about it."

"No, but I'm happy for them." He meant it. Frankie hugged her back. "And I'm happy for me too."

She gave him a searching look. "Frankie, you passed?" She almost squealed.

He nodded, then held his finger up to his lips. "Don't say anything yet. We're here to celebrate my Godchild."

Carol laced her arm through his. "Congratulations, Frankie," she whispered. "You're going to make a wonderful attorney. Shelia had to teach tonight so you can be the lucky man who gets to be my date."

He patted her hand. "Any benefits?" He winked.

"How about this." She kissed his cheek. "I've missed you Frankie Dean Russo. Shelia told me to tell you that she misses you too."

"I've missed you both," he said. "The studying has been intense this last year."

"I can't even imagine. I'm so proud of you." She patted him on the arm.

Together they strolled into the party room and Shawna was the first person he saw. Jesus, she was staring right at him with those bewitching blue eyes. Her hair was hanging down to her waist and she wore a matching light blue mini skirt and clingy white top. It was tight enough to show off all her curves and those incredible legs. His breath caught and once again he couldn't move. His heart was beating so hard that he could barely hear what Carol was saying.

"Frankie, can we sit down? Frankie … are you okay?"

He was finally able to pull his eyes away, but it wasn't easy.

Carol stepped in front of him. "Frankie did you hear me say your name? Are you pulling a Beth Ann?"

"Yes, no, sorry." He glanced at Shawna again, who was talking to a couple of the people who worked there. Holy shit, she was amazing. He scanned her from top to bottom and noticed the way she tossed her head back when she laughed. The dimple in her chin was cute as hell and when she smiled it was enchanting. She strolled over to sit down at an extra long table that had more than likely been set up for the guests. Mother, Mary of God, the way she swayed her hips made his throat go dry.

"Frankie Russo!" Carol was still standing in front of him. She turned slowly, following his gaze. "Well, I'll go to hell." She laughed. "Someone has you tied up in knots. I haven't seen that look since … well shit, I'm not sure I've ever seen you look at someone like that." She pulled his arm. "Let's go sit down." She led him right to where Shawna was, and asked if they could sit next to her.

Shawna gave a tiny grin and nodded. "Of course, I've wanted a chance to talk to Frankie, after all he's one of Beth Ann and Kaylob's best friends." She reached over and touched his arm. "How are you, Frankie?" she asked, then smiled in a way that made his heart skip three to four beats.

Maybe, he was having a heart attack. But with those eyes staring at him, he'd die a happy man.

"Frankie," Shawna said again. "Did you hear me? How are you?" Her lips curved up in what appeared to be a sarcastic smile.

Oh man, she knew what she was doing to him. The brat.

Carol leaned over and cracked up. "Maybe we need to call 9-1-1."

Did someone just ask how was he? That was a very good question because he couldn't seem to figure that out.

At the age of twenty-five Frankie had never had this issue, well maybe once when he was a teenager, but that was for a different reason.

He was a virgin, until he had met a model who was in her twenties. Yes indeedy, they had spent one year sneaking around doing things that must have been illegal back in those days. But, his dad had got a transfer the following year, so he had to leave Novato, and that was the end of that. He never saw her again.

Carol waved her hand in front of him. "Frankie Dean Russo." She called his name and her dark eyes filled with laughter. "Come on pal. Take a deep breath and say hellooo."

He swallowed and did his best to smile. "I'm fine. I can speak." He gave her the shut-the-hell-up look.

"You're so full of it. " She cracked up. "Shawna, do they have a phone here. I need to call 9-1-1 and see if they can come and get his heart beating normally again."

Shawna stood. "I think I'll go talk to my sister-in-law and my brother. Maybe Frankie will be able to speak when I get back." She stood to leave, but glanced over her shoulder giving him the once over.

He caught his breath and stared at Carol, who was snickering. At that moment he wanted to choke her.

"Do you mind? You do know that's Kaylob's baby sister." He reached up and fluffed her hair. He knew she hated that, but she took it in stride.

"Well, she doesn't look like a baby to me." She laughed then added. "Why are you so nervous around her? You're a good looking guy, Frankie, that dark hair and those green eyes. You've caught her attention, I can see that. She's a pretty little thing and I can tell you are enjoying that very much. Does Kaylob know how you feel?"

"I'm not talking about this with you and there's nothing for Kaylob to know." Frankie frowned. "She's too young, and she's my best friend's sister. Let's talk about something else."

He glanced around and noticed that drinks were being served. He sure as heck needed one. One, more like two or three. There were several small groups already laughing and taking the drinks being passed around. Jack and Lenard were talking to Charlie and Tina. John Patterson and his wife were with Kaylob and Beth Ann.

He could tell that everyone there was happy about the news. Nobody ever thought Beth Ann would have a child, but she had surprised them all.

Shawna was talking to some punk guy with blond hair who was checking her out every time she turned around.

"She's twenty, Frankie," Carol said, sighing. "That's not so much younger."

"Hey look, there's Blake. I'm gonna go say 'hi.' Want to join me?" He invited her, but she didn't move and all she did was frown.

"Hell no, I might catch something."

"Oh come on, he's changed and is a good guy. Strike that, he was always a good guy."

"No thanks. I'm hungry and want to find something to eat." She stood and moved through the room.

Frankie watched her go. Wow, he sure as hell hoped he never got on her bad side. Carol had never cared for Blake when he had been with Beth Ann, she made it clear she'd bite his head off if he ever hurt her. Sadly, he was the one that ended up getting his heart shredded.

The whole ordeal was sad. Blake had been in love with Beth Ann and they were weeks away from getting married when Kaylob returned from the dead. There was only one choice for Beth Ann to make, and it hadn't gone in Blake's favor. The great news now, was they were all the best of friends. Pretty cool if you asked him.

Frankie saw Carol stop and talk to Charlie and Tina. They seemed to be an item now and pretty exclusive. Charlie was back in Beth Ann's life after being gone for years and he really liked him, he was a good guy.

He watched as Carol made her way through the room, stopping to talk to different people. Carol was a beauty without a doubt. She had a style that was all her own. If he was being honest, it was her long, lean dancer legs that had caused many a man to beg for mercy. Frankie had tried every which way to Sunday to get her to go out with him. She'd told him he was handsome as hell and loved his dark curly hair and his green eyes. Heck, she'd even pointed to his one dimple, and then said. *Look, Frankie you're just the wrong sex."* She had also told him that if she ever did get the inclination to be with a guy, it would be him, but not to hold his breath.

No complaints though, because he loved Carol as one of his best friends. They had spent a lot of time together when Beth Ann had her nervous breakdown and she had been his rock. That woman was stronger than a dozen men.

"Hey Frankie, what are you doing all by yourself?" He heard Kaylob say just before he sat down next to him.

"I was just thinking about ordering a drink. Actually, I was coming to talk to you and Beth Ann first. How is our little pregnant girl?" He asked.

"Better than I ever dreamed." He rubbed his jaw and Frankie noticed he had red eyes.

Frankie placed his hand on Kaylob's shoulder. "You okay, buddy?"

Kaylob nodded. "I just never dreamed we'd be having a baby and she'd be so happy about it. Before we got here she threw up and then turned around and started singing." His smile widened.

"She throws up and sings. What a trip." Frankie shook his head. "Never in a million years did I imagine that."

Kaylob chuckled. "She's blown me away too. She told me straight up, it's going to be a little girl." He got a far off look in his eye. "Frankie, I hope I'm a good dad."

"Kaylob, you're going to make a great dad. Come on. Let's go get a beer and toast to you being the best father ever." Frankie stood and glanced down at his best friend and saw his eyes fixed on his wife. He'd have to say, he'd never seen a couple so in love. Most people never even dream of having what those two have. It's so rare and he was envious.

Just when he looked up, Shawna was strolling in their direction. He had to leave and get out now. "I'll go get us a beer and be right back." He almost ran off.

* * * *

Beth Ann was standing by the bar, waiting to get a few more drinks delivered to the guests, when she spotted Frankie moving fast. By golly, just maybe Shawna had been right. She chuckled to herself. She had to fight back to keep from laughing out loud when she saw him first trip over his own feet, then dart into the Men's room. She doubted he was in that kind of rush for any necessities.

While she scanned the room, she also saw Blake with some girl she didn't recognize. They were sitting at a table having drinks and were cozy. What in the world was he thinking? By now, he had to know Melissa was crazy about him.

Beth Ann had invited Melissa and she seemed thrilled, and said she was coming. She wondered just how she'd feel, seeing Blake so sociable with the tall drink of bourbon.

With that thought, she moseyed over towards their table. As soon as she arrived, Blake looked up and met her gaze. "Beth Ann, you look wonderful." He rose and kissed her cheek. "How are you feeling?"

"I'm good, throwing up day and night. Not sleeping well, and my stomach yells at me for food all the time. I'm sure I'll weigh a ton by the time the baby is born. But I'm peachy."

Blake laughed. "Well, I don't know about all that, but you look terrific. I'd like to introduce you to Sandra. She's a good friend."

Sandra nodded and gave what Beth Ann would call a fake smile. "Blake, could I steal you away for one minute? Sandra, I promise I won't keep him long."

"Sure." She did another glued on smile, so strong Beth Ann wondered if the glass she was sipping from might stick to her lips.

Beth Ann linked her arm through his and walked him over to where they had privacy, at the corner of the bar.

"Blake did you know I invited Melissa tonight?"

He wrinkled his brow. "No, and she didn't show?" He glanced around. "I have her number if you want to call her."

"I don't want her number. I have that."

"I don't understand, then? I don't know why she didn't come. She might still show up."

"Blake Tanner, do you not get that she's in love with you?" She crossed her arms across her chest.

He grimaced. "Listen, little darlin, I already told you, I will not have my ex- fiancée trying to fix me up."

"I'm not just your ex. We are good friends, all of us." She felt her lip tremble and had no idea why she was so emotional these days.

Blake frowned. "I'm sorry, Beth Ann, I didn't mean to hurt your feelings. You and Kaylob are my good friends, some of my best." He touched her cheek. "But still, you will not be my date planner." His Texas drawl was thick.

"Hey, get your fingers off my wife." Kaylob laughed as he stepped up to join them.

Blake shook his head. "Can you tell your wife to stop trying to fix me up. I have a date." He shook Kaylob's hand and smiled. "She thinks she knows who I should be with."

Kaylob turned his eyes towards his wife. "Beth Ann." He walked around and took her hand. "Sorry Blake, she seems to think her new job is Mrs. Match Maker."

"I'm good at it." She turned, stuck her nose in the air and waltzed away. She'd have a talk with her husband later, since she heard him chuckle when he thought she was out of earshot.

She passed by Dana and Johnny and waved. It seemed as though things were more than heating up with them. She'd heard that they might be moving in together. He was such a big guy and Dana so tiny. He must be six-foot-four and she must be all of five-one, if that. They sure seemed happy. That was it, she needed to call Dana and have some girl talk to find out the scoop.

After Beth Ann spent some time with her sister-in-law and Carol, she was able to laugh and let her hair down. She glanced around the room and saw Frankie at the bar, talking to a group of guys and Blake was laughing with his girl toy.

The one thing she noticed was how all her friends in Riverside had come. Love filled her heart the minute she spied Kaylob staring at her from across the room. The look in his eyes told her they needed a minute alone. She nodded towards his private office and he grinned and mouthed, okay.

"Can you two ladies excuse me? I need to have a chat with my husband."

"Don't be gone all night." Carol looked up from her snacks and arched a brow.

Shawna was staring at Frankie and Beth Ann was sure she saw him glance over at Shawna. Could it be possible she just saw Frankie blush?

* * * *

Frankie stood at the bar, having small talk for no other reason than to avoid the little blonde with penetrating blue eyes. A few times he'd

72

looked over and caught her watching him. Her smile had caused his heart to flip upside down.

When the hell was the dinner going to start? The sooner he got out of this place, the better. He chugged down a hot shot. "Whew!" He shook his head. "That will put some hair on your chest."

The guy sitting next to him laughed, a deep belly laugh. "Trying to knock yourself out there, pal?"

"You might say that." Frankie glanced over his shoulder and saw Shawna talking to Charlie and Tina again. Then he observed Blake letting his lady friend stroke his arm. He'd bet they were going to have some fun tonight. The fox leaned over and whispered in his ear. Whoa, Blake was rubbing her leg in a way that spelled seduction.

Okay, time to stop staring at others having fun. He started to stand when a voice came from the stage.

"Dinner is ready and will be served in the Red Rose Room. Name tags are on the table," a tall guy announced. "Go in and have a seat."

Beth Ann and Kaylob came out from the back and Frankie didn't miss how Kaylob buttoned his top button. Those two were not as sly as they think they are. He also watched Beth Ann smooth out her hair. Yep, they were at it again, he laughed to himself.

He stood and headed towards them, but not before Shawna approached him and threaded her arm through his.

"Well, Frankie, if I didn't know better, I'd swear you were avoiding me," she said in a voice that sent heat to places it shouldn't.

He glanced over at her. "Nope, not avoiding anyone," he lied through his teeth.

They arrived at the table and he exhaled. Finally, he could get away from her, stuff his face, and take his mind off everything.

Chapter Six

The problem was he couldn't get past the way she smelled. Her scent was jasmine with a hint of rose, which fogged his brain. And touching her silky soft bare arm was causing him to have thoughts that were wrong on so many levels.

"Frankie and Shawna," Beth Ann called out. "You two will sit here, since you're the Godparents."

Kaylob walked over and pulled out the chairs.

Shawna drew him over to the table. "This is so nice." She waved at all the settings. "I love all the baby decorations."

Beth Ann held up the cloth napkins. "I know, they look like baby diapers. Look at the napkin holder. It looks like a diaper pin."

Everyone laughed, but Frankie really wanted to turn around and leave. Before he knew it, he was sitting next to the woman who was driving him insane.

Beth Ann continued to show everyone where to sit and while she was talking, an attractive strawberry blonde headed into the room.

"I'm sorry I'm so late. I got behind an accident." She held up a gift.

Where had he seen her? He studied the girl and tried to remember.

"Melissa, I'm so glad you could make it." Beth Ann walked over and embraced her. "You are sitting next to Blake." She waved towards Blake, who appeared uncomfortable.

Blake scooted over and sat between two gorgeous women.

"Lucky dog," Frankie whispered under his breath.

"Did you say something?" Shawna asked.

"No. Nothing that needs repeating," he said a little too harshly. Damn, he was rude. This was ridiculous. He could be polite and not worry about anything. He'd been around dozens of beautiful women.

He'd treat her like family. After all, she was Kaylob's little sister and him and Kaylob were like brothers.

"So Shawna." He swallowed the big hairy lump in his throat. "I hear you're going to work here with Kaylob."

"Yes." She nodded. "I'm enjoying it so much and Kaylob and Andrea are teaching me a lot." Her face glowed with joy. "It's so nice being around my brother," she said quietly. "We missed out on so much time."

"You sure did. I'm happy you two finally got reunited."

The tears in her eyes made his insides melt, and the next stupid thing he did was pick up his napkin and wipe off one little tear that fell from her eye.

When she touched his hand, he felt something he'd never experienced in his life. A surge of desire that almost knocked him off his chair. Shit, this girl was giving him chills.

He moved his hand away and Kaylob saved the day.

He tapped his spoon on his glass. "Can I get everyone's attention?"

The room grew quiet and Frankie saw Jack and Lenard set down their drinks and smile at each other with total excitement.

"We asked you all to be here tonight because you mean a lot to us, and as most of you know, our families live too far away to make it. But they are coming soon."

There was a smattering of applause.

"We wanted to celebrate," he said as he reached down and pulled up his glowing wife. "The future birth of our first child."

Frankie watched Beth Ann clear her throat. He knew her well enough to recognize she was fighting with emotions. "As almost all of you know, I never wanted children. But, when I found out I was pregnant, I immediately fell in love with our baby." Frankie had to swallow his own tears when he saw Beth Ann place her hand on her stomach, as Kaylob wrapped his arms around her. They had been through so much and to see them both so incredibly happy, filled Frankie full of joy.

"Here's to your child," Carol said. "May he or she be as beautiful and smart as her mother."

"Hey there. Let's not forget how smart the dad is," Kaylob said. "If you will all look under your plates, we have a list of names and we want to ask you which one you like the best. Just check it off." He reached out and took a jar off the table. "Place your answers inside."

"For a girl," Kaylob said, we have Stephanie Ann O'Brien, Charolette Missy O'Brien, and Kaylie Maggie O'Brien. For a boy we have, Larry John O'Brien, Thomas James O'Brien, or Shawn Patrick O'Brien."

"But," Beth Ann said loudly. "I know it's going to be a girl, and if anyone wants to make any bets, we could start a gambling pool."

Everyone laughed.

Just then the food started being delivered and Frankie was more than a little relieved.

The evening turned out to be wonderful. Kaylob also introduced his sister to everyone, including Blake, who most definitely scanned her from top to bottom, along with many of the guys who worked there. It was hard not to notice her beauty along with that body.

Luckily for Frankie, he managed to avoid her the rest of the night, and as he walked out to his car after the celebration, he slung his jacket over his shoulder and unlocked his car door. He was safe and maybe he'd make a few calls when he got home. Have some fun and forget about the impact Shawna had on him. He opened his car door with a smile on his face.

* * * *

"Frankie." He turned to see her standing under the dim light. Holy smokes! She was beyond stunning. Her blonde hair was radiant, like strands of silk under the moon. Never in his life had he seen such exquisiteness. It made his legs weak.

She moved closer. "I wanted to thank you for tonight."

"Thank me?"

"Yes, for being so understanding when I started to cry at the table." She stepped into his space.

"No problem. You should probably get inside, it's chilly out here," he said swiftly, as he backed closer to his car.

Before he could say another word she stood on her toes and kissed his cheek. The softness of her lips against his skin, the aroma of her hair, made him lose his mind.

Without missing a beat, he wrapped his arms around her and pulled her into a kiss. A very sweet, soft kiss. Her lips parted and he sampled her mouth that tasted of strawberries and chocolate. This woman rocked his world, and his heart floated out of his chest, somewhere in the nighttime sky. He had to pull away before all reason left him.

"Shawna," he whispered. "I have to go."

"Why," she said lightly into his lips and moved in for another kiss.

If he was smart he'd stop kissing her right now and take a job somewhere far away, but instead he pulled her closer and kissed her deeper.

"Take me to your house, Frankie," she whispered.

"What?" He was lost in the kiss.

"Take me to your place and let's get to know each other," she mumbled.

Just then, some people came out of the hotel across the street and laughter spilled its way into the air. It was enough to wake him from his trance.

"I have to go now." He climbed in his car and shut the door, leaving her standing there, touching her lips.

He backed the car out and fled as fast as he could. What the hell had he just done? That was his best friend's sister and he kissed her. No, wait, she had kissed him on the cheek and shit, he had kissed her. But she sure as hell kissed him back and went in for seconds.

He was convinced he felt the earth tilt right under his feet.

Okay, what he needed was a big tall glass of whisky, vodka, something that would knock his ass out.

* * * *

Beth Ann grabbed her jacket off the hanger and saw Melissa sitting in the corner, reading a menu. Kaylob was loading all the gifts into the car. They hadn't expected anyone to bring presents. It was supposed to be a celebration party, but her dear friends had done it anyway.

Beth Ann headed towards Melissa, then saw Blake walking her way, so she stopped and made a hasty retreat. The other lady he was with had left, thankfully.

Speaking of leaving, where was Frankie? He had shot out of there like the Tasmanian Devil. The one thing Beth Ann was sure of, Frankie was attracted to Shawna and had it bad. As far as she was concerned, they'd make a perfect couple, providing he would settle down. She was going to force him to meet her for coffee and she wouldn't take no for an answer.

Just as she thought that, Shawna waltzed in the door almost floating on air.

"Hi sister," Shawna said, her eyes dreamy.

Beth Ann recognized that look, because she'd seen it on her own face each time Kaylob had kissed her. "Shawna," she said to the girl who was gazing out the window touching her lips. "Ah ha," She tiptoed over. "So he kissed you?"

Shawna's face grew pink. "You saw?"

"No, but I recognize a dreamy kiss face when I see it." She chuckled.

"Beth Ann, he's so incredible. I asked him to take me home, but after we kissed, he ran away. I scare him."

"I think it might be the fact that you're Kaylob's sister. They're best friends and he might feel funny about that, but he'll get over it." She touched, Shawna's arm. "I think you two would be perfect together."

"I like him a lot," she whispered. "But, I'm a virgin and if he found out, he might run even faster. I won't give myself up to anyone before I get married. Not even to Frankie."

Beth Ann nodded. "I understand, sweetie. Just make sure you're honest with him."

"If he ever takes me out, I will be." Her gaze dropped. "I won't give up."

Before they could talk more, Kaylob walked over. "What are my two best girls up to."

"Talking about the baby," Beth Ann said.

"Talking about cooking," Shawna said at the same time.

Kaylob arched a brow. "Now, tell me what you two are really talking about?"

Beth Ann took his arm. "Nothing important."

Blake walked up to them. "I'm taking Melissa home. It's too late for her to drive. I'll see you later, Kaylob. Is this week's pool game still on?"

Kaylob nodded. "Of course, I want to win all your money." He laughed.

"Dream on, pal." He kissed Beth Ann's cheek, shook Kaylob's hand and nodded to Shawna.

"Y'all have a good night."

Melissa hugged Beth Ann and said goodbye to everyone.

"Well," Kaylob said. "Let's look in that jar before we leave and see what baby names they chose."

They sat down and counted all the votes.

"Okay." Beth Ann smiled. "The winner of the girl is Kaylie Maggie O'Brien, and the boy is Shawn Patrick O'Brien."

"I love those names," Kaylob said.

Shawna nodded. "I second that."

Beth Ann touched her stomach. "I wanted Kaylie all along. I adore that name so much, and I love the fact that she'd be named after my gram. And, by some miracle if it's a boy, he'll have your dad's name, Patrick."

"Or when we have a son," Kaylob said.

Beth Ann frowned. "You're a funny man."

* * * *

Kaylob loaded everything in the truck and stood outside, looking up at the sky, Beth Ann and Shawna were inside eating pie and laughing about something. Some inside girl thing, but he had a feeling it was about Frankie since he'd overheard what Shawna had said. He'd noticed how flustered Frankie was around his sister. That was pretty funny; he'd never seen him act like that.

Kaylob still couldn't believe he was going to be a father. There was one thing he knew for damn sure, he wanted to be the kind of father he'd dreamed of having, growing up.

Lillian's words echoed in his heart. They had traveled all the way from Ireland to watch him graduate and surf, which did make him feel pretty special. It seemed as though they did love him. The thing that was confusing is why hadn't he ever noticed them? That sucked. If only he could remember a glance.

What he'd give to remember his birth father. He had memories of the pool and swimming with them, but mainly it was Lillian and her voice.

He closed his eyes and reminisced. *"Swim to Mommy."* Her voice was soft and loving. The smile on her face when he would hug her neck, made his heart flip. He remembered the love, the hugs and the laughter. It had been with him for years, but somehow along the way, the memories faded and he forgot.

Should he forgive her? Could he give her a chance to be his mother? Or would he be bitter forever?

The bigger question is could he ever forgive Harold? The man who never even liked him, but took away the father that did. He needed to confront him. Why would he do that? Did he dislike Kaylob so much that he wanted to hurt him?

"Hey honey. What are you doing out here?" Beth Ann asked.

"I was just watching the stars," he fibbed.

"Do you see our stars? Maybe there is one for our baby too."

"Well, come here and let's look together." Kaylob tried his best to sound happy, but knew deep in his heart that the road ahead would be paved with questions. Ones that he expected to be answered.

* * * *

The next two months slid by in a flash and July was heating up, making Beth Ann feel like a hard-boiled egg. They'd hardly seen Frankie and she missed him. He had shared the news about passing the bar the next day after the party and said he'd be busy figuring out what he was going to do. Frankie had some offers and one was big. Beth Ann wasn't surprised and was proud of him; he had worked hard for this.

Shawna almost took charge at the restaurant, allowing Kaylob to take more time off. They still hadn't found a house, which was frustrating because she wanted out of that townhouse. The thing Beth Ann couldn't get off her mind was Peter. She still had bad dreams about the knife sticking out of his neck. She hadn't meant to murder him and leave Cathy without a father, but she had to get away. He was getting ready to do some bad stuff. The whole thing still haunted her, even after the counseling. There were times she could still feel him hiding around every corner, watching and spying on her. Finding out that those bumps in the night were really him, had freaked her out and she needed to move as soon as possible.

Today, they were looking at a house that held hope. The place was in the neighborhood they loved. When their agent had called and told them a house had come on the market in that area, they were both thrilled. She put the last touches of makeup on, and heard the front door open.

"Beth Ann, I'm home."

"I know, honey, I can hear you." She stepped in front of the mirror and turned sideways. Wow, there was a little bump.

"Kaylob, look I'm fat," she called out. "Come, hurry."

He stood in the doorway. "Fat, huh? Well, more to love." He grinned and scanned her from top to bottom.

"Come here," she ordered.

"Yes, ma'am." He walked over and stood next to her. "What do you need?"

"Look." She turned sideways and showed him her bump.

"That's cute as hell, but sweetheart, I don't think you're fat yet." He reached out and rubbed her belly. Then he slid down to the floor right in front of her and stuck his face into her stomach. "Hello little one. I'm your daddy."

Beth Ann lifted his chin and saw love shining in his eyes. "Oh honey." She slid down to the floor in front of him, their eyes locking on each other. A second later, for some reason she didn't fully understand, they both started crying. Maybe because of the bump in her tummy, or everything they'd gone through, or maybe it was because this child came from pure sweet love. It didn't matter why, all that mattered was that they were crying tears of joy.

They spent the next few minutes loving and cooing to their unborn child. She was a part of them and connected to their souls.

They left a little early so they could do some shopping and pick up some things for the baby. When they were done, Kaylob drove about thirty minutes to the outskirts of Riverside, to a place called Redlands. Not far from the restaurant, about a thirty-minute commute, depending on the traffic.

If they moved there, they would be out of the place that held so many frightening memories. After everything she had been through, that townhouse would never feel like home again.

Kaylob pulled her away from her thoughts. "The people that owned the house transferred and moved away. It's empty and they're anxious." He glanced over at her. "Think about it, two houses on ten acres and a swimming pool in the yard of the smaller house which sits out back. The one place is almost brand new and custom built."

"I am so excited. I hope this is the one. I also hope the swimming pool has a gate around it." Beth Ann cradled her stomach with her hands.

"If not, we'll build one." He sounded adamant.

They found the street, Palmdale Court. The houses were spread out on five and ten acre lots and the area was perfect. Trees lined the road and the houses set far enough off the street so there was plenty of privacy. Some of the people had horses and goats. A dog behind a big white fence came running parallel beside them, barking and wagging his tail. It was almost like he was saying hello.

They saw the For Sale sign and Kaylob slowed down. Once they turned into the driveway, Beth Ann noticed all the colorful rose bushes, some red, yellow, and white. The grass was deep green and well cared for. An old oak tree stood in the center of the yard, giving shade to the lounge chairs and a picnic table. They drove to the front and were thrilled with the circular driveway. It reminded Beth Ann of some of the homes back south, with all the southern charm one could wish for.

Beth Ann sighed and placed her hand across her heart. "Oh Kaylob, I love it."

He nodded. "Me too."

As they stepped out of the car, tranquility drifted through the air. Off in the distance, they could see a few small mountains and rolling hills. There were trees all around. The house sat at the dead end and nothing was behind them or beside them, only open fields. Birds were chirping and hummingbirds were fluttering around the rose bushes.

"This is gorgeous," Beth Ann said.

"I think we found our home, baby,"

She nodded in agreement.

The smell of fresh flowers and cut grass made its way into the air, making her feel like she was home in Novato. The wind rustled through the big old oak tree, near the window. Now, for the first time since she'd left home, she could feel the magic again.

Just then, a car pulled down the driveway. It was Rene the Realtor. She had always been nice and now she was extremely pregnant. At least seven months and waddling. Beth Ann knew she'd be doing that soon.

Kaylob put his arm around Beth Ann's waist as they walked up to meet Rene.

"Are you ready to take a peek inside?" She smiled. "What do you think so far?"

"We love it and yes, we are ready to look inside," Beth Ann said.

Kaylob nodded and took Beth Ann's hand.

The agent got the key and opened the front door. They stepped inside and the first thing Beth Ann noticed was the way the sunlight came through the windows. It shone across the living room floors, highlighting the oak.

They were standing in the foyer, which was larger than their living room at home.

"How big is this place?" Kaylob asked.

Rene looked at her paper. "It's a little over three thousand five hundred square feet and the house out back is twenty-seven hundred, both ranchers. This one has five bedrooms and two of them are master suites. The one out back has four. Both are very open."

"Nice," Kaylob said as they moved past the living room.

It was everything they both loved. They stepped into the master bedroom and saw the double-sided fireplace, Beth Ann was sure they were both sold. Even more so when they examined the large jetted tub that sat on the other side of the fireplace. The master suite even had a little sitting room, which could be a small reading room.

The kitchen had a giant island, walk in pantry, with tile counter tops and floors. The stove was top of the line and Kaylob didn't want to leave once he saw that.

The bedrooms were all extra large. One was a nursery that already had a built-in sound system, so you could hear the baby from every room in the house. Another big bonus included a family room that was warm and inviting.

Kaylob stared at Beth Ann, and in that moment they knew. This is the house. It would be the place they would raise their child and grow old together. They loved it.

"We want it," Kaylob said and Beth Ann nodded.

"But you haven't seen the second house yet. It needs some repairs. The kitchen is a little odd and the carpets need replacing. It was the original house until the owners had this custom home built. So it's ten years old."

"We can fix it and bargain with the price," Kaylob said.

Frankie had told them to say that and make a lower offer. So Kaylob did and it sounded good.

"Alright, but let's go look anyway. I want to show you the pool." Rene waved them out back.

Everything was perfect. The pool was fenced just like Beth Ann wanted. And, the walkway led out back to the other house. Even though the second house did need some repairs, it was wonderful.

They made an offer and had to wait to see if the people took it. They were prepared to offer more if they didn't accept. Beth Ann was praying hard. Even harder than she had as a child about her red hair.

A few days later they got the news. The house was theirs. Because it was a cash deal, it wouldn't take long. Their realtor insisted that they get a home inspection, which they did. The last step was a final walk-through.

Everything was good, so now they had to wait for it to close.

That Friday afternoon, two weeks later, Shawna came walking in the front door. She wasn't wearing the usual smile on her face.

"Hi sweetie." Beth Ann studied her. "Are you okay?"

"I was sure Frankie would at least call me or come around." Shawna glanced down at the ground and shook her head.

"Oh Shawna, don't get too attached to him. I love him dearly and I do think you guys would be perfect, if he would settle down. But see, Frankie might not ever be ready. I wish he would." Beth Ann walked over and embraced her. "I'm sorry."

"No, don't be." She swiped her eyes. "No biggie, and he's just afraid of me anyway."

"Well, he is getting ready to take a new job and had to get sworn in as an attorney. So he has been busy," Beth Ann explained.

Shawna nodded. "Okay, so when do we start packing?" She changed the subject.

"I've already started," she said and pointed towards her bedroom down the hallway. "I put some boxes that are packed in the spare room."

"I am so excited about moving in the back house. I want to redo the carpets and paint and I want to pay for it. I love decorating," Shawna explained.

"It's your place, sweetie, you can do whatever you want. Kaylob and the title company did up the paperwork and are doing something to divide the properties. So, it's in your name. Don't ask me what, because I have no clue. Frankie helped them with all the paperwork," Beth Ann said, then almost bit her tongue. Damn it. Why did she go and bring up Frankie again?

"Oh, that was nice of Frankie. I guess he has been busy."

Shawna and Beth Ann spent hours packing and talking about what they were going to do, and by the time Beth Ann glanced at her watch, it was past noon. Beth Ann couldn't get out of that townhouse fast enough. Just the simple sound of the phone ringing, even after all this time, made her jump. Or when she walked out to the pool, she always had to have someone with her. Would she ever feel safe again? She had faith that the new house would offer her some peace of mind.

The phone rang and she was so startled that she dropped a vase and broke it.

"Damn!" Beth Ann snapped.

"I'll get it," Shawna called out.

Beth Ann heard her answer. "Hello. Yes, she is, hold on."

"Beth Ann it's for you."

"It's somebody named James McFarley. He asked for Elizabeth Ann Rose."

"That's my stage name," Beth Ann said, as she took the receiver from Shawna. "Hello?"

"Elizabeth, this is James McFarley. We met at your show a few years ago, Chorus Years."

"Yes, I do remember you, Mr. McFarley. How are you?"

"I'm good and you?"

"I'm doing well. Thank you."

"I want to get to the point, Elizabeth. This is not about a tour, but I was wondering if you could do the singing in a show. It will be in Beverly Hills at the Grand Night Theater. It's only for one weekend. I'd love to have you."

"Well, I'm just getting ready to move. When would you need me for rehearsals?"

"Not until the beginning of November and the show is the week prior to Thanksgiving. That's a ways off."

Beth Ann touched her stomach. "I have to tell you, I'm pregnant. I'll be showing by then. The baby is due at the end of December."

"Congratulations to you and your husband. If it's okay with you, it's fine with me. Part of the proceeds will go towards the needy and I heard that you support those things." He paused. "It's not much pay, but we can try to give you a bit more."

Beth Ann shook her head. "No, you can give my earnings to the fund. I'll do it for free and I'm looking forward to it. I sing in my husband's restaurant and it will be nice to be on stage again." She felt her heart flutter.

"I wasn't expecting that, Elizabeth, that's very generous. Thank you."

Beth Ann took notes and wrote down the dates, times and address. He mentioned some of the movie stars that would be there and how many people she could invite. She tried to sound calm, but her stomach took a dive. She'd never thought about performing for movie stars and prayed she didn't get stage fright.

When she hung up the phone, she stood there, fretting. Shawna stopped packing and gave her a thoughtful look. "You're going to be in a show?"

"Some famous people are going to be there." She swallowed the lump in her throat. "Some big ones and I know they are just people, but I've never done anything like this before."

"Wow, I don't suppose you can invite others?" Shawna's eyes were big.

"Yes, I can invite up to ten people," she said. "Free of charge."

Shawna jumped for joy just as she heard the front door open and close, then Kaylob walked into the room.

Beth Ann looked his way. "What are you doing home so early?" She moved up and kissed him.

"I have some good news." He smiled and held up some keys. "We are closed and we can move in whenever we want. They had house cleaners scrub both houses from top to bottom and it's ready." He swooped Beth Ann up and spun her around. "We can start moving in today."

"But we need movers and everything." She glanced around.

"Done and done. They'll be here in one hour. I made them an offer they couldn't refuse." He smiled big. "Frankie is on his way over to help too."

"He is?" Shawna and Beth Ann said in unison.

"Yes," Kaylob slanted his head. "What's up?"

"Oh, nothing," Shawna ran to her room and said over her shoulder. "I need to start packing my stuff."

Kaylob crossed his arms and studied Beth Ann.

She didn't give him a chance to speak. "Do you know that I got almost all the bathrooms packed and our room is almost done. I also bought some boxes and bubble wrap, but not sure if we will need those with the movers coming. We could always donate it. I think ..."

"Beth Ann, stop rambling, what is going on?"

"I'm just excited." She laughed and told him all about the show and watched the smile vanish from his face. "What's the matter?"

"Don't you think you should have talked it over with me first?" Kaylob asked tersely.

"You mean, like you talked it over with me when you hired movers today?" She stomped off, feeling angry.

After throwing some of her personal stuff in a bag, she felt Kaylob walk in the room.

"I was acting like a chauvinist pig," he walked up to her. "Can you forgive me for saying that? I'm still moody about the whole family thing. I was wrong to take it out on you."

She glanced up into his eyes. "Of course, I understand, honey." She stood on her toes and kissed him.

He looked around. "I should have asked you if you wanted to go today. I can call and reschedule."

"No." she shook her head. "I want out of here, Kaylob. I'm sorry I didn't wait to talk it over with you, but I really want to do this show for the needy."

"I know, baby, it's okay." He hugged her and the doorbell rang.

Shawna yelled out. "I'll get it."

* * * *

Frankie stood at the door, feeling nervous about being at his best friend's house. Never in all the years he'd known them, had he felt this way. He was thankful that Shawna was getting her own place in the other home. He wouldn't have to see her every time he came for a visit. Well, it was Friday and he had the weekend off. So he just needed to help them and then he could be on his way.

The door opened and, of course, it was Shawna.

"Hi Frankie." She smiled and once again his heart raced.

"Hi." He stuck his hands in his pockets and looked down at the ground. "Can I come in?"

"I don't know, Frankie. Are you going to look at me?" she asked.

He raised his head. "Okay, I'm looking. Now, can I come in?"

"Sure." She barely moved but let him inside.

"Congratulations, Frankie," she touched his arm and kissed his cheek. "I heard the good news."

"Thank you, Shawna." He tried not to notice how soft her lips felt. "Where is Kaylob and Beth Ann?"

"Back in their room, packing some stuff they will need tonight." She turned and walked into the living room.

Holy shit, she was wearing a pair of tight fitting shorts and a top that clung to her braless chest. Her hair was pulled back in a ponytail. Never had he seen a woman so enticing.

"Did you hear that the house has a pool in my back yard?" She bent over and picked up some wrapping paper. That about did him in. He had to look away.

"Yes, sounds great. I can't wait to see everything."

She stood up and said, "Yes, seeing everything means you don't have to imagine what it's like, you can actually find out."

The coy smile on her face made him know she was doing everything on purpose. She was a brat, but the cutest one he'd ever seen.

"Shawna." He frowned. "What are you trying to do?"

"Excuse me?" She acted innocent. "I have no clue what you're talking about."

Before he could say another word, Kaylob walked in. "Hey Frankie, I heard the door, but didn't know you were here."

"Yeah, I was just talking to your sister." He narrowed his eyes at her and all she did was grin.

"Glad you're here. I have some stuff in the spare room. I'd like us to take it over so it doesn't get all packed and hard to find by the movers."

Frankie nodded. "Makes sense, lead the way."

Kaylob turned and headed down the hall, but before Frankie could leave, Shawna winked and he felt his face heat. He instantly frowned at her again. Damn that girl, she had the audacity to laugh.

That little blonde was making his life a mess. Before she came along, nothing ever shook him. He was always the one in control, and usually flirting with women. What the hell?

Frankie and Kaylob got everything packed and loaded into Kaylob's truck. The little stuff went into Frankie's Mustang.

Beth Ann and Shawna stayed behind to get more things ready, thank God.

When they pulled up to the house Frankie was impressed. It was gorgeous.

Kaylob climbed out of his truck at the same time Frankie stepped out of his Mustang.

"So what do you think? Nice, huh," Kaylob said.

"Sure is." Frankie nodded. "Can we sit and have a pop and talk for a minute?"

"Sure. How about on the steps?"

Frankie grabbed two pops off the passenger seat. He needed to talk to his best friend. Sure, it was about his sister, but he had to talk to someone.

They sat down and opened their drinks.

"So," Kaylob asked. "Something on your mind?"

Frankie sat there, wondering how to start the conversation. Should he just blurt it out and tell him, or slowly ease his way into this. It's not every day you tell your best friend you want to date his little sister. Date her? Did he just say that? No, but he sure as shit thought it.

Kaylob nudged him. "You have it bad, don't ya?"

"Have what bad?" Frankie asked.

"Feelings for my sister? I've been there, done that with Beth Ann. I know she's rocking your world."

"I've never had these feelings for anyone, ever." Frankie felt relieved that Kaylob knew. It might make it easier. "She's your baby sister. It's just wrong on so many levels."

"Frankie, if you think I haven't noticed how messed up you've been over this, you're wrong."

"I've been so bottled up it's going to take a corkscrew to get anything out." Frankie ran his hands through his hair.

Kaylob cracked up. "Want me to try and find you one?"

"Are you okay with this? I want to take her out."

"Frankie, don't hurt her. I need to tell you something I overheard Shawna say to Beth Ann." He paused … "I shouldn't be telling you this, but you need to know."

"What?" Frankie asked.

"My sister is a virgin and she wants to stay that way until she's married. That's what I heard her tell Beth Ann, and she has no intention of sleeping with you."

"She's never had a boyfriend?" Frankie rubbed the back of his neck. "She sure is a flirt."

"I don't know about that. All I know is she's never been with anyone. So respect that, okay?"

Frankie nodded. "I will."

Kaylob stood. "Okay, let's start unloading this stuff."

* * * *

Beth Ann looked around at their new house after the movers got done, things looked pretty darn good. Having professionals unpack and put things away was a big help. They even set up the beds and hung their clothes in the closet. There were things still in boxes, but not a lot. Kaylob and Frankie had run to get some food and Shawna went back to her house to get her bed made. She said she was looking forward to sleeping in her own house tonight. She'd never lived on her own before, and even though they were on the same land, she was excited about her independence.

Beth Ann sat down on a kitchen chair, wishing the phone was on. She wanted to call her family and some friends. The phone company would be out on Monday to turn it on. Until then, no phone, no TV, but they had a radio that worked.

Life was good. She was over four months pregnant and excited about getting the nursery set up. Would she be a good mother? She didn't know the first thing about being a mom. What was she thinking? Was she ready for this? She stood up and started pacing. What if she messed up the baby? What if she forgot and left it home alone or left it at the store?

She felt nauseated and made a mad dash into the bathroom. Once she threw up and rinsed her mouth, she raised up and glanced in the mirror, then an ache shot through her abdomen.

She sat on the toilet and continued to feel the stabbing pain while she used the bathroom. "Oh heavens, please no." She saw blood on the toilet paper. When she tried to stand, the ache ripped through her and piercing pain hit her lower back. Before she could think, the room started to spin. Seconds later, the darkness took her.

Chapter Seven

Shawna stood, looking around her new home. It was so pretty and she would add some color and get things set up better, after she had it painted. Maybe, she'd ask Frankie to help, but somehow she couldn't see him with a paint brush or doing any kind of work like that. He had been avoiding her the entire afternoon, but a few times she caught him checking her out.

"I know he likes me." she said out loud to nobody. She finished making her bed and putting up a little end table that would work for now. Tomorrow she would start shopping for furniture and find someone who specialized in wallpaper and design. Thank goodness she'd had her mom wire some of her inheritance to her new account. It was going to be strange to start spending some of her money. Living at home, she'd never had to spend any of her inheritance. She had used her pay from the restaurant. Sure, she had enough to last her the rest of her life and then some, but she was not into buying a lot of fancy stuff. She'd never been like that and her mother had never understood why.

Food. She looked around and realized she was starving. Maybe they'd be home soon with the hamburgers. It was time to go back to the main house anyway. Beth Ann hadn't listened to Kaylob about lifting things and taking a break. Two stubborn women in the family, poor Kaylob, she laughed.

Shawna left her house and passed the pool, which sparkled enticingly. Tomorrow, she'd get a chance to swim and take advantage of it.

When she entered the back door, she called out. "Beth Ann, I'm back. I got my bed set up and everything is ready for tonight."

Silence. Oh, maybe she's laying down. She tiptoed into the

bedroom, but nothing. "Beth Ann."

The bathroom door was shut, so she knocked. "Beth Ann." She turned the knob and opened the door.

"Oh my god. Beth Ann." She was lying on the floor. "Beth Ann, oh no, there is no way to call…" She felt her voice break.

A neighbor would have a phone, she turned Beth Ann over to make sure she was breathing and she was. Just then her eyes fluttered.

"Beth Ann, please wake up." Shawna had tears, but swallowed them back. She had to stay together for Beth Ann.

"I'm bleeding." Beth Ann reached down and Shawna saw the blood on the toilet paper. "Oh, Beth Ann, I'm running to a neighbor's house and I'll be right back. I'm calling an ambulance."

There had to be someone home, she stood and made a mad dash to the front door. She stepped outside and saw Kaylob and Frankie turning into the driveway. With all she had, she ran down to meet them. The minute Kaylob saw her, he threw it in park, then hopped out of the truck, Frankie jumped out and started running too.

"Beth Ann is bleeding and passed out, but she's coming around now," Shawna cried. "I was going to go find a neighbor and call an ambulance."

Kaylob took off running so fast that Shawna couldn't catch him. In the next instant, he came out the door with Beth Ann in his arms. "We need to get her to a hospital." He was frantic. "Let's take my truck."

Frankie drove and Shawna sat in the middle between the two. Kaylob was holding Beth Ann and she kept crying and saying, "My baby. I killed our baby."

Shawna was fighting tears as Frankie kept glancing over at Beth Ann and Kaylob. He didn't say much as he drove, but he was driving fast.

Finally, they pulled up to the hospital, squealing the tires. Kaylob was gone in a flash with her in his arms. He was running full speed into the emergency area.

Shawna climbed out of the truck and bent over trying to collect herself. Seeing Kaylob and Beth Ann losing the baby was too much. This was going to be her niece or nephew and she was the Godmother. She lost it and started to sob.

Frankie stepped up and wrapped his arms around her. "It's okay, she's going to be fine," he soothed.

"But the baby. Oh, Frankie," she cried. "The baby."

At that moment she noticed that Frankie had tears of his own. "I know, I know," he said and held her tighter.

* * * *

Beth Ann felt her clothes being cut off and knew she had lost the baby. The pain in her abdomen did not match the pain in her heart. The few times she saw Kaylob's eyes, she could see the hurt.

All of a sudden, she was rushed into another room, and could hear whispers as they cleaned her up. The nurses were talking to her very softly and acting calm, but she could see the worry etched on their faces. Then the doctor rushed in and started examining her.

They sat her in a wheel chair and took her to the restroom, where they made her pee in a cup. She felt her head spinning from being poked and prodded.

Once she was out of pain, the nurse came in and reached over and patted her arm. "The doctor wants to talk to you and your husband. We are admitting you." She opened the door and told Kaylob to come in.

Kaylob walked in and sat down on the chair next to her bed. "Oh baby." He took her hand and brought it up to his lips. "I was so scared. If I lost you…"

"I'm sorry, honey." Beth Ann felt her lip tremble. "Where is Shawna and Frankie?"

"They are out in the waiting room. They came with us to the hospital."

Dr. Pollack walked in and the look on his face told Beth Ann everything. Kaylob had moisture in his eyes and Beth Ann did everything she could not to fall apart.

"Well Mr. and Mrs. O'Brien." He held a silver clipboard. "The baby is fine right now, but we want to admit you for observation."

"The baby is fine?" Beth Ann cried. "She's still alive?"

Kaylob clutched Beth Ann's hand.

"Yes, the baby has a strong heartbeat, perfect for a little over four months along. We will continue to do some tests, but we are pretty sure you have a urinary tract infection, which caused the pain and bleeding when you went to the bathroom and it can cause nausea. It's very common in pregnancy." He smiled. "You'll be fine."

"But I passed out."

"That is concerning, but Mrs. O'Brien have you eaten today? You look a little pale and you've had some issues with that in the past." The doctor picked up his clipboard and waited for her answer.

She had to think for a minute. "I forgot to have lunch. We're moving."

"Tsk Tsk." He shook his head. "You have to remember to feed the baby. He or she needs nourishment." He met her gaze. "Does that make sense?"

"Yes," she felt her lip tremble.

"Okay," the doctor said. "We are admitting you for the night, but you'll be able to go home tomorrow and follow up with your OBGYN."

Kaylob nodded. "Sounds good doctor and we'll make sure she eats."

"We'll get you in a room, get some food for you, and start running tests, but as I said, this is common."

When he turned and left the room, Beth Ann couldn't hold back, she started bawling and talking at the same time.

"Oh Kaylob, I knew it. I'm going to be an awful mother. Before I started bleeding and passed out, I was thinking I'd forget the baby at home in the crib and go downtown. Or what if I left her downtown in a shopping cart, or in the car and she got kidnapped. I already forgot to feed her."

Kaylob wrapped her in his arms and rocked her. "Sweetheart, you're going to make a wonderful mother. You just have to remember to eat." He gazed into her eyes. "You're never going to forget her. I promise." He brushed the hair out of her face and kissed her forehead.

"Kaylob," she said softly.

"Yes."

"You called her a she." She gave him a weak smile, but at least she smiled and their baby girl was alive.

"I have faith in your visions." He grinned and melted his lips on top of hers. "I love you, Beth Ann."

"I love you too, honey."

* * * *

Frankie sat out in the waiting room, feeling sick to his stomach. His best friends had lost their baby and his heart was broken. Shawna had fallen asleep on his shoulder and he had his arm around her. She had worried herself to sleep and he tried his best to soothe her and tell her it would be okay. There was no doubt that Shawna was one special lady. She shifted and mumbled something in her sleep, so he tucked his jacket around her so she wouldn't get cold. He loved her sleeping in his arms. If he was being honest with himself, nobody had ever felt that good before. Not that he had spent much time holding any of his ladies; he mostly spent time doing other things that didn't involve much thinking.

The doors opened and Kaylob was walking towards them with a smile. That was a good sign. Beth Ann must be okay.

"Shawna, here comes Kaylob," he said lightly, not wanting to startle her.

She stood and waited for him to approach.

"We didn't lose the baby," Kaylob said. "Beth Ann forgot to eat and they think she has a urinary tract infection. But, she and the baby are going to be fine." He rubbed his eyes in fatigue.

Shawna threw her arms around Kaylob. "Can we see her?" Shawna asked, releasing a storm of tears.

"Yes, you can see her and she's okay, honey." He kissed the top of her head and held her for a few minutes.

Once he released her, he turned to Frankie and gave him a big hug. "It's late, so you can't stay too long. Plus, they are going to be running a bunch of tests. They are keeping her, but only for tonight."

Frankie watched Shawna take a deep breath and wipe off her face, then she held her head high and exhaled. "I will pull it together and be strong for my sister," she said adamantly and ran her fingers through her hair.

Damn, not only was he attracted to her, but he really liked her.

"Come on, Frankie, let's go see Beth Ann and our Godchild." She reached her hand out to him and he clutched it.

Kaylob winked and didn't seem to mind that he was holding his sister's hand.

Frankie was happy they hadn't lost the baby and Beth Ann was okay. He couldn't imagine what losing a child would have done to his two best friends. They weren't just his best friends, they were his family and they had been through enough.

* * * *

Beth Ann was anxious to get back home. Kaylob had stayed the night in a chair and she knew he hadn't gotten much sleep. Actually, neither of them had. It was early, but they had to wait for the final word from the doctor so they could leave. Frankie and Shawna had taken the truck home and picked up Beth Ann's car and brought it back. Frankie had also stayed the night at their house. She wondered if they had made out or anything. She'd get the scoop from Shawna when she saw her.

A few minutes later, Dr. Pollack came in the room with his clipboard. "Well," he smiled. "You can go home, it's a UTI, and we are going to order you some medication. Beth Ann, be sure you eat at least three meals a day and are taking your prenatal vitamins. I called Dr. Thomas, your OBGYN and filled him in. It's important, as I said, that you keep up your nourishment. More now than ever."

Beth Ann and Kaylob nodded.

"I promise not to skip meals again." She looked over at Kaylob, who was agreeing.

"She won't doc. I won't let her."

The doctor acknowledged their promise. "Well, young lady, I bet you're anxious to get home to your new house. Now, don't overdo. And, you can resume sexual relations in about two weeks. I want to be sure this infection is gone. So, let's take that precaution for right now."

Beth Ann felt the heat rush up to her face.

The doctor grinned. "Can you handle it?"

Again, they both nodded and Kaylob said, "We can handle it."

* * * *

Shawna woke up just after eight a.m. and felt the warm July breeze coming in from her bedroom window. A bird chirped outside, as though it was singing her a good morning tune. Wait. How did she get to bed? She threw back the covers and realized she still had her clothes on. The last thing she remembered was watching a movie with Frankie at Kaylob and Beth Ann's house. Obviously, she had fallen asleep on him.

She flopped back against her pillow and stared at the ceiling. Frankie was such a special guy. *Oh, now I remember*, the memory of last night started coming back and warmed her all over.

He had held her tightly while carrying her into her house. After he had placed her in bed, he had brushed the hair out of her face. It was something she would never forget. With a gentleness that was hard to describe, he'd kissed her cheek and kept his lips there for more than a few seconds.

There was no forgetting how good it felt to be in his arms. The scent of him was engraved in her mind. It was something extraordinary, spicy with a woodsy fragrance that had lingered from the first kiss. There wasn't much she didn't like about Frankie Russo, right down to the way his pants hugged every inch of his narrow hips.

She got up out of bed and went to her dresser. She was in love with her house and the way her master bedroom window had a view of all the hills and meadows.

However, the kitchen needed work. She would have those ugly cabinets replaced with oak and some nicer counter tops. Plus, she wanted crown molding.

The living room was pretty nice and just needed paint and new carpet. The family room needed a lot. The entire design was wrong. The canary yellow walls with a blue border had to go, however, her master bedroom, mudroom and both bathrooms, were totally perfect.

Beth Ann would be home sometime today and things would get busy. They still had unpacking to do and all of them were going to make sure Beth Ann didn't do any of it.

Right now would be a good time to dive into that pool and still give her time to take a shower and eat breakfast.

She slipped on her bathing suit that was cute, but a whole piece. Maybe this week she'd get a bikini and tan her stomach, it was pretty pale. Once she slipped it on, she grabbed a bathroom towel and headed to the pool, which was set in her front yard and backed up to Beth Ann and Kaylob's back yard. The way the sidewalks led to each other's home was fantastic. They were attached in a sense, but separate for privacy.

Her back yard was full of rose bushes and flowers with a little off white fence that matched her house. She loved it, and could get a kitty now. When she stepped outside, it was already a warm day. The pool looked amazing and she could feel it calling her name.

She laid her towel on one of the lounge chairs that were left behind, then placed her toe in the water and shivered. "Brrr," she said, just before she dove into the deep end and gave her body a chill.

It was refreshing and nippy at the same time. She started doing laps back and forth and was picking up speed.

"Do you mind if I join you?" she heard a masculine voice ask.

Frankie stood by the pool with his swim trunks on.

"Hey Frankie, come on in. The water feels a little chilly, but good."

She watched him as he dove into the water. When he came up she couldn't help but notice how his muscles looked with his skin wet and knew she was staring.

Frankie grinned. "What?"

"Your diving skills are great," she said, then added, "Were you on a swimming team?" Trying to cover her real thoughts.

"No, but I do love swimming. That's why I made sure to bring my trunks. I was hoping I'd have time to do a little."

"Thank you for last night." She moved closer and gazed up into his green eyes.

"Shawna…" He cleared his throat and brought her closer. "I really like you and I think you are a wonderful girl."

She felt it coming. The big letdown. "But," she said.

"I'm not good at settling down and I know you're looking for marriage and a steady guy. I don't want to disappoint you."

"Frankie, I want to get to know you better. Who's talking about marriage or anything serious?" She laughed. "I have no desire to get married for a very long time. I have things I want to do."

"Like?" Frankie asked, pulling her even closer.

It was hard for her to think while being so close to him. She reached out and touched his chest and felt him shiver. "Like, date a bit. I really haven't dated much at all, and I'd like to start with you." She saw something flash in his eyes, but wasn't sure what it was.

Frankie took a long, deep breath. "So let's go on a date. I hope we can do more of this." He leaned down and let his lips cover hers.

"Yes, I would love that," she mumbled when he lifted his head. She didn't hesitate or even play hard to get and kissed him right back. The truth was, she wanted to go on a date with Frankie Russo every day for the rest of her life. But there was no way she'd tell him that.

* * * *

Beth Ann watched Kaylob open the car door for her. She was sure glad they had her car instead of his truck. It was hard enough to climb inside, but it would have been even harder today, because she was really sore.

"Thank you, honey, for having them bring my tiny vehicle. I know you hate driving this thing." She fastened her seat belt and he did the same.

They pulled away from the hospital. "My legs are too long and I feel like a giant." He laughed. "I didn't want you pulling yourself up. When you get home, you are going to rest. No work."

"I know." She pouted. "I wanted to start on the nursery, but I guess it can wait a few more days."

"In a few days we can go shopping for the furniture and a doggie bed."

"A doggie bed?" She was confused.

"Yes, I didn't tell you because we wanted to be sure the pups were all healthy. But Rusty is a daddy and the pups are ready."

"Kaylob, a dog," she said.

"Not just any dog, one of Rusty's relatives." He smiled. "We can pick him or her up whenever you're ready."

"Would right now be good?" Her voice went up five notches.

"I was hoping you'd say that, so when I snuck out of the room and called, I mentioned that we might stop and pick one up before we went home. We should stop by the store first and get what we need."

She leaned over and kissed his cheek. "I have the best husband in the whole world, and I intend to show him in two weeks."

"Beth Ann, let's not talk about it. I think I might die."

"Oh no you won't. There are other ways to make you happy." She nibbled on his ear.

"Baby, honestly, I'm driving. I might crash." He lowered his voice.

She stuck her hand on his lap. "Oh, you are so, so sexy." She touched him in a way that made him swerve.

"Beth Ann," he said in his deep sexy voice. "I'm going to have to pull this car over soon if you don't stop that."

"Oh threaten me with a good time." She laughed and he joined in as they headed to the store.

They stopped by a pet store and picked up everything they needed. From a gate, to a nice doggie bed, toys, dishes and more. They were ready to take their pup home.

Kaylob drove to the outskirts of Riverside and pulled up in front of a small, but adorable house. Once he parked, he moved around the car and opened her door.

"Well, let's go meet our new family member," he said as he took her hand.

They opened the gate and walked up the brick walkway, then knocked on the front door.

Beth Ann heard shuffling inside, then the door opened and an older lady with beautiful gray hair greeted them.

"The O'Brien's right?" she asked.

They both nodded.

"Come in, Charlie has told me all about you. I'm thrilled that you'll be taking one of the pups. My name is Wanda, and I've been an animal rescuer and breeder for years. It's always hard to say goodbye to my babies, but I can't keep them all."

Beth Ann could hear the yelps of puppies, then two came tearing around the corner. One was the most beautiful gold color she'd ever seen. The other one was lighter, but still gorgeous.

The golden pup ran right up to them and barked.

"Hello there." Beth Ann bent down and swooped up the pup. "Aren't you sweet." The doggie licked her face.

She handed the pup to Kaylob and he laughed as he received sloppy kisses.

Wanda smiled. "I think she's picked you, whether you pick her or not."

Kaylob and Beth Ann took turns holding the doggie as they walked through the rooms. There were so many dogs in each of the areas. Never had Beth Ann seen anything so wonderful. A lot of the dogs were rescued and now had love and warm beds to hang out on. They all seemed at ease, and there was a guy petting two beagles. Another girl was taking one of the babies out for a walk.

"You guys take very good care of all these animals. They all look healthy." Beth Ann glanced around.

Kaylob was holding the puppy who had now fallen asleep in his arms, so he couldn't pet the other animals.

Beth Ann was in heaven. So many dogs and some cats too.

Kaylob glanced at Beth Ann. "So do you want to take this little girl home ?" he asked, and kissed the top of the puppy's head.

Beth Ann nodded, then looked at Wanda. "How much do we owe you?"

"You can just make a small donation, if you want, because Charlie was due a free pup for breeding services, but he said to give you your choice. Donations do help us to keep our pets fed and vet bills paid." She walked over and started stroking the little girl in Kaylob's arms. "I'm going to miss her." Wanda's expression looked wistful. "Don't mind me, I always shed a few tears when they leave. Not only because I'm going to miss them, but because they are going to a good home and most of my tears are happy ones."

The phone rang and Wanda held up her finger. "I'll be right back."

Beth Ann leaned close to Kaylob. "Can we make a large donation, honey? This is really wonderful, what she's doing."

He nodded. "The checkbook is in my back pocket. Let's help her expand."

Beth Ann wrote out a check for a large amount, and knew Wanda would be set for a while.

Wanda walked back in the room. "I'm sorry, that was someone wanting to adopt a rescued cat and we have a few that were half dead when we got them. It's so hard to find homes for the cats, so that makes me extremely happy." She sighed.

Beth Ann asked, "Why do people treat animals so bad?"

"I don't know, but thank God for the good people in the world that love animals. So do you want to take this little Goldie locks home?" Wanda gave the pup another stroke. "Could you give us updates and send pictures? Let me show you something." She pointed to another area that had a long hallway.

"Oh my gosh," Beth Ann said. The walls were covered with photos of animals and their new families. It almost made Beth Ann cry. "This is wonderful. What you're doing here is a very good thing."

After spending a little more time walking through the place, they headed towards the front door.

"Thank you, Wanda, and thank you for doing all this for animals." She handed her the check.

"It's what I'm here to do." Wanda lifted the check and her mouth fell open. "Oh my heavens, are you serious?" Tears fell from her eyes.

They both nodded.

"Yes," Kaylob said. "We will donate to you every year."

Beth Ann added. "I will tell some of my friends about what you're doing here, and they will help out too."

Wanda wiped the tears from her face. "Do you have any idea what this will do? I can have another room added and this will take care of my pets for a very long time." She stepped up and hugged them both. "Thank you, thank you," she said, with a tremor in her voice.

They left the house and Kaylob handed the dog to Beth Ann. He opened the car door. "Well, she's sure a cutie." He kissed Beth Ann and the pup.

She climbed in the car, holding her new baby in her arms. "I love her already." The little creature cuddled up close to her neck. "Oh Kaylob, she's so sweet."

Kaylob put Beth Ann's seat belt on, since her hands were full, then he shut the door.

He got inside the car and met Beth Ann's gaze. "So any names come to mind?"

"Yes, no other name will do," she said. "Goldie."

"I love it." Kaylob smiled and added, "Let's get Goldie home."

When they pulled into the driveway and parked, Beth Ann placed her hand across her heart. "Home sweet home," she said softly, and gave Kaylob a long look.

He regarded her thoughtfully. "When we left here yesterday, I thought life wasn't fair." He reached over and stroked the sleeping pup. "That maybe God had it in for us."

Beth Ann wasn't sure what to say, but she gave it her best shot. "We don't always understand where God is when our lives fall apart, but he's always there and he never has it in for us." She reached over and touched his arm. "We are so very blessed, Kaylob. Every day we should find something to be grateful for."

He nodded. "You're right."

They glanced up at the house just as Shawna and Frankie stepped out on the front porch.

They were holding hands, but let go as soon as they saw them.

Beth Ann whispered, "Well, well, looks like they like each other."

Kaylob chuckled. "Frankie asked my permission more or less to ask her out."

"He did?" Beth Ann glanced up as Frankie and Shawna were heading towards the car.

Kaylob opened the door. "I'll tell you about it later."

She nodded and climbed out of the car with the puppy. The minute Shawna and Frankie got close, she raised one finger to her lips. "Shh, we have a baby sleeping."

Frankie and Shawna walked up and saw the cute little bundle in her arms.

"Wow," Frankie joked. "That was a fast delivery and she's almost a redhead." He laughed and nudged Kaylob.

Shawna held out her hands. "Oh wow, can I hold him or her?"

"It's a she," Beth Ann said, then placed the puppy in Shawna's arms. "And her name is Goldie."

Beth Ann glanced at Frankie. "As far as I'm concerned, it is a real baby. She just has fur."

They got everything inside the house and made a place for Goldie in the oversized mudroom, which was right off the kitchen. They had a gate to keep her from having accidents, if they couldn't watch her. There was already a doggie door, but they didn't want her outside by herself yet. She was too small.

They would have to do some potty training and make sure she liked her bed and didn't cry at night. Beth Ann was head over heels in love with Goldie already.

Beth Ann stepped outside with Goldie and placed her leash on for the first time. She seemed fine, like an old pro. The day was exquisite with a slight breeze that fanned its way through the air. Looking off to the west, Beth Ann noticed the meadow that stretched all the way to a large group of trees.

She called out to Kaylob. "Honey, I'm going for a walk."

He came to the back door and stared at her. "Beth Ann, I don't know."

"I'm only taking a leisurely walk to that group of trees." She pointed.

"Beth Ann." He crossed his arms across his chest.

"Kaylob." She crossed her arms too, mimicking him. "The doctor didn't say I couldn't go for a slow walk. Heck, they make people do that when they have surgery."

Goldie barked and glanced back and forth between the two of them. Like she was scolding them for arguing.

Kaylob sighed. "Okay, but be careful and go slow."

"Yes, Daddy." She blew him a kiss and turned to leave.

"Right dear, and daddy says someone needs a spanking," Kaylob threatened playfully.

It was Beth Ann's turn to laugh. "Dangerous man." She wiggled her behind.

Opening the side gate, Beth Ann noticed a trail leading right through the meadow down to the trees. It was wide and had wildflowers speckled all around. Goldie barked at a butterfly and wanted to play, but all it did was sail away into the sky.

"It's okay, honey," Beth Ann said. "Butterflies don't like dogs much." They continued walking.

The buzzing of the bees feeding on pollen, along with birds chirping and woodpeckers pecking, sounded like a symphony. It was truly paradise, reminding Beth Ann once again of her childhood home in Novato.

Once she got closer to the trees, she could hear the sound of running water. This was an unexpected surprise. Nobody had mentioned any of this. She walked to the base of the trees and saw a babbling brook with pebbles. It was like a Zen garden, with a trickling noise that made her completely relax. It was paradise.

"Goldie, can you believe this?" The puppy pulled her towards the running water. There was a little downward trail that led right to the brook.

Once they were at the water's edge, Goldie jumped right in.

"Oh my gosh. You're going to freeze." The pup barked and wagged her tail.

Clearly she loved the water. She was chasing bugs and trying to catch some frogs. Beth Ann was doing her best to hang on. With no warning, Beth Ann slipped on a rock and tumbled into the cold water, losing the leash from her grip.

"Goldie, no," she scolded. The pup looked back and saw Beth Ann sitting in the stream and of course it was time to play. She ran up and started jumping all around, licking her face. Beth Ann had to laugh. She was a good girl and didn't run away. She stayed right there with Beth Ann and wanted to play lick a face and splash bath.

By the time Beth Ann stood up, she was soaking wet and Goldie was a mess.

"Look at us." She laughed hard, imagining what she must look like.

"Beth Ann." Kaylob came running and almost slid down the embankment. "Are you okay." His face was fixed with frown lines.

"Oh yes, I'm fine, just a little wet." She laughed. "Goldie loves the water and decided it was time to catch a frog."

Kaylob got to her and looked her up and down. "You didn't fall and get hurt?"

"I'm okay, I just fell smack dab in the water on my butt. But no, I'm fine, just a little wet and cold."

Kaylob cracked up and looked at her in amusement. "Your face has a little mud on it. We better get you home and give you both a doggie bath."

"Oh, hush." She started to wipe her cheeks, but her hands were covered in some type of slush. "Gross." She couldn't help but laugh some more.

At home, after they were cleaned up, Beth Ann fed Goldie. The poor little thing was so tired, she cuddled down on her new blanket in her doggie bed, then passed out. Beth Ann turned and stared at their new addition and noticed she had one of her stuffed toys in bed with her. Yes, indeed it was time for a few pictures.

Kaylob was in the kitchen, cooking a casserole. The house was filled with a mouth-watering aroma. Frankie and Shawna had emptied the remaining boxes and got all the bathroom stuff put away. The place was looking great.

Beth Ann sat in the living room, staring out the window as dusk settled in.

"Hey lady," Frankie walked in and sat down. "I have to run down to the pay phone and call my neighbor. I want to make sure everything's okay. I think I might have left my doors unlocked. They have a spare key and can check things out for me."

"Go Frankie, you don't want to get robbed."

"Save me some casserole. I'll try to be back before we eat. Is there anything you need?"

She shook her head. "No, but Frankie?"

"Yes." He stood and met her gaze.

"Thank you for being so wonderful." She unfolded herself from the seat and stood.

Frankie moved closer and wrapped his arms around her. "I'm so glad you and my Godchild are okay." He backed up and touched her face. "I love this baby already."

She nodded. "I know you do. I also think you are falling for someone else too."

"I know." He drew in a deep breath. "I really do like her, Beth Ann. So much so, it scares me."

She pulled him into a bigger hug. "Listen to your heart, Frankie," she said softly. Beth Ann leaned back and gave him a wry smile. "Don't lose someone special because of fear."

He kissed her cheek. "Don't worry, we are taking it nice and slow. I better get going," he said. "I'm pretty sure I left it open and I didn't get a chance to tell Mike or Paula I was going to be gone overnight."

Beth Ann waved him off. "Get going," she ordered.

* * * *

Frankie drove down to the little Shop and Go, which was only about ten minutes away. The whole time all he could think about was Shawna.

They had kissed a lot in the pool and what she did to him from a simple kiss was embarrassing to even think about.

He had to go take a shower, but it didn't help, not even a little. So he had to turn the knob all the way to cold. It was a miracle he hadn't developed hypothermia.

He was flabbergasted at the way he had been turned on. After all, he'd kissed a lot of women in swimming pools before, and some were half naked. Not one of them had come close to making him feel so out of control. This was more than just lust. It was something that scared the ever loving shit right out of him.

The parking lot was packed when he pulled up. Crap, he had to park on the street. He hated parking his mustang out there, but his phone call should be quick. He jogged up to the phone booth, stuck in the coin and dialed their number.

"Hello," Paula answered.

"Hi Paula, this is Frankie. I know I usually let you know …"

"Frankie, oh my lord, we've been trying to reach you. But nobody could get in touch."

Frankie heard the panic in her voice. "What is it?"

Chapter Eight

"I'm so sorry to tell you this, but your townhouse caught fire and oh god, Frankie they couldn't save anything. Just a small safe. They said it was fire proof. We have it."

His stomach flipped and everything started to spin. "Do they know what started the fire?"

"It was electrical and started in the place next door. They think that when the electrician redid the wiring, he might have messed up. They're investigating.

"Your neighbors lost everything too. Thank the stars the cat was able to escape from the balcony and was saved."

"Great, at least this is some good news. So only the two townhouses, then?" Frankie asked.

"No, actually the one on the other side got it pretty bad, but they were able to get out and at least theirs is still standing. They said it happened so fast. They could smell a rubbery odor, and the flames just seem to explode, but your place was burned down to the ground. There is nothing to even see."

Frankie rubbed his hand through his hair. "This is awful, Paula, nothing left. Where's Mike?"

He's taking stuff to some of the hotels where the neighbors went. We did sneak around the places and found a few trinkets belonging to the Roberts. They were happy." She sighed. "I'm so sorry Frankie, we couldn't go through your place, it's too dangerous because it's all ash and the fire chief said to stay away. You are welcome to stay with us until you get things figured out."

"No, but thanks for the offer. I'm sure I can stay with my friends out here." He exhaled. "Thank you for hanging on to my safe. I can't help but wonder if I should come on over now."

"No, they have it taped off and it's almost dark. Nobody is supposed to go near the place. Frankie, we feel awful."

"Okay, I need a day to process all this anyway. Thanks, hon. Tell Mike, thank you as well."

He hung up the phone and stood there in shock. What the hell, first Beth Ann almost loses the baby and now most of his belongings were lost. He did have renter's insurance so that might help. Crap, he'd have to start all over again. He needed to call his new boss and hope they'd be okay with him getting things together before he started work.

While he drove back, it started to sink in, everything was gone. Pictures of his family, but he should be able to get those back. He had sent out duplicates to almost everyone. Thank God he had put his degrees in his safe along with some other jewelry and things which had been passed down to him. His dad always told him to get a fireproof safe, keep all important papers and things inside, in case of a fire and he had listened, thank goodness. But what about his clothes, shoes, socks, and other things? Shit, his dress suits, all gone. He'd been buying those for years so he'd have a collection when he became an attorney. He sure hoped his insurance would cover some of the cost.

By the time Frankie got back it was pretty dark and he was shaken up. He walked up to the front door, and his legs got weak. It was like a sledge hammer had just knocked the wind out of him and he couldn't seem to catch his breath.

* * * *

As soon as Frankie walked in the door, Beth Ann knew something wasn't right. "What's wrong?"

Frankie sat on the couch and rubbed his hand through his hair. He looked like a man who'd just lost his best friend or his whole world.

"Frankie." Beth Ann moved closer. "Kaylob," she yelled.

Kaylob came running in, with Shawna behind him. "What's the matter?" He ran next to Beth Ann.

"Nothing with me." She nodded towards Frankie.

Frankie glanced up with glassy eyes. "My place burned down and there's nothing left but a fire proof safe." His voice cracked. "I lost everything."

Kaylob sat next to him. "Shit Frankie, I'm so sorry." Kaylob put his hand on his shoulder. "What can we do, should we go check the place out?"

"Not this evening, it's too late. My neighbors said they have it roped off and the fire chief said to stay away."

Beth Ann repeated. "What can we do, Frankie?"

"If you don't mind, let me stay here for a few weeks, until I find a new home." He swallowed. "I hate to ask. I know you guys need your space."

"Don't be silly," Beth Ann said. "Our casa is your casa. Who put us up when we were homeless?"

Frankie glanced up at Shawna. "Sorry guys, I know this puts a damper on this happy day with the new pup and your new home."

Shawna smiled and sat on the coffee table in front of him. "Frankie, why don't you stay in the house with me? I have four bedrooms, plus I could use some help with my house." She touched his arm. "I'm so sorry this happened."

"Hell, I don't even have a bed," Frankie said dryly.

Kaylob perked up. "We have a spare bed. It's the one we had in the apartment. It's in storage, but it's a double, so it's a pretty good size. It's still early enough, even though it's dark. We could pick it up tonight after dinner. We could take a peek and see what else we have over there. We have a unit filled with some stuff from our townhouse and everything from the apartment. You can take whatever you need."

Beth Ann nodded. "We were going to donate it anyway. Now you can have first dibs."

"Cool. That helps a lot. I had renter's insurance and I'll find out what they cover." Frankie exhaled.

Shawna spoke up again. "So will you stay with me?"

Frankie nodded. "Sure, I'll help you fix your place the best I can. I painted once."

"Once." Shawna repeated.

"I guess it's time to learn." He did a half shrug. "I will need to go buy some clothes, like tonight. What I have on is it, and the swim trunks I brought over."

"I have a lot of clothes ... some I've never even worn." Kaylob grinned. "I'll get some together for you. At least until you can go

111

shopping."

"Thanks a bunch. But you are a little thicker than I am. So, not sure how well your pants will stay up." Frankie chuckled.

"Hey, what are you saying?" Kaylob patted his belly and everyone laughed, which seemed to break the gloom.

Kaylob was thick, but hard as a rock and, as far as Beth Ann was concerned, the sexiest man alive.

They all stood and Frankie said, "I'm starving, is the food ready? I need some comfort food."

After the wonderful meal, Frankie and Kaylob took off to the storage with large flashlights, while Beth Ann and Shawna cleaned the kitchen.

Beth Ann glanced over at Shawna. "So, what's going on between you and Frankie?"

"We kissed a lot in the pool," Shawna said. "He was honest and told me he's not looking for anything serious."

"How do you feel about that?" Beth Ann asked.

"I lied, Beth Ann." Shawna set down her drying towel. "I told him I didn't want anything serious. I was honest about not dating much, and I told him I wanted to start with him." She sighed. "What I left out is the simple truth. I would like to date him every day for the rest of my life."

"Let's sit down," Beth Ann suggested. "They'll be gone for a bit, but I do need to check on Goldie and see if she needs to go out first."

"I'll go with you," Shawna said.

Beth Ann crossed the room and stepped into the mudroom. Goldie was still sleeping, so she squatted down. "Come on, girl. Let's go outside." The poor little thing could hardly stand.

"Aw," Shawna giggled. "She's really tired."

Beth Ann picked her up and carried her out to the grass. She did her business and stared at Beth Ann, with a please carry me look. So of course, she picked her up, kissed her face and put her back in bed. The baby was out as fast as a light.

"I hope she's okay." Beth Ann wondered if she should be so tired.

"She's just a pup, they sleep a lot. And, she's had a lot of activity and attention today."

"True." Beth Ann nodded. They headed into the living room. "Now about Frankie. Maybe you should date a few guys. Make sure you don't get too attached."

"I did get asked out by Howard, the bartender at the restaurant. He wants to take me to dinner." Shawna gave a little smile.

"Well, sounds like a good idea. You might not get so attached to Frankie, at least until he's ready to settle down."

"Frankie asked me out, too. I better make sure it's not on the same night."

"Good idea." Beth Ann agreed. "When are you going out with Frankie?"

"This week. So to be safe, I'll go out with Howard next week."

After chatting for another hour, Beth Ann saw headlights flash across the wall from the truck pulling into the driveway. "They're back. Just remember, Shawna, to everything there is a season. Do you know the song by the Byrds, *Turn Turn Turn*?"

"I think I've heard it. Can you sing it for me? The guys will be carrying the stuff into my house."

Beth Ann thought for a minute and started singing. "To everything. turn, turn, turn. There is a season." When she got to the last line Shawna had tears. "A time to love, a time to hate. A time of peace, I swear it's not too late!"

Shawna wiped away her face. "You made me cry." She crossed the room to Beth Ann and they both shed a few tears.

"We're being silly," Beth Ann said. "We shouldn't be crying."

"You almost made us cry, too," Kaylob said, nudging Frankie. "Here Frankie, you can borrow my tissue." They both wiped their eyes, but there was no doubt they were being smarty pants.

Kaylob pointed outside. "We better go finish what we were doing." He pretended to cry.

"Okay I'm coming, boo hoo. Let's go," Frankie joined in.

Both wise guys exited the room. Shawna and Beth Ann stared until they were gone. Then they turned their attention to each other for a long minute, and did the only thing they could do. Laughed like hell.

* * * *

Frankie was happy with what they found in storage and was putting

113

the finishing touches on the room where he'd be staying for the next two weeks or so. He didn't want to stay too long because, well, just because.

There was a light knock on his door. "Come in."

Shawna poked her head inside. "I'm making some tea. Would you like a cup and are you hungry?"

"No food for me, but tea sounds good. What can I do to help?" He waved around his temporary room. "Pretty nice, don't you think?" He tried to act happier than he felt.

She nodded. "Looks better than mine."

"Thanks to all of you. I have a roof over my head and a bed to sleep in. Not to mention lamps, end tables and a dresser. Even a little TV," he pointed.

"I'm still sorry that you lost all your stuff, Frankie. That can't be easy."

"Well, I had some nice furniture and a quilt that my grandma made. That can never be replaced. But I didn't have a lot of personal items, although I had some. I'm happy I had that safe." He felt his spirits fall, because as the evening had gone on he was remembering more things that he had lost. One was cards from friends and family. Not all those were in the safe.

"Come on." She waved. "Let's go have tea."

He followed her down the hallway and the way she moved her hips was more than a little enticing. Holy smokes, she was sexy and he wondered if she was swaying like that for his pleasure. Well, it was taking his mind off other things, like the suits that he'd spent hundreds of dollars on over the years.

Once he entered the kitchen, he had to wince and she caught him doing so. It was the ugliest kitchen, he'd ever been in. He glanced around and tried not to make a face.

"I know it's awful." She giggled. "But it's very large. Look at all my counter space and storage. I have a walk in pantry." She opened it up. "Look at this, a lazy susan. I love it."

Frankie nodded. "That part is nice, but … The colors and counters. What were they thinking?"

"Not sure," she said as she glanced around. "It is ten years old."

Once she made the tea they both sat down at the ugly table that matched the ugly kitchen. "So they left you a table and chairs. Nice," Frankie said.

"Well, at least it's some place to sit until mine gets here." She blew on her tea.

"Shawna," Frankie cleared his throat. "I want to make sure us staying together doesn't give you the wrong ideas."

"Wrong ideas," she repeated. "About?"

"How serious this is. I want to lay all the cards on the table."

"Frankie, I understand. You already made that clear, and besides, I'm going out with Howard next week. I'm fine Frankie, I told you I wanted to start dating."

"Howard? You mean the bartender at the restaurant?"

"Yes, that Howard," she said.

"Oh." For some asinine reason, her dating someone else bothered him. But he lied. "Well, good. I won't worry then."

"Great, no need to worry." She seemed completely unfazed.

After they had tea she stood and yawned. "Time for me to go to bed. Oh, by the way, what night did you want to take me out. I don't want to make any other dates on that same night."

Now that really got under his skin, but he put on his best smile. "How about tomorrow night?"

"Sounds great. I'm looking forward to it," she said, then stood and sashayed out of the kitchen.

Frankie sat there, thinking about Howard kissing her and didn't like it one little bit. But since these were his rules, what choice did he have? This was all his doing and he should be happy about it, right?

He needed to take his mind off Shawna's date with Howard and make a note to call his insurance company first thing Monday morning. Although, he knew if it was caused by the electrician doing a shitty job, his insurance company would not have to pay. He placed his head in his hands and hoped like hell the owners of the building had made sure the guy was licensed. If by some chance he wasn't, it was going to be a pain for everyone.

* * * *

Shawna crawled into bed after brushing her teeth. So, he wanted her to date and not get serious. Fine, that's exactly what she'd do. She punched her pillow. "I'm going to change his mind."

She turned off the light and could hear the shower running. She would sure like to peek at him, but that wasn't a good idea. Maybe once she closed her eyes, she'd fall asleep fast and stop thinking about Frankie.

But apparently closing her eyes wasn't enough, so she tried counting butterflies, then tried thinking about the ocean back home. Okay, she'd try humming, but nothing was helping. By the time it was 3:00 a.m., she got out of bed, slipped on her silky robe, and headed out to the kitchen. What she needed was a large cup of passion flower tea to calm her down and stop her racing mind.

She filled the tea kettle with water again and turned it on. Once it whistled, she pulled it off fast so she wouldn't wake Frankie. Then she grabbed the biggest cup she could find. As she drank, she thumbed through a *Country Home* magazine and saw some decorating ideas she wanted to do. There was no doubt in her mind, she'd fall asleep now. When she passed by Frankie's room, the door was slightly cracked open, so she stopped and listened. She could hear the sounds of his breathing, which told her he sure as heck wasn't having a hard time sleeping.

Lightly she pushed on the door and stepped inside his room. The sight of him made her lose her breath, it was stuck deep inside her heart. He was naked and the moon lit up the back side of him, which caused her to respond in a way she'd never experienced.

Her reserve had always been to wait until she was married, but in that moment, all she wanted was to climb into bed and ask him to be her first. Instead she backed away, and got one more long delicious look. After a few seconds and her heart throbbing, she backed slowly out, and closed the door.

Her hand went across her heart and she whispered, "Oh my. Calm down my beating heart."

With that, she went into bed and fell asleep and had dreams of Frankie the entire night.

* * * *

Beth Ann awoke to the sounds of barking. She reached for Kaylob,

116

but came up empty. Was he gone? He wasn't working today, so where was he? She heard the bark again and tore out of bed, heading towards the mudroom.

She arrived at the puppy bed, but Goldie wasn't there. The barking was coming from outside. She opened the door and saw Kaylob and Goldie running around the back yard. It was one of the cutest things she'd ever seen. He was sprinting around and the pup was chasing him.

Beth Ann stepped out on the steps and Kaylob glanced up. "Hey sleepy head, or should I say ..."

Beth Ann said it for him. "Sleeping beauty." He had always said that.

"Sweetheart, you're a beauty, but maybe you should get dressed."

"What are you talking about?" She glanced down and remembered she had on a little tiny T-shirt and undies.

"We do have a male guest and although he's my best friend, I don't want him seeing you naked."

"Why? I already did." Frankie raised up from the lawn chair and whistled. "She's a foxy little flasher, no doubt."

Beth Ann knew it was an inside joke about one time when she accidentally walked out naked in front of him. She'd never live that down. Her cheeks heated and she dashed inside with Goldie on her heels. She ran into the bedroom and pulled on a pair of blue jeans and a flowered shirt that buttoned down the front.

She bent down and pet Goldie. "Hey girl. You were playing with daddy this morning. Did you have fun?"

She barked like she understood, then turned and ran out of the room.

Beth Ann laughed, but knew from now on she'd be sure she got dressed before she went outside.

In the next instance Goldie was back with her toy in her mouth. She dropped it on the floor and barked.

"So you want to play." She picked it up and played fetch for a few minutes.

Once Beth Ann got outside with Goldie, Kaylob and Frankie seemed in a deep conversation.

"Hey guys, what are you up to?"

Frankie turned and gave her a weak smile. "I need to go check out my place this morning. I can't get in touch with my insurance company until Monday. But I can go pick up my safe, and check the place out."

Beth Ann nodded. "Do you want us to go with you?"

"Not you or Shawna. It might be dirty and dangerous. But I would like to steal your husband, if that's okay."

Kaylob turned and gave her an amused look. "Glad you got dressed."

Frankie stood. "I'm going to go fix something to eat for your sis. She was up late last night. I thought I heard her up after three this morning. She's still sleeping."

"I could cook breakfast," Kaylob said.

Frankie's eyes widened. "Who could refuse that kind of offer. I'm going to get a few things done and I'll let Shawna know if she wakes up. When should we be here?"

"Give me some time to spank my wife and that should only take a few minutes. Breakfast should be done in about forty-five."

"Okay, have fun," Frankie said as he walked away.

Beth Ann stood with her hands on her hips. "Oh, right. You just try it."

Kaylob was out of the chair and swung her up in his arms. The minute he put her on the ground, he did what he'd always done, tickled her knees.

"Who's the boss?" he growled. The game began, only this time it was with a new member of the family, who thought she was supposed to lick Beth Ann while she was on the ground. It was her playtime too. They both howled with laughter and Beth Ann couldn't help but scream a little while Kaylob held her down.

* * * *

Frankie could hear Kaylob laughing and Beth Ann squealing. They really had something special, but the truth was if she was his wife, he wouldn't want her prancing around half naked either. Beth Ann was a fine looking woman all the way around. He had accidentally seen her naked once when she thought he was Carol, and came out to flaunt her muscles. Man oh boy, he had seen all of her. No matter how beautiful she was, he loved her as his best friend and wouldn't trade that for the world. Not even when Kaylob was missing. There was a minute when they both thought maybe they should be together, but it was a fleeting thought.

Frankie went down the hall to his room, and made his bed. He checked out some of the clothes that Kaylob had given him. The shirts and boxers were fine and the socks were still in the packaging. But the pants were just too wide. He wasn't as big and husky as Kaylob. He hung them up and put everything else in his dresser. What he needed to do was make a list of everything he had to replace. He also had to get in touch with his new boss to see if he could put off starting work for a few weeks. There was a lot to figure out. He was still worrying about the insurance thing.

The whole fire situation sucked, and it was a bit odd living with someone he was about to start dating. There was no way he wanted her to get too serious, at least that's what he kept telling himself, but hell, that might just be bullshit. He was still bothered by the fact that she had a date with that Howard dude. He remembered seeing him check her out last time he was at the restaurant, along with that chef guy with the fake blond hair. He was pretty sure his name was Ralf.

He picked up a notepad and grumbled, then headed out to the kitchen. A list and coffee sounded good. Before he could get the coffee going, he heard shuffling sounds coming towards the kitchen. The minute he saw her, he almost dropped the pot. She had a little white T-shirt and good lord, he could see right through it. He turned his head, but it was too late, maybe Kaylob's baggy jeans would be good, because right now, his pants were too tight. What the hell is the deal with women and those little shirts?

"Good morning, Shawna." He filled the pot up and started looking for the coffee.

Shawna crossed the room and pointed to the cabinet. "It's right here." She opened the door and pulled the coffee can down. He kept his head facing the other direction as he couldn't look at her without springing into action. Never had he seen someone so foxy with messy hair and no makeup. Not to mention the natural scent of her was making it hard to focus.

She moved closer and stared at him. He tried to only look at her face. It was a fighting effort.

"Are you okay, Frankie? You seem tense." She reached out and touched his arm.

"Not really," he blurted out. "I know this is your house, but Shawna…" he looked down and shivered. He wanted to touch her, to feel her skin, and bury his nose in her neck.

"What?" Shawna questioned.

He lifted the sleeve of her shirt. "Do you think you might want to get dressed? I can see through that and …"

She stepped back and looked. "Whoa, you're right. I'll go get on my robe." She left the kitchen in a hurry.

Holy hell. He blew out a breath. He'd never asked a woman to get dressed before. That was a first.

He finished the coffee with trembling hands and sat down to start on the list. Shawna returned, dressed in a cute pair of white shorts with a sky blue top. He was glad she didn't slip on her robe. She had her hair in a ponytail and her face was still without makeup. She was smoking hot.

"So," Frankie asked, "you had problems sleeping last night?"

"I did. New place and all." She blushed and he wondered why.

"Kaylob is making us breakfast, then we are heading over to my townhouse or what used to be my place."

"What are you writing?" Shawna asked as she walked over to the cupboard, pulled down two cups, and poured some coffee for them both. "Do you want cream or sugar?"

"Just black, thanks."

She put cream and sugar in hers and carried both cups over to the table. He watched the way she stood on her tip toes when she went back and returned the sugar to the cabinet. His heart leaped into overdrive.

She sat down. "It's really hot, so be careful."

"Thank you." That wasn't all that was hot.

"Thank you for making it." She blew on her coffee. Pointing to the paper, she asked again, "What are you writing there?"

"Oh, a list of what I need to purchase. At least to get me through until I get the check from my insurance company." He paused for a moment. "I guess I should say hopefully I will get one. It all depends on what caused the fire. I know the insurance company will pay. I'm not so sure about the electrician."

Shawna peeked at the list. "I hope they can help you fast. That's looking like a lot of stuff."

"So far I wrote down towels, clothes, shoes, socks, ties, and some business suits. I have to start my new job." He sighed, picked up his coffee cup and took a small sip. "There's so much stuff I didn't even think about."

"Do you think the electrician will have to pay?"

"Well, it all depends on what the investigators find. If it was started by electrical issues, it may be the fault of the guy who just finished doing the work. In that case, he would be liable."

"Oh, that makes sense." She stood. "I just hope they find out soon."

"Me too." He sighed.

"Frankie?" Shawna said softly.

"Yes?" He watched her move closer, then was surprised when she sank down on his lap.

"I watched you sleep last night," she said, placing her lips closer to his.

Without missing a beat, he kissed her and got lost in her deliciousness. She tasted of coffee and sweet cream. In seconds, he melted like a marshmallow that was dropped in hot chocolate.

Everything felt right, holding her, kissing her, just being with her.

"Frankie," she whispered again. "I like you a lot."

"Oh, and I like you too. Maybe too much," he moaned into her lips.

In another move that surprised the hell out of him, she slid her hands under his shirt. "Frankie, if I ever broke my rule, I would want it to be with you." She kissed his neck and pain hit him all over.

She straddled him and put her arms around his shoulders. "I enjoyed watching you sleep last night. You have a very sexy ..."

He placed his finger to her lips. "Shawna, you're driving me crazy."

"I'm sorry. I just like being close to you and I'm smart enough to get that you don't hate it." She kissed him again. "As a matter of fact, I'd say you're loving it right now." Her gaze locked with his.

"You're going to be the death of me." He groaned and shifted her over a little.

"Or maybe I'll be the life of you." She stuck his hands around her waist and shifted closer.

"I've never met a woman as sure of herself as you," Frankie said.

"That might be true, but what I'm sure of…" She studied his eyes. "Is that this is where I belong, right in your arms."

"How would you know if you haven't dated all that much?"

"That doesn't mean I haven't dated at all. I've been kissed and cuddled. It just never meant anything before. Frankie, I knew from the minute I saw your photo that if we ever met, something magical would happen."

He laughed. "Well, let me tell you, something is happening alright. I need to go take a very long cold shower."

"I would join you, but I need to unpack a few things." She stood.

"Shawna are you trying to tease me or torture me?"

"No," she said in a stern voice. "I'm not a tease, I just love being close to you."

"Me too," he admitted and stood up. "However, I also respect you and I will not push you into something you're not ready for. I know you've never been with a man before."

"Oh, Beth Ann told you?" She sounded hurt.

"No." He shook his head. "Kaylob overheard you tell Beth Ann that you weren't going to sleep with anybody until you got married, not even me." He stepped closer and put his arms around her. "I'm going to be honest, Shawna. I've slept with a lot of women. I started when I was fourteen. I'm okay with this." He exhaled. "Okay, maybe not okay, but I respect your choices."

"Thank you, Frankie."

"For?"

"For not making fun of me." She glanced down. "I just want to save myself for my wedding night."

Frankie felt a pain in his chest as he thought of her getting married and letting another man touch her. He needed to get a grip. He'd never cared about anything like that before.

"We better get going, little lady." He tried his best John Wayne impression.

Shawna giggled. "What about your cold shower?"

He smiled and kissed her neck. "I guess it can wait. I'm starving."

* * * *

Two weeks later, Beth Ann stood in front of the mirror staring at her stomach. There was no hiding the bump now. She was legitimately showing and knocking at five months. Kaylob had returned to work and Beth Ann was counting down the minutes until he got home. It was only 1:00 p.m., so it was a long time until tonight. She couldn't wait to make love with her husband again.

She looked at Goldie, who was chewing on her toy. That goose seemed to be her favorite. Beth Ann was sure it was because it did have an odd squeak.

"Hey girl, want to take a walk?" Goldie was up and ran to the other room. "I guess that's a yes."

As she headed out to the living room Goldie came flying from around the corner with her leash hanging out of her mouth.

"Oh my gosh, you understood me? That is unreal, you are so smart."

The doorbell rang and Beth Ann went to answer it, but not before she peeked through the peephole. She still didn't feel safe enough not to look.

It was the postal carrier who was holding a letter. She opened the door. "Hi."

"Is Kaylob O'Brien here?"

"No, but I'm his wife."

"Okay, I need you to sign here." She held out a clipboard and Beth Ann signed on the x–spot, glancing at the envelope. It was from Dusty Clark. Why would she be sending a certified letter to Kaylob? That was some girl he'd dated back in junior high. She had left town a few months after they'd stopped seeing each other, and nobody had heard from her since. The rumor was her parents had sent her to live with an aunt because they were gone all the time. Beth Ann had been relieved and happy she was gone.

Now, here Beth Ann was holding a letter in her hand, wondering how she'd found Kaylob and what was inside.

Chapter Nine

She needed to call him and let him know and hoped it wasn't any bad news. He was going through so much already with finding out about his birth parents. All he needed was more stress. He already had problems with his blood pressure.

Beth Ann picked up the phone and called the restaurant. "Seven Nights Seven Roses, fine dining."

It was Beverly, the hostess. "Hi Beverly can I speak to Kaylob."

"Sure thing, how are you feeling?"

"Really good and very pregnant, thank you."

She heard the phone go on hold and the music started.

"Hey sweetheart, everything okay?"

"I don't know." She paused. "You got a certified letter from Dusty."

"What?" He seemed shocked. "Dusty, from Novato?"

"Yes."

"Can you open it?" Kaylob asked.

"Sure." She laid down the phone, unfolded the letter and started to read.

"Okay, here we go." She cleared her throat.

Dear Kaylob,

I never thought I'd be writing this letter to you and I know it's been years. I guess there is no way to say this, but to get straight to the point. I have a son and he's a wonderful boy. He's smart and the kindest young man you could ever imagine." Beth Ann took a breath. *"Let me back up a little. I've been diagnosed with stage four bone cancer. There is no cure. My son's name is Tylor Thomas Clark and he's never known his father. Kaylob, I'm pretty sure you're his dad. I admit there was one other guy and I've sent him a duplicate letter, only I'm not sure he's the dad. I was with him twice. As you know, we were together for an entire summer, and well, we rarely missed a day. His eyes remind me of you and although he has brown hair, he's kind and giving just like you were. Would you be willing to do a paternity test to find out? He needs a living parent.*

Beth Ann paused, feeling a little sick, but forced herself to continue reading.

Enclosed is his picture and age and date of his birth. You will see it matches up to the timeframe when we were together. I've loved raising him and never really needed another parent, until now. I know you might be angry with me for never telling you, but you were in love with someone else. I know you, Kaylob, and you would have wanted to do the right thing. You always wanted to do the right thing, because you are a good person. I could have never done that to you.

There was silence on the other end of the phone line.
"Kaylob, are you okay?" asked Beth Ann.
"Not really," he said. "Is that all?"
"No, there's more. Shall I continue?"
"Go ahead," he said.

From what I hear you are married and very happy. So I hope this doesn't do anything to damper that.
Enclosed you will find a card that you can call and make arrangements to have the blood test done. It's up to you. But know, if I don't find Tylor's dad, he has no living relative that will take him. He will have to be placed in a foster home.
I only have about six months, so please don't wait too long.
Thank you
Dusty

Beth Ann felt like crying. She was sad about the boy and about the mother dying of cancer. For whatever reason she didn't feel jealous. Instead, all she felt was a deep sadness. She also thought about how the truth had been kept from Kaylob, and how it was possible that a child of his, had been going through the same situation. Well, not the same, but close enough.

"Kaylob?"

"I'm coming home." Then the phone went dead.

Beth Ann picked up the picture and couldn't see any resemblance. Maybe he looked like Dusty's side of the family. He looked to be around thirteen, which would be about right. Beth Ann's heart sank. She couldn't imagine what it would feel like, leaving a child behind, and not knowing his fate. She sat on the couch and cried.

About thirty minutes later Kaylob came rushing in and the minute he saw her, his face dropped. "I know that must have been hard for you to read, but remember that was a long time ago."

"Oh honey." Beth Ann touched his face. "I'm not jealous or anything like that. I just feel bad."

"Really?" He looked surprised.

"Really." She hugged him.

"My baby has really turned into a grown-up woman." He studied her. "There was a time when you would have thrown a fit."

"Well, that time has passed. I trust you, and I know you love me, and you know that I love you. We have trust and faith in each other." She met his eyes. "Right now we have to worry about this poor young man and Dusty dying." She felt her voice break. "Kaylob, that is so sad."

He nodded. "It is. Can I see the picture?"

She handed it to him and he shook his head. "I'll have the test, but he doesn't look like my side of the family, at all."

Beth Ann agreed. "I'm glad you're willing to take the test. We don't want anything like what you went through going on." She gave him a long, lingering kiss. "I'm very proud of you, that you're not angry."

"No, how can I be? She's dying." He looked sad. "But you're right, I don't want history repeating itself."

Beth Ann nodded in agreement. "Let me make you some coffee."

"No," he said as he took her arm. "I know this might seem strange. But can we please make love. I need to feel you close and it's been two weeks. We can make the arrangements tomorrow." He looked around. "Where's Goldie?"

"We were getting ready to take a walk and she had her leash." She glanced around. "She must have got tired of waiting. I better go check on her."

They found her in the laundry room just waiting by the back door. "Ah Kaylob, can we take her for that walk first."

He smiled tenderly. "Of course. How can we refuse anything so sweet?"

Kaylob put on her leash and they headed out the front door. This would be the first walk down the main road and it should be fun for Goldie. They passed by neighbors and some of the dogs wanted to sniff and say hello. Her little tail was wagging a mile a minute.

As they walked in silence. Beth Ann finally spoke up. "So every day for a whole summer, huh." She arched an eyebrow. "That explains a lot."

"Like?" He stopped and met her gaze.

"Like the way you made love to me that first time. I mean, I knew it wasn't your first, but I guess I didn't know how much experience you had."

"I didn't just learn that from her, there was this other girl too." He winced. "Shit, never mind."

"Oh really? She was before me?" She held his gaze.

He nodded. "We didn't go all the way, but—"

"I get it Kaylob. As you recall, we got good at fooling around too, without going all the way."

"Yeah, but with you I saved all the really good stuff until we finally did go all the way."

She smiled. "Yes, you did, and you really have a knack for that good stuff. I guess we should get back now." She wanted her husband in a bad way.

"You got it, mama." He grinned.

They couldn't get home fast enough. They gave Goldie a bone and some fresh water. Just as Beth Ann was locking the gate and entered the kitchen, Kaylob swept her up.

"Me man, need my woman," he groaned.

Beth Ann giggled. "Me woman, need my man."

He took her into the bedroom and placed her on the bed. Slowly he took off her shorts and stared at her lacy black underwear.

"Beth Ann you know what I want you to do for me?"

She nodded and slipped off her panties. She moved back up on the bed and gave him his favorite dessert. He watched and as he did, he gave her some of what she loved too. They teased and observed each other until they couldn't stand it anymore. Afterwards, he hovered over her, and gazed down into her eyes.

"Beth Ann, I can't get enough of you. Watching you do that is something that drives me over the edge."

Beth Ann wrapped her legs around him. "I feel the same with you and it drives me crazy with desire." She loved what he did more than she could put into words.

He lowered himself gently, giving her all the love he had to share. They moved in perfect harmony, going deep into each other's soul. Beth Ann couldn't help but love the way he said her name over and over again. In the end she must have been loud, because he covered her mouth with kisses and laughed when Goldie barked.

* * * *

Frankie made another trip to the store after work. All he'd done today at his job was to get his private office partially set up. He still needed to get a desk and it should be there in about a week. After that, he'd start working full time. The suit he'd bought today was pinstripe and the thing was expensive, but he couldn't imagine wearing it every single day. The investigation should be over this week and he should be getting a check from someone. He still hadn't found out if the electrician was licensed or not. Thankfully, he still had some savings left.

There was also a chance that he'd find his own place soon. He sure liked the Redlands more than Riverside, plus he would be closer to Shawna.

He was looking forward to getting home and seeing her tonight. They had been having so much fun. Every day for the last two weeks they had been together, swimming and going out to eat, plus hanging around at the nearby park. It had been nice because Shawna had taken the time off work to get her place fixed up. They had also done some hot and heavy making out. Cold showers were becoming a daily event.

He was proud of himself for not pushing to take things too far. Last night they had kissed, held hands and danced alone in the house for hours. He cared about her differently than anyone he'd ever been with. The fact was, he loved her company, and was handling not making love to her better than he imagined.

He thought about Debra; he had liked her, but it was more about the sex. Man, the woman had been wild and crazy in bed. But he'd never had deep feelings for her and she deserved better. He had heard through the grapevine that she was engaged to her childhood best friend. That was a nice thing, she had someone who loved her the right way.

The first time he met Roger, he could see the guy had deep feelings for her. Debra was blind to it, but from what he heard, Roger was smart, and let her know right after she moved out of his house. Frankie was happy for her.

When he got home, he saw Kaylob's truck was there. Oh, two weeks, he laughed. Kaylob had been dying and voiced it. There was no way he was going to knock on their door.

He pulled down the other side of the private driveway. They had cleaned it up and got all the weeds pulled. It was nice to have a separate one. Shawna was going to get it paved because right now it was rock and gravel.

He parked the car and was glad to see that Shawna was home. The feeling inside his heart grew thinking about how he was getting used to being with her. Maybe he'd take her out to dinner tonight. He picked up his bags and headed towards the front door. Just as he got to the step he heard a car driving down the driveway.

"Who is that?" Oh, maybe the decorators. She was going to hire someone to put up the crown molding and do wallpaper. He stood waiting.

As soon as the guy stepped out of the car, Frankie's heart started to race. It was Howard from the bar. What the hell?

"Hey Frankie," Howard said with a big grin. "Shawna told me she was letting you stay here and about the fire. Man, sorry to hear about that."

The guy was friendly, so Frankie just nodded.

"Did Shawna forget something at work?' Frankie questioned.

"No, we have a date." His eyes lit up way too much.

Just about that time the front door opened. "Oh, hi Frankie. Hey Howard, come on in, I'm almost ready."

Frankie stepped inside and went directly to his room. He set down the bag and felt instantly irritated. Why would she date him now? They had been spending every day together, and somehow he got it in his head she had changed her mind about dating other guys. Of course, he had told her to go out with other people, but that was in the beginning. Hell, they'd only been dating for a little over two weeks. But for him, he felt like he'd been with her all his life and waiting a lifetime to find her.

He wanted to go throw Howard out of the house, but he knew he had no right. What he needed to do was buck it up and act like a man. He would be moving soon anyway and wouldn't have to watch this. Why didn't he tell her the truth? Well, maybe because he hadn't known it himself.

Not until this very moment.

Taking a deep breath, he strolled out with a big smile on his face. Howard was sitting in a chair, waiting.

"I hope you two have a great time tonight." Frankie tried to sound okay, but knew he failed. "Would you like a cup of coffee or some water?"

"Sure, I'll take a glass of water and I'll make sure to show her a good time," Howard said with a smile.

"What's that supposed to mean?" Frankie almost growled and met his eyes dead on.

"Just what I said. I'll show her a great time."

Before Frankie could speak, Shawna came prancing down the hallway. She wore a cute white skirt and a simple button down sweater that clung to her breasts. She looked amazing. The skirt was short and showed off her stunning legs.

Howard stood. "Wow! You look beautiful." His eyes scanned her with an expression that made Frankie see red.

Frankie hadn't even noticed the flowers that Howard was carrying.

"These are for you." He grinned as he handed them to her.

"Thank you, Howard," she said, inhaling their scent. "They smell great and are very beautiful."

She turned with the flowers and left the room. Frankie followed her.

Once they arrived in the kitchen, Frankie was shocked to see things were being torn apart.

"What happened in here?" Frankie asked as he looked around.

"Oh, the construction started today. It's going to take about a week or so. But when they're done, it should be perfect."

"Great," Frankie responded then asked. "So where is he taking you tonight?"

Shawna smiled. "I didn't ask. He said it had great views that were beautiful."

"How special."

"I know, isn't it?" She placed the flowers in a vase, filled it with water, then carried them back out without even glancing Frankie's way. He sat down at the table fuming, but trying to hide it. What the hell did she see in this guy? He looked like a body builder with muscles everywhere. It was abnormal. Why would she want to go out with some muscle bound guy anyway?

After a few minutes he heard her call out, "Have a nice evening, Frankie. I should be back sometime tonight."

"Bye!" He tried to sound normal again. "Wait, did she just say, she *should* be back?" What was that supposed to mean? He tossed the magazine, some home decorating thing, across the room.

Okay, get a grip. You told her to date other guys. Yeah, you big dope. Why the hell did you go and do that? He got up and ran to snoop out the window. When he saw the ape holding her hand, it took everything he had not to go out there and act like some crazy, jealous man. He could see it in his mind. Punching the guy in the nose and then running like hell. Shawna would be furious and he knew that wouldn't get him many dates. Hell, that wouldn't get him any dates.

Soon as they pulled out of the driveway, he flopped on the couch. Shit, he was falling for her and needed to move the hell out. He couldn't do this.

It took a couple of seconds to calm himself down. He got the newspaper and started calling apartments. What he should do is find another place and do it now. Maybe he could move out this weekend. That was only two days away and that would be great.

What he needed was to go get laid. That would get his mind off her.

He picked up the phone and dialed Nanette.

"Hello?" she answered in her friendly tone.

"Hi, this is Frankie. How have you been?"

"Not good, I need my Frankie fix," she whined.

"What are you doing right now?"

"Waiting for you. My door is open."

"I'll be right there."

Yes, he was going to have some fun tonight. He wished he really felt more excited about it. That would happen though. Whenever he got to her apartment, she always had something fun waiting for him. That girl was a sexy thing and very adventurous. Just what the doctor ordered.

He'd write a note to Shawna so she'd know he wasn't coming back tonight.

* * * *

Shawna had tried her best to enjoy her evening out with Howard and if she was being honest, she'd have to say, he was a sweet guy. They had gone to the Desert River Café, but her heart wasn't in it. She wanted to get home and see Frankie. The evening went by in a blur and Shawna was glad it was over.

Howard pulled up in the driveway. "I'll walk you to the door. It looks dark."

Where was Frankie's car? She glanced around. It wasn't there.

Howard got out of the car and opened her door. "You should leave an outside light on," he said as she stepped out.

She nodded. "I know."

They arrived up to the door and he kissed her cheek. "I hope to do this again sometime, Shawna." He stared at her. "But I have a feeling your mind was somewhere else or with someone else."

"Well, it was a lovely evening," she lied.

"Don't lead me to believe we have a chance, if it's not the case. I can handle it and I understand. I think you're hung up on Frankie and I would venture to guess, he's got it bad for you too," he paused. "He was steaming because I was taking you out."

"You're right about me being crazy for him. But I'm not so sure he has those kind of feelings for me." She felt her heart sink.

"Believe me," Howard touched her arm, "Frankie is head over the moon for you."

Shawna stood on her toes and kissed his cheek. "Thank you, Howard."

He nodded and left. She opened the door and walked into a dark quiet house. Frankie was not there. She looked at her clock on the wall. It was past ten. Maybe he went out to eat.

She walked into the kitchen and saw a note.

Shawna, won't be back tonight. Hope you had a great time. Later, Frankie.

Tears built in her eyes. Maybe he didn't like her as much as she thought. He wasn't coming home, which meant only one thing, she needed her sister-in-law.

* * * *

Beth Ann was asleep in Kaylob's arms when barking woke her up. She whispered, "Sleep honey, you have to get up early. I'll take her out."

"Okay, thank you baby," he mumbled. Clearly tired after a day of making love and worrying about the outcome of that letter. Kaylob had been through so much. Finding out he'd been lied to almost all his life and now this. Holy smokes, when would he get a break? They both deserved some peace from the stress. The reality was, she was still having nightmares about Peter at least once a week. Maybe she needed to go back to therapy soon. Sometimes she felt like a monster for killing him and worried daily about little Cathy.

Once inside the mud room, Beth Ann saw Goldic by thc door. "You need to go out, girl." She turned on the back light and opened the door.

She saw Shawna walking slowly down the path towards the second house. "Shawna?" she called out.

"I'm sorry I woke you." Shawna turned around and started to cry.

Beth Ann let Goldie out and hurried down the sidewalk. "What's the matter? Did your date go bad?"

"No, well, yes, but only because I didn't want to be out with Howard. I wanted Frankie. I got home to an empty house and a note that said he wouldn't be back tonight."

"I'm sorry, honey," Beth Ann wrapped her arms around Shawna.

"Why don't you stay with us tonight and we can stay up and have some tea and talk. You don't work tomorrow, right?"

Shawna nodded.

"Come on, let's go inside." Beth Ann called Goldie and watched as she ran up the steps and got into her bed. Before she left the room, she kissed her head and covered her with the baby blanket. "Good night, girl."

Beth Ann stayed up with Shawna until she fell asleep on the couch. It was just before two in the morning. She didn't want to wake her so she covered her and dimmed the lights. Poor Shawna, maybe falling in love with Frankie wasn't such a good idea. Her and Kaylob were sure he was falling in love. Well, they must have been wrong. Or had they? He was pretty damn stubborn.

She had a good mind to go tell him a thing or two. How dare he leave her a note saying he was going to be out all night. Nothing like making it obvious that he was with another woman. Of course, Shawna did go out with Howard, so he didn't really do anything wrong. Maybe he thought they needed privacy. Oh well, she'd have a long talk with him anyway.

She quietly climbed back into bed and Kaylob's arms went around her, pulling her closer. There was no doubt in her mind just how blessed she was. Kaylob was the best husband in the whole world.

Thank you God, she said wordlessly.

* * * *

Frankie sat at the bar drinking another beer. He was pathetic and needed to get his ass home in bed. It was after two and they had already said last call, but at least he had the rest of the week off. It was fine with him not to start work yet. He needed a small vacation. Everyone had said, *Frankie, take a few months off after you get out of school, have some fun.* That's what he should have done.

The bartender was a nice lady, not bad to look at either. Tall, tan with jet black hair. But shit, that didn't do him any good. He hadn't even showed up at Nanette's. At least he'd called her and said he had something come up. Right, what came up?

He wasn't even sure what was wrong with him. Ever since he'd met

Shawna, his life had been spinning out of control.

The lady behind the bar smiled. "Sorry, handsome, we are going to have to ask you to leave. Closing time." She wiped the counters and started cleaning glasses.

Frankie stood and dropped a twenty-dollar bill on the counter. "Can I use the phone to call a taxi? I've had too many beers to drive. I'll be back tomorrow to get my car."

"Taxi is already here. I had a feeling you'd need one," she said.

"Thanks, beautiful." He winked, took one last drink and headed outside.

The taxi was there waiting so he waved and the guy pulled up.

"Come on in. Where are you heading?" the short, dark haired, man asked.

Frankie gave him the address.

It was a long silent drive and when they arrived, he got out on the street. He didn't want the crunching of the car pulling up in the driveway to wake Shawna.

He walked up to the house and put his key in the door. Once he entered, he went directly into the kitchen. Shawna had tea every night and he wanted to see if she found his note. The evidence was clear, she wasn't home. The note was still there and no tea was made.

It might have been late when she came in and maybe she went straight to bed. He bet that's what happened.

He tiptoed down the hall and saw her bedroom door was open and her bed untouched. She hadn't come home? A sharp pain stabbed him right through the heart. That could only mean one thing; she must like Howard a lot.

A half hour later, after sitting on her bed, he knew he needed to get some sleep. His heart was torn up, his stomach raw, but he had nobody to blame but himself. Shawna had moved on. Hell, he hadn't even bought her flowers. All he'd done is make her coffee and fix her sandwiches. Sure, he'd taken her out to dinner twice, once Chinese and the other Mexican food. They'd had fun and laughed and played in a nearby park later. He'd pushed her on a swing and they had acted like two kids. Afterwards, they had built castles in the sandbox.

Every day they had grown closer and enjoyed being together. This had gone on for two weeks and something had happened during that time. Something he'd never experienced with any woman.

His throat clogged with pent-up emotions. Maybe he was just emotional over everything. His home had burned down to nothing and Shawna had been there for him. He'd never felt so pampered and cared for. The facts smacked him, he had grown dependent on her smiles and those sweet kisses. If he got quiet, she'd find a way to make him smile and it always worked.

Maybe he could make her change her mind about Howard.

After all, she had told Frankie she liked him a lot and belonged in his arms. Last night they had made out in the pool and she had taken his hand and placed it on her breast. It was over her wet bathing suit, but still, it had been sweet. When her nipples got hard, so did he, and she knew it.

The way she looked up into his eyes had done him in. When he pulled her closer she knew just how badly he wanted her. She had surprised him and pressed her body against his and touched him in a way that almost made him fall apart.

What he had with Shawna though, wasn't based on sex. Sure, he wanted her, but he loved being with her. Just holding her hand and strolling under the stars. Those moments, over the last two weeks, had made him feel more alive than ever before.

Admit it, Frankie. You're in love with her. He had no choice but to stop trying to lie to himself. He knew the truth and now it was more than likely too late. She was going to end up with some gorilla who brought her flowers.

He climbed into bed and closed his eyes, his head felt like it was going to explode. The room started spinning before he passed out.

* * * *

Beth Ann awoke and heard Shawna talking. From the sounds of it, she was speaking to Goldie. There were little barks and Shawna was giggling.

Kaylob had left for work at O dark thirty and she wasn't sure of the time. He had kissed her and called her sexy mama. That much she remembered.

Beth Ann slipped on her robe and shuffled down the hallway. She followed the sounds that were coming from the family room.

"Good morning." Beth Ann greeted them with a smile.

Shawna glanced up and Beth Ann gasped at the circles under Shawna's red-rimmed eyes. "Oh my gosh." She moved over next to her and lifted her chin. "Shawna, you cried all night, didn't you?"

She nodded. "I'm sorry. Every time I woke up, I thought about Frankie with another woman and I fell apart. I've never hurt like this before."

Beth Ann was sad and angry all at once. "Did you see if his car is back?"

"I've looked every hour, since four this morning. He never came home."

Beth Ann placed her arm around Shawna. "I'm so sorry you've been hurt. I have a good mind to go kick his ass."

"No, he was more than honest with me. I was the one that kept thinking I could change his mind. It's my fault."

Beth Ann shrugged. "He could have waited until he moved out to start his playboy lifestyle."

Goldie barked and headed towards the back door. "I need to let her out to go pee."

Shawna nodded. "Kaylob took her out this morning, but I pretended to be asleep. I didn't want him to see my eyes."

Beth Ann stroked her arm then headed to the mudroom to let Goldie out. She stepped outside, and the little girl took off running towards the back fence. She was after something.

As she glanced out at the scenery, she noticed the blue sky had puffy white clouds hovering above the mountains. It appeared like an oil painting.

"Hurry girl," Beth Ann said.

There was a movement in one of the lawn chairs and she started to yell, but saw it was Frankie.

"Hey Beth Ann, letting the dog do her business?"

"Frankie, where's your car?" She looked around.

"I went to a bar last night not far from here and tied one on. I had to get a taxi. I was going to ask you or Kaylob to give me a ride. I would've asked Shawna, but she stayed out all night." He appeared torn up.

"She did huh? With her date?" She gave him an amused look.

He nodded and swallowed. "Yeah, with Mr. Gorilla man. He brought her flowers."

"Well, I guess she took your advice and started seeing other people."

"I guess so." He looked down and Beth Ann could see he was in pain. "I'm such an idiot."

Chapter Ten

"Yes, you are. Don't go anywhere. Can you watch Goldie for a second? I need you to see something."

"Sure." he said, looking confused.

Beth Ann ran in the house. "Shawna," she called quietly.

"Yes? Are you okay?" Shawna asked.

"I'm fine. Come here and look at something."

Shawna followed her into the mud room. "Look out the window. But don't pull back the curtain all the way."

"What?" She slightly pulled it to the side and saw him. "Frankie, but when?"

Beth Ann turned her around. "He took a taxi home because he was so drunk. He was just trying to drink away his pain. He thinks you've been gone all night. He's torn up, Shawna."

"Oh God," she went to the door. "I have to go to him."

"Go." Beth Ann swallowed, feeling sentimental.

"I love you, Beth Ann." Shawna hugged her. "You're the best friend and greatest sister I could have ever dreamed of." Her voice broke.

"Get out there," Beth Ann ordered.

* * * *

Shawna stepped out the back door and moved down the steps.

"I don't think Goldie wants to come inside. She's enjoying the sunshine," Frankie said, turning around as he spoke.

His eyes opened wide and his mouth fell open. "Shawna. When did you get home?"

She put her finger to her chin. "Let's see, around ten last night. I stayed with Beth Ann and Kaylob. You said you weren't coming home all night."

He moved closer. "Shawna, did something happen? Jesus, your eyes are all red. Did that Gorilla hurt you?" He scowled.

"Nobody hurt me," she said softly. "I thought you were with a woman last night. I guess I got upset."

He stepped even closer. "I only wanted to be with you and there was no woman."

"You weren't with anyone?"

"No, I wanted to be with you," he said. "Shawna, I love you. I want to spend my life with you. Please don't date anyone else."

"Frankie, I love you too." She threw her arms around him. "I've loved you since the first time I saw your picture."

"I wasn't sure what happened when we met, just that you knocked me off my feet," Frankie said. "Shawna, this is really fast, but I know I've found the right girl." He got down on one knee. "I also know that this isn't romantic." He sighed. "I'll do it again and buy you a ring. But I want to ask you something."

"Frankie," she said, tears running down her cheeks.

"Will you be my wife and let me love you forever?"

"Are you sure I'm who you want, Frankie? I only want to be married once in my life."

"I'm more than sure." He swallowed hard with tears in his eyes.

"I will marry you and be your wife forever and I don't care how fast we fell in love." She threw her arms around his neck and shed more tears, but this time it was from joy.

Just that minute, the back door opened and Beth Ann stepped out onto the porch. She was sniffing too. "Oh my gosh. That was so sweet. Yes, I was listening."

Beth Ann ran down the stairs and hugged them both. "I'm so happy for you guys. I don't even know what to say."

Frankie laughed as he wrapped his arms around Shawna. "Say that you'll convince Kaylob that this is a good thing."

Beth Ann's lip trembled. "I will. He will be happy. We already suspected you guys were in love. We were waiting for you to figure it out. And well, Kaylob made me stay out of it. Now, go be together and savor this time. Come on Goldie, let's eat."

Shawna laughed when she saw how fast Goldie took off up the

stairs. She had learned what eat means, there was no doubt about that.

She took Frankie's hand. "Let's go home." And it was home.

* * * *

They entered the house, tumbled on the couch into each other's arms. Frankie felt happier than he'd ever been in his life, knowing Shawna was going to be his wife. She was his girl and he was never going to let her go.

"Shawna, I'm so sorry I didn't tell you sooner, but honestly, I wouldn't face up to it, and last night seeing you with Howard, I knew."

"It's okay. I should have never gone on that date." She kissed him.

"Did he touch you?"

"If you count holding my hand and kissing my cheek good night. He also told me that you were head over the moon for me." She met his gaze.

"That makes me very happy. I love you and never want to share you again."

"You won't, because very soon I'll be your wife."

"Yes," he said and nodded. "So you want a big fancy wedding or a simple one?"

Shawna stared into his eyes. "How do you feel about that and what kind do you want?"

"I'm okay with whatever you want." He kissed her neck. "I just hope it doesn't take too long," he growled.

"Frankie, I have a confession."

"What?" His stomach flipped.

"I don't want a big wedding, I'd rather go to the justice of the peace and skip all that."

"Shawna, all girls want to have a big wedding." He pulled back, studying her face.

"No, I really don't. I don't need all that. All my life was fancy balls, sweet sixteen. I hated it. I don't want to dress up in a fancy dress and have that stuff." She scrunched her nose. "I'll do it for you." She leaned on his shoulder. "But only for you."

"Ah sweetie, I don't care about all that either. I never have."

"Really?" She smiled big. "You don't care about it either?"

141

He shook his head. "When can we get married?" he asked, shocking himself at the fact that he didn't want any delays.

"I'm ready when you are. We could do it now," she said and stared into his eyes. "Who should we tell?"

"Just Kaylob and Beth Ann. Carol will kill me, but maybe we could have a reception afterwards," Frankie suggested.

Shawna's voice went up. "That's a great idea. I was ready yesterday."

Frankie explained in detail what they had to do. "We have to go to the County Clerk's office and get a marriage license. Bring valid ID, usually two forms and we can get married by a judge, county clerk, priest, minister or rabbi of any religious denomination."

"How do you know all this?" Shawna questioned. "Did you almost get married before?"

"Hell no. I've never even gone steady." He laughed. "Sweetie, your future husband is an attorney." He kissed her again. She was cute, no doubt about that.

"Oh, of course." She giggled.

After spending hours making plans, Frankie knew they had to tell Kaylob and Beth Ann. All he could do is hope that Kaylob didn't knock his block off. He was marrying his little sister, after all.

"We need to go down to the mall before we do anything."

"Why?" Shawna asked.

"Because I'm buying our wedding rings and your engagement ring."

"Frankie, we're only going to be engaged for barely twenty-four hours. How about just the wedding rings."

"No can do. You are going to get an engagement ring. It will match the wedding rings. I can skip the wedding, but not this."

"Alright, my wonderful, fiancé. I would love that."

"Shawna Cynthia Rafferty, I'm crazy in love with you." He pulled her on his lap.

"Frankie Dean Russo, I'm insanely in love with you." She turned around and straddled him. "And I can't wait for the wedding night." She wiggled on his lap, moving her hips.

"Jesus, Shawna." Frankie grunted and adjusted her. "Are you trying to kill me before our wedding?"

"No, I'm just showing you how well we're going to move together."

"Oh, yeah." He picked her up, laid her on the couch and moved between her legs. He showed her just how wonderful their movements would be. "I have no doubt that we are going to be hot together."

"Oh Frankie," she sighed, kissing him deeply.

One thing Frankie knew for sure was not one part of him was afraid of marrying Shawna; he was over the moon in love with her.

For a long while they teased and kissed and his little cutie was moaning his name. Not only was he looking forward to making love with his wife, but he was looking forward to making a life with her and having babies.

"Oh shit." Did she want kids he wondered?

"What?" Shawna said breathlessly.

"Do you want children someday?"

"Yes, of course. I want babies. Your babies."

He moved against her again, watching her eyes tear up. "Am I hurting you?"

"No Frankie, I just feel like breaking my own rule. I want to feel you inside of me."

"We better stop before I help you break that rule." He sighed and crawled off her. "I think we've tortured each other enough for one day. Let's get to the mall." He reached out and took her hand.

After they got dressed and cleaned up, they left. Tomorrow they would be getting married and that was going to make him a very happy man.

* * * *

Beth Ann paced around the house. She was happy about Frankie and Shawna and noticed they had left together a few hours ago. The thing that had her on edge was that note from Dusty. If Kaylob ended up being the dad, that would change their life in a big way, they'd have a teenage son. This afternoon he was going to stop and do what he needed to do for that paternity test. He had also mentioned taking a trip to see Dusty. She was living in Arizona and he wanted Beth Ann to go with him. That would be odd, but the woman was dying and she wanted to be supportive, not only to Kaylob, but a woman who was leaving her son behind.

As Beth Ann dusted in the family room and did light chores, Goldie was playing with her goose. They had bought her a lot of other toys, but that was her favorite and she carried it into every room she was in.

"Beth Ann, I'm home."

"I'm in the family room," she called out.

The minute he walked in, her heart skipped a beat. How could a man be so sexy and beautiful? Kaylob was getting more handsome as he aged. At twenty-seven, he was hot. She moved towards him and watched his lips curve up in a mischievous smile. It's like he could read her mind.

"I'm glad you're home." She stood on her toes and kissed him.

He looked around. "Are we alone?"

She nodded. "Yes. How did it go?"

"They took my blood. We should know in a couple of weeks. It's a lot to deal with. I still am dealing with my own stuff of being lied to about my parents. Now I might have a child who hasn't been told that I may or may not be his dad." He studied Beth Ann.

"Honey, no matter what, we'll go through this together. We are a strong team."

"You're right. Now, about us being alone…" He swooped her up in his arms. "I need you."

"Kaylob," she said, laughing, "You had me yesterday, over and over again."

"We have to make up for two weeks." He looked down at Goldie and sat Beth Ann down. "Oh, we have a child now, I keep forgetting." He nodded at Goldie, she hadn't even looked up from chewing her toy.

Beth Ann gave him her best sultry look. "I could give her a bone again." She touched his chest.

"Grrr. You have such nice fingers." He raised them to his lips and kissed them.

Just about that time they heard a knock. "Well, so much for my afternoon delight." He frowned.

Beth Ann followed him into the formal living room and watched as he opened the door. It was Shawna and Frankie. Beth Ann noticed the sparkle in Shawna's eyes and Frankie was happier than she'd ever seen him.

"Come in." Kaylob said, trying to smile.

Shawna looked uncertainly at Kaylob. "Are we interrupting something?"

"No," he said. "I was trying to take advantage of my wife, but I can do that later."

"Kaylob!" Beth Ann tried not to laugh.

Shawna and Frankie walked in holding hands.

"Come on into the family room. Goldie is having goose," Beth Ann said.

Once they entered the room, everyone took a seat. Beth Ann was sure that Frankie and Shawna were there to tell Kaylob they were engaged. She couldn't wait to help with the wedding. Shawna would look so beautiful in her wedding gown; she'd look like a princess.

Frankie cleared his throat. "Kaylob, Beth Ann, Shawna and I are engaged and ... As Beth Ann knows, she saw me propose."

Shawna held out her ring. "Isn't it beautiful?"

"Yes," Beth Ann crossed the room to get a better look. "Oh, Frankie, this is gorgeous." It was a lovely solitaire diamond ring. It was gold and platinum, very delicate and perfect for her hand.

Shawna and Beth Ann hugged. "I'm so happy for you guys." Beth Ann turned and glanced over at her husband, whose mouth was literally hanging open.

"Kaylob, aren't we happy for them?" She gave him a stern look.

He nodded. "Yes, very," he said, then stood, giving them both a big hug. "I guess in truth, I'm a little shocked."

Frankie laughed. "Who knew I'd find my true love in the way of your sister."

"So when do we start planning the wedding?" Beth Ann interrupted with excitement.

Frankie and Shawna both sat back down. "Should I tell them?" Frankie asked Shawna.

"No, let me. This was my decision." She glanced between Kaylob and Beth Ann.

"I don't want a big fancy wedding, and neither does Frankie." She reached for Frankie's hand. "I would have done it for him, but I hate all that fancy stuff."

"That's okay," Beth Ann said. "We can make it simple. Maybe use our back yard or that little church down the street."

Shawna shook her head. "No. We are getting married tomorrow and we are doing it downtown, simple and fast."

Kaylob spoke up as he and Beth Ann sat back down. "This whole thing is pretty fast and the wedding's tomorrow? That's really sudden." He frowned. "What's the rush?" He stared at his sister's stomach, then over to Frankie.

"Kaylob, I'm still a virgin." She blushed. "However, we want to get married now. A nice small wedding, and we would like to have the reception at the restaurant. We were also hoping that Beth Ann would sing with the band."

Beth Ann couldn't believe they didn't want a big wedding, but it was their choice. "I'd love to sing." She glanced over at Kaylob.

"Why the rush?" Kaylob asked again and looked between Frankie and Shawna. "Aren't you two jumping into this? You've only been dating for a few weeks."

Frankie shook his head. "No, I've played around with enough women to know that Shawna is my one and only, from this point forward. I love her, Kaylob."

Shawna nodded. "I knew the minute I saw his picture." She smiled at Beth Ann.

"True story," Beth Ann said. "I was there and showed her the wedding album."

"I don't know." Kaylob shook his head. "I think you two should wait. Give it some thought and in a few months if you want to still get married, do it then."

Shawna stood and moved closer to him. "There is nothing to wait for. Please be happy for us. We love each other deeply." She stared down at him.

"I'm trying," Kaylob said. "But it feels way too fast."

Beth Ann frowned. "Try harder. Remember Gram and Nicky and remember how Cole made you wait. Gram and Nicky were kept apart by family members and missed all those years. Aren't you the one that told Patterson when you meet the right person, there's no need to look around anymore?" Beth Ann met his gaze dead on, then watched Frankie stand by Shawna.

After a few minutes of uncomfortable silence, Kaylob cleared his throat. "You're right. I'm being ridiculous. I know all too well how it feels to be told to wait for a commitment with someone you love. We will support your decision." He stood and hugged them both again. "Congratulations."

Beth Ann could tell he meant it and wondered what he was talking about when he said he knew how hard it was to wait for a commitment. All Cole had ever told him was he had to wait to make love, or at least that's what she thought. She'd make a mental note to ask him later.

Shawna's lip trembled, clearly overcome with emotion. "I'll tell mom and grandma after we are married. I hope they can come out for the reception. They have their passports, so it shouldn't be an issue. We were just in New York a few months back."

Kaylob nodded. "How soon after the wedding do you want the reception?"

Frankie sat back down. "How about Saturday? Is that enough time?"

"Sure," Kaylob said. "We'll make it work."

Shawna grinned at Kaylob and Beth Ann. "So, will you come tomorrow and stand up for us?"

They both agreed and were happy to do that.

"So Frankie, guess I should take you to a strip club and suffer sitting through it for your bachelor party."

Beth Ann knew Kaylob was kidding. He was far too young to want to die.

Shawna glared at Kaylob. "The only bachelor party he's having is with me. He's had plenty of those since he was fourteen."

Frankie and Kaylob both laughed and the subject was not brought up again.

The day was lovely. Kaylob whipped up dinner early and made his chicken Marsala and twice-baked potatoes with baby carrots. They all had wine except for Beth Ann; there was some new information coming to light about babies and alcohol. She didn't want to chance it.

After dinner, Kaylob brought out a wonderful chocolate cake he had baked at the restaurant. He'd followed a new recipe from some famous guy in Chicago. Beth Ann made the coffee while they talked about the next day.

Once the table was cleared, they poured coffee and each took a good-sized piece of cake. Beth Ann took the first bite. "Holy sugar rush, this is so good. I had this in Chicago. Yum. I never thought I'd taste it again."

Everyone took a bite and made groaning noises. Kaylob tilted his head and studied Beth Ann. "What restaurant were you at?"

Beth Ann couldn't remember the name. "It was some fancy place." She glanced down. "Shit, that was the first time I met Peter." All of a sudden the cake didn't seem so exciting. She once again saw the knife sticking out of his neck. Guilt slammed into her and Cathy popped into her mind.

They all looked at her and nobody said a word. Why did she still feel guilty? Peter was a total monster who just happened to have the sweetest little girl Beth Ann had ever worked with.

"Well, that's the past," she finally said and knew she needed to change her thoughts.

She didn't want to damper the special night and took another big bite. There was no way Peter's memory would take away the delicious taste of what her husband had created. "Yum," she said again. "Honey, you did great. I think this is better than anything I've ever tasted."

"That was on your date with Blake, right?" He arched a brow.

"Yes," she said, but left out the part about him feeding it to her.

"So did he have a piece too?" Kaylob asked.

She watched Frankie lay down his fork and Shawna was taking a sip of wine.

"Frankie, you're not going to finish that? I would eat it, but I'm already so full. I better go take Goldie out because she's hasn't been out for a while. Kaylob, did I tell you that she knows what eat, means? When I say it, she takes off and waits by her dish." She laughed, trying to change the subject.

Shawna spoke up. "True story. I saw it."

"The other day when I asked her if she wanted to go for a walk she went and grabbed her leash." Beth Ann noticed that both Frankie and Kaylob looked at each other and were trying to stop from laughing.

"What?" Beth Ann demanded. "Is so funny?"

Both busted up and couldn't seem to stop.

Finally, Frankie caught his breath while she and Shawna watched the hyenas.

"I'd heard about you doing this from your husband, but I'd never seen it before." Frankie's face was red from laughter. "You're right, Kaylob, she does ramble and she is cute about it."

"Ramble." She glanced at her husband, who was holding his napkin to his mouth. Obviously trying not to crack up again.

Shawna smiled, reached over and took her hand. "I thought what you were saying was just fine." She frowned at the guys.

"Thank you. So you want to go shopping? It's still early." Beth Ann asked, ignoring the two goofballs.

"Yes and by the way, can I spend the night with you?"

"What?" Frankie stopped laughing and his face dropped. "Why?"

"Because," Shawna smiled, "I may not want a big wedding, but I don't want you to see me in my wedding dress and for other reasons, like what almost happened today."

"Okay, too much information." Kaylob stood. "Come on, Frankie, let's go find something to watch on TV and have a little man to man chat." He at least had a smile on his face when he said it.

"Well, Shawna, let's go find your wedding dress and get away from these laughing hyenas." Beth Ann stood and stuck her nose in the air.

* * * *

The next morning Shawna woke up and almost forgot where she was. It took a minute for her to remember she was in Kaylob and Beth Ann's spare room, but she could hear noises coming from the kitchen where someone was banging pots and pans.

Today was her wedding day and she had found the perfect dress. She and Beth Ann had spent the entire evening shopping and had located it in an old vintage boutique on the east side of town. Thankfully, they had stayed open to let her look around. The dress was a beautiful ivory color, that was all lace and true vintage in a 1930s style. She loved its classic silhouette with its full circle skirt and short sleeves. The main material was tulle, with an elegant lace neckline and a few lace appliques on the skirt. The best part was she could wear it for more than just a wedding dress. It was classy, yet simple. The surprise was it was a size six and fit her perfectly.

She glanced around. She should eat breakfast, then afterwards, Beth Ann was going to do her hair and makeup. There was a big part of her that wanted to call her mom and Grandma, but they would try to talk her into a big wedding, and she just didn't want all that. All she wanted was to be married to her very sexy, hot-blooded fiancé. The man she wanted to spend her life with.

She threw the covers back, stood and twirled around the room, just like she had when she was little. Today her dream was coming true. It had always been to fall in love with the perfect guy and she had, and he loved her right back. That would make this day the best day of her life.

There was a knock on the door. "Come in."

Beth Ann peeked in. Her hair was piled on top of her head in a ponytail looking like Pebbles from the Flintstones. She was so adorable.

"Hey, Miss Bride-to-Be. Are you ready to eat breakfast? Kaylob's making pancakes, eggs, and some wonderful fresh fruit. I did the coffee." She smiled grandly.

"I am. Can you believe it? I am marrying Frankie today." Shawna grabbed Beth Ann's hand and they spun around like two little girls.

"I'm so excited for you." Beth Ann stopped spinning. "Think about how wonderful it is that you are marrying our best friend. We are going to live right here, side by side."

"It's a dream I didn't even know I had, until now," Shawna said and her heart overflowed with love.

They ran out to the kitchen laughing and carrying on while Kaylob cooked. Every now and again he laughed with them. It was a happy morning. Even Goldie was excited. Shawna didn't know why, but maybe animals could feel the energy.

* * * *

Beth Ann couldn't believe how fast the morning zipped by. She was in high spirits about the day, and the only thing that made her feel a little off was that letter. They hadn't told Frankie and Shawna because this was their happy time.

They would tell everyone later, or maybe they'd wait until they got the results in two weeks. That was when their lives could change.

Beth Ann slipped on her new chiffon pink dress. It was romantic and feminine. She loved the way it had the v-cut down the back and was so light. The skirt of the dress flowed out enough that her belly bump didn't show.

"Wow, you're a knock out, baby." Kaylob walked over and kissed her neck. "That back is a little revealing." His brows scrunched together.

"It only shows off my back. I thought you would love it." She pouted.

"I do, I do. You look amazing. It's fine." He smiled and pulled her into his arms.

"Thank you, honey. It covers my bump."

"Oh Beth Ann, I love that bump. It makes me proud, and it's sexy as hell," he growled. "By the way, have you noticed your breasts?" He cupped them. "Wow!"

"No, but I guess you have."

"You bet your sweet bottom I have. They have doubled in size."

"Well, I guess what I heard was right." She frowned.

"What's that?" he asked.

"That you're a big boob guy." She pulled his hands away.

"Beth Ann, stop that. I only love one set of boobs, and that's yours."

She was being silly, but she couldn't help it. What would happen when they went back to normal. Would he like them as much?

"Beth Ann." He moved up and pulled her back in his arms. "You are the most perfect and beautiful woman in the world. I love everything about you. Even when you act sixteen again."

She looked up at him and grinned. "I guess I'm being silly."

"You guess." He leaned down and kissed her deeply. "Want me to show you how much you turn me on?"

"No, silly. We have to get going. We have a wedding to attend."

"Beth Ann." He looked troubled.

"Yes."

"How would you feel if the boy is mine and we take him in? Are you sure you'll be able to handle it?"

"Of course. He's a part of you so I'd love him." She meant it, but in her heart she prayed he wasn't Kaylob's.

The minute Beth Ann stepped out into the living room, she placed her hand across her mouth, then said, "Oh my gosh, Shawna, you are radiant and glowing."

Shawna smiled as she searched Kaylob's face.

"Honey," he said as he walked towards her. "You are beautiful." They embraced in a gentle hug.

Shawna swallowed hard. "You're built so much like our dad. It makes me feel as though he's here with us." She chewed her bottom lip. "I miss him so much."

Kaylob looked far away for a moment, then he brightened, but Beth Ann recognized it was forced. "I wish he was here for you. But since he's not, I'll step in." He moved backwards and held her hand. "Frankie is going to fall to his knees when he sees you."

They got everything together and Kaylob said, "Frankie and I will meet you guys there. Don't come outside until we're gone." He gave them both a kiss goodbye and left.

Beth Ann pointed towards Goldie. "I'm leaving her doggie door open. The fence is completely secure so she'll be okay," she said to Shawna as she walked in and put down some dry food. "There you go, girl." She pulled the cover off the door and Goldie jumped up, wagged her tail and ran into the yard.

"Well, that answered that. She knows how to use it." Beth Ann laughed.

Shawna was pacing. "Beth Ann, what if Frankie changes his mind?"

"What? Change his mind? He better not. We'd kill him." Beth Ann meant it.

"Maybe I twisted his arm? I should have let him make love to me." She flopped down on the kitchen chair.

"Come on, silly. Frankie isn't marrying you for sex." Beth Ann laughed.

"How do you know?"

"Well, because he never had any issues getting dates or sex. He started fooling around when he was young. I never had any clue he had gone all the way, but I knew he was fooling around." She paused. "Shawna," Beth Ann said as she pulled her up. "He's never asked anyone to marry him. I know he's deeply in love with you. I can see it in

April's Secret Storm

his eyes."

"You're right, I'm just being nervous."

Beth Ann nodded. "Yes, you are. We've been best friends since grammar school. I've never seen him like this. Remember, I told you that he said, *someday when he turned thirty something, he wanted to find love like me and Kaylob, and he wouldn't settle for anything less.* It just came a little earlier." Beth Ann touched her heart. "He's been waiting for you all his life."

"Let's get to my wedding," Shawna said just above a whisper.

Once they arrived at the City Hall, downtown, they found the right area and walked through a set of double doors. The place was nice. There was an archway with beautiful flowers, which must have been set up for weddings. Beth Ann had not expected it to be so pretty with the wood paneling that went part way up the wall. That was a special touch.

Shawna waved around. "This is so sweet, Beth Ann. I love it." She stood staring around the room.

The only thing missing was Kaylob and Frankie. Where the heck were they?

Finally, a white haired man walked in, dressed in a dark robe with a white cloth around his shoulders. He walked up and smiled towards Shawna. "Are you the bride?"

"Yes," she nodded.

"I will be performing your wedding. My name is Judge Bernard Williams. It's nice to meet you. "They shook hands.

A few seconds later Frankie and Kaylob came running in carrying a bunch of flowers. They both looked so handsome, Kaylob in his dark blue suit with a light blue tie, and Frankie in a dark pinstripe suit with a vest underneath. She hadn't seen Frankie in a suit very often, but she could see Shawna's approving gaze. He was handsome, there was no doubt about that.

The flowers they were putting around were a beautiful, ivory color with pale blues and some red. Those guys had to be the most wonderful men in the world. Beth Ann smiled at Kaylob and he gave her a dazzling grin and winked.

* * * *

Once Frankie stood in the spot up by the judge, he felt his heart explode when he saw his soon-to-be wife. She was the most stunning woman he'd ever seen. Her soft smile, put a spell on him and drew him in. He was a taken man and he knew he was going to love every minute of it. He looked at her incredible ivory dress, so perfect in every way. Her hair hung down in golden curls, her eyes sparkled like diamonds, which left him with unshed tears.

Kaylob and Frankie had set up all the flowers and a lady came in and turned on the music. They dimmed the lights and lit some candles. The setting was simple and beautiful.

Frankie took a deep breath when Kaylob held out his elbow and Shawna wove her arm through his. They slowly strolled towards him, as though they had rehearsed the entire thing.

It took everything he had not to sink to the ground. How in the world did he get so lucky? This incredible beauty had fallen in love with him and agreed to be his wife. There would never be a day that he wasn't grateful.

Beth Ann stood up front looking gorgeous, as usual. He was one ecstatic man to have his two best friends there to stand up for them. Maybe he should slap himself in the face to see if he was dreaming. Imagine, the first girl he'd ever fallen in love with was the girl he would spend the rest of his life with.

The events had come so fast his head was spinning. As he stood gazing into Shawna's eyes, he was so hypnotized that he hadn't heard what the judge had said. He needed to pull his mind back to the man's words.

"Do you, Frankie Dean Russo, take this woman, Shawna Cynthia Rafferty, to be your lawful wedded wife. To love, honor, and cherish her, through sickness and in health, through times of happiness and travail, until death do you part?

"Yes, I do." Frankie felt the air stick in his throat and had to cough to get it out.

"Place this ring upon her finger and repeat after me."

"With this ring, I thee wed, and forever pledge my devotion," Frankie repeated the vows, then the gentleman turned to Shawna.

"Do you, Shawna Cynthia Rafferty, take this man, Frankie Dean

Russo, to be your lawful wedded husband. To love, honor and cherish him through sickness and in health, through times of happiness and travail, until death do you part?

"Yes," she nodded, with tears in her eyes.

"Place this ring upon his finger and repeat after me."

"With this ring, I thee wed, and forever pledge my devotion," Shawna repeated.

"You came to me as two single people and you will now leave as a married couple, united to each other by the binding contract you have just entered. Your cares, your worries, your pleasures and your joys, you must share with each other. The best of good fortune to both of you and may God bless your lives."

He nodded and said the final words.

"I now pronounce you, husband and wife. Mr. Russo, you may kiss your bride."

And so he did. He wrapped his arms around his wife and kissed her deeply. On that day, Thursday, July 31, 1975, Frankie Dean Russo and Shawna Cynthia Russo became husband and wife.

* * * *

Beth Ann and Kaylob acted overjoyed as the rounds of hugs began. Beth Ann must have taken at least sixty pictures and kept saying over and over, "this was such a romantic wedding."

Shawna smiled and pulled Frankie close. "Let's go home. As much as I love you in that suit, I want to get you out of it." He had to gather his bearings because those words rocked his soul.

"Oh no, we are not going home tonight and we won't be home for a full week. We *will* go to the reception on Saturday, that's a given. But this is our honeymoon, and there are construction workers all over the place. I want you alone." Frankie arched a brow.

"Oh, you're right." Shawna agreed. "We would have no privacy."

Frankie took her hand and looked into her eyes. "I rented the honeymoon suite across the street from the best restaurant in Riverside. You know, the one your brother owns." He grinned. "For two nights we have a honeymoon suite, then for five nights we have another one, in Palm Springs. Paid for by Kaylob and Beth Ann. Our wedding gift." He turned and smiled at them. "Thank you both so much."

"Thank you for the lovely gift." Shawna went over and hugged them. "I hadn't even thought about the construction workers."

"No worries about them," Kaylob said. "We will make sure they keep on task. If we have any questions that we don't know or understand, we can call you."

Shawna turned to Frankie. "We have to go home and pack."

Frankie shook his head and pointed to Beth Ann. "She got everything ready for you for the next week."

Beth Ann nodded. "Yes and I also threw in a few new things."

"Oh wow. You are both wonderful." She smiled and her lip trembled.

Everyone hugged again and said their goodbyes. Frankie led his wife outside to his Mustang. He opened the door and gave her a lingering kiss before she climbed in.

Once he was in the car, he glanced over. "Are you ready to start our honeymoon?"

"Yes," she said and didn't even hesitate.

Frankie, however, had to loosen his tie. He was feeling nervous and was going to take her out to dinner and dancing before they even started their night together. The truth was, he'd never made love to a woman who'd never made love before. He wasn't sure how to work things. He almost asked Kaylob, but that didn't feel right, since Shawna was his sister.

They could always wait a few more days. It didn't have to start the night of the honeymoon. Did it?

They pulled up in front of the hotel right across the street from Kaylob's restaurant. Saturday would be their reception and Beth Ann had said she'd contact all their friends and family in Ireland, so Shawna didn't have to deal with it and Kaylob still hadn't wanted to talk to any of his parents. Frankie couldn't say he blamed him, though. He needed time.

Frankie had already told his parents and of course his mom had bawled. They weren't going to be able to make it, but they were coming for Thanksgiving.

"Frankie, are you okay? You're really quiet." She turned and met his gaze.

"I was just thinking about our reception party. By the way, did Kaylob and Beth Ann seem a little tense underneath their smiles?" he wondered.

"Yes, I thought it was just me. But I could feel them worrying about something and well, I didn't mean to overhear this, but I was in the bathroom and they were talking a little loud. I heard Kaylob ask Beth Ann if she would accept the boy, if the test showed he was the dad."

"What?" Frankie's mouth fell open. "Kaylob would never cheat on Beth Ann."

"Maybe it's from the past?" Shawna said.

"There weren't that many women from his past. I think only one to be honest." Frankie paused, deep in thought. "That was years ago."

"Well, he said the boy, not the baby."

"Whoa," Frankie shook his head. "That would be Dusty Clark. She was the only other girl he was ever with. He was fourteen and she was eighteen."

"Wow, she was way too old to be with a fourteen-year-old boy."

Frankie decided he better change the subject. "Let's check in and hopefully someone will carry up our luggage." He got out, walked around the car and opened the door for his new bride.

Once they were inside and told the front desk person who they were, the bellman came and gathered their luggage and the desk clerk asked, "Could you take these up to Mr. and Mrs. Russo's room?"

Frankie loved the sound of their names and repeated, "Mr and Mrs. Russo." Shawna smiled.

The guy at the front desk also said, "Congratulations, let us know if we can get you anything. We pick up food from any local restaurant, plus the place across the way has the best food in town."

"I know the place well," Shawna chuckled.

The man handed Frankie the keys. "Here you go and your luggage should be up soon."

They took the elevator and went up to the top floor. The minute they stepped inside the room, Frankie stood, gawking at the place in awe.

Shawna stared and couldn't seem to move. "Oh my word. Can you believe this? Look at all the flowers and candles. So romantic. And all this food." She waved her hand around.

Just then, there was a knock on the door, so Frankie went and opened it. There was the bellman, standing by a cart with all their luggage. Frankie waved him inside, and watched as he set the suitcases in the private bedroom. Once he came out, Frankie thanked him and handed him a good size tip. He congratulated them again and left.

Frankie and Shawna walked around looking at all the delicacies, wine, crackers, cheese, and even some chicken wings with fried zucchini. They would *not* have to leave their room tonight, but he wasn't sure how he felt about that part, so he focused on the food instead.

There was soup and fresh baked French bread, with two different types of dessert. The bowl of ice with shrimp looked delicious and the fresh strawberries accented everything.

There was a note that said: *You have more in the fridge by the bar. You won't have to go out for dinner for the two days you are there. We will bring breakfast to you, if and when you're hungry. Whatever time it is in the morning, you call us. We will have it sent to your room. Seven Nights and Seven Roses, dining staff. We love you Shawna, and congrats to you and Frankie.*

"I think Beth Ann and Kaylob were behind this," he said.

Shawna nodded and was extremely quiet. It appeared she was taking in the entire scene, maybe making memories, just as he was.

The room was quite elegant with a full length bar across the southern wall. A golden sofa, set in front of a dark wood fireplace, against the north wall. Next to the large picture window was a small dining table, big enough for two.

He strolled over and walked through the set of double doors, leading into the giant size master suite where the guy had put their luggage.

His eyes caught sight of the Jacuzzi tub that set off to the far side of the room. A bottle of champagne had been placed in the corner, chilling in ice with two glasses perched on each side.

As he turned, he saw Shawna open up the curtains behind the dining table. The view was amazing. It seemed as though you could see the entire city.

"I bet at night with all the lights, it's a sight to see," Frankie said.

He moved slowly across the room and paused, observing the

beautiful woman who was now his wife. Her eyes clung to his and the softness of the love curled around his heart and left him speechless.

As he approached her, his gaze fell to her lips, then he swept her into his arms. "Oh my lovely wife. I never in my wildest dreams imagined what this would feel like. I don't know if I can put into words just how much love is in my heart when I look at you."

"Frankie." Shawna's eyes shone with joy.

The warmth of her melted his insides. She wrapped her arms around him and the emotions were overwhelming. For the next few minutes they just held on to each other, savoring the tenderness of their love.

He tipped his finger under her chin, lifting it just a touch, then melted his lips across hers. He savored the sweet honey taste of her mouth and felt it all the way into his soul.

After a few minutes of kissing, Shawna finally pulled back and whispered, catching her breath, "I'm going to see what Beth Ann packed, because I want to change."

"Find something comfortable. I want to go dancing at the new club downtown."

"Dancing downtown?" She seemed confused. "Don't you want to stay here and just be together?"

"We will be together. I'm not letting my wife miss out on anything."

"Frankie, I'm not twenty-one yet."

"That's okay, they have stamps. It's the kind of club that you can get stamped if you're not twenty-one. You can't drink, but at least you can go dancing. Besides, you're almost twenty-one."

She nodded, turned, and strolled out of the room.

Frankie started to pace. Why hadn't he done some research about this? He was sure making love with a virgin wasn't much different. Maybe they should wait a few days. Christ, he'd never even talked to anyone about this, and didn't know anybody besides Kaylob who'd been with a girl who had never had sex before.

Shawna entered the room. Holy shit! She was wearing a red lacy thing that left nothing to the imagination. He felt his heart to see if it had stopped beating, or if he was dead.

Chapter Eleven

He cleared his throat. "I don't think you can go dancing in that. I'd end up in jail."

"Why would you end up in jail? I am the one wearing it." She giggled.

"Because I'd have to beat up a lot of guys," he quipped.

The way she moved across the room made him swallow the knot that was stuck in his throat. But he was still having a hard time breathing.

"We're not going dancing. I want to be with my husband." She waltzed over and flipped on a radio that sat on an end table. The song that came out was pretty new and it seemed perfect. *Lovin' You* by Minnie Riperton. "Loving you has made my life so beautiful."

When she moved closer, the view was even better, and the idea of dancing out in public faded from his mind.

"Frankie," she whispered. "Why are you so nervous?" She pulled him closer.

"Nervous? What makes you think that?" He heard his voice crack and backed up.

"Frankie Dean Russo?" She put her hands on her hips, and oh lord, what lovely hips they were. As a matter of fact, everything about her was exquisite.

"Okay, fine, I admit it. Shawna, I've never been with someone who has never done it before. I don't want to hurt you."

"Frankie, my sweet husband. You are not going to hurt me. I'm so ready for you, every single part of my body aches for you." She moved closer again and took his hand. "Come on, we are going to make love, and you are going to teach me *everything*, and in return, I will help you understand when I'm ready."

Once they were at the end of the bed, she let her gown fall to the floor. His head started spinning in circles. Never in his life had he seen anyone so gorgeous. He reached out and touched her breast and her nipple hardened. Then, he leaned down and kissed all around, using his tongue on the tip. Oh, man, never had he felt like this. He raised up and stared into her eyes.

"You are magnificent, Shawna, in every way. I love everything about you."

"Oh Frankie." She moaned. "I love everything about you too."

As the magic of the candle lights danced all around and music played in the background, the moment was captivating. The mystery of this woman, who now was his wife, made desire wash through him like the heat from a volcano, blistering his insides.

"Frankie," she said lightly. "I want you." She took his hand and guided his fingers to feel her readiness. "See how much I need you," she shivered and had tiny tremors. He slowly moved his fingers, feeling her wants and needs.

"Oh, Mrs. Russo." He stayed right there for a few more seconds, feeling his legs weaken. So before he fell, he lifted her onto the bed and gently laid her down. He couldn't take his eyes off her exquisiteness.

He took a step backwards and slowly slipped off his jacket. Next was his vest, keeping an eye on every inch of her. Then he started unbuttoning his shirt, one button at a time.

Watching her, watching him, filled him with even more desire, so he moved his hand to his pants, then inched the zipper down. He gazed into her steamy eyes and let his slacks fall over his hips. There was no hiding how much he wanted her.

Shawna's eyes heated with something he'd never witnessed. What she did next, surprised and thrilled him, she got on her knees and tugged off the rest of his clothes. He followed her gaze, as she drank in every inch of him.

Her soft, delicate hands sent shivers from the top of his head down to his toes. Never had anyone's touch torched him the way hers did. He glanced down, realizing what she was doing to him. He had never had this experience and wasn't sure what to do. He didn't want to come apart, not yet.

Just before she moved backwards on the bed, she reached up and pulled him down. When he parted her legs and started kissing every inch of her thigh, a soft moan came from deep within her. Good god, the look on her face, the sound of her voice, created a tsunami of desire that flooded through him.

Nibbling and tasting the flavor of her, he slowly moved up to her breast and savored each one as he gently explored the love of his life. He knew he'd have to go slow and wanted to relish every second.

"Oh, Shawna, you are so ... incredible. I love you."

He trailed kisses down until he came to that special place that took him to another world. In slow, easy movements, he showed her the secrets of his mouth and all that he could do. He drank from her sweetness like a starving man.

She squirmed. "Frankie, you are making me ..." she trailed off, groaning, and he knew she was trying to stop herself.

"It's okay sweetie, let it happen," he mumbled. "You are so very sexy."

Once again, she shuddered and moved her hips. He relished her flavor, making her moan his name over and over again. He felt a tremble run through her, then she let out a tiny scream. The second she completely surrendered, he damn near joined her. He was damp with longing as she continued to release her passion. And oh yes, she was warm and perfect in every way. She tasted of sunlight and pure sweetness. Nothing he'd ever experienced could compare.

"Frankie," she called his name. Her voice was low and raspy. The minute she wrapped her legs around his waist and adjusted her body, he knew what she wanted. So he lowered himself to her, taking it nice and slow, going to the edge before sailing over.

"Shawna, I love you."

"Frankie, I love you too." She pushed her hips up to greet him.

With one last motion, he moved deeper, then felt some resistance. He slowed down, moving softly, until at last he joined her. When he did, he heard her moan and cry at what he prayed was pure pleasure.

"Oh Shawna," he moaned shivering all over. "Are you okay? Did I hurt you?"

When she didn't answer, he stared down into her beautiful blue eyes. "Are you okay?"

"Yes, Oh yes. I wanted to enjoy this moment." She started to move. Pushing her hips up to his. "Love me, Frankie."

With that request he knew he had to comply, so his lips took hers in a deep, wet savoring kiss and he entered a point of no return. She was a fine wine, and he was addicted.

Finally, after they both came to a gentle stop, Frankie rolled off and pulled her close to him. He knew he'd have to make love to her again and again. It was going to take some time for him to gain more control. Not only because of the way they fit together, but this was his first experience of *making love* to someone he cherished.

Shawna lifted her head from his chest and glanced into his eyes. "Frankie was that good for you?"

He laughed. "Good for me? Oh hell, Shawna. I just realized, I was a virgin too."

"What?" she looked perplexed.

"I've had lots of sex, but I know now that I have never made love with anyone. The feeling was so intense I had a hard time controlling myself."

Shawna climbed on top of him and wiggled. "Well, we better practice again. Being virgins and all."

That entire day and night was spent making love and getting to know each other's body and soul. It was the sweetest and most precious moments of his life. He knew now that he'd spend the rest of his life loving one woman. And oh, what a woman she was.

He had a feeling he had met his match, in every way.

* * * *

Saturday morning Beth Ann and Kaylob got up early. They needed to head over to the restaurant and check on the set up for the reception. Thank goodness she'd been able to get Sarah to help out again. She had been their wedding planner and was happy to help them with everything.

They had closed the place to the public and were just using it for the party. However, they would let some of the regulars come in for drinks.

Lillian and Edna would be arriving early afternoon, but had decided to come straight from the airport to the restaurant. It was a surprise for Shawna. They were going to stay with Beth Ann and Kaylob and she hoped that Kaylob would be okay with Lillian, at least during the party.

As she was getting ready to leave, Beth Ann glanced around at her new house. "Holy midnight, I should have cleaned better."

All she could do is hope everyone would understand. After all, she was pregnant and hadn't been in the house that long. Beth Ann's mom and Stanley should be there soon. Maybe her mom would help with organizing. That had always been her mom's specialty. Living on the road with three children left her little choice.

Denny and Lisa were coming too. It was going to be nice to see everyone. She hadn't seen them since she found out she was pregnant. Jackie would be riding with her mom and Stanley, but Harold made his excuses, as usual. It made her angry he wasn't coming. *The coward.*

"Hey baby, where's my black pants?" Kaylob said, acting frustrated.

"I don't know, maybe where you left them," she said and laughed.

"Thank you so much," he snapped.

Gosh, he was really in a mood. She finished putting on her shoes and stepped into the closet. He was rummaging through his dirty clothes.

"Kaylob why would you be looking in the dirty clothes. If you find them, you can't wear them."

"And why not?" he turned and glared at her.

"Because, they would be dirty."

"Maybe I don't give a shit." He kicked the basket over.

What in the world? She hadn't seen him act like that since he got home from the POW camp. When he stood up glaring at her, she felt her bottom lip tremble. She hated her emotions these days. Everything made her cry.

"Whatever," she said and walked out of the room. She went and found Goldie and together they went out back.

A few minutes later she heard the back door open and he stepped out on the patio. "Baby, I'm such an ass. I'm so sorry. You didn't deserve that."

"What's really the matter?" she asked.

He walked closer and wrapped his arms around her. "I don't want to see any of them right now."

"Any of whom?" She glanced up at him.

"My parents, both sets. I'm still pissed off and even more so at

Jackie and Harold." He kissed her head. "But, I shouldn't take it out on you. I love you and I'm very sorry."

Ah, that was it. Today he'd have Jackie, Lillian and Edna all together. Although, Beth Ann was pretty sure he was okay with Edna.

"I understand, Kaylob. They are only staying a few days. Your dad's not coming, and if you're that uncomfortable, just work a lot or we could have them stay somewhere else."

He shook his head. "I can't do that, although, staying somewhere else does sound better. But it's my sister and my best friend's reception. I'll do the best I can. I'm also stressed about other things too. Beth Ann, I've been thinking, I was careful with Dusty, I always used a rubber because I didn't want to get her pregnant. I don't understand." He shook his head.

"Honey, maybe he's not your son, and if he is, we will work it out." Her gaze clung to his. "Try not to worry. I'm with you every step of the way, like I said." She laid her head on his chest.

"Okay," he nodded. "Have I told you that you are the most beautiful, sexy and wonderful woman in the world."

"Never," she lied and they both laughed.

All of a sudden, Goldie let out a loud yelp. Both ran to her side and kneeled down in front of her. A bee fell from her mouth. She was whimpering and crawled into Beth Ann's lap.

"Oh, my poor baby." Beth Ann pouted. "She got stung by a bee in her mouth." Beth Ann carried her inside and Kaylob grabbed her baby blanket.

"Poor girl." Kaylob rubbed behind her ears. "I hope she's going to be okay."

Beth Ann nodded. "Me, too. We should take her with us and keep an eye on her. We could put her in the office."

Kaylob nodded. "I agree. I'll get her bed and a toy."

"Make sure to get her goose."

* * * *

Beth Ann observed family and friends crying and carrying on about Frankie and Shawna. Lillian seemed to be taken with Frankie and that made her and Kaylob breathe a sigh of relief, even though Beth Ann had not seen Kaylob smile once in Lillian's direction. Frankie and Shawna were blissfully happy. Shawna had told her privately that Frankie was the most gentle and loving man in the world and had made her first time amazing.

Beth Ann had always suspected that about Frankie. Once they had kissed a very long time ago and she remembered how sweet his lips were. She had always wanted him to be with Carol, but now she understood that God had other plans, not to mention, Carol was gay. Her disinterest in men might have been an issue.

She felt happy as she looked around the room and saw Carol holding Frankie's arm. Shelia and Shawna were laughing and eating some shrimp that had been placed on the table.

Blake was there with another one of his women friends. Once again, Beth Ann was disappointed he wasn't with Melissa. He was going to keep playing around until he lost her. She shook her head and turned away, then saw Gram and Nicky walk through the door.

Gram hurried towards her. "Oh my sweetness, look at you." She touched Beth Ann's stomach, and tears filled her blue eyes. "You look wonderful." She gently pressed both hands on Beth Ann's stomach. "And the baby, she's strong."

Gram looked amazing with her white hair flowing freely and Nicky was as handsome as ever. His silver hair with his white jacket showed off his Italian skin. They made a very handsome couple.

Nicky gave her a big hug. "How are you feeling?" He smiled, but his green eyes showed concern.

"I'm good now. Just getting fat." Beth Ann placed her hands on her tummy.

Nicky laughed. "You look beautiful." He hugged her again. "Have I thanked you lately for bringing your grandmother back to me? I'm one happy man." He glanced over at his wife and his eyes sparkled with joy.

Her and Kaylob had found Nicky, and had talked him into surprising Gram at their wedding. He was Gram's first love. It was so sad how Gram's family had made her marry another man. Now, after so many years apart, they were together and obviously happy.

Nicky excused himself, kissed Gram's cheek, then headed over to say hello to Stanley. The two guys had hit it off and loved talking mechanics.

"Gram, oh my gosh, you called the baby a she. I know it's a little girl. I saw her in a vision once a long time ago when Kaylob was still missing.

Gram smiled. "Well, I'm usually right about these things, and I would say it's most definitely a little girl."

"There was also a golden dog." Beth Ann remembered the bee sting. "I have to check on Goldie. She got stung by a bee in the mouth."

Gram held her arm. "Is her mouth swollen?"

"Yes, her tongue seems red too."

"We might need to get some Benadryl," Gram said. "She needs to drink some ice water. Did you get the stinger out?"

Beth Ann shook her head. "No. Oh my gosh, I'm a terrible person."

"No you're not, you just didn't know. Let's go to her." Gram's eyes had shadows of worry, which made Beth Ann's stomach flip.

Beth Ann motioned for Kaylob as they hurried towards the office. He was talking to some tall woman with a big chest who worked as the new hostess. She reached up and touched his hair and got a little too close. As far as Beth Ann was concerned, that was not acceptable.

She saw red, but tried to cover it up. Why was she touching her husband's hair and getting so cozy?

Kaylob finally got there, and Gram explained what she wanted to check out with Goldie just before they stepped into the office. Beth Ann paused and shot the harlot a long nasty look. The tart had the nerve to give her a smart-ass grin. Did she not understand that this was her husband and she could fire her?

They entered the office and Goldie was sleeping. The pup seemed very sad, but Kaylob held a flashlight so Gram could see while she examined Goldie's mouth.

"Hi Goldie," Gram said. "This is a heck of a way to meet me, isn't it. There it is." She reached in with a cloth and pulled out the stinger. "Got it. Now, get her some ice or at least put it in her water dish. The swelling should go down. Hopefully, she will be back to herself in no time. If not, like I mentioned, we will need to give her a small dose of Benadryl."

"Thank you, Gram, you saved the day," Beth Ann said.

Kaylob gave her a hug. "You're the best, thank you."

"Now, I need to go use the ladies room. I'll meet you back out there afterwards." Gram hurried out the door.

Beth Ann got down on the floor with Goldie. "Poor baby, wonder if she needs to pee."

Kaylob shook his head. "Flo took her out for us."

"Who's Flo?" Beth Ann wanted to thank her.

"She's the new hostess. A very nice girl and great worker."

"Oh yes, very nice and I noticed she likes your hair." Beth Ann glanced up at him.

"My hair?" he asked.

"Yes, your hair. She was playing with it a few minutes ago."

He laughed. "No, she was taking something out of my hair. You were here when I hired her."

"Yeah, well she wasn't touching your hair." Beth Ann didn't like that one bit and was sad they'd lost Beverly, but she got married and moved away.

Kaylob reached down and stroked Goldie's head. "Do you see that? Your mommy is one jealous redhead."

"Shut up," said Beth Ann as she stood to leave.

He took her hand and told Goldie they'd be back soon. "Let's go beat up that wicked woman for touching my hair."

Beth Ann wanted to smack him.

* * * *

The band finally showed up and Beth Ann got all the songs together. As she stood on stage, she glanced around at all the family and friends. Denny and Lisa were hanging out with Blake and the newlyweds. They were all holding up glasses and toasting to Shawna and Frankie. He had his arm protectively around his wife and Beth Ann inhaled deeply. She could feel the love all the way across the room. Blake, on the other hand, was checking out one woman after another. He was at the far end from being in love.

Blake must have felt her staring, because he turned around and smiled. His twin dimples flashed, then he winked. Beth Ann gave him a soft smile and there was a secret exchange. It was a bond between them that would always be there. For a split second, when she stared into his blue eyes, she thought they looked sad and her heart sank. She would always have a special place in her heart for him because he had not only been her fiancé when Kaylob was missing, but he had been a very supportive and a dear friend. Now, they were like family and him and Kaylob had forged a special friendship during her kidnapping ordeal. She reached down and felt her baby and wondered if Blake was sad because he didn't have children yet. He had told her when they were engaged that someday he wanted them. She prayed he would find love again. All he'd been finding lately were women he tossed aside after a few dates. He was right back to where he was before they got together.

"Are you doing okay? Everything alright?"

She hadn't seen her mom come up on stage.

"Yes, Mama. I feel fantastic. Just a little fat."

"Fat, oh you silly girl. You are paper thin with a tiny bump," she drawled. "By the time I was four months, I was waddling. Make sure you're feeding my grandchild." Her mom's eyes filled with moisture. "I'm so elated to be called Grandma."

"I think that's pretty clear, since you've sent thirty baby shirts that say 'grandma loves me' or 'behave or I'll call my grandma,' And, I can see it in your eyes." Beth Ann giggled. "I am feeding this baby a lot, Mama. Believe me, Kaylob is always cooking my favorite foods." She glanced around for her husband. "Where is that husband of mine? He's usually out here when I get up on stage."

"Oh, he had Goldie on a leash and it looked like he was taking her out back. He said she was feeling better and was hungry."

"Gram saved the day," Beth Ann said.

"She does that a lot." She smiled and kissed her daughter's cheek. "I can't wait to hear you sing. I'm going to go down and talk to Frankie and Shawna. They are such a lovely couple."

The band started warming up and her mom left the stage. A few seconds later, Kaylob was standing off to the side, holding Goldie. He was pointing towards her and Goldie was actually watching. It was so cute. Sarah walked over beside Kaylob and gave the dog a scratch behind the ears. Thank God for her, there was no way Beth Ann could have set this whole thing in motion.

The decorations were perfect. Sarah had used pale blues and mauve, with some light reds. It was elegantly done, even though it was such short notice.

Billie from the band nodded and said, "We're ready when you are, beautiful."

"Okay." She took the microphone.

"I'd like to ask the newlyweds to come out to the dance floor. I've thought long and hard and decided this song would be perfect for them."

Frankie shoveled himself out of the booth and stretched his hand to Shawna. As she took hold, cameras started flashing.

The way Frankie crossed the room with Shawna's arm weaved through his was magnificent. Every female seemed to be in awe, including Denny, who might be a tad bit envious. When she was young, she had a giant size crush on him.

Beth Ann glanced around and was pretty darn sure every female tongue was hanging out. Except Carol, who had a wide grin and gazed at him with complete admiration.

Shawna and Frankie came across like a prince and princess. Frankie was dressed in a dark blue suit that opened up in the front, with a corduroy vest and a casual shirt. It was extremely attractive. Shawna wore a pale blue cocktail dress with short sleeves. The bodice showed off her flawless figure and the scalloped neckline was perfect for her.

Shawna's movement and style showed she had been raised with class and etiquette. There was an air about her that you could see and feel, but in no way did she come across as a snob or stuck up.

Beth Ann glanced over at Kaylob and they did their love signs to each other. Then she touched her heart, and waited for Frankie to take Shawna in his arms.

"I have chosen an Elvis Presley song," Beth Ann said as she gazed at them. "To Frankie and Shawna, may your love be in full bloom every day for the rest of your lives."

The lights dimmed and the band hit the first note.

"Wise men say only fools rush in. But I can't help falling in love with you." Billie harmonized with her. His voice was rich and deep.

Shawna's lip trembled and Frankie pulled her closer. They were so perfect together, even the way they moved in harmony to the beat of the music. Beth Ann knew she had picked the right song as Frankie glided Shawna around the dance floor.

"Some things are meant to be, take my hand, take my whole life ..." And when she hit the last note she realized that Frankie had a tough time concealing his emotions when he swiped at his eyes.

Beth Ann felt tears burning, but continued on. This was a first. She'd never seen Frankie so emotional. The closest time was when he had left Novato when they were kids. But he had turned and ran away before it happened. This touched her heart like nothing had in a long time.

When she finished singing, she walked down the stage and embraced Frankie and then Shawna. Kaylob handed off Goldie to her mom and came out on the dance floor and tapped on Frankie's shoulder.

Another song started to play and it was a beautiful one by Elton John called "Your Song." The band started playing and Billie's voice enchanted the room.

"I'm stealing my sister for a dance," Kaylob said. Then, just as Frankie turned to ask Beth Ann, Lillian appeared.

"Could I have this one dance with Frankie?"

Beth Ann stepped back. "Of course."

It was beautiful to see Kaylob with his sister and Lillian with Frankie.

Lillian and Edna had been very quiet and she hoped they felt at home. Maybe they were just trying to give Kaylob some space. He had spent very little time talking to them.

Just then there was a tap on her shoulder. "Can I have this dance?" Blake's dimples flashed. "And, no matchmaking attempts?"

"You got it." She walked into his embrace.

The one thing Beth Ann and Blake had discovered when they were kids and engaged, was that they could heat up the dance floor. They had incredible rhythm together.

"So darlin, how are you feeling?" Blake pulled her closer and lifted her hands in the correct position to do a slow foxtrot.

"I'm feeling great. Just fat."

"Fat, where?" He winked. "You can show me if you want."

"Blake," she said, smacking his arm.

Brenda Ashworth Barry

"Think we can make that husband of yours jealous?" He gave her a mischievous look.

"No. I'm worse than he is. Earlier we almost took someone out back and beat the crap out of her."

Blake laughed. "Now, *that* I'd have to see. What did she do?"

"She was touching his hair and got a little too close, as far as I'm concerned."

"Oooh, that harlot." He spun her around and pulled her back again.

After a few more spins, Kaylob walked over and tapped Blake on the arm.

"Okay, cowboy, I want my woman back."

"Damn, man, you are one stingy dude." He handed her over to Kaylob. "Now don't be letting any women touch your hair." He laughed and walked away.

"What did you tell him?" Kaylob looked annoyed. "I'll never hear the end of this."

"Oh, just how Flo was in your space, touching your hair. And, how we might just have to fire her."

"Elizabeth Ann Rose, you want me to fire her because she touched my hair?"

"Yes, I do as a matter of fact." She wasn't kidding. "She also gave me a smarty pants look."

"Beth Ann, stop this. You know I don't give a shit about anyone but you."

"Good, then you won't have any problems firing her."

The music stopped and she left him standing there. Beth Ann noticed that Blake's smile faded when she stomped off the dance floor.

She strolled over to Charlie and Tina. "How would you like to meet Goldie?"

They both nodded and followed her into the office. Goldie bounded over to see Beth Ann and give Charlie and Tina a big wet kiss. She was most definitely feeling better.

The phone rang, then Charlie and Tina waved goodbye, to give her privacy.

"Seven nights and Seven Roses," Beth Ann answered, just as Kaylob walked through the door.

"Yes," a man said. "We are calling to make a reservation for August seventh."

She handed the phone to Kaylob, and started to leave, but he caught her eye and pointed towards the couch.

After he finished, he crossed the room and sat by her. "Baby, do you really want me to fire her?"

"No." She leaned over on his arm. "I don't know why I'm being such a brat."

He rubbed her belly. "Maybe you're tired. I'm taking the day off tomorrow and you are going to sleep in."

"I love you, Kaylob Shawn O'Brien."

"I love you too." He wrapped his arms around her and nibbled on her neck. "I could just eat you."

She giggled and stood. "Come on, we better get back out there. I still have songs to do."

The night ended up being magical with Frankie and Shawna dancing and loving on each other. However, everyone could see they wanted to get back to their hotel room. They were the definition of newlyweds.

Things started thinning out after Frankie and Shawna left. Flo was still hanging around, helping the crew to clean up. Maybe she was a good worker and Beth Ann knew she had to be fair.

Lisa ran over to her. "Finally, I get some time to talk to you."

Lisa looked so pretty with her dark curly hair hanging down to her shoulders and her blue dress that matched her eyes. They had been best friends since the sixth grade.

"You look wonderful, Beth Ann." She waved for Denny to join them, but Denny seemed pretty busy flirting with some guy up at the bar.

"Thank you, Lisa, I've missed you so much." Beth Ann hugged her.

"I know, me too. I can't wait until the baby is born. You should see how big Benjamin is. He's a handful."

Just about that time Denny came strutting over. She was obviously giving the guy a good show. People had always compared her to Sally Field, but somehow she was not as wholesome. The truth was, Denny loved being with men and made it no secret. She thought it was only fair for women to be allowed to have as much fun as they did.

"Whoa, he's one hot, rich papa." Denny laughed. "He's taking me out to dinner tomorrow night."

Lisa frowned. "You don't even know him. That's dangerous."

Beth Ann had to agree. "Denny, this is Riverside, it's not always safe."

"It will be fine because you and Beth Ann will be at the table behind me, right here and this guy even owns a yacht. He's not from Riverside. He's from some island in the Caribbean."

Beth Ann and Lisa glanced at each other and had to crack up.

"I heard the food is good and hell he owns a Yacht," Lisa finally said. "What do you say, Beth Ann?"

"I say, I'll be here." Beth Ann looked over at the guy and a chill ran up her spine and it wasn't a good one. "Yes," she said, trying not to sound worried. "We will be here the whole time."

Later, Beth Ann was walking around, picking up plates, when Goldie came running out. A lot of their friends and family had decided to get hotel rooms. Her parents and Jackie, Edna and Lillian, were all staying with them. They had five bedrooms so there was more than enough room. Plus, Shawna had told Denny and Lisa they could stay at her and Frankie's house, but there was no room service and no pampering, so they got a room at the hotel across the street.

Beth Ann had at least talked Nicky and Gram into staying on the property in their new RV. They were like two little kids, wanting to play with their new toy.

Beth Ann saw Goldie trying to eat the food that had fallen on the floor, so she scooped her up and laughed. "Okay girl, you're going back into the office until we go home."

Once she opened the door, she saw Flo sitting on the chair in front of Kaylob while he wrote in his appointment book. The other woman's eyes flickered over Beth Ann with disinterest before she looked away.

"Oh, hi," Beth Ann said as she entered the room and sat Goldie down near her water dish. "There you go, girl. Drink some more water."

Kaylob finished and Flo stood. "Thank you, Kaylob. I'll see you tomorrow." She left without looking Beth Ann's way.

Kaylob finally closed his book and smiled. "We booked in three parties this weekend." He glanced up and his smile faded the minute he looked at Beth Ann's face.

Chapter Twelve

"Are you okay?" He stood and walked around to her.

"No. I'm not okay. I'm trying to be, but she's really pretty and has those really big things that are called boobs. I know she likes you a little too much."

"Oh baby," he laughed. "She's not after me, and I don't care about her big things, no matter what they're called. All she wanted was to tell me she had to get off early Monday because her grandma has cancer and they are doing her first treatment. She was very upset."

"I said hi and she never even looked at me."

Kaylob lifted her chin. "I think she just wanted to leave fast because she was almost crying."

"Alright," Beth Ann said. "I'll stop."

"Let's get home and get Goldie to bed." Kaylob pulled her up. "And let's get my big baby girl to bed so I can take advantage of her."

Beth Ann shook her head. "Our families are there. I think you'll have to wait."

He looked at the door and grinned. "We have a lock. Everyone's busy and I have a bone for Goldie."

With that thought, Beth Ann moved over to the door and locked it.

* * * *

Later that evening, Kaylob tucked Beth Ann in bed. She was down for the count. They had made love in his office after the party ended. It was always like the first time with Beth Ann, the only difference was they knew each other's secret desires.

Her eyes had closed before her head hit the pillow. Just as he leaned down to switch off the bedside lamp, his heart stuttered when he noticed Beth Ann was glowing. He had to catch his breath at the sight of her.

There was no way he could put into words how grateful he was. He was sure glad that everyone besides Jean and Stanley had decided to stay out back at Shawna's place, now Frankie's too. That way he didn't have to worry about running into them and having to make small talk, when all he felt like right now was yelling at Jackie, his mom, or so called mom, who had lied to him his entire life.

He kissed Beth Ann's head and brushed the hair from her face. "I love you forever and a day," he said tenderly.

He trod softly out of the bedroom and made his way into the mud room. Goldie was crashed as well. The poor girl had been traumatized by that damn bee sting. When she felt a little better, she had gotten wild, running and playing with everyone. Even Nicky and Gram had played fetch with her in the backyard. She was a good girl and he was happy to have a dog, or as Beth Ann would say, a child with fur.

As he entered the kitchen, he glanced around and noticed how great things looked. Everything was clean and the island was beautiful. Jean had her handiwork all over the house and he knew darn well she'd helped Beth Ann get things done. She was a gem and he loved her like a mother. The house was quiet, all except the ticking of the old clock that hung on the wall. They'd had that timepiece since they were first together. Beth Ann refused to give it up and honestly, he didn't want to either.

He crossed the room and opened the refrigerator. With ease, he pulled out the milk carton and looked over his shoulder. Now, this was a rare chance to eat at night. The food patrol officer was asleep, he thought and chuckled. "Cookies…yum." He spotted the ones on the counter that Gram had brought. Yes, he'd have a few, well, maybe four or five. He grabbed them up and quietly opened the cabinet, then pulled down a plate for his midnight rendezvous.

While he sat eating cookies, savoring every delicious bite, he thought about if he'd known Dusty was pregnant, *would* he have married her? Yes, he would have and she was right; he would have been a very unhappy man. He thought about Gram and Nickolas, and shivered. He couldn't imagine not having Beth Ann in his life or being torn apart from her again. It was bad enough that Cole had made him wait so long to ask her to go steady. He'd never told Beth Ann that her brother had threatened to send her away to live with Gram in Salem. He'd bought her a going steady ring when she was fourteen, but when he got to her house earlier that day before her party, he had the brilliant idea to show Cole. That sure as hell hadn't gone over well. Cole had told him he better take it back or he'd never see her again. So he did. He'd never told Beth Ann the whole story because, hell, he wasn't sure why? Why hadn't he?

Just as he was taking a bite of his last cookie, he heard a sound. Beth Ann stood there looking disheveled. That made him want to scoop her up and take her back to bed. He would never get enough of her. He'd felt like that since the age of fourteen. She had electrified him from the first moment she touched him.

"I woke up and you weren't there," she mumbled.

"Come here, my little minx." He waved her over and pulled her down on his lap, then kissed her neck.

She giggled with the same precious melody she'd had since they were kids. His sweet wife put her arms around his neck and laid her head on his chest. God, he loved this; her in his arms, while she listened to his heart beating.

She raised up and took his last half of the cookie. "How many did you eat, Mr. O'Brien?"

"A few." After she finished chewing, she said, "Take me to bed. I need you to hold me."

With that, he stood with her in his arms and carried her to their room. She curled up next to him and instantly fell asleep once more. He whispered a prayer of thanks.

"Oh, my gosh." Beth Ann suddenly shot up and put her hand over her stomach.

"I'll call 9-1-1," he said, as he hit the floor and went sliding.

"No, Kaylob!" she cried and laughed at the same time. "The baby just moved."

"What?" He finally stood and stared at her.

"She's kicking and moving. Oh, Kaylob, come and feel her."

He moved over to the bed and placed his hand on her bare belly. There was movement, then he felt the baby kick, making his heart thump extra hard as a lump formed in his throat. Their baby girl was in there and he could feel her.

"Oh, Beth Ann," he said, his voice husky with emotion. "Our baby, our precious child."

She nodded and placed her hand on top of his. "Kaylie Maggie O'Brien will bring us more joy than we ever imagined. She will have golden hair and blue eyes just like her daddy and today August, 2nd 1975, is the first time we felt her move."

* * * *

Blake woke up and realized he had overslept. He glanced at the woman in bed next to him and couldn't remember her name. She was a gorgeous redhead and he sure as shit remembered what they had done last night. On a scale from one to ten, she was way past ten, which was something he didn't experience that often.

After the party, he'd gone down to the bar around the corner and that's when she waltzed up to him, knocking the air right out of his lungs. That had never happened before either, except with his ex-fiancée, who had done that to him since childhood.

All he knew was the woman lying in his arms was almost as gorgeous as his ex-fiancée. And man, was she a sexy kitten. The essence of her was enthralling. Her scent was natural with a sweet, succulent overtone.

Speaking of his ex-fiancée, she had practically been glowing last night. If the truth be known, dancing with her still stung a little, but not like it had in the past. He supposed he'd always have a weak spot for Beth Ann.

Kaylob was his buddy though, and a good man. One time, Kaylob had busted him. He'd been staring at her and Blake had winced and said, "Sorry, pal. Sometimes she still takes my breath away."

Kaylob was so cool about it. All he did was say, "Hey, I know all about how Beth Ann can capture your heart and never let go. Besides, I trust you, Blake, you're like my family."

Blake appreciated the trust and treasured their friendship. So he tried like hell to put the past away, and he'd done a damn good job of it.

He gently lifted her head off his chest and kissed her lips. She was sleeping peacefully so, he rolled off the bed and glanced down at this beauty. Holy hell she was gorgeous. It was hard to pull his gaze away.

But he needed to get dressed, so he slipped on his boxers and grabbed his pants. What he wanted was mouthwash, usually these rooms have something like that. The taste in his mouth was like Texas in August, dry as hell.

Once he rinsed his mouth, he made his way back to the bedroom and finished getting his shoes and socks on. He had to get out of the hotel before she woke up. He never liked sticking around the next day, no serious shit. He put on his shirt and while he buttoned it, he took in her shoulders and the way her neck curved. Damn, everything about her was perfect.

He'd leave her a note or call her later, maybe a second date might be nice. Did he have her number? Christ, he really didn't know. He knew they took their own cars, because she insisted on it. However, some things were fuzzy, because they had finished off those little bottles of booze in that half pint fridge.

Just as he buckled his belt, she opened her eyes and holy smoking hell, they were spicy blue. He'd never been with a redhead that had blue eyes before.

"Good morning, beautiful." He smiled and found his wallet.

"You're leaving?" she asked.

Oh no, here we go. Women always tried to talk him into staying. Clingy is what he called it. Trying to find a way to spend the morning with him. Cook him breakfast, try to get personal. Yada yada yada. He'd seen it all.

"Yeah, sorry about that darlin. I've got to get home, get changed, and go meet clients." He lied smoothly, cause he actually had the day off. "If you give me your number, I could call you."

"Oh no, I can't give you my number." She sat up and covered her breasts, taking away the glorious view.

"It was a good time, but we don't need to talk again," she said.

"Uh, okay, whatever you say." He had to admit he was shocked as hell. "Sorry to hear that, but it was a really awesome night. I hope you enjoyed yourself. I didn't hear any complaints."

"Everything was more than I imagined. But, I'm getting married next weekend and well, I wanted to have at least one fling." She pushed the hair out of her face. "He's the only guy I've ever been with and I knew I wanted a one-night stand, but had no idea how to go about it."

"Well darlin, you did a fine job." He grinned.

"When you walked in, I knew it had to be you." She paused. "I'm glad it was, but it was only one time. I'll never do it again. I don't think Arnold would understand."

"Ah, I'd have to say that's more than likely a true statement." He finished his tie and gave it a tug. "I'm not sure this is a good way to start off a marriage, but I'm sure as heck no expert." He slipped on his jacket. "Well, you have a great life and congratulations." He bent down and kissed her head. "It was really nice meeting you. I had a fantastic time."

"Thank you Blake, it was really nice." She blushed. "I enjoyed everything."

"The pleasure was all mine." He started to leave, then paused. "What's your name?" he turned and asked.

An amusing smile crossed her lips and her eyes sparkled. "Ginger," she said lightly. "Just call me Ginger Rogers."

"Okay, Ginger Rogers, thank you and take care."

She stood, and the sheet fell just enough for him to see her magnificent body, which showed a very large bruise on her hip. With a fast move, she tugged it up.

Blake crossed the room and stood in front of her. "I hope I didn't do that," he said as he lifted the bed sheet and studied the bruise.

"Oh no, I did that horseback riding." She glanced down. "I have to get going too. Wedding cakes." She smiled, but it didn't seem genuine. "I have to go taste testing with my fiancé."

"I see." He grinned and flashed his twin dimples. Girls always like that, but she seemed unfazed.

All she did was turn away. "Have a good one."

The minute he stepped outside, he felt a loss and wished he could go back inside and make love to her again. But that was a no no in his rule book.

The damn hotel had been packed when they got there last night and now he had to trek down the street to where his car was parked.

He climbed into his Jaguar and stuck the keys in the ignition. Damn, too bad about her getting married, there was something about her that was steamy and sassy. Something that reminded him of another redhead.

He drove off before understanding dawned on him. She had used him for a piece of ass and showed him the door. Now, that was a change, something that had never happened before. He shook his head and wondered if he was losing his touch.

By the time he got home to his Palm Springs townhouse, it was past ten a.m. Traffic was a mess out there. He walked in the door and Dana and Johnny were carrying one of his big plants.

"Hey, Blake." Dana smiled and Johnny nodded.

"What's going on with the plant?" Blake asked, as he opened the front door for them to carry it out.

"It left a mess on the floor," Dana said. "I'm going to clean the spot and try to get it to stop leaving a ring." She sighed. "The new housekeeper needs to keep an eye on it too, so I'm leaving her a note."

"Get a fake one," Johnny said, as they set it down on the front step.

"Fake?" She shook her head. "Oh, by the way." She came back into the house. "Melissa called and wanted to talk to you. She said it's important."

"I have to get going," Johnny said. "Do you need me for that plant anymore?"

Blake watched Dana smile. "No, I'll see you later," she whispered and kissed Johnny's cheek.

Damn, Johnny blushed. That girl had him wrapped, but they both seemed happy. He trusted Johnny with Dana and knew he'd take good care of her.

She stood at the door, watching him leave.

"Dana," Blake said.

She turned giving him a look of curiosity. "Yes."

"Why are you still working for me? You went to school and spent hours learning how to be a court reporter."

Her face softened. "I love being here and doing this." She gestured around the room. "Blake, you're the only family I have. I don't want to work full time, sitting in court." She crossed the room and hugged him. "I love you."

God dang it, he felt all choked up. "I love you too." He caught his breath. "Now get to work before I fire you."

She pulled back and held his gaze. "Oh, you big fake, Blake Tanner.

You're just a softie and I know it."

Blake kissed her forehead and headed to his office. What was with all these emotions today? Was he going through male menopause or something?

He shook it off and walked into his home office. The desk had mail piled for two days that he needed to attend to, but not before he called Melissa.

She'd been staying away from him lately and he felt bad. The girl had been crushing on him for years. The truth was, she had grown into a gorgeous woman and there was no hiding her great body, but he just wasn't interested.

He didn't hold the right kind of feelings for her and he didn't want to hurt her. There was no way he'd pretend to feel something that wasn't there. That was bullshit and that kind of stuff still pissed him off. He thumped his knuckles on the desk.

"Shit." He shook his hand, which smarted from the pain.

He picked up the phone and held it. Speaking of Beth Ann, she had sure pushed the hell out of him getting together with Melissa, but he was going to have to disappoint her. Because this wasn't about who she wanted him to be with. Blake had made a decision that he'd never get tied down again. No commitment of any kind, no love, no living together, nada. And that was that, signed, sealed, and decided.

One time on the airplane headed to Hawaii, Melissa had caught him off guard and planted a sizzling kiss right on his lips. Oh sure, he'd responded to it, but after a few seconds he had pulled everything back. The only feelings he'd allowed himself to have are the ones that drive a man hard.

Which returned his thoughts to last night. The redhead, Ginger Rogers, he chuckled. Now, that was one girl he'd like to see again. But it was just his luck, she was getting married.

Although, seeing her again would have been purely for sex.

He had gotten used to coming home again to an empty house. Or at least that's what he told himself. Maybe, he should get a dog or a bird. No, a bird would be too noisy. Okay, a goldfish would be perfect; how much trouble could they be?

When he finally sat down still holding the phone, it rang.

"Good morning, Tanner and Associates," Blake answered.

"Blake, it's me."

"Hey Kaylob, what's cooking?"

"Thought you might want to have dinner with us tonight. We're celebrating the movement of our little girl."

"The movement of your little girl?" Blake questioned. "Goldie looked like she was moving around fine the last two times I saw her."

Kaylob cracked up. "No, our baby. She moved last night."

"I hate to say this pal, but how do you know she's a she."

"Beth Ann said so and you should know by now, she's always right."

"Kaylob Shawn O'Brien." He heard Beth Ann scolding in the background. "I heard that."

"Well, you want to meet us at the restaurant this afternoon? Dinner's on us."

"Sure, congratulations to you both." He looked at his watch. "What time is dinner?"

"Let's say six."

"Sounds good, see you then."

"Those two are funny." He had to laugh, then picked up the phone and dialed Melissa's number.

"Hello," she answered.

"Hi there, it's me. You called."

"Hi Blake. I was wondering if we could talk this afternoon?" She sounded serious.

"Sure, is everything okay?"

"I just need to talk to you. Can you meet me around five or five-thirty?"

"I can, but I have to meet Kaylob and Beth Ann at six for dinner."

"Oh, I'm meeting them too. Why don't we meet at the restaurant early? That way we can talk first."

"Sounds good." Blake agreed. "I'll see you there at five."

"Okay, see you then." She hung up.

"Wonder what that's all about?" He was worried, but decided he needed to relax and take it easy. Last night had worn his ass out.

Blake hung around the townhouse and opened up all his mail and made sure to file everything in the right order for his replacement for Dana. She'd be starting next week, since Dana was going to be working part-time at court reporting.

Man, it was nice to have a day off and be able to work out of his home office. He was going to miss Dana. Not only had she worked as his house manager for years. She'd taken care of a lot of his home office paperwork and phone calls. After Beth Ann had broken his heart, she'd been there to help him pick up the pieces. Now, she and Johnny seemed to be in love. She was still going to work for him part-time, but his life was crazy, so he needed someone to fill in the hours she'd be gone.

Later he went out to the pool and took a swim. It was always hot in Palm Springs in August. The scenery was pretty damn good though. He watched some foxy babes in their bikinis strutting around the pool—one of the perks of living in a townhouse. But after Ginger, he wasn't in the mood. Even though one of them kept smiling and wiggling her cute little bottom at him.

The memory of last night played out in his mind like a sex movie. He had been sitting there minding his own business drinking a beer, when this redhead came out of nowhere and asked, "What's your pleasure?" Then she touched his leg in a way that made him rise to the occasion. Usually, nothing ever happened that fast, but she had turned him on, and turned him on hard.

Fifteen minutes later they had taken off to a nearby hotel, only in separate cars.

She hadn't been shy, which was amazing since she'd claimed she'd only been with one other guy. It reminded him of the way Beth Ann seduced him that first time. Only they'd known each other since childhood.

If he was being honest, last night was the best he'd ever had. Man, she was full of energy and desire, which begged the question. Was she getting what she needed from her fiancé?

He still couldn't wrap his brain around the experience. Even today he was feeling the burn. Christ almighty, six times. No wonder he couldn't think about sex. Except he was, but only for a repeat performance, with the almost-married Ginger Rogers.

Oh well. He glanced at his watch. It was time to get ready to meet

185

Melissa and go to the dinner party. He took off from the pool, but not before he noticed one of the girls checking him out. Today he'd have to pass, he was done in.

When he walked back into the bedroom to change out of his swim trunks, he thought about Beth Ann and Kaylob. Nobody should ever have to go through what they had. It hadn't helped that he had been a complete ass when Kaylob got home from the POW camp. Beth Ann had never loved him as much as she loved Kaylob and he knew that now, but hadn't wanted to believe it back then.

However, when he saw the look on her face as she walked down the aisle to meet Kaylob, there was no room for speculation. She was head over heels in love with that man and had been all her life. He had no choice but to walk away and accept what had smacked him in the face.

But after the kidnapping, he and Kaylob had joined forces to find her. Somewhere along that journey, they had started to really like each other and became good buddies.

Blake had to admit that he loved the guy like a brother, but Beth Ann he'd never love as a sister, although he wanted her happy and she *was* with Kaylob.

As hard as it was to believe, he really enjoyed watching the two of them together. They could inspire people to find the person they were meant to be with. Not him, though; he was done. Once was enough and besides, he enjoyed all the women in his life.

He stepped in front of the mirror. His socks matched his shirt, his belt matched the color of his shoes, and his tie matched his pants. That made him ready. He went into his closet and noticed one of his white shirts was hanging with the blue ones. Crap, the new housekeeper didn't understand his system. Dana had spoiled him and knew how he liked everything. He pulled it down and placed it in the right area. There, now he was ready. He took in a deep breath, knowing everything was organized.

Shit, was he anal or something? Beth Ann had made up that song about him.

Speaking of the happy couple, he wished Kaylob would move their restaurant to Palm Springs. It would be so much closer to his house, but not so much for them. Maybe someday they would make that choice. His business would boom even more than it already had. The guy was the best chef from here to the Texas border. There were some mighty fine restaurants in Dallas and maybe a few he liked more, but only because of the sexy ladies who waited tables. But as far as the food, they had nothing that compared to Kaylob's place. He should have named it that. Instead, he used words like Seven Roses and Nights? What were flowers and numbers all about? Someday he'd have to ask him.

He pulled up to the restaurant and saw that Melissa's car was already there. A worry hit his gut. Had she gotten herself in some kind of trouble? Man, he sure as hell hoped not. The problem was that ever since she had come to work for him at his Palm Springs office, he felt like he was responsible for her. Her daddy was a good friend and business associate.

He walked into the restaurant and the first thing he saw was Kaylob wiping down some tables. He hadn't taken two steps, when Kaylob turned to greet him. "Hey Blake, you're early. The party isn't for another hour or so."

"No, I'm here to meet Melissa first." He glanced around. "I saw her car out front."

"Let me ask Flo." Kaylob walked up to the woman at the hosting station. Blake saw Kaylob say something to her, then she stepped so close that he had to back up. The look in her eyes told the entire story.

Blake shifted uncomfortably. Holy hell, Beth Ann was right. That woman had the hots for Kaylob. He noticed that when Kaylob turned to pick up some menus, she moved her chest right into his back and once again Kaylob had to move away.

Kaylob frowned and pointed towards Blake. He sure seemed uncomfortable.

Flo came striding towards him, with Kaylob walking behind her. Kaylob was keeping his eyes everywhere but on her. Man, she had enormous breasts and it was clear that Kaylob didn't give a flying crap. The man was in love and only had eyes for his wife. Blake respected that.

"Flo will take you to Melissa." Kaylob said.

She nodded with a glued-on smile. "Follow me." She started walking towards the back and Blake almost laughed. If she swung her ass any harder, she was going to dislodge a hip. The girl must have a big hole in her screen door or as they say, a screw loose, 'cause she didn't seem to understand Kaylob wasn't interested.

Blake hesitated a moment before he followed. "Hey Kaylob. I've been thinking. I do believe that Beth Ann is always right." He did a half shrug before trailing after the not-so-subtle Flo.

He glanced back and saw a perplexed look on Kaylob's face and had to chuckle.

He found Melissa was sitting at a secluded booth in the back dining area, looking nervous. "What in the name of Texas pie was going on?"

Chapter Thirteen

He sat down and Flo handed them both menus and brought back two glasses of water.

Blake saw Melissa fidget with the napkin. "Okay little darlin, what's up?" He saw that her brown eyes were laced with shadows of sadness.

She opened her menu. "We really shouldn't eat, because they are having a dinner, but I could have coffee."

He nodded. "Coffee it is."

They ordered and waited for the waitress to bring it to them before they started talking.

"Blake," Melissa said, her chin quivering. "I want to quit working for you."

"Can I ask why?" He took a drink of his coffee and looked long and hard, searching her face.

"Because." Tears flooded her cheeks.

Damn, had he done something? "What did I do" Blake felt awful. "Did I say something to hurt you, or do you need more money?" He reached out and touched her hand, but she pulled it away and sat there, without speaking, wiping her eyes.

She finally composed herself and took a deep, shaky sigh. "No, you've always been good to me and treated me like a little sister. I feel like you've wanted to protect me and take care of me."

"Then what?" he asked.

"Blake, I spent the last few years waiting for you, hoping you'd fall in love with me." She inhaled and more tears flowed. "But, I know now that, that, you don't and won't." She couldn't finish.

"Ah, little, darlin, you are a beauty, and I think you are really sexy. But, I can't love anyone. I think you know that. My heart was torn up and it's never going to be whole again. I loved and lost and sadly, I lost any ability to love again." He reached out for her hand and this time she let him hold it.

"I'm sorry, Blake." She dried her tears and shifted straightening her shoulders. "I still can't work for you. I need to move on. I want to love someone and be loved back. I can't do that working for you."

"Of course." There was no choice but for him to understand. He felt sad because he did love her, just not the way she wanted. "When do you want to leave?"

"As soon as you can spare me. I know Dana only works for you part time now since she got a job at court reporting. I don't want to leave you in a bind."

"I have someone that fills in on the days Dana is gone and hey, I can find someone to take your place," he said. "But Melissa, I will miss you and I'm grateful for all the support you've shown me over the years."

"How soon can I leave?" she asked, then sipped her coffee.

"Whenever you're ready." He laid down his napkin.

"Can I leave right away? Like today?"

He nodded. "Yes, I can call the agency, they'll send someone out."

"Thank you. Blake." She took another sip of her coffee. "Could you tell Beth Ann and Kaylob I'm sorry, but I need to get packed and ready to move."

"Wow. You're moving?" He was shocked.

A little smile hit the corners of her lips. "I'm going back home to Eureka, the small town I grew up in. I want to be around my friends and family. My sister wants me to move in with her. She's got a little house and a job for me." She stirred her coffee. "She runs an art gallery and I'm going to work in sales. She said it's really busy and she could use the help." She placed her napkin down and stood. "I'll be near the ocean again too."

Blake rose and embraced her. "Melissa, you're a special lady and someday you will meet the right man." He stepped back with his arms on her shoulders. "And he better treat you right or he'll answer to me."

She moved forward and gave him a sweet and tender kiss. "Take care, Blake. I'll get in touch after a while."

He nodded and felt a lump in his throat. It was hard to say goodbye because he was really going to miss her. After a few seconds of standing there, staring at her as she walked away, he headed to the bar.

Kaylob walked up and put his hand on his shoulder. "Hey buddy, everything okay? You look like you lost your best friend."

"Oh, Melissa just quit, she's moving back to Eureka. Said she needs a fresh start and can't do that around me." He needed a beer.

"You are going to just let her go without a fight?" Kaylob asked.

"Yeah, I love her like a little sister. I just don't have the right kind of feelings for her. Beth Ann was right. She did seem to have deeper ones than I knew for me."

"Sorry," Kaylob said. "But it might be better for her."

"Yep. Now, speaking of your wife." He nodded towards Flo. "I think she's right more than you know."

"What?" Kaylob said.

"Take the word from someone who's been around the block a hundred and one times. She's right about that chick."

"Shit, that must be why Flo was changing into her uniform when I walked in my office. I almost fell out the damn door. Shit, Blake, she was standing there with almost nothing on."

Blake could only do one thing. He bent over laughing. "Is she hot?"

"Hell no, I was too damned shocked to even think about that."

"Well, pal, I think you have your answer."

"I'm calling Frankie to see if I can fire her because of what she did."

"I bet you can. She was naked in your office and I saw her sticking her chest into your back."

"That started bad today. I thought maybe it was just an accident, but Andrea and I work in close spaces and that never happens." Kaylob wiped his forehead. He flipped around and stared at Flo. "Screw it, I'm firing her ass. I'll deal with the outcome later."

Blake watched with amusement as Kaylob walked over to Flo, said something he couldn't quite make out, and pointed towards the door. She stood there, looking like a woman ready to kill. Kaylob left, then a few minutes later he crossed the room and handed her a check. Afterwards, he darted into the kitchen. Hot chili peppers, she stormed out the door and didn't even look back.

Wow, Kaylob was a devoted husband. Blake had to smile, he already respected Kaylob, but even more now.

A while later, Blake sat at the bar, waiting for the gang to get there, when he felt a tap on his shoulder.

"Are you stalking me?" A set of blue eyes met his. A smile flirted with the corners of her mouth.

"No, but I think you're stalking me, since my friends own this place." He laughed.

"I came in to talk to the owner, Kaylob, about my bridal shower, but had to meet with someone else," Ginger explained. "I didn't expect to find you here. I love his wife's voice. I saw her in a show once in Colorado."

"What, don't you read the tabloids?" Blake questioned.

"No. Why?"

Blake shook his head. "No reason. I've known Beth Ann and Kaylob since childhood."

"Wow, how neat." She smiled and sat down.

"Want a drink? Some food? Another fling?" He stared into those hot sexy eyes and continued. "I'm up for it if you are." He trailed a finger down her cheek and said lightly, "You're beautiful."

"Hmm," she said. "A drink sounds good."

He asked Howard to bring her a glass of Chardonnay. "I saw you drinking that the other night."

"My favorite. Thank you."

Howard brought the wine and they both thanked him.

Blake lifted his glass. "To Ginger Rogers. May her life be filled with happiness and satisfaction."

She raised the glass to her lips and the minute her tongue went over the edge, his pants got a tad tighter. He needed to stop staring at her mouth.

"So, the big day is this weekend?"

"Yes," she nodded, but there was something missing in her eyes. A spark of joy, happiness, any hint of excitement.

"So tell me, Ginger. Does your fiancé make you happy?"

"Yes, of course," she answered too quickly. "I just needed to try something, and you were that something. Thank you for the wine and for last night." She rose. "I have to get going."

Blake reached out and playfully took her arm.

"Ouch," she whispered, then moved away.

"Sorry, I didn't mean to hurt you." He saw shadows cross her eyes. What was that? he wondered. He'd hardly touched her.

"You didn't." She kissed his cheek and then almost flew out the door.

Something didn't feel right. He stood from the bar and rushed out of the restaurant. He spotted her sitting in a car, so he approached. Once he got closer, he could see she had her head down on the steering wheel.

He stood back for a minute and thought about turning around. The last thing he needed was to get involved with a woman who was getting married in a few days and was obviously unhappy. But he couldn't just turn and walk away.

Why? That would be the smart thing to do, but he'd never been all that bright anyway.

He tapped on the window. "Ginger?"

She wiped her face and rolled it down. "So, you are stalking me." She laughed, but it sounded forced.

"Can I come in and sit with you for a minute?"

She nodded. "Sure, for a minute."

He walked around and climbed in the small car. Once inside, she wouldn't meet his gaze, so Blake touched her arm and gently rolled up her sleeve.

"Holy hell." It was black and blue and those weren't there last night. But he had spotted one on her hip that she said was from horseback riding.

She pulled her sweater back over her arm and looked out the window.

"He gets angry and I was late for the first cake meeting. When we got home, he showed me just how important it is to be on time."

"Why are you marrying this asshole?" Blake asked.

She didn't answer; all she did was sit there in silence.

"Ginger?" he reached over and touched her silky cheek. "You are exquisite. Why would anyone want to hurt you? Why would you stay with someone or worse, marry that person?" He was confused.

She swallowed and seem to be gathering words. "I really can't tell you, but I have to marry him and my dad really wants this and my mom too. It could be dangerous if I don't."

Blake reached over and took her hand. "But, I'm sure they'd want to know if he's hurting you. Does he do this often?"

She nodded. "Yes, often."

"Jesus, I'll go kick his ass. What a piece of work," Blake growled.

"No." She shook her head. "My parents are so excited about this wedding. I need to go. I shouldn't have said anything. I'm sure in time he'll stop."

Blake's stomach turned. He wanted to find a way to get her to stay. "Hey, don't leave. How about you join me for dinner? Or we could go be alone," he said gently. "I have a nice place not too far from here. About twenty, thirty minutes."

"I can't." She shook her head. "If I don't get back, it could get worse."

He couldn't force her, but he could do this. "Listen." He pulled out his wallet. "Here is my address, it's a townhouse. If you want to talk, get away, escape." He handed her a spare key and his address on a business card and made sure there were two of them. "Use my place. I have two guest rooms and I don't care which one you take. Even if I'm not there, or whenever you need it, you can stay as long as you want. Dana or Johnny will be around off and on...they work for me, but they are some of my best friends too. Dana is like my little sister and a real nice girl."

She held it in her hand not saying a word.

He brushed the hair out of her face and that's when he saw another bruise by her hairline.

"Jesus Christ. This guy is a monster. Darlin, tell your parents, they wouldn't want you going through this, and if they do, divorce them. Believe me, if he's doing this now, it's only going to get worse." Blake kissed her cheek and exited the car, but leaned back in the window. "You'd be safe at my place."

He stood by the door to the restaurant, watching her. She sat there holding his address and key in her hand, then started her car and drove away.

More than likely he'd never see her again, but at least he tried. Why the hell did men have to do that? Beat on a woman. He didn't know much about the pigs who did that kinda crap, but he was sure as hell going to try to learn more about it.

* * * *

Thirty minutes later, Beth Ann got to the restaurant and the first person she saw was Blake sitting alone at the bar. Just like when they were kids, she stepped up behind him, put her hands over his eyes and asked, "Guess who?"

"Let me think? Could it be Angie Dickinson with her uniform on?"

Beth Ann laughed when he turned around. "Yes, that's me and you're under arrest."

His twin dimples flashed. "Well, I just spoke to Ginger Rogers, so I'm not surprised."

Beth Ann shook her head. "How many of those have you had?" she asked and pointed to his drink. Blake had always had a great sense of humor, with just the right amount of sarcasm.

"Not enough." He took a large sip.

"Have you seen my husband?" She glanced around.

"Yep, I sure did. Last I saw him he was in a conversation with Flo. You know the tall lady with the big ones."

"Yes, I know all about her and her big things," Beth Ann sighed as she set her purse on the counter. "She's got a thing for Kaylob, but he'll have to figure it out for himself."

Howard walked up. "What can I get for ya, beautiful?" He grinned at Beth Ann.

"Seven-Up would be great. Thank you, Howard."

Blake smiled. "Well, you know that your husband has such a big heart, he rarely sees people as bad or doing things that might be sneaky." He took another sip of his beer.

Beth Ann nodded. "I know."

The thing about Kaylob was he'd always been like that. It was one of the many things she loved about him.

Howard set the Seven-Up in front of her. "On the rocks," he said with a wink.

"Thank you, handsome." She smiled.

"Mrs. O'Brien, are you being a flirt?" Blake asked.

Beth Ann chuckled, then saw Kaylob approaching. "Here he comes now, don't tattle on me."

Kaylob arrived and kissed Beth Ann's cheek. "Hi there," he said, and turned to Blake. "Who was the redhead you were talking to? She looked familiar. She seemed upset when she left and I noticed you followed her outside."

Blake nodded. "She was upset. I met her last night and I think she's in trouble, but she was coming here to talk to you about a wedding party or something."

"Ah, someone else must have handled it."

"Really?" Beth Ann interrupted. "What kind of trouble?"

"The kind where she's getting married this weekend to a man whose hobby is beating the shit out of her."

"What?" Beth Ann and Kaylob said in unison.

"Long story. I'll tell you more later, but we're here to celebrate some good news. So the baby is moving around."

"She's kicking me good." She rubbed her stomach.

Blake stared at Beth Ann's stomach. "That has to be exciting."

"Do you want to feel?" Beth Ann asked.

"No, maybe later." His eyes cast a hint of pain and Beth Ann felt bad. What was she thinking?

Blake changed the subject. "You might want to keep an eye on your wife here. She was flirting with Howard." He winked and the smile was back in his eyes.

"Is that so? I guess I should fire him too," Kaylob said.

"Too? Did you fire someone else?" Beth Ann asked.

Kaylob got up. "There's Jack and Lenard. I need to go make sure the table is set up before everyone else gets here."

Blake laughed. "Don't even ask me about anything." He stood and raised his hands. "I'm going to the restroom." He strolled off and Beth Ann observed every single female in the place stop and stare. Even the ones that were with their husbands.

She giggled and told herself *better Blake than Kaylob*. She'd already put up with Flo. Speaking of which, where was she? Beth Ann glanced around, but didn't see her anywhere. Good, maybe she had the night off.

After a few more minutes, Jack and Lenard were coming towards her, while Blake and Kaylob stood over at the table in a deep conversation. Those two seemed to be up to something.

"Look at you," Jack said. "You are glowing." He embraced her.

After she hugged Jack, it was Lenard's turn to place his arms around her. "You look wonderful, Beth Ann." He backed her up and glanced at her stomach. "You're hardly showing though. By the way, I'm so sorry we missed the reception, but we just got back in town last night."

"It's okay, you're here now and look, I am showing." She turned sideways and showed off her bump.

"You are," Jack almost cried and Lenard nodded.

"How cute is that." Lenard grinned and they all laughed.

The three of them were making their way over to the table when Carol and Shelia came in the door and headed right for her.

Carol smiled as she approached. "Let me feel that little kicker."

Carol and Shelia, both took turns feeling her baby move, while the guys laughed and carried on, ordering some beer and wine. A few minutes later all the family arrived. Gram and Nicky were holding hands and Edna and Lillian were talking to her mom and Stanley. Just seeing everyone together made her heart swell.

This was such a special occasion and she sure hoped Kaylob would be okay. He'd been so distant with everyone. When Jackie took off this morning for the airport to go home, he'd already left for work and didn't even say goodbye.

Kaylob announced, "We made up a salad bar if anyone wants some before dinner. There's crab and all kinds of fixings. Just follow me."

Jack and Lenard followed Kaylob, while the rest of them took a seat. Blake stayed put, drinking his beer, but there was no missing the look that passed between him and Carol.

"By the way," Blake said, "Melissa won't be here tonight. She's moving back to Eureka and stopped working for me today."

Beth Ann couldn't believe what she was hearing. "Oh, my gosh, and you let her go?" Why couldn't he see how much she loved him. That made her want to shake him a good one.

Carol and Shelia rose. "We're heading over to that salad bar. We're starving."

"Okay." She watched as they strolled away, along with everyone else who appeared to be getting out of dodge. She shot a look at Blake.

He held up his hands. "Don't go there. I already told you we're only friends. Beth Ann, and you can't force feelings. You out of all people should know that. Either you have them, or you don't."

"Blake."

"Beth Ann." He shook his head. "I don't want commitment. I like being alone. I have plenty of girlfriends."

That was a big fat lie and she knew it, at least the part about liking to be alone. "Okay, fine." She blew out a breath. "Then tell me more about this lady that's in trouble?"

"Not tonight. This is a happy time."

"Look." Beth Ann crossed her arms and gave him a pointed look. "I'll leave the Melissa thing alone, but at least share with me about this lady that's getting hurt by her boyfriend."

"Fiancé," Blake corrected.

"That's awful, Blake. I hope she will be okay."

"Me too. She was black and blue, with a gash and bruise on her hairline."

Beth Ann felt bad for a woman she had never met. "That's really sad. What's her name?"

"Ginger," he said, just as Jack and Lenard came back with their salad dishes piled high. Before Blake could share any more information, everyone started showing up with their salads, so Beth Ann had to get up and go get a plate herself. She saw Lillian and her parents hanging out together. Kaylob had stayed clear. It was obvious he was avoiding Lillian and even Edna. He pretended to be busy until the three had left. Her mom and Stanley had stuck around though, and there was no doubt her mom was worried about Kaylob and was heading over to talk to Beth Ann.

"How is Kaylob with all this, honey?"

"He's not good, Mama. He is pretty angry and confused. It's going to take him a while to get over it. Plus, he has some other stuff going on right now that I can't talk about."

Her mom glanced over at him. "Should I talk to him about his parents? You know I was estranged from my mom and dad and …" She swallowed. "They died before I ever had a chance to make up or talk to them again."

Wow, Beth Ann was blown away. Her mom had never brought them up at all. She didn't even know all the details, but didn't want to ask right now.

"No, I think right now he just needs to be the one to talk about it."

"Okay. I'll see you back at the house. I'm feeling pretty tired."

As the evening went on, Beth Ann was worn out and noticed Blake was sitting up at the bar talking to Howard and Kaylob. Her husband was at least laughing with them. It was hard to see the hurt in his eyes every time he glanced at Lillian. He had finally sat by Edna once, when nobody was around, but once Lillian came back, he stood, pointed towards the kitchen and left.

The next hour, she spent with Gram and Nicky, but they were exhausted too. It was time for them to head out on the road early the next morning, they were going to the Grand Canyon.

She said her goodbyes and would be seeing them again at Thanksgiving, but of course that didn't stop her from shedding a few tears.

Since the guys were all busy talking, Beth Ann crept into the office and pulled off her shoes. Being pregnant really did make her extra tired.

The last thing she remembered was laying her head down on the desk and thinking of the stranger who was being beat up by her future husband and how cute it was to see Lisa sitting with Denny, chaperoning her on her date.

* * * *

After eight days of married bliss, Shawna awoke to the sound of the ocean and crooning of the seagulls. Frankie had brought her to Huntington Beach, instead of Palm Springs. It was a wonderful place and Beth Ann and Kaylob didn't mind that they had moved their honeymoon spot. They still insisted on paying for it. All she'd done was mention that she missed the sea, and Frankie had changed their reservations.

She peered over at her sleeping husband and noticed the supple smile planted on his lips. Quietly, she rose from the bed and made her way to the window, feeling a feathery breeze brush against her skin. Oh, how she loved the salty, sweet aroma that brought visions of Ireland. The ocean had always been a place where Shawna found peace, even in the midst of a chaotic world.

"Hey," she heard Frankie say. "Where is my wife and my good morning kiss?"

Shawna turned around and had to smile when she saw Frankie's hair in such a mess. It was all over the place, with curls that covered his forehead. He was so sexy.

"I'm right here, watching the waves and the seagulls. This place is truly magnificent." She moved over to the bed and curled up next to him. "Did I thank you for bringing me here?"

"Oh yes, Mrs. Russo. You thanked me very well last night." He kissed her neck. "More than once."

"Come and see the ocean. It's spectacular," Shawna said. "As a matter of fact, let's go for a short walk before we order room service."

"I need my morning dessert first," Frankie whispered into her ear.

Tingles hit her neck and traveled to every other part of her. "Frankie."

"Yes?" he put his hand on her bare stomach and moved his fingers gently.

"Oh, Frankie, I need you."

* * * *

After a few more minutes of teasing and taunting, Frankie felt her tremble and a wave of desire rushed out to greet him. Then, a tidal wave of emotion and ecstasy pulled him under. What they experienced next was euphoria, which rippled through them at the same moment.

They stayed as one for a long time, not wanting to part. With reluctance, Frankie rolled over and pulled her with him. "Ah, you take my breath away."

"I don't think that's true, Frankie." She looked up into his eyes.

"I can promise you do, and why would you think you don't?"

"Because, I would say you were breathing just fine. As a matter of fact, I thought you were going to hyperventilate." She giggled.

"Mrs. Russo, you are a funny lady."

She smacked his bottom and ran into the shower.

He was right behind her and thought maybe he'd just take that naked wife of his over his knee. That might be fun. Frankie grinned at the thought.

Later that day, as they strolled hand in hand near the ocean, Frankie saw a lady that looked sad and stared at her. He wondered why some pretty redhead would look so forlorn and all alone on the beach.

Shawna gave him a sidelong glance. "Should I be jealous?" She followed his gaze to the redhead.

"No, of course not. Look at her. She appears to be crying," he said.

Shawna peeked over. "Oh, Frankie, you're right." Her face fell. "Should I go talk to her?"

"No, but it reminds me of the way Beth Ann looked when Kaylob was missing, and then when he was pronounced dead." He shook his head. "I thought .... we all thought .... we were going to lose her."

"How awful." Shawna came to a standstill and studied Frankie. "Did you and Beth Ann ever? You know, get together in any way? I mean I'd understand because you both went through a horrible loss."

"No, we never did. I think it crossed our mind for a minute. She offered once, because she thought it was what I wanted." He sighed. "But I told her I'd rather have her whole heart as my best friend, than half her heart as her boyfriend."

"Oh, my." Shawna placed her hand on her heart. "That's a sweet thing to say."

"Funny," he laughed. "Beth Ann told me that was the sweetest thing I'd ever said to her and she cried."

"Wow. How wonderful."

"You know, though," Frankie said. "She kept saying she didn't want to live when Kaylob was gone." His voice cracked. "We should never feel that way."

"What do you mean? I can understand feeling what Beth Ann did."

"No," he said sharply, then realized he'd snapped, so he gentled his tone. "I would want you to live, and go on, find love again, be happy."

"I guess I understand," she said sadly.

"So please don't ever think that. If I were to ever die, I'd want you to live and love again." He touched her heart. "I'd go on living in your heart forever, but I'd want you to move forward."

He felt Shawna tremble.

"Don't worry though, I'm not going to leave you."

"Thank you," she said and held his hand just a little tighter.

They continued strolling down the sandy beach, leaving the tall redhead with the sad blue eyes behind. Frankie couldn't help but think about the pain she must be feeling. For that reason, he said a silent prayer that whatever she was going through, she would end up fine. Just like Beth Ann.

* * * *

Beth Ann couldn't believe the end of August had arrived and September was knocking at the door. It was sticky and hot, making the air outside so oppressive it took her breath away. Even more now, since she was almost six months along. She finished hanging the curtains in the nursery and heard the front door open.

"Beth Ann, I'm home."

"I'm back here in the nursery," she answered and stood admiring how nice everything looked. Frankie had given her a bad time about doing things in pink and white. He kept insisting that the baby could be a boy and said a boy wouldn't want pink.

Frankie and Shawna were home from their honeymoon and as happy as ever. They got their kitty cat from Wanda at the animal rescue and Goldie loved her dearly. The cat and dog were fast becoming best friends. Frankie was working at the new law firm and was gone long hours. Shawna was working too, but would putter while waiting for Frankie to come home. Beth Ann would swear Shawna had it almost as bad as she did.

"Hi," Kaylob said, walking in, holding an envelope. "This was out in the mail and it's the results."

Beth Ann's legs got weak and knew this was the moment of truth. Would their life change forever?

Chapter Fourteen

"Do you want me to open it?" Kaylob asked, with fear in his eyes.

Beth Ann nodded and swallowed the lump in her throat. "No matter what, we will be okay. We have plenty of room to take him in and we will love him." She smiled and meant it.

He slowly opened up the letter and unfolded the official looking form.

Beth Ann's heart raced as she watched his face. "Kaylob," she whispered.

He sighed and ran his hand through his hair, just staring at the paper.

Oh my gosh, he's the father. She took a deep breath and prepared to be brave and strong for him. "It's okay, honey, we can get one of the spare rooms decorated and make it really nice."

"No," he shook his head. "I'm not the father." He scooped her up in a hug. "I feel so bad and guilty. I was not prepared to be a father to a teenager I've never met. However, I would have done it if he were my son. I sure as hell wouldn't have let him go through what I have. The boy could be damaged for life. I mean, think about it, he's losing the only parent he's ever had. He'll need someone to step up to the plate." He kissed her neck and stepped back. "I need to call Dusty."

Beth Ann nodded in agreement. "I hope his father will do the right thing."

"Me too." Kaylob said and took her hand. "Let's go call. I want you on the other line."

Beth Ann nodded.

Kaylob dialed the phone number that was on the letter and Beth Ann picked up the other line.

The phone rang and eventually a woman's voice, sounding tentative, answered. "Hello?"

"Hi, Dusty, it's me Kaylob." He sounded nervous.

"Hi, Kaylob, it's so nice to hear from you."

"Beth Ann is on the other line, only because I asked her to be."

"Hello, Beth Ann." She sounded sweet.

"Hi Dusty."

There was a moment of awkward silence, which Dusty broke. "Anyway, I know you're not Tylor's dad. I got a call from Larry today and he's a match. He is going to come and meet with Tylor and start taking him for visits while I'm still here." Her voice trembled.

Beth Ann felt tears building. This was just too sad. She needed to get off the phone.

"Dusty," Beth Ann whispered. "Is there anything we can do?"

"That is very sweet," Dusty said. "But everything is going to be fine. Larry has a good job as an engineer and his wife is excited to meet Tylor. She's never been able to have a child, so this must be God's plan. I had him for thirteen years and now they will have the pleasure of being parents to him. He's truly wonderful."

A huge wave of emotion ran through Beth Ann. "I have to go let Goldie, our dog, out," Beth Ann said, trying to keep her voice strong. "You're in my prayers Dusty."

"Thank you so much."

Beth Ann hung up the phone and heard Kaylob continue talking. She reached down and felt her baby girl and a pang of grief hit. The sadness of leaving your child had to be heartbreaking, something Beth Ann didn't want to imagine. Besides losing a child, what worse pain could there be?

* * * *

Shawna stood in the kitchen, admiring how wonderful everything looked. The remodeling and redecorating was very close to being done. She called for her new Siamese baby. "Sasha. Here kitty, kitty." She opened up a can of food and tapped on the can.

"Meow." Sasha came in the room and stretched, then slowly went to the food, purring like a little engine. She was such a sweet girl, with pretty blue eyes. The new pink collar looked adorable and the little bell jingled when she pranced around.

Shawna had always loved cats. To be honest, she loved all animals.

Someday they'd more than likely get a pup too, but with Goldie and Sasha being best buds, it was like they had a dog already. Goldie would come to the back door and bark for Sasha to come play. They would roll in the grass and sleep next to each other. It was so sweet.

Funny, Sasha was nothing like Goldie. When you said food to Goldie, she would run to her bowl and sometimes put the whole thing in her mouth. One time she carried it out to the living room, dropping it on the floor and barking. She and Beth Ann had both laughed so hard that their sides hurt.

Shawna opened her bag from the mall. She had bought new light yellow place mats and matching napkins. Frankie loved the color of the kitchen now. It was light yellow with white crown molding. The counter tops were a speckled tile and the floors matched. It was truly gorgeous.

She smiled as she glanced around. Frankie was getting off early today and she had some big plans for him. A romantic dinner with her wearing her new nightie after they ate. That would be his dessert. She went over and opened up the box and held it up.

"Ooh la la. This should drive him wild," she said to the sheer baby doll with crotchless panties. She'd never worn anything like that, and she hoped nobody had done that for Frankie either.

Actually, Beth Ann had shown her a pair that she had bought when the new Fredricks of Hollywood store first opened in the mall. Obviously, Beth Ann hadn't thought before she had confessed that they had driven Kaylob wild. When it occurred to her that she'd said too much to his little sister, Beth Ann had blushed.

At first Shawna was a little shy about walking into the store. Even so, she had wanted them so much that she waltzed in and picked them up. There were many other ladies there smiling and holding up all kinds of sexy lingerie.

Shawna placed the nightie back inside the little box and set it on the kitchen chair. Then she set the candles on the table. Tonight she was cooking Steak Diane with steamed potatoes and asparagus. It was one of Frankie's favorites. The last time she'd cooked it for him was the second night home from their honeymoon. That evening had been so much fun. They had waited until Kaylob and Beth Ann had turned off the lights and gone to bed. Then she and Frankie had gone skinny dipping. Frankie had done things to her in the water that made her see heaven. Not only had they made love twice in the pool, they had made love again when they went to bed.

What touched her heart even more were the words Frankie had whispered as they lay in each other's arms.

"Shawna, my love, what we have is so powerful that my heart explodes each time we make love," he murmured. *You are everything to me. I always dreamed of having love like this, but I didn't know how magnificent it would feel.*

He had secured his arms around her, then nuzzled close to her neck, drifting off to sleep. That night as she listened to his soft breathing, she had cried tears of joy, love, and happiness. She was over the moon just thinking about growing old with him.

The other exciting part was they had stopped using protection. Shawna hadn't told anyone, but when she got pregnant, she planned on shouting it to the world.

They had talked about waiting, but the truth was, they didn't want to wait. They wanted children and more than one. Maybe three or four. They would have to build onto the house, but that was okay too. Frankie was supposed to get a good size check this week from the electrician, because it ended up being the guy's fault. She just wanted to put Frankie on the title for the property, but he wanted to put money towards it. He was paying all the bills for the remodel and wanted to pay for the driveway and a new tile roof. He wouldn't let her do anything until he paid for those things. Her husband was a stubborn man.

As she put the finishing touches on the table, her heart skipped extra beats, just anticipating their night together.

Once she pulled down the plates and got the pan out, the phone rang.

She knew it was Frankie, saying he'd be there any second. He did that almost daily.

"Hello?" she said, brightly.

"Shawna?" a female voice said.

"Yes, this is she."

"This is Dana, Blake's housekeeper. Well, part-time housekeeper. I tried to call Kaylob and Beth Ann but their phone is busy."

"I can get a message to them."

"No," Dana said, and sounded odd.

"Is something wrong? Is Blake okay?" Shawna asked.

"Yes." She sounded nervous.

"What is it then?" Shawna asked again. "You're scaring me."

"I work as a court reporter and well, there's a hostage situation over here at the courthouse. You might want to turn on your TV."

"Court house?" She felt the room spinning. "Does this involve Frankie?"

"Yes, I'm sorry Shawna. But he's in the courtroom where it's happening. There have been gunshots fired. We know some people are wounded, but we don't know how bad."

Shawna dropped the phone and ran with every bit of strength she had to Beth Ann and Kaylob. Without knocking, she ran into their house crying. "Kaylob, Beth Ann!"

"What?" Beth Ann must have heard the panic in her voice because she came running. "What's wrong? Where is Goldie?"

"Out in the backyard, laying in the sun waiting for Sasha." Shawna started to cry and a pain ripped through her heart.

"Then what has you so upset?" Beth Ann reached out and gently held her arm. "What is it, sweetie?"

"Frankie is at the courthouse and there has been a shooting." She tried to catch her breath, then said, "Dana called and said he's in the room where the shots have been fired. Some guy is holding everyone hostage and some have been injured."

"Kaylob," Beth Ann yelled. "We need you, now!" Shawna heard him hang up the phone, then he came tearing into the kitchen. "What's the matter?"

Beth Ann filled Kaylob in on everything and Shawna watched his face pale.

"Let's go turn on the TV," Kaylob said, and they both guided Shawna into the family room.

* * * *

Beth Ann took Shawna's hands and turned her around. "He is going to be okay. I know it." She wished she really did.

"Okay," Shawna said, but the flood of tears that trailed down her cheeks said otherwise.

They all sat on the couch, flipping through the stations, trying to hear everything they could about the incident.

The phone rang and made Shawna jump. She was clearly full of nerves. Kaylob jogged over to pick up the receiver.

"Oh, hi Dana. Any news?" He paused, listening to what she said, then he turned to face them and cupped his hand over the mouthpiece. "They just got off the phone with the police and they know a judge has been gunned down. They don't know if he's dead, but the shooters are demanding a van and are taking some hostages."

Beth Ann covered her mouth as Shawna stood, but she needed to stay calm so she helped Shawna sit back down and squared her shoulders.

Before she could take a breath, the doorbell rang. She touched Shawna's arm and whisked into the formal living room to answer it.

Johnny and Blake stood on the front step, looking out of sorts.

"Blake, Johnny. Hi," said Beth Ann, glad to see them.

Johnny's face was etched with worry.

"Dana's on the phone with Kaylob now." She opened the door and Johnny brushed past her, rushing into the other room.

Blake met her gaze with a worried look. "You okay, darlin? We heard about it on the radio and were in the car heading back from Riverside."

Beth Ann nodded and pointed towards the other room. "Shawna's a mess. Frankie was in that courtroom where the shooting took place."

"Jesus. That we didn't know, we were worried about Dana and wanted to use your phone. We were just down the street." He looked sick as they headed into the other room.

Johnny was just hanging up the phone with Dana. "She'll call us back if she hears anything else."

The next hour dragged by and the men paced. Shawna fell silent just staring out the window.

Kaylob glanced at Beth Ann. "I'm going to make some coffee after I take Goldie for a walk. She's a little stressed. Where's the big coffee maker?"

"It's in the mud room, in the lower cabinet, next to the door."

He nodded and left the family room. When he returned, about twenty minutes later, he was carrying coffee on a tray in two carafes with mugs and all the condiments.

Everyone headed toward the coffee and started filling their cups. It seemed to be a welcome distraction. All except for Shawna; nothing could pull her eyes away from staring out the window. Unless it was a report on the TV.

A little while later the news showed the hostages being led into a van. They were so far away that it was hard to see. The newscaster reported that a judge had been killed and that six people, jurors and attorneys, were taken in the van.

Shawna, let out a gasp. "I think the last one walking was Frankie. It looked like a pinstripe suit," she cried. "That's what he was wearing today."

Kaylob stood by her. "Honey, the camera man was so far away, it's hard to tell." He led her back to the couch and they sat down. "It's okay, Shawna, he's going to be alright." He soothed and took her hand.

Goldie stayed by Shawna's side and laid her head on her lap. Shawna kept touching her head and stroking behind her ears. In some ways, the dog seemed to comfort her.

Beth Ann touched her stomach and knew she needed to call Frankie's family. His mom and dad might not even know. But what could she tell them? All she knew was he'd been in that courtroom.

"Kaylob, Shawna, should I call Frankie's parents?"

Shawna took a breath. "Frankie wouldn't want to worry them and besides, they are traveling and I have no idea how to reach them. They are living in their motorhome right now. Since his dad retired, they have been traveling all over. They usually call us when they get to each stop." She wiped away a tear. "They are coming for Thanksgiving." She looked at her wedding ring morosely. "He has to be okay. We have our whole life ahead of us and I love him. He's my best friend."

Kaylob stood and walked over to the window, gazing out. Beth Ann couldn't help but wonder what his thoughts were. Did he believe that Frankie would be okay?

Beth Ann glanced across the room and saw that Johnny was reading a magazine and Blake was standing by the window as well. They were being awfully quiet, like they were trying not to intrude.

Beth Ann nodded. "He will be, I promise."

Goldie let out a whimper, like she knew Shawna was crying. She was such a good dog.

Kaylob turned and said to his sister, "Remember, Beth Ann is always right." He was trying to ease her tension, but nothing worked.

The television was playing commercials and had just started back into some daytime soap opera when the news reporter broke in. "We interrupt this program again with an update of the hostage situation at the courthouse in Riverside. There has been a big shootout and some people have been injured. Our latest report is that some of those people have been killed. We will return as soon as we have more information."

The phone rang again and Kaylob crossed the room and answered it. "Hi Dana, yes, he's here. Any news?"

He listened intently, his face grave, pacing in a tight circle around the phone.

"We saw that on the TV. Any names? One attorney? One judge and some of the kidnappers. Okay, thanks, here's Johnny."

Shawna didn't look up. She just sat there. It was already three and no word on Frankie. The knot in Beth Ann's throat sank down to her stomach. What Shawna was going through was something Beth Ann understood. It's like sinking into a black hole and trying to breathe. The look in her eyes was way too familiar.

For that reason, she knew all they could do is keep faith that Frankie was okay and support Shawna. When Kaylob was reported missing, they had given up on him way too soon. That had hurt Beth Ann. No way would she do that with Frankie.

Beth Ann knew everyone needed to eat, so she busied herself in the kitchen, heating up the homemade chili and making sandwiches.

Blake came in the kitchen. "Can I help?"

"Sure, how about getting the smaller plates, bowls and napkins." She pointed to the cupboard.

He started gathering the dishes while she got the sandwiches all together.

"Blake, did you ever hear from that lady? The one whose husband was beating her."

"No, never heard from her again."

She saw a hint of disappointment.

"Did you like her?"

"I didn't know her all that well, but she seemed nice."

Beth Ann sighed. "I hope she's okay."

He nodded. "Me too."

They got the sandwiches all done and started putting them on a plate when she heard Goldie bark and the front door open.

"Let me go see what's going on. That's the first time Goldie has left Shawna's side."

Beth Ann walked into the formal living room and saw Frankie standing there, casual as can be, scratching behind Goldie's ear.

"Hi," he said lightly to Beth Ann.

"Frankie?" Her lip trembled as a few tears trailed down her face. "You need to go to your wife."

He embraced her, then leaned down and kissed Beth Ann's cheek. "I love you too."

She touched his face. "Thank God you're safe."

Beth Ann spotted Blake coming out of the kitchen with the sandwiches. His smile spread and his twin dimples flashed.

She followed Frankie into the family room, where Shawna was standing once again, staring out the window, her back to everyone. When Kaylob saw Frankie, his eyes got wide and the room went silent.

Frankie stood behind Shawna for a few seconds, but she was so lost in her worry she didn't notice. Finally, Frankie reached out and touched her elbow. "Honey, I'm home." At that point, everything seemed to happen in slow motion. Shawna turned and threw her arms around her husband.

She buried her face in his neck. "Frankie. Oh my God, I love you." Her knees buckled. He steadied her, but she couldn't stand, so he lifted her into his arms. She hung on for dear life and Frankie used his shoulder to wipe away his tears. Take me home, Frankie," she sobbed.

"Thank you, everyone. I was safe. They didn't even know I was an attorney. Most of us made it out okay. I'm sorry I worried all of you, but I couldn't get to a phone. I'll be back in a bit. I need to be alone with my wife for a little while."

Kaylob touched his sister's hair and walked ahead to open the back door for them. Beth Ann was dying to know what had happened, but knew the whole story would have to wait until Shawna was settled down.

* * * *

Frankie carried Shawna all the way down the path and managed to open the back door. When he arrived in the kitchen, he saw the table set and knew she had planned dinner. He decided tonight they'd order out.

He set her gently on the couch, but she refused to let go of him. "I was so scared. I would have wanted to die too."

"Don't say that, sweetie, please." He took his thumb and wiped the tears from under her eyes. "We talked about this remember?"

"Sorry, I was just so afraid, Frankie. I didn't know what to do."

"They didn't even know I was an attorney, like I said. They were mostly after the judges. They seemed to think they were worth more ransom and they could get what they wanted." Frankie kissed her forehead. "They thought I was just some guy in the courtroom because I was only there observing. Holy hell, it sucked seeing the judge gunned down." His stomach rolled at the memory.

"I'm so sorry you had to see that." She kissed his eyelids, then his nose and both cheeks. "But I'm so happy you're home."

"Me too, sweetie, me too. I just wanted to get home to you. They wouldn't let us leave for hours and I couldn't use any phones." He shook his head. "I knew you'd be worried."

"Frankie, make love to me," she whispered. "I need you so badly."

With that, he picked her up and carried her into the bedroom. With a slow, easy motion, he slipped off her clothes and then his own. Unlike any other time, they both moved slowly, savoring every moment, every touch that could have been lost forever.

When they joined together as one, they both cried and couldn't seem to get deep enough into their love. The afternoon turned into evening and Frankie called Beth Ann and explained he'd see them tomorrow morning. He needed his wife to be in his arms and she needed the same. Beth Ann seemed to completely understand and said they were turning in early anyway. The stress from the day had probably wiped her out.

He slipped back in bed and made love to his incredible wife all over again. What dawned on him was one of the most fearful days of his life, turned out to be the most unbelievable intimate moments with his wife. Beth Ann always said, sometimes good things come from bad events. Maybe she was right.

Each time they joined together, it was slow and easy, moving deeper into the smoldering love. Shawna had never cried out like she did that day, saying his name over and over. Frankie knew one thing for sure; he'd thought that their lovemaking couldn't get any more perfect, but he was dead wrong. The way they moved, never taking their eyes off each other, planted a forever seed of adoration in their souls.

* * * *

Five weeks later, Beth Ann sat in her kitchen, feeling like a blimp. What she needed was to go get some maternity clothes, but holy ugly alert, they were anything but attractive. At least the ones she had seen in some of the department stores. There was another shop she'd heard about, though, maybe she'd try there today because everything was getting tighter by the day.

She spoke to her baby. "You are eating a lot, little one." The baby shifted and she placed her hand on her stomach. "Wow," she blinked back tears, as a powerful wave of love rolled over her. Never in her wildest dreams had she imagined that, in October of 1975, she'd be feeling so much passion towards her unborn daughter.

"Hello? Beth Ann?" Shawna's voice startled her. She was coming in through the mudroom and of course Goldie ran out to greet her. Goldie loved Frankie and Shawna. They were her other family.

"I'm in the kitchen," she said. Today Beth Ann was wearing shorts and her half top, letting her belly get some air.

Goldie stood in front of Beth Ann and barked.

"What, girl?" She reached down and stroked her head.

"Hi Beth Ann, how are you feeling?" Shawna glanced at her bare belly and smiled.

"Good. Just giving the baby some fresh air." She stared down at her balloon belly.

Goldie barked again and started wagging her tail. Then she stuck her nose right into Beth Ann's stomach and started licking.

Beth Ann giggled. "Goldie, that tickles." She moved her away, but she came back and put her chin on Beth Ann's stomach.

"What is she doing?" Shawna laughed.

"Since the baby started moving, Goldie seems to be curious about what's in there." She chuckled. "She barks when she sees the baby kicking around."

Beth Ann stood, though it took a little effort. "Have you eaten? Kaylob made some wonderful blueberry muffins and I have fresh coffee."

"I would love some. I have the day off today. I had a bug or something for a couple days. I was throwing up."

"Frankie told us that you didn't want to come over because you were afraid of giving it to me. Are you feeling better now?"

"Yes, much. You know I never get sick. It was a surprise."

Beth Ann finished making the coffee and put the muffins on a plate. Shawna stood to take the muffins to the table when Beth Ann saw her turn green. She dropped the plate on the counter and ran to the bathroom.

Beth Ann stood outside the door, listening to Shawna heave, feeling amused. She had a pretty good idea that the flu was not the issue.

"Shawna, can I get you something?" Beth Ann called out.

"No, I just need to rinse my mouth."

"There is some mouth wash in the medicine cabinet."

"Thank you."

Beth Ann turned to go back to the table. That's the way it hit Beth Ann when she first got pregnant. The smell of food sometimes made her throw up and it would hit at all hours.

A few minutes later, Shawna walked in the kitchen and plopped down, pushing the muffin away.

"I guess I'm not over this bug yet," she said and lifted the coffee to her lips. "Yum, this tastes good though."

"Well, I think that you better plan on this bug sticking around for let's see, maybe the next seven, eight, nine months." Beth Ann arched a brow.

"What?" Shawna met her gaze. "Oh, my cows!" She counted on her fingers and stood, clearly excited. "I am late." She placed her hand on her stomach. "We stopped using birth control a few months ago."

Beth Ann touched Shawna's stomach. "I would bet you are."

"I need to find out for sure before I tell Frankie," Shawna exclaimed.

"How far along do you think you might be?"

"Maybe four or five weeks. I'm not sure. But," Shawna glanced down and for the first time Beth Ann saw her blush.

"What?" Beth Ann asked.

"The day of the hostage situation, Frankie and I made love so many times, I lost count. That was at least five weeks ago."

"Would you like to see Dr. Thomas, my doctor? He's a very good OBGYN."

"Yes, when do you think he can get me in?"

"Let me call and ask." She moved over to the phone and dialed his number.

After explaining to the office it was for her sister-in-law and why she needed an appointment, they got her in later that morning, due to a cancellation.

"I'm going to change and get ready, I'll be back in twenty minutes," Shawna said.

"Okay," Beth Ann agreed. "You want to let Sasha and Goldie stay in the mud room together? That way they can go in and out."

"Sounds great. I'll bring Sasha and put her cat box out on the patio. She likes going out to use it anyway."

"They will have fun together. They always do." Beth Ann turned to go get ready. Wow, if Shawna was pregnant, their children would grow up together. How cool would that be?

They arrived at the doctor's office ten minutes early. Shawna fidgeted and must have paged through at least ten magazines.

Finally, a nurse Beth Ann had never seen before, entered the waiting room. "Shawna Russo."

Shawna followed the nurse back while Beth Ann waited.

While she sat reading an article about nursing, she noticed women looking at her belly. Yes, she needed some maternity clothes and maybe they could go shopping on the way home. After a few more minutes, she thumbed through another magazine, reading the latest gossip on Blake. Stuff she knew was made up. That was something she didn't miss, all those paparazzi's and BS magazines. Blake was still being followed because of his millionaire and playboy status. It appeared as though he was back to being one of America's most eligible bachelors.

A while later, Shawna came out and waved, heading straight to the reception area.

"Doctor wants me to set up another appointment for two weeks," she said to the lady with salt and pepper hair. Once she finished getting a card and sticking it in her purse, she smiled at Beth Ann.

"I have to go get some blood work, but he's sure I'm pregnant."

Beth Ann hugged her. "That's the same thing I had to do. After you're done, can we run by that maternity store in the mall? I need some new clothes badly." She looked down at the tight shirt that hugged her belly.

"Yes," Shawna agreed. "I want to buy something too. I think I'll be wearing a maternity top when Frankie gets home, maybe pick up a baby toy." She laughed. "I'm going to surprise him."

By the time Shawna got the blood test and they left the mall, it was way past lunch time. Beth Ann had new maternity clothes in tow and had decided to wear one of the new pink empire tops that gave her room to breathe.

Beth Ann looked over at Shawna as she put the keys in the ignition. "Want to go to lunch at Café Delight? I hear it is a cute place with great food."

"Sounds fun," Shawna said and smiled.

They pulled up to the place and Beth Ann managed to roll out of the car. It was getting to the point where, at seven months, she was going to have to be rolled everywhere.

Shawna came around to her side. "You okay?"

"Yes, so long as my legs hold up." Beth Ann chuckled.

They strolled into the Café, arm in arm. The minute Beth Ann stepped through the front door, she spotted a familiar face.

"Oh my gosh! Shawna, we need to go." Beth Ann pulled on her arm.

"Why, what's the matter?"

Beth Ann dragged her into the restroom. "That girl sitting at the first table, the little blonde?" Beth Ann explained. "That's Cathy, Peter's daughter. I think the lady that's with her, is her mom. Although I've never met her." She exhaled. "I killed her father."

Shawna took Beth Ann's hand. "You didn't kill him. In a sense, he killed himself. You fought him off."

"Tell an ...." Beth Ann counted, "almost eleven-year-old that."

Shawna nodded. "I see your point. We can find somewhere else."

Just as they turned to exit, Cathy walked into the restroom and stood staring at Beth Ann.

"We were just leaving," Shawna said, taking Beth Ann's hand again.

Cathy's eyes filled with what looked like sorrow. "I know you hate me and I'm sorry for what my dad did, but I'm not my dad."

Beth Ann couldn't believe she heard her right. "What?"

"I'm not my dad. I'm not evil and I would never hurt anyone." A tear slid down Cathy's cheek. "Please don't hate me anymore. I'm sorry. I didn't know what he was doing."

"Hate you?" Beth Ann stepped closer. "I could never hate you. I thought you hated me." Beth Ann pulled Cathy into an embrace. "I'm so happy to see you again."

Shawna stepped over to the door. "Why don't I stand outside. I think you two need privacy." Shawna opened the door and Beth Ann heard her speaking to someone, who was asking about Cathy. It must have been her mom, but she didn't come in.

Cathy hugged Beth Ann back. "I've thought about you so many times, but my mom thought it might be best if I left you alone. I know my dad was a monster. I hate him for it."

Beth Ann released her and put her hands on Cathy's shoulder. "Honey, I know your dad did some bad things, but he wasn't a monster and I feel awful that I took him away from you. I never meant to do that. He was not well, but that doesn't make him all bad. I do know he loved you very much."

Cathy's eyes widened. "I can't believe you are defending him."

"I understand your dad was mentally ill, honey. That's what we heard." She held Cathy's gaze. "That means he couldn't help how he was."

"Thank you for saying that." Cathy hugged her again. "And for not hating me."

"I'm so happy that we ran into each other." Beth Ann studied the pretty girl. "I think about you often."

"Me too," Cathy said, then pointed to Beth Ann's stomach. "You look pretty and you're going to have a baby."

"I am, and I feel very sure it's going to be a little girl. I hope she's just as smart and brave as you are, sweetie."

With that said, Cathy went back into her arms and gave Beth Ann another hug. After a few more minutes, the lady who ended up being Cathy's mom came in and was thrilled when she found out Beth Ann wasn't angry or blaming Cathy.

That day ended up being one of the most healing days of Beth Ann's life. She found out Cathy didn't hate her. Also, Beth Ann had discovered something important about herself. She had truly forgiven Peter, and herself for killing him. She hadn't meant to take anyone's life, but he was getting ready to hurt her and she had to protect herself. That whole experience was put to rest and now she could breathe a peaceful sigh of release. Cathy was doing well and making good grades. It had to be God's plan for them to run into each other. They had exchanged phone numbers and agreed to stay in contact.

Later, when they arrived home, they pulled into Shawna's driveway, since it was closer to Beth Ann's back door. Once they got out, they spotted Frankie dozing in the back yard, in one of the lounge chairs by the pool.

"He's home early," Shawna said.

Beth Ann got her packages and whispered, "Let me know how it goes after you tell him."

Shawna gave her an exuberant grin and headed towards her sleeping husband.

Goldie ran up to greet Beth Ann when she stepped through the gate to her yard. She couldn't wait to try on her new clothes, but even more, she wanted to tell Kaylob what had happened.

Right now, she had to get ready. Tonight she would be singing at the restaurant and there might not be many nights of working left. Kaylob was worried she was too far along and needed the rest. Her overprotective husband was a worrywart. But she agreed with him, because lately he'd been quiet and he'd told her he felt like he was an orphan. He had made it clear, he didn't consider any of them as his parents. She was saddened he was so hurt over everything. After he told her that, she'd waited for a bit and reminded him, her parents loved him like a son. That seemed to help a little, but his eyes were still filled with pain.

* * * *

Shawna quietly went into the house and changed into her maternity top. Then she grabbed the baby rattle and headed back outside.

She could see Frankie was still sleeping, so she strolled over to him, leaned down, and kissed his lips.

"Ahhh, such sweet lips. I wonder who they belong to?" Frankie whispered.

Shawna laughed. "Only one set of lips better be on yours."

He flashed his cute dimple and opened his eyes. "I only want my wife's lips on me." He pulled her down into the chair with him. "Where were you? My last client canceled and I wanted to spend some time with you."

"I had some errands to run with Beth Ann. She had to buy some maternity clothes and I had a few things to do as well."

Frankie wrapped his arms around her, but said nothing about the top. So Shawna shook the rattle and he looked at it.

"Oh, cute, a new toy for Sasha. She'll love that," Frankie said.

Oh brother, this was not going to be as easy as she thought. So she kissed his cheek and stood right in front of him.

"So, I bought this new top today." She turned in a circle. "What do you think?"

"Nice." He unfolded himself from the lounge and pulled her close. "Anything you wear looks sexy."

How could he not notice she was wearing a maternity top? Now she had to figure out what she was going to do.

Frankie smiled. "What do you want to do for dinner tonight? I don't want you to have to cook, so how about we order takeout, or go out?"

Shawna shrugged. "I guess takeout would be good."

"How about Chinese food?" Frankie asked.

"Sure, that would be great." Shawna tried to smile.

They entered the house and Shawna laid the baby rattle down on the coffee table. There was nothing left for her to do, other than to outright tell him, but when? Before dinner, after dinner, in bed?

She watched as he picked up the phone and dialed their favorite Chinese restaurant.

"This is the Russo's and we want our usual," he said. "Chicken chow mein, sweet and sour pork, and how about some shrimp-fried rice." He picked up the baby rattle and started shaking it.

Shawna noticed him examine it, then he shook it some more. After a few seconds he scanned her and looked back at the toy. He shook it one more time, then his eyes widened.

He dropped the phone along with his jaw. "We're having a baby?"

Chapter Fifteen

She nodded and whispered, "Yes."

He turned back to the phone and said, "Just bring the food, my wife is … we're ... Oh my hell … a baby, our baby." He hung up.

Shawna laughed. "Frankie, they more than likely think you meant I was having it right now.

With that, he enveloped her. "Oh sweetie, I can't believe it. We're having a baby." He spun her around and yelled, "Yes," and pumped his fist into the air. "You are making me the happiest man in the world."

"I still need to call the lab first thing in the morning, although the doctor was sure."

The smile on Frankie's face widened. "So how far along and when is the baby due?" Frankie went and grabbed a note pad.

"What are you doing?" Shawna was confused.

"We have to make a list of everything we'll need."

Shawna laughed. Frankie had a thing about lists.

"We are pretty sure I'm heading into my second month. So it's very much in the beginning. I think you can relax."

Frankie still picked up the notepad. "Diapers, football, baseball bats, and uniforms." He glanced up at her. "Well, Beth Ann has everything in pink and white."

They both laughed and waited for the Chinese food to be delivered. When the delivery boy came, he brought extra food because the restaurant thought it was going to be a long night. Frankie tried to explain he meant his wife was pregnant, but the guy didn't speak much English. They gave the young man a large tip to make up for the misunderstanding.

* * * *

Time had passed and it was one week before Thanksgiving. Beth Ann was cleaning and preparing for everyone who was coming. Their house was going to be packed with relatives.

She heard a knock on the door and Goldie flew to the formal living room, her tail wagging. Beth Ann followed, expecting it to be Frankie or Shawna coming back from the doctor's office.

She opened the door and was shocked to see her in-laws standing on her doorstep. "Harold, Jackie, what a lovely surprise. We weren't expecting you guys until Thanksgiving."

Harold nodded and Jackie glanced at her stomach. "Look at you," she said, clearly delighted. She walked in and gave Beth Ann a big hug. Harold gave her a gentle hug and she led them into the family room, motioning for them to sit down. "Are you staying until Thanksgiving? We have plenty of room."

"No, not sure we'll be here for Thanksgiving." Harold shook his head. "That's why we're here now."

"I see." Beth Ann couldn't think of any other response to this odd statement. "Is there anything I can get for you?"

"No," Jackie said. "We need to talk to Kaylob." She glanced at Harold and he nodded.

"Let me go call him." Beth Ann went into the kitchen, let out a deep breath, then dialed his number.

"Seven Nights and Seven Roses," Kaylob answered.

"Hi honey, your parents are here."

"What? They drove all this way and didn't let us know?"

"Yes, and they want to speak to you."

"Jesus, I'll be there as soon as I can."

Beth Ann said goodbye and decided to make a pot of coffee, but before she did, she went and spent a little time talking with Kaylob's parents. This was going to be a long afternoon. She excused herself to go get everything set up on the serving tray.

After she got the coffee made and was carrying all they needed towards the family room, she heard the front door open. Kaylob walked in the kitchen with trepidation in his eyes.

"Hi, baby." He walked over and kissed her forehead, then took the tray out of her hands. She pointed towards the family room. "That was fast, did you race?"

"No, I got lucky and the traffic was mild."

They walked in together, but Beth Ann wasn't sure if she should stay. "I can go take Goldie for a walk and let you guys talk."

"I'd like you to stay if you would," Kaylob asked, then set the tray down on the coffee table in front of his parents.

Jackie rose and hugged Kaylob, but Harold just nodded.

"Okay, so let's get right to the point," Kaylob said. "Why are you here?"

Beth Ann and Kaylob both sat down on the love seat across from them.

Jackie nudged Harold and he cleared his throat.

"It's my fault that you were never told about your birth family. Your mom, uh, Jackie wanted to tell you when you were sixteen, even younger, but I forbade it."

Kaylob rubbed his hand through his hair and Beth Ann watched Jackie stare straight ahead, her eyes full of shame.

"Why? You never liked me!" Kaylob snapped.

"The hell I didn't," Harold said. "You never liked me after you spent time with your birth dad. I could never measure up."

"I was a child. How could I make a decision like that?" Kaylob's eyes flared.

"You did," Harold said and frowned. "You cried for them every time they left and you wouldn't come near me."

"I know I cried. I remember you hitting me because of it." Kaylob frowned. "You also called me a sissy pants."

"That was wrong," Harold said gruffly. "I shouldn't have let my hurt feelings wash over onto you."

Kaylob's eyes widened and he seemed to be at a loss for words.

Jackie spoke up. "We love you, Kaylob. I love you, you were the only sunshine in my dreary life."

"Is that supposed to make me feel good?" He stood. "That I was there to cheer you up in your dreary life? I had no childhood. I worked at the age of six, helping with laundry, taking care of things that my parents should have been there taking care of, instead of making me do it." He stared out the window. "I didn't get to play like other kids, because I had to cheer up my mom." He turned around and anger shadowed his eyes. "Where was my dad? Gone, missing in action, while I dealt with things no child should have to deal with."

Beth Ann unfolded herself on the couch. She was sad because Kaylob was right, he shouldn't have lost his childhood. She went over and stood close, taking his hand in hers, showing him support.

"You're right, Kaylob. There was no excuse for what we expected you to do. But," Jackie looked down and her voice cracked. "I loved you with every bit of my heart. In my soul you were and will always be my son."

Kaylob's expression softened. "I believe you. But, you're right. I should have been treated differently. But to go so long without telling me the truth. That is unforgivable."

Harold stood. "Don't blame your mom. Or even your birth mother. Blame me. I've been the idiot who didn't know how to show love and I didn't want them telling you. I broke the agreement, all because I was jealous. If you need to hate someone, hate me. I deserve it." His voice seemed to waver. "They begged and pleaded with me for years and all I ever did was fight with them." He turned and glanced at Jackie. "I'd yell and carry on. I am to blame for your mom's depression. She never got that way until I cut her off from Lillian, her best friend." He turned and walked to the window, gazing off into the distance. "I know it's too late to say I'm sorry. I don't expect you'll ever forgive me. But I'm sorry anyway, son, and just for the record, I do love you and always have."

Jackie started crying at this admission. Beth Ann picked up some tissues and handed them to her.

This was not only emotional for Beth Ann, but shocking too. Harold had just come clean with everything and said he loved Kaylob.

Harold finally turned around and Beth Ann was even more surprised to see the grief in his eyes.

Kaylob hadn't said a word, but kept looking between both of his parents. She wondered if he was going to say anything, or just walk away. She prayed not, because it was clear they both loved him. Please God, let him forgive them, she whispered inside. It would bring him peace again and she knew it. This had been going on for months.

Kaylob stood. "I need some fresh air." He stormed out of the room.

Beth Ann felt her legs get shaky. "I'll be back. I need to go talk to him."

When she walked out the back door and found him sitting in a chair and Goldie by his side, she knew he was upset.

He looked up at her with puzzlement etched in his eyes. "I don't know how to feel. So many years he never said he loved me, why now?"

"Why not now?" Beth Ann pulled up the other chair and sat across from him. "It's all come out. Maybe he doesn't want to waste anymore time with you. He's not getting any younger and you know he doesn't look well."

"I noticed that too." Kaylob's eyes held hers. "Do you think something's wrong with him and that's why he's doing this?"

"I don't know, but if he were to pass away tomorrow, how would you feel? Would you be okay with not forgiving him?" Beth Ann asked.

Kaylob went silent and stared out at the mountains. She couldn't read his thoughts or figure out what he was feeling. After about twenty minutes, he stood and held out his hand.

Once they got back inside, Harold and Jackie both glanced up at him.

Kaylob walked over to Harold. "Why haven't you ever told me that you loved me before now?" he asked. "Is there something wrong with your health?"

"Besides getting old, not that I know of. The only excuse I have is I'm an idiot." He stared at Kaylob and rose. "It's true, though, son. I do love you and I guess that, in my twisted head, I thought taking you surfing and flying kites showed you love." He shook his head. "But I know it was not enough and I failed badly, and getting older and this baby coming, I don't want to miss out anymore, but it's not just up to me, it's your call."

"I don't know how I feel right now." Kaylob shrugged. "But, I do know that I want you to be a part of our baby's life."

Jackie stood. "Kaylob, I'm so excited about the baby and being in her or his life."

"Me too, Mom," he said. "I want you to be a part of her life." He glanced at Harold. "I want you to be too, so long as you treat her right."

Harold cleared his throat. "You have my word, son."

Things slipped into silence and Jackie and Harold sat back down.

Kaylob moved over to the window and stared out for a while, then turned around. "There is one thing I know. Who I am today is a result of the two of you. I don't think I'm such a bad guy and I'm damn glad I grew up in Novato." He shot a loving look at his wife.

Beth Ann finally spoke. "I can't imagine anything different. And, Kaylob Shawn O'Brien, you are the most wonderful man I know."

He gave her a pleased look. "I had to become the man you saw when I looked into your eyes."

Jackie nodded. "Kaylob, you were always wonderful. I couldn't have asked for a better son."

"Well, I did some things you don't know about, but I wouldn't have ever met the love of my life if you hadn't adopted me." He kissed Beth Ann's cheek. "I wouldn't trade that for the world." He paused. "I wouldn't trade the days in Novato or the kite and surfing experiences, for any other life." He met Harold's eyes dead on.

"I love you too, Dad, and I love you, Mom. I'm not a hundred percent happy with everything. How I found out I was adopted is the hardest, but I'm going to work extra hard to forgive the two of you. I want our child to have all her grandparents."

What was more surprising is when she saw Harold shed a tear and say, "Time heals all wounds and I hope it can heal yours."

Beth Ann had to pull back her emotions. This was a happy day.

After everything was said, they sat down and had coffee, talking about the baby. Beth Ann and Kaylob showed them the nursery and they both looked confused when they saw it was all in pink and white, so Beth Ann explained.

By dinner, Harold and Jackie finally said yes for Thanksgiving. They even agreed to stay for the week. Beth Ann was pleased when Harold went with Kaylob to work the next morning. He said he wanted to see what his son did, and spend some time with him. That touched Beth Ann, maybe as much as it did Kaylob. More than anything, she was thrilled Kaylob had so many people that loved him, and Kaylie was going to have tons of grandparents who would spoil her rotten.

* * * *

December rolled in with the season of storms. She could hear the droplets of rain splattering against the window. The sky was filled with ominous, dark clouds. The last time she'd seen the sky pouring like this was when Kaylob had come home from his first tour in Vietnam.

November, on the other hand, had been nice. The weather had stayed perfect, but it had been busy. Beth Ann had performed at the Beverly Hills Grand Night Theater and there had been many movie stars in attendance, who were friendly and complimentary towards her singing. Most had wanted to know when the baby was due and were excited for her and Kaylob. One of the best parts was having most of the family there. She had been able to get extra tickets because they wanted to see her sing on a big stage again. Beth Ann had to admit the experience made her miss Broadway, though not enough for her to leave Kaylob and their life behind. Doing shows locally would be awesome, though.

Frankie's mom and dad were in love with Shawna and were thrilled with the news of the baby.

Beth Ann touched her heart. Gram and Nicky were like two little love birds, finishing each other's sentences and laughing about it. It was so good to see them together and they all enjoyed her show. It had been great fun.

Right now the lightning and thunder was making her nervous, but not as bad as it was scaring Goldie, who wouldn't leave her side. She heard a bolt of lightning shake the house.

"Come here, girl." She picked her up and carried her over to the couch. "You'll be fine." She gave her some love and turned up the music to try and drown out the noise.

* * * *

Across town, Frankie watched as two doctors stood around with the funny machine called an ultrasound. They had made special arrangements for it to be used on Shawna. Just the thought made his stomach churn from nerves. She seemed as healthy as a horse and had been eating well, so he wasn't sure what the problem was or why all the fuss.

The minute they were done, Doctor Thomas looked between him

and Shawna and patted her on the arm. "Once you get your clothes on, let the nurse know and she'll lead you to my office."

Frankie nodded and the two doctors left. He could see the worry on Shawna's face and he tried his best to give her a genuine smile.

They were led in silence to the doctor's private office, where they sat, holding hands. After what seemed like forever, the doctor walked in, carrying a chart.

Once he sat down, he looked again at the two of them.

"Do either of you have twins in your family?"

Frankie shook his head and Shawna spoke up. "My great-great-grandma had twins, but one died at birth," she said.

"Well, I guess it decided to skip a few generations, because you are pregnant with twins."

"I am?" Shawna choked up. "Two babies?"

Frankie felt a large lump in his throat and had to swallow it down. He just sat there nodding, until he had the presence of mind to ask, "Doctor, how hard will this be on my wife's health?"

"Well, she's at a good weight and we will need to see her often. More than likely she'll need to have a C-section, but she's young and healthy and we don't see any issues at this point." He studied Shawna. "You're a chef, right?"

"Yes, I work at my brother's restaurant."

"You'll need to cut back your hours and rest more. I don't want you working after five months, because with twins, it's double the pressure."

She nodded. "That won't be an issue. I'll talk to my brother when I get home today."

Frankie agreed. "He already wanted her to stop." He took her hand up to his lips and kissed it.

"Okay, we'll see you again in two weeks." The doc rose and shook both their hands. "Congratulations."

They both thanked him and left.

Once Frankie opened the car door, he smiled. "Okay, let's go tell Beth Ann and Kaylob. Two babies. I have to get my notepad. We have to buy more stuff. Two footballs, uniforms, gloves, bikes."

"What if it's two girls?" Shawna stood staring at him while the rain pelted her umbrella.

"Two girls. God would not do that to me," he said. "I would have to buy a gun."

"What?" Shawna crawled into the car and closed her umbrella.

He got into the driver's seat and put the keys in the ignition. "To keep the boys away."

"What about with boys? You have to worry about them too."

"With boys you only worry about one hot dog. With girls you have to worry about the whole pack."

"Frankie Dean Russo!" she scolded.

He started the car and drove off. "It's true."

Frankie and Shawna pulled up and saw Kaylob's truck was there. They were both home, so they headed straight to their house.

"Knock Knock," Frankie called out as they entered. "I hope they're decent."

"We're in the family room," Kaylob called back.

"Is everything okay?' Frankie noticed Kaylob's face appeared strained.

"Well." He glanced at Beth Ann. "Lillian called and wanted to know if she could come out when the baby is born. But Jackie and Harold want to come too."

"Mom and Grandma can stay with us," Shawna said. "We have the room and everything is all done with the house."

"Okay," Kaylob nodded. "I'm trying really hard to forgive all of them, but sometimes I still find myself being pissed."

"The most important thing is, you're trying and letting them be a part of your life." Shawna moved across the room and gave him a big hug. "I'm proud of how far you've come in eight months. Some people would have taken years or maybe never."

"I'm proud of you too," Beth Ann glanced between the two of them. "Now tell us about the baby. I've been pacing all morning."

"We don't have a baby," Shawna said.

"What?" they both said in unison and Frankie noted their eyes fell.

Frankie grinned. "We have two babies."

"Twins?" Kaylob asked.

Beth Ann stood. "That's some really good news."

"By the way," Frankie said. "When we came through the mud room

Goldie hid under the blanket and only peeked out at us. Is she okay?"

"Lightning, she hates it." Beth Ann tried to jump up and down but couldn't. "Twins. I'm so excited."

Kaylob chuckled, helping to steady her. "I bet they are going to be girls. Karma." He winked at Frankie.

"No way. Boys," Frankie argued.

Shawna laughed. "Frankie said, with a girl you have to worry about a whole pack of hot dogs and with a boy you only have to worry about the one."

Frankie glanced at Kaylob's face as it went pale. "So," Frankie said. "What's wrong Kaylob, did that just dawn on you?"

All he did was nod and all Beth Ann and Shawna could do was chuckle at him.

Frankie and Kaylob were not laughing.

* * * *

Weeks later, on Christmas morning, Beth Ann stood in the family room near the fire. It had been exceptionally cold outside, but it was toasty near the flames. Even Goldie had not wanted to go outside as much and loved laying by the fireplace. She and Kaylob were going to spend the day alone, and hadn't done that in years.

As she went to sit down, she heard a pop, then felt a big gush of water run down her legs. Kaylob was in the kitchen getting ready to put in the turkey.

"My water just broke," she yelled.

He ran into the family room, eyes wide, staring at the water pooling at her feet.

"Our baby is coming," she said, keeping her voice nonchalant after she'd witnessed his melt down when Lisa went into labor. Jesus, he'd about knocked himself out cold running into the wall.

"Our baby!" He suddenly looked a little panicked. "Let's get you to the hospital." He jogged over to give her a quick hug, then released her and practically flew out of the room

"Oh no," she whispered and hoped he would stay calm, then heard a loud crash. Before she could say anything, another stabbing pain shot through her. She had to sit down before she fell.

Crack, thump. Oh lord, what in God's name was he doing?

"Kaylob, are you okay?" she called out. No answer. "Oh no, I hope he didn't knock himself out."

After a few minutes, she managed to make her way over to the phone. Thank God for Shawna and Frankie.

"Please answer," she bent over as another pain tore through her.

"Hello," Shawna answered.

"Can you please come," she grunted. "I'm in labor and I think Kaylob might have knocked himself out."

"Oh my stars. On our way," Shawna said and hung up.

Beth Ann trudged her way back over to the couch and tried to do some deep breathing. Another loud crash rippled through the house.

"Kaylob, what are you doing?" she called out again. Goldie whimpered and licked her hand. "It's okay girl." She scratched behind her ear. "Daddy is just freaking out a little."

A few seconds later, Shawna and Frankie came rushing in the door.

Frankie sat next to her. "Where's Kaylob?" He sounded winded.

Beth Ann held her stomach, but pointed. "Back there." Goldie barked like she knew something was going on. "Don't worry," Beth Ann soothed her.

"I'll go check on him." Frankie tore out of the room, but at least he didn't run into any walls.

Shawna went down next to her and held her hand. "Remember your breathing." Shawna exhaled.

The pain started to go away, so Beth Ann took a long deep breath.

"Well, this is it. Our baby girl is making her way into the world." She glanced down at her wonderful dog. "Goldie's excited. I think she might know."

Shawna gave Goldie a scratch behind her ears. "My niece is on the way and Goldie is excited to be getting a human sister."

A few minutes later Kaylob came roaring into the room with a suitcase and wide eyes. "I'm getting your stuff in the car," he said, leaning down to kiss Beth Ann's head again.

She winced and bent over. "I think the pains are really close together. About five or six minutes apart."

"What can I do?" Shawna asked.

Kaylob's eyes grew wider. "Oh baby, should I call an ambulance?" His face dripped with sweat and worry flooded his eyes.

"No! Owweee! This is a big one," she cried and held her stomach.

Kaylob's hands trembled. "Let me get your suitcase in the car, then I'll carry you."

He picked up the suitcase and started to tear out of the room, but tripped over the throw rug and down he went with a thud.

"Shit, I'm okay." He jumped up and headed out again, almost forgetting the suitcase. "I got it. I'm fine," he said again, holding it up. Once he finally got going, Goldie was on his heels barking like she was scolding him.

Beth Ann glanced at Shawna and even though she was in pain, they both howled in laughter.

Frankie came out and looked around. "Where's Kaylob and what's so funny?" He held up a bag.

"Oh, he just slipped on the rug and hit the floor. He's okay." Beth Ann was still chuckling.

Frankie shook his head. "He asked me to grab the diaper bag, but he pointed to the wrong closet. I was looking everywhere and when I turned around, he was gone. Is this a diaper bag?"

Beth Ann nodded. "Yes."

"I don't know if it has everything you need." He handed it to Beth Ann. "You want to check?"

Beth Ann looked inside. "Everything is here." She frowned. "Kaylob went out to put my suitcase in the car. He's taking too long. I hope he didn't fall down and crack his noggin."

Frankie laughed. "Let me go help. I might have to turn the hose on him." Goldie barked and ran to the front door. A few seconds later she was back, right by Beth Ann's side.

Beth Ann held Shawna's hand and another pain rippled through her. "I guess I better get to the hospital because now…" She glanced at her wrist watch and felt stressed. "They are like less than five minutes apart. We need to get Goldie's bed ready and make sure she has a bone and fresh water."

Shawna stood. "Do you want me to get you a glass of water or ice? I can do that, then get Goldie all set up."

"No, I'm okay for now. Just make sure the doggie door is open."

"Okay." Shawna took off towards the mud room and called Goldie.

Beth Ann kept an eye on the time and noticed four minutes and twenty seconds had passed, when another pain hit.

In the next instance, Frankie came tearing into the family room. His look was one of confusion.

"What?" Beth Ann asked just as Shawna re-entered the room.

"He's gone, along with the car." He placed his hand on top of his head. "Where the hell did he go? I thought maybe he went to get gas. But, why would he do that without telling us?"

Beth Ann sighed. "He went to the hospital. He'll be back in about," she glanced at her watch once again. "Ten or fifteen minutes, unless he figures it out on the way and depending on how much traffic there is. It's not far from here."

"What, are you serious?" Shawna said.

"Holy hell, I should have turned the hose on him," said Frankie.

"He was panicking and forgot I wasn't in the car. He'll be back." She shook her head.

"Shit." Frankie paced, waving his hand all around while mumbling curse words, looking just like an Italian. "Should I go ahead and take you?"

"I think I can wait, but if he takes too long, then yes. You might need to take me."

The three of them waited and Beth Ann kept track of her pain for the next ten minutes. They would roll over her like a freight train, every four minutes.

Frankie was pacing and Shawna held her hand. Every now and again Shawna would touch her own stomach. Soon enough, she'd be going through the same thing and Beth Ann would be there for her, every step of the way.

"Oooh, craaap." She bent over. "This one is bad." Beth Ann was crying from pain.

Frankie moved to her side. "Let's get you into the car."

"Please Beth Ann, I'm worried," Shawna begged.

Beth Ann nodded and knew they were right. She needed to get to the hospital. They both helped her stand. "I don't know what I would have done without the two of you."

Just as they got to the front door, Kaylob pulled up in the driveway. He hopped out and was making a mad dash towards them, his face frantic. "I'm so sorry, Beth Ann, please forgive me."

"You went to the hospital, didn't you?" Beth Ann asked with a grin.

Frankie was on one side and Shawna on the other, helping her stand.

"Yes." He stepped up and scooped her up in his arms. "I'll carry you. How did you know?"

Beth Ann laughed. "I saw what happened with Lisa and I just knew." She wrapped her arms around his neck and kissed his cheek. "My strong, brave husband. Are you okay? I heard you crash into the wall in the bedroom."

Kaylob gave her a shy smile as they reached the car door. "The bunny slippers tripped me up and I hit the wall."

"Uh oh, they are really out to get you." She shook her head. "They already gave you rabies once."

"Rabies?" he gave her a confused look.

"Remember when you had foam all over your toe? The bunny slippers tripped you up then too, when you hit your head? Oh … that's right, it was toothpaste." She giggled harder, but another pain hit just as he slid her into the car.

Frankie interrupted their banter. "We'll take our car and meet you guys there. Kaylob, you will make it to the hospital, right?"

"Funny, Frankie." Kaylob shook his head. "Of course. The nurses are waiting for us. They might be waiting with a straight jacket, though."

Beth Ann laughed in spite of the ordeal. Her husband was a funny man.

Kaylob buckled her in, then climbed inside. Beth Ann glanced over at him.

"Kaylob."

"Yes, baby."

"Just breathe." She showed him how.

* * * *

Blake didn't know what to do with himself when he woke that Christmas morning in Palm Springs. Everyone he knew was busy with family or with their wives and husbands. He'd always spent this day with Dana, but this year she was meeting Johnny's family, who had all flown in and were having a big get together at Johnny's house. They'd invited him, but he'd passed it up. This should be Dana's time to get to know her future in-laws. Dana had been worried about how he would spend the holiday, but he had lied and told her he'd be spending his day with a lady he'd met.

His love life was to the point where nobody asked their names. Why? Because it was always a new one. Although, for the last few months he hadn't seen many ladies at all. The truth was, he'd take them out for dinner and that was it. He had gone to bed once with one of his regulars, but there had been no emotions, and so therefore, there had been no heat.

Dana had made him some of her Christmas stew and that was always good stuff. She'd also left him a couple gifts. He figured he'd spend the day eating stew and opening up some of the presents he'd received.

That was okay. A lot of people spent the holidays alone. Right? He turned on the radio and Elvis sailed out, *Blue Christmas*. Crap, that certainly wasn't the song he wanted to hear. He tried switching the station until he came to *Rocking around the Christmas Tree* by Brenda Lee. Now, *that* he could listen to.

Blake puttered around downstairs for a bit, then finally went to the artificial tree that Dana had put up and grabbed the gift from Beth Ann and Kaylob. He felt his heart sink.

"Knock it off," he said out loud to nobody. Every damn year at Christmas he got a little sad because at one time he and Beth Ann had been planning their life together. The wedding was supposed to have been in February. That, of course, never happened because Kaylob had turned up, very much alive.

How would it have been to live his life with someone who never really loved him the right way? Besides, the most important thing was that Kaylob had made it home. He was happy about that. They were some of his best friends and he cared about them. He'd always have deeper feelings for Beth Ann, but that was okay, because she was right where she belonged.

He sat on the couch and slowly opened the present. It was a picture of the three of them standing by his birthday cake. He had a smear mark of chocolate on his lips and his white shirt. Good night, he laughed when he read the words on the frame, *Miracles can happen*. The bottom, read *Friends Forever*.

They were trying to say he was a neat freak and he knew it was true. Everything in Blake's life had to be in order. Beth Ann had even made up a song once about his packing. He laughed, remembering her singing it to him.

He'd painted his life the way it was. But enough of this cowboy pity party. He wasn't going to sit around on Christmas Day feeling sorry for himself. Maybe after he opened his gifts and had a big bowl of Dana's delicious stew, he'd go out and perhaps get lucky. Something had to be open.

Then, oddly, he thought about what his life might have been like if he had got together with Melissa. No, he couldn't even go there. It's better to be alone, than marry or be with someone under the pretense of love. Besides, she deserved better than that. The bottom line was, no commitments, no ties, and no love. He'd made that rule and he was sticking to it.

Just as he got up to go make some coffee, the doorbell rang. Who the heck would that be on Christmas? Oh, he bet it was Dana, checking on him before things got crazy. But that was odd; she never used the doorbell.

He got to the front door and swung it open. A set of blue eyes locked onto his, and he shook his head to see if he was imagining things.

"Hello Blake," the redhead on his doorstep said. "I know it's been months, but you told me once that if I ever needed a safe place, I could come to you." She held up the card, as if he could forget giving it to her, and glanced around, shivering. "I need that place."

He stepped back, his heart feeling a mixture of sorrow and excitement. Sorrow it had come to this and excitement that something so utterly unexpected and enjoyable had happened on Christmas Day.

"Come in."

She seemed a little unsteady so he took her elbow and started to walk her inside. Just as she stepped across the doorjamb, her eyes rolled back in her head and, damn, she was falling. He scooped her up in his arms and carried her to the couch.

Lord almighty, what should he do? Call an ambulance. He listened to her breathing. She was still alive, thank God for that. He adjusted her and glanced at her neck. Jesus, Joseph and Mary, someone had tried to choke her. He couldn't believe what he was seeing, so he pulled her shirt open a tiny bit more. "Holy hell, she's covered in bruises."

That was it, he needed to call the police.

Her eyes started fluttering, "Blake, I'm sorry."

"It's okay, darlin, I'm calling for help."

"No, please don't. He'll find me," she pleaded weakly. "He would kill us both."

This was not the Christmas Day he had planned. He thought it was going to be a boring and lonely day. What he hadn't expected was for a woman he had met months ago to show up at his door, beat to hell.

"Ginger, I need to get you help. You're hurt badly." He felt horrible.

"Blake, I'm sorry. He'll kill me though." Her voice sounded hoarse. "Please don't call anyone."

He lifted her fingers and his stomach rolled. She had burn marks on her hands. "What the hell?"

She glanced down. "He used my hands to put out his cigarettes. I've been trying to escape for a week, but he had me tied up and told my parents I had gone to visit a sick friend." She tried to sit up, but winced at the effort. "I finally escaped when he fell asleep. He'll be looking for me."

"Ginger, you need to let me call the police."

"No." She shook her head slowly. "His brother is the police, the chief of the police. They have power and money. Please." She started to cry. "I should just leave. It's Christmas and I thought you'd be gone away somewhere. I'm sure you have people coming over." She tried to stand, but lost her balance.

He caught her and helped her back down. "I'm going to call a client who's a doctor," he said grimly. "He owes me a favor."

He moved across the room, picked up the phone and dialed.

"Merry Christmas, Adam's residence."

Blake breathed a sigh of relief that his friend had picked up the phone. The less people he told, the better. "Hi Greg, Merry Christmas to you. This is Blake Tanner."

"Well, what a surprise. I hope you are having a great day."

"I know this is Christmas, and I hate to take you up on that favor, but I have someone who is badly hurt and she can't go to the emergency room, nor can she call the police."

Greg was silent for a moment. "Do I want to know why she can't go there."

Blake pursed his lips. "I'll explain more when I see you."

"So she's badly hurt?"

"Yes, I think it's pretty serious."

"I could meet you at my private office. Nobody's there and I can be there in fifteen."

"Thanks so much, Greg. I'll see you then." He got the address and placed the phone back on the receiver.

Ginger was shaking her head. "I can't go. I already told you." She was trying to stand again.

"Look, this is his private practice and nobody's there today. We can go and be safe. I'll pay for it."

"I can't let you do that." She looked around at his townhouse and frowned.

"Darlin, do you know who I am?" He met her gaze. "This place is just temporary."

"Yes, you're Blake Tanner, your card said so and you just said it on the phone."

"I can see you have no clue about my life." He gave her a small smile. "But, let's just say, I can afford to pay."

She fell back weakly on the couch. "I'll pay you back."

"Alright, let's just go."

He got her in the car and made his way across town without breaking too many speeding laws. The last thing he wanted to do was get pulled over by a cop and have this asshole find out where she was. She had on a wedding ring so she must have married the scum bag.

Once he pulled up to the private office, he moved around to the passenger side to help Ginger out. She was pale and he practically had to carry her.

The minute they got to the door, Blake saw Greg coming to open up for them.

"Hey, Blake."

He looked over at Ginger, and though his eyes widened for a moment, clearly shocked, he kept a calm demeanor. "I'm Greg and what's your name?" He closed and secured the front door.

"Ginger," she said lightly.

"Let's get you back to the examination room." He helped her walk and while he did, his brow wrinkled.

Blake stayed in the waiting room as Greg steered her down the hall, figuring she wanted her privacy, but Ginger stopped and turned. "Blake, are you coming?"

"No, I figured you'd want to be alone with the doc." He tried to smile, but knew he didn't do well.

"Please come with me." She glanced at Greg. "Is it okay?"

"Sure," he said and nodded for Blake to follow. "We'll both step out, while you slip on the gown."

"Okay, thank you," she said, her voice trembling.

Greg opened the door. "The gown is on the table. Do you need any help?"

She shook her head. "No, I can do it."

Once she closed the door Greg gave Blake a curious look. "What the hell happened to her?"

"Her husband or fiancé, I'm not sure, I haven't seen her in months, so I don't know if she married the guy or not, but by the wedding ring on her finger, I think she did."

Greg shook his head. "I don't know the extent of all he did yet, but from her neck and those cigarette burns on her hands, I'd say this guy deserves to be put away."

Blake nodded. "I agree, but she's very afraid of him. When I mentioned hospital or police, she said her brother-in-law is the police, and got very upset." Blake took a deep breath. "That's why I called you."

Greg nodded. "I'm glad you did." He knocked on the door. "Is it okay for us to come in?"

"Yes," she replied, sounding weak. She had managed to get up on the examination table by the time they walked in. Seeing her like that almost broke Blake's heart. He'd never seen a woman beat before and never imagined anything like this.

* * * *

Blake watched as the doc walked up and touched her arm. "Sweetie, I need to take a look at some of your bruises. Do you have any other burns, besides the ones on your hands?"

She shook her head. "No."

He looked at her back and listened to her breathe with his stethoscope. "I need to do an x-ray. Are you having trouble breathing?"

She nodded. "A little."

He took her vitals and examined the bruises that covered her arms, legs and stomach.

Blake turned his head and couldn't believe what he was seeing. She was almost a solid mass of black and blue. He wanted to go kill this guy. Who does something like that? This type of abuse, or any kind for that matter, was out of his realm.

"Should I step out?" Blake asked.

"No. Stay." Ginger's eyes were fearful and she held out her hand.

He went by her side and held it, squeezing gently.

After Greg finished examining her, he said, "I need to take some pictures of your bruises. Would that be okay? I'll keep them hidden in your file, just in case you ever need them."

She agreed and sniffed, but no tears came. At that moment Blake was proud of her. To walk away from this and stay so strong, his admiration soared.

Greg snapped picture after picture, then asked, "How long has he done this to you?"

"Since we got engaged a little over a year ago." She glanced down at her hands.

"So you are engaged to him?" the doc asked.

"No." She nodded and Blake could see she was embarrassed. "I married him ..." She paused, then added, "I tried to call it off, but he threatened to kill my family and make me watch." Her voice trembled. "He said he'd kill me after he killed my mom and dad. My baby sister's away at college and he said he'd go rape her and kill her too." She broke into a sob.

Greg stooped down so his eyes were level with hers and he patted her on the shoulder. "I'm sorry that he did that to you. You don't deserve this kind of treatment. You know that, correct?"

She finally nodded.

"Good," he said. He took his stethoscope. "Can you breathe in and out for me again and try to breathe deeper this time."

She did, but Blake could see her wince. Man, the guy had done a number on her.

Blake needed to excuse himself. Anxiety clenched his chest. This guy was a worthless piece of shit and he wanted to go show him how it feels. He imagined getting Johnny, Kaylob, and every big guy he knew to go and pound on his sorry ass.

"I need to go use the restroom. I'll come right back." He managed to make his voice sound normal. "Greg? Can I use your phone? I just need to check in with my friends." He smiled reassuringly at Ginger.

"Sure, help yourself. I have to take her down the hall to x-ray anyway." He focused on Ginger. "I want to get a look at your lungs and ribs."

"Okay," she said with a shaky voice. "Thank you, Blake."

With that, he nodded and left. Once he got out to the waiting area, he walked back and forth for a while. Powerless was the only word he could come up with.

After a few minutes of burning off some steam, he went into the private office and closed the door. He exhaled and dialed Kaylob's number, but there was no answer. Next, he called Frankie's house, no answer there either. He'd call again later. He wanted to see if Ginger could stay there, where she'd be safe. They had that big guest room with a nice big bathroom and sunken tub. It was risky at his town house since she'd had his card, which had his phone number and address on it. The guy might have seen it and he wanted to keep her safe.

He made another call. "I need to make reservations. This is Blake Tanner."

Once he was done with his calls, he knocked on the door and Greg answered it.

"Good news," Greg said. "Her ribs and lungs seem to be fine, but she's got a pulmonary contusion, with no blood, and she seems to be sore, but breathing better and she can cough. I don't need to suction and thank goodness the bruise inside is mild." He glanced at both of them. "She also has a slightly bruised rib. She will need to rest for the next few days, in bed. No work and not a lot of walking. If she starts to have any trouble breathing, she will need to go to the hospital."

Blake breathed a sigh of relief.

Greg turned and gave a long, steady look at Ginger. "You should be staying in the hospital for observation."

She made a noise of protest. "I don't want to stay in any hospital."

He gave Blake a questioning look. "Can you keep an eye on her? You don't have to stay up all night, just close by."

Blake nodded. "No problem." He studied Ginger, who looked a bit nervous.

"I want you to call me tomorrow morning and let me know how she did tonight. We will be closed, but I can come in if I need to." He walked to the sink and washed his hands. "I'm going to get you some pain pills I have here in the office and write you a prescription. Please take them tonight. They will help you sleep and right now that's what you need. Plenty of rest. Not just for your lungs, but for your entire body."

"Okay," she said softly.

"Ginger," the doc said and touched her arm. "You need to get away from this man. Any guy who would inflict this kind of damage to his wife, and make the threats that he did, is sick and dangerous."

She nodded. "I know. I left with almost nothing. I grabbed my overnight bag which has a few things in it, but only a few things. And some hidden cash. I can pay you with what I have."

"No, not necessary. There is no charge for this visit. We will leave and let you get dressed."

She looked overwhelmed as she sat there, blinking in the bright lights of the office. "Thank you so much."

"You're most welcome." He shook her hand. "Go ahead and get dressed. We'll be right outside."

Once they stepped out of the room, Greg motioned to move further away. "I'm going to write her a prescription for something stronger, just in case. I know she's scared, but you need to try to talk her into going to the police."

Blake agreed. A few minutes later Ginger came out and he helped her back to the waiting room while Greg got the pills and prescription.

He settled Ginger into the most comfortable seat, then asked. "Do you think he knows where I live?"

She looked stricken. "You gave me two cards and one is in my top drawer at home." She sighed. "I had them in two places so I could get to them if I needed to run."

Blake took her hand. "We'll stay in a hotel tonight. Normally, I can get security, but I let them go for the holiday. Both guys are with family."

"Blake, that's too much money."

"Stop worrying about money. If you weren't so hurt, I'd take you out of town on my company's private plane. Maybe later I can get you away from here."

"Private plane?" She seemed confused.

"I own one of the biggest real estate companies in California, with other locations around the globe. So stop worrying about money."

She swallowed. "Oh, you're *that* Tanner. I've seen your for sale signs, but they don't have your picture, only pictures of other people."

"The pictures are of my top agents." He gave her an amused look.

Greg entered the room with the medication and prescriptions. "Take these when you feel pain." He held up the bottles. "These antibiotics are for those burns. I marked down how much you should take. Here, I also grabbed some cream to treat the wounds on your hands." He handed everything to Blake, after he placed it all in a small bag. "Make sure she uses that cream. Those burns could get infected."

Blake nodded. "Thanks Greg, I owe you now."

Greg shook his head. "My reward will be to hear that this man gets locked up before he kills someone."

Ginger met his gaze. "I need some time, that's all. I have to make sure my family is safe."

With that, they both shook Greg's hand and exited his office.

Once Blake got her inside his car and climbed in himself, she took a deep breath. "Blake, I don't know how I'll ever repay you. I mean, you hardly know me and you're doing all this."

He stuck the keys in the ignition. "I don't know, I feel I know you pretty darn well." He gave her a flirty smile and saw a small grin tug at the corner of her mouth. "I only want to ask you one thing."

"Okay." Ginger studied his face.

"What's your real name?" he asked her gently.

She stared into his eyes. "My first name is really Ginger. My maiden name is Roberts."

"So you're really Ginger Roberts." He started the car and drove towards the hotel.

She nodded. "I am."

"Well, Ginger Roberts, it's a pleasure to be spending time with you again. I'm just sorry it's under these circumstances." He kept his eyes on the road. "We will be staying at the Colony Manor. I booked the largest suite they have. It's very private and has a homey feel to it. Lush gardens and private enclosed patios. You can relax and get sun without the world seeing you."

"Okay." She sat silently for a moment. "Are you sure about this?"

"Yes, darlin, I'm sure."

"It's just you're under no obligation to help me." She played with her purse.

Blake took a minute to give that some thought. It was true, he wasn't under any obligation. Even so, he liked Ginger and wanted to help her. Hell, he'd liked her from the minute he met her after Frankie and Shawna's wedding.

"I want to do this, Ginger." His eyes clung to hers. "I wouldn't have given you my card and stuck a second one with it, if I didn't want to see this through. Remember, I saw the bruises before."

They drove in a comfortable silence for over fifteen minutes before he finally pulled the car up to the hotel. It was off the beaten path and didn't look like anything other than an upscale townhouse.

"Wow!" she exclaimed, perking up. "I've never seen any place look like this." She stared down at her clothes.

"It's okay," he said and smiled. "I'll go get the key and pull around to the residence. You don't have to see anyone today."

"I left everything in my car. I didn't bring a lot, but a few things I'll need," Ginger said.

"No worries. I'm getting you settled and I'll go pick up your stuff. I'll just need the keys to your car. I'm going to park it in my garage."

"Mr. Tanner," she said lightly.

"Yes." Her eyes filled with tears and he wanted to hold her and tell her everything was going to be okay.

"You're a wonderful guy." She leaned over, wincing slightly, and gave him a kiss on the cheek.

His heart exploded with something and he wasn't about to try and figure it out. Not right now. He needed to get her to bed and go pick up her clothes. Also, he needed a few for himself, then he'd get those prescriptions filled.

* * * *

Two hours later, Beth Ann wanted to kick the holy dickens out of something. She was in a private delivery room, wondering how long this would last. Doctor Thomas, her OBGYN was sitting down at the end of the table, between her legs, while Kaylob held her hand. There was a nurse near the doctor, handing him things and she wondered if there was a knockout pill on that tray anywhere.

"You're doing great, baby." Kaylob wiped the sweat from her brow with a cool washrag, which the nurse had handed him earlier.

"Okay," the doctor said. "Push."

Beth Ann strained and groaned and gave it her all. It took everything she could muster to push.

"Good job. We're almost there." He glanced up at her.

Another contraction hit and it was the biggest yet. She felt a burning sensation, then she let out a small groan and a partial cry. "Holy midnight."

"Now, Beth Ann, push harder. This is it." The doctor ordered and she wished she could clobber him, but instead she gave it her all.

With one giant push, she strained and felt sweat dripping from her face. "Arrrrgh!"

"Baby's coming," the doctor called out. "I got her."

The baby wailed and her little voice engraved it's way into Beth Ann's soul.

"Here she is." The doctor held her up. "She's a beauty, and has a great set of lungs."

All Beth Ann wanted was to hold her baby girl.

Once she was cleaned and wrapped in a pink blanket, they placed her in Beth Ann's arms. She inhaled deeply and loved the fragrance of her newborn baby. It was hard to describe the scent of her precious child. The only words that came close was pure, sweet, and heavenly.

"Oh, Kaylob, look at our little Kaylie," she said weakly. "She's perfect." Beth Ann never understood the meaning of a mother's love until that moment.

Kaylob reached out for his daughter and the minute he took her in his arms, tears trickled down his cheeks. "My baby girl. I love you." He kissed her head and tried to wipe off his tears. The look on his face made Beth Ann's heart swell so much, she was afraid it would burst from the love growing inside.

In that precious moment with the doctor and the nurses gathered around, Beth Ann knew that their lives would never be the same.

Kaylie Maggie O'Brien weighing six pounds and twelve ounces, was born on December 25th, 1975. And what a beauty she was, their little Christmas blessing from God. For a long while they took turns holding their daughter.

Beth Ann touched her nose. "I think she has your nose, honey, and I know she has your blond hair."

"But, she has your curls and your beauty without a doubt." Kaylob grinned leaning over his baby girl.

"Kaylob, look." Beth Ann pointed to her chin. "She's got yours and Shawna's cleft."

"Ah," Kaylob said. "It sure looks that way."

Awhile later, Beth Ann was taken to her room. Of course, Kaylob wanted her to have a private one, so she did.

Kaylob sat by her bed, just watching their new little daughter. He just couldn't seem to get enough of her. The door opened and they both glanced up.

Shawna and Frankie were being led in by a nurse.

Beth Ann smiled and whispered to Kaylie. "Your uncle Frankie and Auntie Shawna are here to meet you."

Kaylob stood and hugged them both.

Shawna moved over next to the bed and took the baby gently from Beth Ann's hands. "Oh my goodness, look at this precious baby girl." Her voice was soft and trembled.

Frankie stepped closer and kissed Beth Ann's head. "For just having a baby you sure look gorgeous."

"Thank you for being such a good liar and a dear friend," she teased.

Shawna handed the baby to her husband and surprisingly Frankie acted like a pro.

He held the baby and grinned at Kaylob. "A Christmas miracle and she's going to be a little knock out." He rocked her back and forth, then kissed Kaylie's cheek. "Just look at you. I'm your Uncle Frankie."

Frankie held her for a few more minutes, then gave her back to Beth Ann. He pulled out one of his famous lists. "I called everyone last night."

He named off the names: "All the parents, every one of our friends in Novato. And all our friends here and of course everyone at the restaurant. I tried to reach Blake, but there was no answer."

Beth Ann felt content. "Thank you, Frankie."

Shawna nudged him. "Tell her about Lisa."

"Oh, right." He chuckled. "I called her from the hospital when you first got here. Per Lisa's orders. She yelled and said you better not have the baby before she gets here and not to push."

They all cracked up. Unlike Lisa's labor that lasted for more than twenty-four hours, Beth Ann's had only lasted a little over three. She was thrilled that Kaylie had actually arrived on Christmas Day and couldn't think of a better gift than the birth of her daughter.

Kaylob stood. "I need to stretch my legs and by the time Lisa gets here, we'll be just about heading home. They are releasing her tomorrow morning."

Just then a nurse came in. "It's time to let our new mother get some rest." She moved next to the bed and reached out to the baby. "We need to do some tests, just standard." She smiled and cooed at Kaylie.

Reluctantly, Beth Ann handed her over. "Okay, I'll try to rest."

The nurse nodded. "You should get as much as you can before you go home. We really would like you to stay a few more days."

Beth Ann shook her head. "No, I'm looking forward to being at home and I'll have plenty of helpers, believe me."

Everyone in the room agreed.

"Okay." She held the baby gently. "We are also going to give her a bath and get her all cleaned up for you." Beth Ann felt her eyes droop and everyone must have noticed. Kaylob gave her a soft kiss.

"I'm going to see what they have to eat. I'm starving. Want me to bring you anything?"

"Jello, if they have it." She couldn't keep her eyes open.

Frankie whispered to Kaylob, and Beth Ann barely made out what he said.

"We'll stop by and pick up Goldie and take her home with us."

That was the last thing Beth Ann remembered before she drifted off.

* * * *

The next morning, Blake woke and wasn't sure where the hell he was. Then it all came drifting back. He was at the Colony House. He glanced over and saw Ginger resting peacefully. Damn, she was a beautiful woman. He couldn't help but notice the way her curls hung around her face. Her skin was creamy with a natural blush. Somehow she reminded him of Beth Ann. It was the hair color and her curls, but it was also her skin tone. Of course Ginger was not tiny like Beth Ann. She was medium height and fuller all the way around, but the way her body filled out was nothing but hot.

What's gotten into you? He disciplined himself and knew he needed to boot his ass out of bed. The last thing she would want was him getting turned on, which he was. So cowboy, turn your brain down another trail.

The place had three bedrooms and he'd definitely move into another one tonight. This one had two twin beds, which worked out well, because he was able to keep an eye on her.

There was no way he could begin to understand what her husband had done. Jesus, he studied the marks on her neck before realizing that just thinking about what that asshole did made him steam. He quietly shrugged his covers off, pulled up his pants, put on his shirt and went downstairs to the living room. The place had an olden day charm, with all the comforts of home, and right now it offered more than his small townhouse.

It had a piano room, game room and the best part was, it was very secluded, with palm trees and plants all around. A cement wall covered in ivy and jasmine surrounded the entire back yard. Ginger could go outside and sit in the sun or soak in the hot tub and feel safe. The waterfall feature would help to soothe her. After what she'd been through, she needed it.

Maybe it would be best to just stay put for a while. The place had great security and she wouldn't have to go out until she was ready. He could get the resident chef to come and whip up meals for them. Marty was the best cook in the place, and a good guy. He always kept quiet about who was staying in the residence. A lot of movie stars loved this place, so he'd better reserve it for as long as he could. There were other suites on the property, but he always liked this one for its extreme privacy. He'd go ahead and take it for the next two months. Hell, he needed some pampering anyway. The massages they gave were out of this world.

He picked up the phone and dialed zero. "Good morning, Mr. Tanner." It was Amber, one of the regulars at the front desk.

"Hi darlin'. Can you book me in this room for two months? I'm going to be putting my townhouse on the market and I need a home away from home, until I find my next place."

"Sure Mr. Tanner. I'll book you in and put down that you may need it longer, just in case you don't find a place."

"Good idea. As a matter of fact, normally it takes three months to close escrow. You have my credit card, so just book it in for the next six months. Go ahead and charge me for the entire time. Also, please let my guest have anything she needs. I want her to feel comfortable during her stay."

"Alright, Mr. Tanner. Do you want me to add her name to the paperwork?"

"She wants her privacy, so keep everything in my name. How about we just list her as Mr. Tanner's friend, Mrs. Rogers."

"Of course," Amber said. "Anything else?"

"Please tell Carl that if my guest needs to go somewhere, I'd like him to drive her and watch out for anyone following them." He sighed and didn't want to give out too much information, but needed to keep her safe. He was going to have to hire a bodyguard for her when she was ready to go out again.

"Of course, Mr. Tanner. I will alert the manager and security."

"Thank you, Amber. Also, can I get Marty to whip up some breakfast this morning? I'll also need dinner for tonight. We can handle lunch ourselves."

"We will take good care of you and Mrs. Rogers while you're here, you have my word."

"One more thing," Blake said. "I need someone to pick up some clothes and toiletries for my guest." He paused for a minute. "Tell Lois if she'll do this for me, I'll let her match what she picks up, and I promise to give her a nice tip."

"What size is your guest?" Amber asked.

"I would say a size eight or nine and she's about five feet, ten inches tall. Her shoe size is eight. I checked it out last night after she fell asleep. I know women don't like to tell anyone what size shoe they wear, which seems a little odd." He chuckled. "So all kinds of shoes, undergarments, and any other things a woman might like. Also, I would like her to have some of the finest lotions and perfumes. I want to make sure she has all she needs."

"If Lois can't do it, I will be happy to," Amber said.

"Then, the same goes for you, Amber. If you do, you can match item for item of what you like, with a tip at the end. And don't skimp, get her plenty of stuff."

"You're so generous, Mr. Tanner."

"I try," he said before he hung up.

Blake picked up the phone again and dialed Beth Ann and Kaylob. After about six rings he realized they weren't home again. Strange. He glanced at the clock and knew that it was pretty early for them to be gone.

Next he dialed Frankie.

"Hello," Frankie said, sounding dead tired.

"Hey, I'm trying to get in touch with Kaylob and Beth Ann. Where are they? Everything okay?"

"Yes, they should be back by noon. Beth Ann had the baby yesterday."

"Wow! No kidding. Boy or girl? Let me guess. Girl."

"You got it and she's a beauty. We tried to call you last night, but you didn't answer."

"I know. I had a bit of an emergency myself. Frankie, can you come and see me today. I have a friend I want you to talk to. She's in some trouble."

"What kind of trouble?" Frankie sounded nervous.

"The kind where her husband beat her black and blue and also made threats against her family. He's a dangerous man and his brother is the Chief of Police in Riverside. Seems he thinks he can get away with anything."

"Holy shit, Blake, this is serious. How badly was she hurt?"

"The guy did some internal damage and used her hands as an ashtray."

"That's awful. Sounds like he needs to be put away. What time should I come over and can I bring Shawna? She might be of some help."

"As soon as you can get here and yes, bring Shawna. That might help Ginger feel more comfortable."

"We can't stay too long. We have to be there to help Beth Ann and Kaylob."

Blake let out a long sigh. "I'll wait a few days before I come and see the baby."

"I don't think they'll let you get away with that." Frankie laughed and added, "I'll see you soon though."

Blake gave him the address and hung up, then heard a knock at the door. He went and opened it to a smiling Marty.

"I hear you need breakfast for two." He winked and waved towards his stainless steel cart on wheels. "I brought everything but the kitchen."

Chapter Sixteen

A while later, Marty left and the table was covered with food. Blake sure hoped Ginger woke up soon and wondered if he should carry some stuff up on a tray. She might have a hard time with those stairs. He had helped her last night, but who knows how she would be feeling today. He decided he'd better check on her.

Just as he was about to go upstairs, he saw her standing up at the top. She was in a pair of white PJs, looking sleepy with her hair a mess and rosy cheeks, which were pale yesterday. Man, she was a vision of delight, even with her half-asleep eyes.

"Do you want me to help you down?" he asked.

"No," she gave a tiny smile and slowly took each step. He met her halfway and helped anyway. Her vanilla scent almost knocked him down the stairs. The minute he took her arm a herd of desire galloped through him. He needed to stop this and stop it now. She was beat up, with damage to her lungs and ribs. He thought about the bruises and burns and pulled his mind out of the dirt.

Ginger sniffed the air. "Wow, something smells wonderful. Do you cook?"

Blake laughed. "No, I barbecue meat and vegetables, and stick some potatoes in the oven. That's about it. Marty came and made our breakfast which awaits us in the formal dining area. Coffee is ready and tea too." He took her by the elbow and led her to the dining room.

"Marty?" She finally asked when they entered the room and sat down.

"Yes, he's a wonderful chef, not as good as Kaylob, but who is?" He pushed her chair in for her.

"Blake, this place is amazing, I didn't see much when we got here, because you took me upstairs and made me go to bed right away. I saw a piano, just now." She smiled. "I haven't played in so long. Is it allowed?"

Blake nodded. "Yes, it's allowed." He removed the covers from the top of all the platters. "As you can see, there is a lot of everything."

"I'm starving, and Blake?" she said, glancing at him.

"Yes."

"I'm not a dainty eater." She smiled wryly. "I normally run daily and work out a lot, so I can eat what I want. Or I used to."

"You stopped eating or working out?" Blake asked.

"Both." She looked away, clearly not wanting to make eye contact.

Blake hated to see her looking sad, so he reached out and lifted her chin to face him. "Hey darlin, you can eat all you want."

She cleared her throat. "Arnold, my husband, told me I was too fat and he would lock up the food. He wanted me skinny, but didn't want me running. He said that it would make my ..." she flushed. "Breasts sag. He also wanted me to get them reduced to be smaller. Nothing I did, seemed to please him. Actually, nothing about me made him happy. I wonder all the time why he even wanted to marry me."

Blake's eyes went to her breasts, then slowly moved up to her face. "Well, I think that husband of yours needs to be put away." He shook his head. "Not only is he an abusive asshole, but he has a screw loose if he saw you any other way than perfect."

Ginger gave him a tiny smile. "Thank you."

"Let's chow down." He picked up a fork and handed it to her.

Blake honestly enjoyed watching her eat. He hated going out with women who picked at their meal like a bird. She loved food and that was one more thing he enjoyed about Ginger. There was just something about her that was special.

Watching her use her tongue to lick the frosting off the cinnamon rolls made him have to shift around in his seat. If she had any idea what she was doing to him just eating, she'd want to flee the room.

Nothing could happen between them right now. She was vulnerable and he was helping a friend and nothing more.

Besides, he had his number-one rule: no romance, no love, and no getting tied down. Those were his rules and he was sticking to them.

"Penny for your thoughts," Ginger said, her eyes searching his face.

253

"Darlin, I'm not use to talking about my thoughts with anyone."

She laid her napkin down. "Please tell me."

Should he tell her? He didn't want to upset her, but he didn't want to lie either. He could refuse to say anything. For some reason, though, he wanted to share with her.

"The way you've been hurt is awful. I don't understand men that hurt women." He reached out and took her hand. "We are not all like that and I would never purposely hurt a woman. I did make a couple cry in my younger days, but not because I hit them or anything like that. I was just a player and fooled around, at any cost."

She gave him an encouraging smile.

"Now, before I'm with anyone, I tell them my rules up front," Blake added.

She nodded. "I remember your speech."

"Oh shit, I was toasted that night. What did I say?"

"You said, 'don't fall in love, because I don't do commitments of any kind. This is purely sex.' Then you added, *"if you're okay with that, then take off your clothes and get on your back."*

Blake could feel the heat rise in his cheeks. "I didn't say that, did I?" He felt like an ass.

She chuckled. "Well, not the clothes or the back part, I just added that to see the look on your face."

"I see." He laughed and shook a playful finger at her, which she caught and grinned.

He was glad they could play together and she seemed to trust him. After what she'd been through, he didn't want to make her afraid in any way.

"Why is it you don't want a commitment?" she asked.

"I tried that once and it just didn't work out. I got hurt," he said in a deep gloomy voice that shocked even him.

Apparently, she didn't mind because she moved her hand into his. "I'm sorry you got hurt. What happened?"

"Doesn't really matter now." He stood and took the dishes over to the sink and heard a knock at the door. Oh, crap. He forgot to tell Ginger that Frankie and Shawna were coming over.

She frowned and a dark shadow of fear seemed to loom in her eyes.

"I'm sorry. I forgot to tell you that a couple of friends are stopping by. You want me to help you go upstairs to get dressed?"

She shook her head. "I'll just stay out of the way."

"No," he shot over his shoulder as he headed to the door. "I called them over to talk to you. Frankie is an attorney."

"What?" she snapped, which made him stop where he was. "I didn't say I wanted to talk to an attorney, not today." She stood gingerly and left the room.

"Crap," he muttered to himself. Why hadn't he checked with her first?

He made his way to the front door feeling awful. He'd pulled Frankie and Shawna away from the celebration of Beth Ann and Kaylob's new baby girl.

He slowly opened the door. "Hey Frankie," he said, shook his hand and kissed his wife's gorgeous cheek.

"Wow!" Frankie glanced around. "What a place."

"Let me give you a tour." Blake motioned them in. "Can I take your jackets and your briefcase?"

"Actually, I will need my case." He slipped out of his jacket, then helped Shawna to pull off hers.

Blake's eyes went to her stomach. "Wow, very pregnant." He smiled. She was a lot larger than Beth Ann, although he wasn't a hundred percent sure how far along she was.

"Twins." Frankie placed his hand on her stomach.

"Two?" Blake looked back and forth between them both.

Shawna laughed. "Yes, two."

"Well, let's get your wife off her feet." He took their coats and hung them on the hooks.

They went into the living room and Blake switched on the gas fireplace. It was a bit chilly.

Once they all got comfortable, Blake cleared his throat. "I'm so sorry for calling you guys out today. Ginger is just not ready to talk to anyone yet. I should have asked her. She's been through so much."

Frankie nodded. "Understood. Where is she?"

"Upstairs." Blake pointed.

Shawna appeared sad. "I knew someone who was knocked around

by her boyfriend in Ireland. All of us tried to get her to stay away from him. But she wouldn't leave him."

Frankie finished. "Her friend was killed, stabbed to death," Frankie clutched her hand.

Shawna met Blake's eyes. "She was only seventeen." A tear trailed down her cheek. "She was my best friend since childhood. I still miss her."

"Sorry Shawna. It never dawned on me that this might be hard for you," Frankie said softly.

"No," Shawna spoke up. "If I can help even a little, I want to try."

Ginger entered the room. "Thank you, Shawna. I'm Ginger and I'm afraid I just panicked. I need an attorney." She met Frankie's eyes.

"I'm sorry, Blake, for acting so rude."

Ginger crossed the room and shook hands with Frankie and Shawna. "It's nice to meet you both." She then sat next to Blake. "I can't thank you enough for coming. I know I have to stop living in fear."

"I feel like I've seen you somewhere before," Shawna said.

Ginger tilted her head. "I thought the same thing about you both."

"I agree," said Frankie.

Blake reached out and took her hand. "She's been at Kaylob's restaurant a few times."

"Ah," Frankie said, then opened his briefcase pulling out a legal notepad.

Blake felt Ginger stiffen. "You okay?"

She nodded and swallowed.

"First, I have to ask this," Frankie said. "Are you okay that Shawna and Blake are in the room with us?"

"Yes," she said agreeably.

"Okay, what is your husband's full name?"

Ginger inhaled. "Arnold Reid Parker."

"Tell me everything you know about him. Include his education, where he went to school, and how you met."

After a few starts and stops, Ginger told them everything she could about this excuse of a man. Blake listened with interest. They had known each other since college and he had been charming and kind. How does someone like that change? Or was he just hiding it?

She had liked him, but hadn't wanted to get serious. From the sounds of it, her parents had pushed her. They liked his charm and money. Her family didn't have a lot of money and had wanted more for their daughter. He wondered what they would think if they saw what that monster had done.

As Ginger continued her story, Blake was surprised to find out how she had tried to break it off with him so many times during college. This idiot would beg and plead, even going as far as to threaten suicide. Once she gave in and agreed to marry him, he turned ugly.

So as far as Blake was concerned, he had more than likely always been abusive. There was no way that someone got like that overnight.

Frankie set down his notepad and looked up at Ginger. She was visibly shaken and looked pale.

"We will put him away for a very long time. You are talking kidnapping and domestic abuse. I would bet there are more women who fell prey to him." He sighed. "I would like to have him investigated. You can't be the first. Men like him normally have done this before."

"Oh, my God," Ginger said, looking shell shocked. "There was a girl before me, Katie Long, from high school. After they broke up, her parents sent her out of town to live with an aunt and nobody ever saw her again."

"Interesting." Frankie picked up his pad again and started writing.

"Rumors were that she got pregnant. But Arnold said she got in some trouble with drugs and her parents sent her to live on her aunt's farm. Nobody ever believed him and thought he was just protecting her reputation. What if they were afraid of him?"

Frankie took down the name. "We will check it out. In the meantime, let's file a restraining order to keep him away from you."

"Do we have to tell him where I am?"

"No," Frankie said. "He will not be told."

Ginger looked relieved.

"I want to make sure he can't hurt my sister. He has said he'd do horrible things to her."

Frankie frowned. "We'll need to talk to your sister, make sure she's safe until we get him locked up."

Ginger nodded. "Good idea." She sighed.

"Can you continue?" asked Frankie. "Or do you need a break?"

"Let's get this done," she said. "I've waited too long."

Frankie and Ginger continued to talk for the next hour. Frankie took notes and Ginger started remembering names of girls in college that had hated her husband. Blake wondered what she studied in college, but decided to wait until later to ask.

After Frankie had gotten all the information he thought he needed, Shawna and Ginger went into the kitchen and got some drinks. Blake was aware that the two ladies were laughing and seemed to be hitting it off. That made him feel good.

About fifteen minutes later, the two beauties returned with the pops and Blake could see a newly-formed friendship. The four sat and talked about Beth Ann and Kaylob's new baby girl and they all wondered how she knew so clearly it was a girl.

Just as Frankie tucked his legal pad back in his binder there was a knock at the door.

"Excuse me." Blake stood. "Those are more than likely some things I ordered."

When Blake opened the door, he saw three of the property's employees standing there, laden with a lot of packages.

"Thank you. Would you mind putting these items in the piano room and the food in the kitchen."

They nodded and carried them inside. At least Amber had done what he asked and bought Ginger a lot of things.

Once Blake entered the living room again, Frankie and Shawna stood. "We need to head back and get over to Beth Ann's house," Frankie explained, apologetically. "Shawna's mom and Grandma are going to be coming in from Ireland, and we have a lot to do since they will be staying with us. Everyone is excited to see the baby."

"Of course," said Blake.

Ginger tried to get up, but Shawna went over and gave her a hug.

"Please sit," she said. "You need your rest so you can heal up."

"It was so nice to meet you both." She turned to Frankie. "I can work out payments or look into a loan. I also dream of going to work when I'm better. I never had the chance to do anything regarding a job, being married to Arnold and all."

Shawna reached out and touched Ginger's arm. "Please let me cover this for you." Her eyes were shiny with unspent tears. "I couldn't help my best friend, but I can help a new friend."

Ginger smiled gratefully. "Thank you, Shawna, and I will pay you back some day. I promise."

"You'll pay me back by getting him locked up. I'd like to see every man who batters a woman put away."

Ginger nodded. "Me too. Thank you again. I don't know what to say."

Shawna smiled. "No need to thank me. You're helping me to heal my heart by doing this."

After they left, Ginger pulled herself off the couch and walked up to Blake, putting her arms around his neck. He was taken back by how close she was, but only because he felt like she belonged there. She fit perfectly.

"Blake, I'm so sorry for being short with you earlier. I hope you can forgive me."

He embraced her gently with ease. He didn't want to hurt her. "Nothing to forgive. I have something I want you to see." He released her and led her slowly into the piano room.

"These are yours." He pointed to all the packages. "I hope you like them."

"But how? When?" The look on her face was priceless. She covered her mouth and tears flooded. "Blake, it's too much."

"Open them. Please." Blake nodded towards the items.

She crossed the room and started opening up some of the boxes. With each item she opened, he heard her gasp with surprise, which deeply touched him.

"Blake, I can't believe you did this for me. They are beautiful." She touched her heart. "Nobody has ever done this before. I've never had clothes like this." She moved down on the loveseat. "How am I ever going to repay you for all this?"

"No need." He sat next to her and stared into her amazing blue eyes. Without thinking, he moved his head down and placed his lips over hers. There was no explanation as to why he did it, but he loved the taste and the softness of her mouth. She tasted like maple syrup and cloves. Jesus, her fragrance was making his head spin. When she responded with a small moan and her tongue moved across his, he was coming undone for the first time in many years. Sure, he got turned on over other women, but this was something different and he knew it.

He gently pulled her onto his lap and wrapped his arms around her. There was no missing how badly he wanted her. He had to stop before he lost his mind with desire.

"Ginger," he whispered. "I have to stop." He moved her back. "That was wrong of me. You've been through so much and the last thing I want to do is take advantage of you."

She leaned forward and put her fingers across his lips. "No, Blake." She was silent for a second. "I have thought about you almost daily. I know you are not interested in anything serious, but I think you're interested in me, and I know I am interested in you."

He started to protest, but she took her finger and placed it over his lips again. "Shhh, just kiss me."

With that, he gently embraced her and a feeling swelled that was intense and strong. It was an emotion he hadn't felt since being with Beth Ann. Ginger was bringing his soul to life again. All those lonely dark hidden parts were now flooding with passion. His heart was beating strong and oh, lord have mercy, he was lost in her kisses.

* * * *

Two days later, Beth Ann was sitting in the nursery, fighting to stay awake while she was breastfeeding Kaylie. They had family all over the house, which was wonderful, except she hadn't had much time alone with her baby girl. She watched her daughter puckering her little lips and wanting more, so she needed to switch breasts. Just like the doctor had told her, she didn't switch until the one breast was empty. She'd also been putting a safety pin on her bra to alert her to what breast she had used last time. It was helping, considering how sleepy she was.

There was a knock at the door.

"Come in," she called out.

The door opened and Lisa stepped in. "Look at this precious picture. Can I get the camera?"

"No!" Beth Ann frowned. "I don't think Kaylob wants me showing off my breast to the entire world."

"Selfish man." They both laughed.

"When you're done, I want to hold her." Lisa stared longingly at the baby. "She's so beautiful." She walked over and touched her little head. "Look at all those blonde curls."

"I know." Beth Ann's heart grew extra large. "Her daddy's hair color and I bet her eyes will stay blue."

"And your curls," Lisa said. "I bet she'll be talented like her mommy."

"I hope she can cook like her daddy." Beth Ann chuckled. "Not like me in that department."

"So how are you feeling?" Lisa gestured subtly downward.

"I sure hope I'll be able to make love again."

Lisa laughed. "You will and everything will be back in place soon."

Just then Kaylie stopped nursing. "I need to burp her." She shifted the baby.

"Can I do it please?" Lisa reached for her.

"Yes," Beth Ann placed her bundle of joy in Lisa's arms.

Lisa held her like a pro and patted her back. "Terry and I want a little girl so bad."

"You do?"

"We are trying again." She sighed. "You know how long it took with Benjamin and he's a handful." She laughed. "He keeps us going. And you know what else?" Lisa's eyes sparkled with laughter.

"What?" Beth Ann waited.

"Everything you've heard about the terrible twos is such a lie."

"Really? That's good to know." Beth Ann started cleaning up the changing table. "I always wondered about that."

"The truth is you need to quadruple how hard you heard it's going to be." Beth Ann met her gaze, making them both laugh.

"If you do have a little girl, what will you name her?" Beth Ann busied herself with folding the baby diapers.

"Maranda Rose." Lisa nodded. "Terry and I both want a daughter named after his grandma."

"Wow! I love that name and you know a daughter with the name Rose in it has to be very, very special."

Lisa smiled. "How did I know you would say that?"

They both cracked up.

"Hey there ladies, breakfast is ready and I want my baby girl." Kaylob's face turned to mush every time he so much as glanced at his daughter.

Lisa handed her over and grinned. "If you guys are planning on eating, she'll want to eat again too."

"I just fed her," Beth Ann said.

"Doesn't matter, that's how it works." Lisa laughed. "You'll learn. Mama hungry, baby hungry."

Kaylob nodded towards the kitchen and her and Lisa left while he held his baby girl. Beth Ann could see he wasn't too keen on sitting down at the table with everyone. She prayed that someday things would heal between him and his family. They were trying so hard to make up for the past. But in truth, it was going to take more than a few months for him to get through the pain. He had said it wasn't because they gave him up. They were young and kids, people make mistakes. However, all the secrecy had hurt him the most. Beth Ann prayed every day that Kaylob would work through things so they'd be able to have family gatherings and she wouldn't have to see the pain in his eyes. The day had to come where they could be a big happy family, right?

* * * *

Across town, Blake had just parked his car in front of his townhouse. He leaned over and kissed Ginger. "You sure you don't want to come in? I just need to grab some more clothes, since I'll be staying longer than I thought."

"I'm sure. The doctor said not much walking."

He winked. "Won't take me long. Johnny and Dana are here. They're going to want to meet you. If you don't mind, I'll invite them over later after we go to see the baby."

"I can't wait," she said. "I love babies and I'd love to meet them."

She reached out and touched his arm. "Have I told you how wonderful you are?" She moved closer to his face.

"A few times," he whispered into her lips. "But I don't mind hearing it again."

She pressed her soft mouth against his. "I could get very used to all this. Not sure that's so smart," she said.

"I think you are very smart." He grinned. Jesus, he was crazy about this woman. After spending a few days with her, he felt as though he'd known her all his life. Was he ready to break his own rules?

He pulled away from her lips and saw Dana step out on the front porch. She must have seen him pull up.

"There's Dana now." Blake pointed. "Want to say hello?"

"Yes, I would."

He opened up his side and stepped out into a beautiful brisk day. He waved to Dana and crossed around to open up the door for Ginger. Dana was coming down the steps and heading in their direction, when a car backfired. That's when he saw Dana fall. Jesus, she must have lost her balance. Then another backfire.

Ginger screamed. "Oh my God, Blake it's him!" She pointed. "He's got a gun!"

Blake stepped in front of Ginger and became transfixed on the man standing across the street by the telephone pole, holding the rifle, aiming it their way. Dana was down on the ground bleeding from her arm, so he shoved Ginger back in the car. He stood in front of the door and yelled. "Johnny!"

Just as he took a step towards Dana, Johnny was out on the front porch with a handgun of his own, aiming at the asshole. "Drop it," he yelled. "I will kill you, you sonofabitch," Johnny glanced down at Dana and fear flickered in his eyes.

Everything happened so fast. Johnny's handgun roared as bullets left the chamber. Blake heard another round of shots seconds before he felt the burn in his hip. Then something warm flowed down his leg. As soon as he touched it, blood dripped from his fingers. He dove towards Dana when heat tore through his back.

Things started to spin and he saw Johnny firing again. He could hear his car being hit and the sound of bullets hitting metal. Ginger, he thought. He managed to crawl her way, but when he pulled himself up to the window, he found her slumped over in the seat, with blood streaming from her temple.

"Oh, hell, no," he cried. He tried to open the door, but everything was going black and he couldn't hold himself up. Jesus, he was falling. All he heard was the thud of his own body hitting the ground, as though it were happening to someone else, and the last thing he saw was blood forming around him.

The story continues with, The Seasons of Forever- Book Six.

Follow the Seasons of Love and War Saga.

Book 1: Seasons of Love and War
Book 2: December Road
Book 3: The Journey of Elizbeth Ann Rose
Book 4: June's Stolen Rose
Book 5: April's Secret Storm
Book 6: The Seasons of Forever

Coming Soon

The Seasons of Forever, Book 6 of Seasons of Love and War

About the Author

Brenda Ashworth Barry's first book was a memoir titled, Healing the Voices Within, which was never published but sponsored on a local TV station and flew off the shelves at her Healing Center in Redding California.

Her most recent work is a six-part saga of star-crossed lovers separated by the war in Vietnam, entitled Seasons of Love and War. Brenda worked for over five years to bring the six part Saga alive.

Brenda lives in Roseburg, Oregon, by the Umpqua River, and has raised four children three birth children and one adopted born in her heart. Her husband, who was in the military for 21 years, gave her help and encouragement while writing her novel. When she's not writing she can normally be found walking the trails with her husband and their little dachshund, or in their RV enjoying nature.

Twitter: @sunsetsky52
Website: http://www.brendaashworthbarry.com
Facebook: www.facebook.com/pages/Seasons-of-Love-and-War-Author-Page/411210412247684
Blog: brendabarry.blogspot.com
Blog: brendabarryashworth.wordpress.com

www.ingramcontent.com/pod-product-compliance
Lightning Source LLC
Chambersburg PA
CBHW020821260626
47169CB00003B/770